"Fantasy and Sci-fi are some of the most popular genres in movies and literature. Yet what a tragedy that so many of this generation, both inside and outside the church, are missing the greatest adventure ever told. In *The Millennium Chronicles* Doug Hamp shows his readers just how utterly amazing the future world will be according to the prophecies of the Bible. Whatever the reader believes about bible prophecy, reading *The Millennium Chronicles* is a great way to engage the hunger of imagination with the realities of the future."

—John Di Bartolo, founder of Middle-earth Network

"Science fiction meets Bible fact! In *The Millennium Chronicles* Doug Hamp takes future events revealed in the Bible and makes them come to life. This epic journey is a must-read for both Christians and fans of science fiction!"

—Gonz Shimura, producer of *Age of Deceit*, Canary Cry Radio

"*The Millennium Chronicles* is a page-turner based solidly on the Word of God!"

—John Sutherland, senior pastor, Calvary Chapel Elko, NV

"In *The Millennium Chronicles* author Doug Hamp has managed to weave into one engaging novel all the major elements of what the Bible speaks of as 'The Day of the Lord.' A powerful work, reminiscent of C. S. Lewis and J. R. R. Tolkien."

—Gary Cowan, senior pastor, Calvary Chapel East Albuquerque

"This is the most fascinating read I have ever experienced. It is absolutely brilliant how God inspired Doug to write such a remarkable story through use of Scripture. I learned so, so much! This is a work that all believers must read! The three DVDs are helpful in understanding even more of the book."

—Phil Richardson, Founder, Telios Education Solutions

"*The Millennium Chronicles* is a 'novel' approach to the unfolding of future biblical events, excellently documented from Scripture. Quite a thought-provoking read!"

The
Millennium
Chronicles
Road to the Final Rebellion

by Douglas Hamp

*A future-historical novel of Lucifer's final assault
against the New Jerusalem*

The Millennium Chronicles

Copyright © 2014 by Douglas Hamp; www.douglashamp.com

www.themillenniumchronicles.com

Cover by Frederick Briggs

Scriptural allusions are inspired by the Holy Bible: International

Standard Version. Copyright © 1996-2012 by The ISV Foundation.

First printing November 2013

ISBN 13: 978-1492795520

ISBN 10: 1492795526

Printed in the United States of America.

To Mom:
Thanks for believing in me!

Acknowledgments

I would like to thank first and foremost my wife for giving me the time to write this labor-intensive book and for helping with the proofing. Thank you Randy Stucky for the many, many hours you spent going over my early manuscripts helping the story take flight. Thank you Candy Outlaw for putting on the finishing touches! Thank you Frederick Briggs for steadfastly working on the cover and patiently honing it until it was "just right." Thank you Bob Rico for helping think through many of the foundational ideas contained in this book. You have been a great mentor. I would also like to thank Norma Hance for the keen eye you showed as a proofer. Thanks also to Norm Robinson for believing in me and encouraging me to write this. Thank you also Mike Hoiden for giving important feedback on early drafts. Finally, thank you Renee Story for formatting the book for publication. There are many others who also read a portion of the book and gave helpful feedback. Thank you!

Using this Book for Small Group Study

Small-group Bible studies will benefit from going through the study guide after reading the book because the many verses will require much reflection and discussion.

To help with the process, I recommend that you first read this book for enjoyment as a likely scenario of how things may come about and then read it again. You can also consult the following resources available at www.douglashamp.com in which I explain the timing of the new heavens and earth, the purpose of the millennial sacrifices, the Highway of Holiness, and the purpose of the River of Life and the Tree of Life.

1. The companion nonfiction book, *The New Heavens and Earth*, forthcoming in 2014, deals with the biblical, linguistic, and theological underpinnings contained in this story.

2. *The Millennium Chronicles* teaching videos

   a. The Second Coming and Armageddon

   b. The Millennium

   c. The Final Rebellion

3. Free, downloadable study guide with all of the scriptures used in this work is available at www.themillenniumchronicles.com.

Contents

After one thousand years of Yeshua's glorious reign upon the earth, Lucifer and his minions have been released from the Abyss. They have had one year to gather the nations together to attempt the final assault against the City of Adonai.

Prologue

THE STARS SPARKLED more brilliantly than ever before and the sun shone seven times brighter. Even the moon's reflection was equal to the sun in the former age of darkness.[1] Still, their light paled in comparison to the light beaming from the City of Adonai.[2]

The City rested on top of the world, beautifully situated on the northern pole of the earth[3] ever since the time of the Hebrews' Trouble when the planet had tottered like a drunk. The City rose up more than thirty times higher than Mount Everest, the highest mountain in the previous age. Far below, on the surface of the earth, the City was laid out as a square surrounded by walls of precious stones.[4] Mile-wide platforms surrounded one level of the City with another above it. As it rose, the sides tapered up like a mountain, or a step-pyramid, encased with diamond-like gold from the top to the bottom. Behind the translucent gold, on each platform, spires and towers covered with gemstones climbed upward, adorning the City in splendor. On the uppermost platform in the midst of the Twenty-four Elders—exactly at the center of the pyramid-shaped City—the light of Adonai, brighter than the sun, refracted off the precious stones in a million different shades of color like rainbows all around.

The River of Life flowed in multiple streams down the side of the mountain, bringing joy to the inhabitants of the City and beyond. Lush rivers were flowing in previously barren heights and fountains were gurgling in the midst of valleys; pools of water abounded. The contiguous ocean of the former age was gone and the earth was now covered with vast patches of green, dotted with massive lakes.

On every lofty mountain and every high hill were brooks and canals running with water.[5] The hills were covered with deep green grass and vibrant green foliage of grand cedar trees, acacia, myrtle, olive trees, and fruit trees of every kind. There were cypresses, box trees, and pine trees in what were formerly deserts.[6] The sweet aroma of vibrant flowers and fruit saturated the air. The very depths of the earth and the mountains and the former waste places had all broken forth into singing, resonating in deep and gentle harmony with the song of the King, which he sang over the New Jerusalem, his beloved City for the past thousand years.[7]

The sublime song was abruptly interrupted by the sudden shouts of battle and the thunderous movement of billions of shadowy figures of darkness rushing in to sack the City of Light, exactly three hundred sixty days after being liberated from their prison.

360 days earlier

1

The Escape

ON THE SURFACE of the earth, two illustrious beings emerged from the massive, golden, gemstone-covered temple. Their bodies looked like dazzling gems; their faces emitted flashes like lightning, like the rays of the sun.[1] Their arms and feet shone like polished bronze.[2] Their clothing was shining[3] whiter than any snow[4] and they wore belts of pure gold around their waists.

They walked past six guardhouses, artfully engraved with palm trees, until they passed through one of the eastward, ten-foot-tall gates in the mile-long wall that encircled the temple.[5]

"With great satisfaction I tell you that the time of the Covering is over," Adam said to his companion Michael, as they crossed a bridge over a river. Michael recalled the first time Adonai had offered the life-force of an animal as a covering for Adam and Eve, which was necessary when they were mortals. Adam glanced knowingly at Michael as they shared the memory of that ancient day of shame.

They continued walking alongside the crystal clear River of Life that proceeded from the very throne of Adonai and of Yeshua at the apex of the mountain.[6] The water collected in a pool before the throne and looked like a sea of glass, clear as crystal.[7] Half of it flowed to the Western

Sea and the other half flowed to the Eastern Sea, branching off into multiple streams on the way down the mountain, making glad the City of Adonai.[8] One branch flowed under the Temple and came out of the eastward threshold where it continued toward[9] the eastern territories and its water flowed toward the Eastern Sea (formerly the Salt Sea). The Living Water had transformed the Sea so that it could support all kinds of living creatures that thrived abundantly. Wherever the River flowed, everything lived!

A pair of fiery horses[10] adorned with bells inscribed with 'Holiness to Adonai' galloped past the massive temple structure on the ornate street overlaid with gold.

Michael stopped suddenly. "He's coming," he solemnly said to Adam, looking south, to the gate of the Abyss.

◎ ◎ ◎ ◎ ◎

Under the surface of the earth, deep in the lowest recesses of the Abyss, on a remote slope of that ancient pit devoid of light,[11] the unbreakable, everlasting chains[12] that had fully immobilized Lucifer for the past thousand years began to shake. He knew that the time of his emancipation was at hand.

How he loathed his prison of darkness in the belly of Tartarus, the lowest rung of the Abyss. A foul and putrid stench of sulfur and rotting flesh, like the smell of death, permeated the stale, lifeless cavern of despair, while wailing voices and gnashing teeth were faintly heard[13] far above them. It was here in this place, thousands of years earlier, in the days of the Great Deluge, that some of Lucifer's Watchers had been imprisoned until he had acquired the Key and released them[14] before being ingloriously cast into the Abyss himself.

Lucifer was still seething with rage over his last debacle. He had been on the verge of victory when Adonai's mighty Angel swooped down with that unbreakable chain and single-handedly bound and thrust him into the pit, sealing him in and locking the gate with the Key.[15] This same Key had once been in his possession after he had robbed Adam and Eve of the earth and left them in abject slavery, bound their entire lives by the fear of death.[16] Both this Key of death and the Key of the Abyss[17] had been in his possession until Lord Yeshua intervened on behalf of the mortals and repossessed the Keys and the Scroll of Destiny.[18]

The unyielding and relentless chains that had shackled his neck, hands, and feet, shook violently and suddenly broke open. Immediately Lucifer ripped them off and cast them aside. Finally free, he stood up from his bed of maggots, shook off the blanket of worms that had smothered him,[19] and watched as the chains confining his entire Watchers' army also fell away. At that moment they all roared mightily, like a horde of lions seizing their helpless prey, shaking the Abyss. The reverberation traveled out of their dungeon and up the jagged shaft, where it crashed against the mighty door and fractured the great seal that the powerful Angel had placed over it one thousand years[20] earlier. Thus the din of their voices escaped to the world above, announcing their return.

All eyes were on Lucifer, eagerly awaiting instructions from their leader.

"The Adamites have had one thousand years of Lord Yeshua their King ruling with his rod of iron,"[21] Lucifer said sarcastically, "while we have been unjustly locked away in the Abyss. Now we shall go and test the hearts of the Adamites to see if they truly desire him as their King." After a brief pause he continued slowly and deliberately, "Or to see if perhaps they missed me. I know their hearts, for they are utterly deceitful and incurably wicked![22] They have served him for these past thousand years because they had no choice! We shall go and liberate them from their oppression!"[23] he boasted, holding up the chains that had fallen off him. "I guarantee you; there will be billions of defectors who will march with us to sack Adonai's City of Light[24] because the Adamites are weak and feeble-minded!

"My unjust incarceration these past one thousand years has only given me time to calculate every possible combination of scenarios and their potential outcomes. As you know, our battle with Adonai has never been one of might, for he is stronger and we cannot defeat him that way. Ours has always been a battle of legality, which is his greatest weakness; we shall exploit it to the fullest. Our strategy is simple and our victory is certain because Adonai is obligated to keep his word; he cannot lie.[25] He has magnified his word above his name[26] and therefore any contradiction of his word will create an irreparable rift in the cosmos that will force him to abdicate his throne.

"Each of you must go out to your former regions," Lucifer said to Prince Parás, lord over the land of Persia. Then turning to Prince Yaván, lord over Greece, "You must oh-so-subtly share our plan of attack," he smirked. "Then I will climb up to the peak of Jerusalem, the City of Adonai, and set up my throne."[27] The legions of the underworld cackled in the darkness, eager to realize the final fall of the Adamites and even Adonai himself.

"Take courage, brothers," Lucifer proclaimed, gazing at the faces of countless Watchers, who were once luminous Angels resembling Adonai's image but now were disfigured like Lucifer. "Our sacrifice to restore justice in the cosmos is nearly complete. Soon all of the Adamites will learn their true place—at our feet!" Rekindling the ancient hatred in the hearts of the fallen, he cried, "Now, great ones, destined to rule the cosmos with me, let us rise, never to fall again and, henceforth, never to taste defeat! We shall feast on the life-force of the Adamites!"[28]

Immediately, he and countless hordes shot upward as if from cannons to the world above them. In just moments they reached the massive gate which had shut them in and smashed through it, sending it flying thousands of feet into the air and landing miles away. Hundreds of millions of the rebel Watchers launched through the smoke that billowed from the dungeon of deepest darkness out into the agonizing light of Adonai, exposing their sunken cheeks and shriveled arms and legs on their drab grey, disfigured and grotesque bodies.

They hovered for a moment as they transformed themselves into Angels of light, masquerading as Angels in Adonai's service, just as they had done in the previous age, though their light had a bluer hue to it than that of their counterparts.[29] Their hideous true-selves could not endure Adonai's blazing brilliance. They then flew out like balls of lightning in every direction, returning to their former regions.

A strange shadow of darkness began to fall upon the pristine planet for the first time in a thousand years.[30] "I feel the same awful wickedness, greed, and depravity[31] emanating from Lucifer that I came to know seven millennia ago," Adam said, surprised at the foreboding he felt from the release of his ancient nemesis. Adam looked at the lush orchards brimming with vibrant flowers of every color that flanked the street. He breathed in the fragrance of apples, passion fruit, peaches, oranges, and fruit of every kind that permeated the pure, uncontaminated air. The light of the rays of the setting sun shimmered through the wings of a thousand beautiful blue butterflies clinging to the side of one of the tall, majestic trees that were home to animals of every sort. Hummingbirds drew nectar from the flowers on the fruit trees. A warm glow emitted from every leaf, every blade of grass, every wing, every creature. A lion rollicked with a deer, and animals everywhere were enjoying one another.[32]

Adam observed one of two grey wolves that were lying down together with a lamb nestled between them. It warily raised its head, tilted it sideways, and thrust back its ears for the first time in a thousand years. "It senses the same bloodthirsty, invincible, and willful arrogance that has characterized Lucifer ever since he intruded upon my wife and me in the Garden so long ago, covered with all of his brilliantly colored precious gems that refracted his light in every direction."

"We met his gaze yet suspected nothing," Adam said, recalling his first encounter with the deceiver. "Eve and I simply admired his beauty, for none but Adonai himself compared in splendor. His presence was not surprising, for Adonai had stationed him in Eden to keep Adonai's special places."[33]

Michael nodded, remembering the treachery of Lucifer, once a member of the divine council of the Angels[34] on the Mountain-City of Adonai and Guardian cherub to Adonai himself![35] "There has been no noble thing that the mortal Adamites could not have during the past thousand years," he said, looking down at the sparkling crystal clear water and the many fishermen who had plenty of room to spread their nets along the banks of the River.

"And yet," continued Michael, finishing his thought, "many have ungratefully lingered; waiting, imagining, anticipating his ascension." Turning his head back toward where Lucifer and the Watchers had re-entered earth's atmosphere, he added, "Now Lucifer has returned and he and his minions will slowly begin sowing seeds of discord, just as before, so that they may eventually dare to show their faces to the Adamites and encourage them to rise against their Maker."

Adam walked down to the riverside, cupped some water, and let it pass through his fingers, remembering how Lucifer's subtle scheme had excited his pride and desire to be wise.[36] Falling into the carefully laid trap, Adam had sunk his teeth into the deadly fruit,[37] savoring its flavor while Lucifer looked on, masking his devilish delight.[38]

Adam thought to himself, *Not only have earth's inhabitants been abundantly satisfied with the fullness of God's house, but they have even been invited to drink from his River of delights! Indeed, with Adonai is the Fountain of Life and it is in his light that we see light.*[39] *How sad it is that just as the ancient Hebrews in the previous age forsook him, the fountain of living water, and carved for themselves broken cisterns that could hold no water,*[40] *so too now some will prefer Lucifer, who is nothing but a broken cistern full of putrid water.*

Adam turned to look, with Michael, in the direction Lucifer had come from the Abyss. "Adonai has placed before them life and death; they must choose their destiny."

357 days later

2
The Final Village

"THEY ARE READY and waiting, my Lord," Prince Yaván said to Lucifer. The sound of thousands of Adamites from the village of Koinonia, eager to hear how they could be liberated from Adonai, filled the air. The sky was uncharacteristically dark. A shadow lingered in every place where Lucifer was welcomed. He had come to the village to personally oversee the final persuasion, as there was no room for mistakes. He was the father of lies[1] and no one could spin them as he could.

The villagers could see the two beings with brilliant, shining bodies decorated with gemstones walking toward their village. Their radiance had a cold bluish hue; it was almost ominous, as if the light were hiding a shadow of darkness. Many perceived these beings as standing taller and nobler than any Adamite. One of the two exuded an air of great power, confidence, and authority characteristic of the anticipated Great Liberator.

"I have been encouraging them to follow their passions and pride for the past year," Prince Yaván reported. "The entire land, including this village, has been waiting for you, their Great Liberator, to come and set them free from the upside-down kingdom of Yeshua!"

"Who founded this village of 'Koinonia'?" asked Lucifer.

"A certain immortal named Antipas was the founder and ruler of the village of Koinonia. He was one of ten to whom Yeshua had granted authority over such villages as a reward for loyal and faithful service in the previous age. Though there were many men named Antipas in the former age, I believe it may have been the very same Antipas that we so meticulously disposed of in Pergamum, where your throne was. He held fast to the name of Yeshua and would not deny his loyalty to him[2] even though we turned up the heat unmercifully."

"Antipas," Lucifer said, remembering the many mortals he had destroyed throughout the millennia. "Of course I remember him—he was 'well-done' when he finally passed through the veil. If he founded this village then I suspect that same devotion and loyalty must still be present. Tell me more about him."

"As an immortal equal in power and knowledge to an Angel," Prince Yaván began, "he directed the early mortal villagers in the building of the roads and bridges and all the infrastructure of Koinonia. He taught them how to work together and to consider the needs of others[3] by assisting in the construction of one another's homes,[4] which were made of crystal, gold, lapis lazuli, gemstones, and other abundant resources."

"I can see the infrastructure!" barked Lucifer. "What else do you know about him?"

"When a disagreement arose among the villagers, Antipas was the one who heard their complaints and, because his authority was given to him by Yeshua, his decisions were binding.[5] He believed the greatest and most exciting times of the year were when they went to celebrate the feasts of Adonai. For centuries they used to go up to the Mountain of Adonai, to the house of the King of Jacob, so he could teach them his requirements and they could follow his standards."[6]

"With such a foundation, what makes you think that they will join our rebellion now?" Lucifer asked with consternation.

"I perceive that they will offer no resistance, my Lord," Prince Yaván said. "They appear willfully ignorant of the former times and share none of the loyalty to Yeshua like the survivors who went through the time of the Hebrews' Trouble, nor the early generations. Unlike these villagers, the first villagers of Koinonia, who had only weeks earlier come out of the time of the Hebrews' Trouble, truly appreciated the things that were missing in their village."

Prince Yaván pointed to the doors which did not have a lock and key mechanism.

"They appreciated that locks were no longer necessary on doors, nor was intense labor required to obtain the raw materials necessary to produce such devices. As survivors of the previous age, they also valued the absence of extreme temperatures on the earth. They realized that everything was different in the kingdom of Yeshua: there were no obstacles to overcome, no wars to win,[7] no diseases to cure, no crimes to solve, no factories to manage.

"The first villagers also valued how the degeneration was gone from the earth and how it now yielded great quantities of food with very little effort,"[8] he said, pointing to a bushel of oranges and then a bushel of plums and another of grapes. The fruit, slightly dry from lack of rain, still looked delicious. "The villagers here and now have no concept of what they have," he added, pointing again to fruit trees all around with dry, withered fruit. "They do not understand the mouth-watering taste of the fruit in this age that no chemical or fertilizer of the old age could approximate. They don't understand that with no insects to infest or weeds to compete with, no insecticides or herbicides are needed.

"The first villagers brought here by Antipas recognized that the professions they once held were no longer needed,"

Yaván continued. "There were no doctors, surgeons, or nurses because there was no sickness or disease. They were glad that the old economy was gone, never to return.[9]

"These current villagers, however, have no recollection of the previous age for the most part and increasingly are controlled by their own appetites. They will believe whatever you tell them because they love the darkness more than they love light![10] Over the past year I have observed that they have become haters of Adonai, proud and boastful.[11] They also complain about having to take their wealth to the New Jerusalem and how unfair it is that the Hebrews receive it."

"Then they have been waiting for me, their Great Liberator, to come and set them free from the upside-down kingdom of Yeshua!" Lucifer remarked. "It is just as I told you in the Abyss: 'The greater serving the lesser is foolishness,'[12] which I have always fought against; these Adamites appear to agree."

"It is not as though you *desire* to be the greatest," Prince Yaván flattered, "you simply *are* the greatest.[13] The Adam-ites ought to be serving you, and now they desire you to be their master."

"Oh, how we were betrayed those seven thousand years ago!" lamented Lucifer. "I remember well the day Adonai formed the worm! The betrayal was not forming a body from the dirt, the *adamáh* that resembled himself, or even when Adonai condescendingly slouched over the lump of dust and breathed into him.[14] It was when he gave such a lowly creature complete dominion of the earth[15] and then expected *us*, his glorious messengers of flaming fire,[16] to be servants[17] of Dusty and his kind!"

"It was so easy," Prince Yaván smirked, "convincing Adam and his helper to violate Adonai's directive, which merely proved how unworthy they were of our service."

"I remember the looks on their Adamite faces when they realized their folly. The moment everything changed for all time. That moment was priceless," Lucifer recalled with contempt.

"And you were right to expose them!" Prince Yaván said. "They and their kind are worthless pieces of dirt, bits of dust ready to disintegrate back into the ground from which they came. Naturally, when you, the paragon of form and beauty, the very one that Adonai created as the sum of all things, the paradigm against which all else was measured, the epitome of wisdom and beauty,[18] were expected to act like a slave to the one made of dust,[19] then it was apparent that Adonai had transgressed his own laws of hierarchy—that is the very essence of evil! We, your lesser brothers, shared your outrage over such a scheme to enslave us all to an inferior race. We are truly the greatest of Adonai's achievements and we serve no one," Prince Yaván said with outright disdain.

"A glorious day it was when they began dying," Lucifer gloated. "They no longer absorbed and emitted Adonai's light[20] and had to hide themselves when Adonai came looking for them.[21] They were overcome by death, which eventually left their bodies separated from their life-force and estranged from their beloved Adonai."

"It all worked so easily, according to your brilliant plan," said Prince Yaván. "Thanks to you we were freed from having to serve the worms. Never again would they be able to exist in his presence[22]—that is, were it not for Yeshua."

Lucifer grimaced. "Yes, but Yeshua's deed cannot be repeated; thus Adonai has played his ace.[23] There will be no way for him to counteract the treason the Adamites are now committing."[24] Lucifer sighed with satisfaction.

"And now billions of the Adamites have joined us, demonstrating once and for all the foolishness of the race of Adam and the inverted economy of Adonai," Prince Yaván scoffed. "Adonai loves the Adamites and even relinquished his life-force for them and yet they will be delighted to have you back."

In the village center, a man stepped up onto a beautifully crafted platform made of sapphire and diamond. "They are almost here!" he shouted excitedly. Korah, the oldest person in the village, still looked youthful at 870 years of age.[25]

The villagers erupted in anticipation and excitement.

3
Ben-Oni

BEN, A HANDSOME young man slightly over six-feet tall with light brown hair and a sturdy build, watched intently from his second-story bedroom window as the two shining ones approached. The youngest member of the village, having just turned 20, Ben often contemplated how he had never been to the City of Jerusalem to celebrate the Feasts and wondered why his father never spoke of them.

As far back as Ben could remember his father had been distant and cold, taking little interest in him. He knew his father had doubts about his parentage because occasionally he would say something like, "I really don't understand how you could be my son. You are so different from the others." Yes, he did have a different look from his father and siblings but what did that matter? He was still a son and a brother. As all these thoughts churned in his head and ripped at his heart, quite suddenly he found himself thinking about his mother. After all these years, he could barely remember her, but he wondered, *Did my father treat her the same way he treats me? Did she run away to escape his cruelty or some dark secret?* For whatever reason, she had abandoned him to a family that questioned whether he really belonged to them and took special delight in treating him as an outsider.

19

This past year had been especially confusing as his father often spoke quietly and confidentially with Ben's many older brothers and sister about how better off they would be without Yeshua. "If we were to govern ourselves," his father had said, "with each of us doing what is right in our own eyes, then 'do what you will shall be the whole of the law.'[1] We would never need to go up to the City of Jerusalem ever again." Ben had managed to eavesdrop even though he had been shut out of the meetings. His heart ached at being excluded from his father's secret plans.

When his father and brothers had specifically forbidden him from coming to the village square to hear the Great Liberator, he knew his pain couldn't get any worse. He had felt their patronizing gazes of disdain: "Stay here," they said; "you are too young and naïve to understand what the Great Liberator is going to say."

"He probably still thinks that Yeshua's kingdom is fair," Ben had overheard one brother say to another as they headed out the door to the village square.

Ben watched as the shining ones walked past his window. There were so many questions that he yearned to ask someone else, someone other than his family or fellow villagers. He wanted to learn what really happened. *I desire to know the truth,* he thought. Just then a beautiful deep-blue butterfly flitted by his window, which had no glass in it for there was nothing to keep out, such as cold weather or pests, nor was there hot or cold air to keep in. Ben reached out and the butterfly landed gently on his right index finger. He admired the intricate detail and artistry of its exquisite design.

The light emitting from its wings glowed in the subtle shadow that had recently settled upon the village. Ben suddenly remembered the legend that everything used to glow incessantly because of the light of the King—though he had never before witnessed this phenomenon. *Perhaps the legend is true because only a good and compassionate being would make such beautiful things,* Ben thought, staring at the butterfly until it flew away. As he thought about what he had just seen, his spirits began to lift. He had made a decision.

Ben stood up and walked deliberately to the mahogany door of his bedroom, over the floor covered with planks of cypress, and through the cedar-lined hallway decorated with ornamental buds and open flowers that gave a palatial yet homey feeling.[2]

He could already feel hope welling up inside as he opened the massive, solid-sapphire door of his house. The house itself, made of translucent gold, was adorned with transparent precious stones that reflected a spectacular spectrum of colors. The original builders of the house obviously intended the building materials and all the embellishments to bring joy and warmth to the hearts of the occupants.

Ben looked around to make sure his brothers and father would not see him and then ran to the back of the crowd directly opposite his house. Korah was just about to say something important.

"My fellow villagers," Korah began, "for hundreds of years the people of this village went up from one new moon to another to serve Adonai.[3] We also made the yearly trek to celebrate the Feast of Tabernacles, which was in reality a grand celebration when Adonai had dried every tear[4] and was dwelling among his people. There was celebration with great rejoicing because such a just King was in our midst.

"However, everything changed three hundred years ago when Nabal and his wife Talia, members of our village, died in the presence of Yeshua. They were accused of being disloyal.[5] The official story, which we have long disputed, was that when they went to Jerusalem, they boasted they had given a certain amount of gold and silver to Yeshua when in fact they had not—not even close. They were accused of desiring the praise of Adamites more than the good blessing of the King.[6] It was said they had violated the same principle as Lucifer did in the beginning. They had a proud look and a lying tongue[7] and when confronted, they lied and denied it. When they then went into the temple, where Yeshua sits judging, to receive the Covering, suddenly fire went out from the presence of Yeshua and consumed them so that they died before him.[8] That was when I decided to stop going to celebrate the Feasts. I admit, I was at first afraid that I too might suffer their fate. However, the more I considered what had happened, the more I began to realize that I ought to be able to do what is right in my own eyes. The next year, several people followed my lead until finally after twenty years most people in the village stopped going altogether. To my satisfaction, any mention of the Feasts is shunned and I can honestly say that I have not missed them.

"However," Korah continued, "after some time of not going up to the City to celebrate the Feasts, Yeshua decided that we were not worthy to receive rain and our beautiful vegetation became dry and mostly unfruitful. The dirt itself, the *adamáh*, was still good, and while there has been some produce, it has not been in the abundance we enjoyed during the first several hundred years of Yeshua's rule.

"We eventually received reports of similar things occurring around the earth. There were, for example, the people of Egypt who did not go to Jerusalem to take part and then had no annual river overflow. And Yeshua sent a plague to strike the peoples who did not come to observe the Feast of Tabernacles.[9]

"There were some among us who remained loyal to Yeshua and said he was doing this to help us see that he was the source of blessing—that we had refused to acknowledge him as King and had become slothful in our service toward him!" Korah said spitefully. "The lack of rain, they claimed, was to make us remember him rather than harbor secret resentment. Well, I tell you, when they left here with high hopes of finding the River of Life and the Tree of Life to allow them to enter the City, I bid them good riddance!"

The villagers cheered in approval. People in the crowd began speaking to one another, saying "The Great Liberator is telling people all over the earth that we ought to be able to do as we want."

"The Great Liberator's ways are easy and his burden is light,"[10] another said to his neighbor. "He doesn't require anything of us and he doesn't demand that we go and pay homage to him. He would not rule with a rod of iron."[11]

"Now that an option to finally choose against Yeshua is presenting itself," Korah said, "I believe it is time to act. The Great Liberator is the one who truly championed the cause of the Adamites. He and his cohorts have a better plan for our lives by helping us live as we want to live—freely and without constraints." Korah glowed with anticipation of the new reality that awaited them. "We will be able to throw off the oppression of Prince Yeshua, son of Adonai![12] They are here! Make way and let them pass!" he commanded. "Welcome, O Great Liberator!"

24

4

The Great Liberator

"NOBLE CITIZENS OF the glorious land of Yaván," Prince Yaván ascended the platform and greeted the people of the village with a voice that sounded like the flowing of many waters.[1] He looked around, smiling and stretching out his hands as if summoning them to listen carefully. The villagers squinted from the bluish light that emanated from his body. "I have the pleasure of introducing the former vizier to Adonai himself who was in Eden and was in the City of Adonai.[2] He is the one I have been telling you about and speaking of in villages throughout the land of Yaván this past year."

Lucifer stood behind the Prince, looking intently at the people in the crowd. He made eye contact with Ben and immediately Ben felt charged and invigorated by this commanding figure, drawn to his might and power. And yet despite this attraction there was something in, or perhaps it was something missing from, the eyes of Lucifer that made the hairs of the back of Ben's neck prickle.

"You know that the first to put forth his case seems right," the Prince continued, "until someone else comes forward and cross-examines him![3] I, therefore, implore you to listen as the Great Liberator shares his story of how he risked everything to bring you true freedom from oppression—a quality you value as did your ancestors before you. Your fathers in the previous age, under my domain, were part of one of the greatest civilizations ever known to the Adamites. Through the efforts of one of the Great Liberator's grandest visionaries, Alexander of Macedonia, the culture and fame of the land of Yaván spread throughout the known world. Your poet Homer was read for nearly three thousand years. Your sculptors set the standard in artistic expression of the human body, and your philosophers were the envy of the ancient world. It is written in the Chronicles, 'A good name is to be chosen rather than great riches,'[4] yet you had *both* fame and fortune because I, Prince Yaván, granted you such success.

"Your form of self-governance, democracy, became the ideal that the western world attempted to copy for millennia, and it gained you respect in the eyes of the world in the previous age. You believed that people should rule themselves, and I do not doubt that such a noble desire yet remains in you to return to this lofty ideal.

"I know that Adonai would commend you for your faithful service to him these past thousand years," Yaván continued. "You have sacrificed your own personal freedom to fulfill his desires. What king would not be pleased with subjects like you? You have denied yourselves to serve him and the Hebrews, the people that he has chosen. I know that for these past thousand years Yeshua has been ruling you with a rod of iron.[5] There has obviously been peace on the earth—who would dare oppose such a dictator who has vowed to shatter any who would oppose him?" he said, smashing his fist into his hand. "Ask yourself, if given the opportunity, how might you govern yourselves? I can only wonder if you have ever had the opportunity to truly choose your own path."

The people were spellbound by the possibility of being free and many shook their heads as they considered all that had been denied them over the last thousand years.

The Prince pressed on, "Certainly, it is written in the Chronicles that 'he who is spiritual judges all things, yet he himself is judged by no one'[6] and 'if we judge ourselves, we will not be judged.'"[7] He carefully crafted Adonai's own words to make them say what Lucifer had instructed him to say. "You are able to discern both good and evil[8] and, therefore, are able to decide what is right in your own eyes[9] and be your own masters."

The villagers were enraptured with what they heard. Korah seemed to be in agreement with everything, as well.

"My noble citizens, because you value freedom, I implore you to listen carefully to the words of the Great Liberator." With that, Prince Yaván stepped to the back of the platform. His words were already sinking in and taking effect, like venom.

Lucifer came forward and looked out at the people, gauging their response. "They are ready to be harvested," he communicated telepathically to Prince Yaván. "You have prepared them well."

Lucifer remained silent, letting the anticipation of his words build. The crowd stood mesmerized by his stunning glory and apparent strength. It seemed that their Liberator had come.

"Tell us how to be free!" someone in the crowd finally shouted out. The villagers roared with enthusiasm. Ben was awestruck by the shining ones and overcome by the excitement in the air.

"Shortly after the creation of your race," Lucifer began methodically, "I realized that Adonai had proposed," he paused, "an ... unbalanced constitution. He required that the older should serve the younger,[10] the stronger should serve the weaker,[11] that you must love your enemy,[12] the first had to be last and the last first,[13] and he who would be the greatest had to be the servant of all.[14]

"I have sought since the beginning to restore balance to the cosmos. Adonai created me first, as the greatest, wisest, and most glorious of all of his creatures.[15] I have been fighting for your freedom ever since.

"That which Adonai advocates is upside down. However, since I was able to grasp the concept, I have no fear that you, being lovers of wisdom like your forefathers, will be able to grasp it, as well." Lucifer smirked inwardly at his cunning tongue.[16]

Suddenly, something like a stunning three-dimensional color hologram appeared in front of the crowd. They could see all of the animals from lowly creatures like insects, worms, termites, and lice at the bottom of the hierarchy to increasingly larger animals such as mice, ferrets, wolves, lions, and elephants.[17] "There was the mighty Behemoth, once called the sauropod dinosaur, a name derived from your ancient tongue," Lucifer pointed out, "who ranked first among the creatures of Adonai, and then even the mighty Leviathan. Adonai himself boasted of these majestic and powerful dinosaurs[18] and wrote in the Chronicles concerning Leviathan, 'There's nothing like him on the earth; he was created without the ability to fear. He looks down on everything that is high; he rules over every kind of pride.' Clearly, Adonai was right to take pride in those creatures," he continued. "No one would have expected him to boast of the lice or worms or mice because everything had its own place in the order of the cosmos.

"You see, of all the magnificent and majestic creatures Adonai called into existence,[19] he said that I am the one he made more wonderful than any other.[20] I was the most beautiful of all. Think of me as a hand-crafted mold from which all casts are formed. Adonai stated that I was the sum of perfection, that I was full of wisdom and simply perfect in beauty.[21] I was endowed with unimaginable splendor for I was covered with brilliant sardius, glistening golden-topaz, sparkling diamond, beryl, onyx, deep reddish jasper, translucent blue sapphire, prismatic green emerald, and red-hot carbuncle.[22] The beautiful gems covering me refracted the light continually, making my appearance all the more dazzling. Truly, no aspect of aesthetic beauty was withheld at my creation. Any Adamite living today would have mistaken me for Adonai himself[23] and fallen to the ground in awe of my splendor.[24] Even the workmanship of my harps was prepared for me on the day I was made.[25] I was created for a great purpose; I was the anointed cherub, the Angel, and according to Adonai, the most beautiful of all the sons of Adonai. None is as magnificent or wise or brilliant as I, Lucifer,[26] the Great Liberator.[27]

"My rank was among the stones of fire that are the four cherubim who look like bright coals or brilliant torches with electricity,[28] like gleaming amber and lightning flashing among them.[29] They support the throne of Adonai and I walked in their midst. Yet I was the anointed cherub, who protected a large region in the Garden. I was above the throne of Adonai, an exalted position and duty which he gave me. I was also charged with overseeing certain sanctuaries in Eden.[30]

"Consider how dishonored ..." Lucifer said, looking sad-faced at Prince Yaván, who nodded his head in agreement, "disgraced, even ... ashamed you would feel if your father were the sovereign over a vast realm, and having invited many choice and stately guests to a dinner, were to have a conversation with a vagrant, ignorant, half-witted, menial, vile ... serf."

Prince Yaván nodded knowingly, aware of Lucifer's hatred of the Adamites.

Lucifer thought of another illustration, again making it appear as a hologram before the crowd. "Or like Phidias, your renowned sculptor, paying homage to a boy who could merely lay stones one on top of another. Worse yet," he continued," it would be as if Alexander, your greatest and most brilliant strategist, after routing King Darius had returned to the camp and washed the soldiers' clothes." Lucifer silently recalled his own even greater indignation when he had seen Yeshua stoop down and wash the feet of his followers.[31]

"This is how completely contrary the Maker has acted toward the obvious order of the creation." Lucifer loathed the Adamites more than ever and Adonai for expecting him, the anointed cherub who covers, the greatest of all, whom Adonai himself placed at the top, to stoop down and slavishly serve creatures made of dust. Obviously, such shameful behavior would undermine the dignity of the entire established hierarchy.

But Lucifer was not through: "The imbalance I discovered ran even deeper. Let me ask you: would Adonai delight in his creatures if any of us should gaze toward the heavens and observe the sun, the moon, the stars—the entire array of the sky—with the intent to worship and serve them, mere objects created by Adonai?"[32]

"No," the people shook their heads, surprised by this question.

"And I believe that we would all agree that only Adonai is worthy of our service." The people were about to answer when he hurried on with another question. "And is it not Adonai's desire that he alone should be served as King?" Lucifer made eye contact with key leaders in the crowd, who nodded in agreement. "Adonai is indeed the only One worthy of our service for he is mighty and powerful and his glory cannot be given to any other.[33] You see, Adonai stated in no uncertain terms that we ought to be destroyed if we should make carved images for ourselves—all sorts of images in the form of any animal, any winged bird or any creeping thing, or any fish in the sea—images of anything lesser than himself.[34] Therefore, we Angels had an impossible choice."

Continuing along this cunning line of rhetoric, Lucifer said, "Consider for yourselves: would it not, therefore, be contrary to the order of how Adonai made the cosmos for the Angels, who are mighty, to be servant spirits to those who would inherit salvation?[35] Is it not unreasonable, perhaps even irrational, for us to serve someone lesser than ourselves? Certainly serving Adonai, the King of kings is a duty worthy of our rank. Yet would it not have been a contradiction for us to serve creatures lesser than ourselves, such as those of the race of Adam?" And then he slyly injected, "Would it have been right for the glorious Angels to have served Adam, made of the *adamáh*?

"Then I submit this for your consideration: can anyone serve two masters? Will he not hate one and love the other, or be loyal to one and despise the other? We Angels concluded that we could not serve both Adonai and Adam!"[36] Lucifer's heart was full of cursing and bitterness[37] as he led the crowd one step futher down this line of reasoning: "If serving Adonai required us to serve Adam, then could we really serve Adonai?"

5

The Request

ANTIPAS LOOKED UP at the massive city he was about to enter—the great City of Adonai. There was simply no city like it anywhere; Mount Jerusalem, the holy mountain, was the joy of the entire planet![1] Each time Antipas entered, it was as if it were the first time. He was awestruck by the massive gates made of solid pearl, the walls covered with gemstones.[2] As he walked on the solid-gold streets, he admired the towers[3] made of rubies that studded the rising slope of the city. The light of Adonai glittered off the precious stones in a million different hues. Antipas looked up to the top of the city, higher than any mountain ever before—so high that it dwarfed by many magnitudes the tallest mountain of the previous age.[4]

More than eleven months had passed since Lucifer and his Watchers had ascended from the Abyss and still Ben, the last free-born citizen of Antipas's jurisdiction, had not been transformed. Antipas knew that he had to warn him, for Ben was a mere youth[5] and had not lived enough years on the earth to be afforded the opportunity to be transformed. Antipas wanted Ben to know the grave danger he would face from the lies of Lucifer; hence the reason for this visit to the King.

"If only I could tell Ben," Antipas recalled sharing with the great Abraham days before, "how slanderous Lucifer really is and how wonderful Adonai is—I know he would make the right decision and come to the City. I attempted to send the Chronicles myself this past year but ever since the shadow of Lucifer appeared, communication over the Ether has been blocked repeatedly by his forces. Should I take it to him myself?"

"No," Abraham had answered. "Take the Chronicles and go to Adonai. He will send one of his most seasoned messengers, an Angel, to personally deliver it to the young man," instructed Abraham.

"How can you be so sure that he would send an Angel for just one Adamite?"

Abraham beamed, remembering his own experience. "In the previous age, I pleaded with Adonai for the life of another. I wondered if he would destroy the righteous with the wicked[6] and was not disappointed. He sent two of his Angels to deliver my nephew and his family.[7] He will do likewise for your last of kin." Abraham's words encouraged Antipas. There was hope his request would be granted.

Antipas then rose on the wind, up to the council located on the uppermost platform[8] of the City, on Adonai's great mountain.[9] He set down on the sapphire pavement[10] and at once felt the imposing, weighty presence of Adonai. He looked and saw in front of the throne lampstands burning with seven flames which were the seven spirits of Adonai.[11]

There was Adonai, the great and high King, Lord of all lords sitting gloriously before his elders,[12] high and lifted up. He sat on a fiery throne that rested on the cherubim, who were actually wheels of blazing fire,[13] and a river of fire flowed from his presence.[14] He had the silhouette of Adam[15] whom he had made in his own image and likeness.[16] Antipas suddenly realized that it wasn't that the King looked like Adam but that Adam looked like the

King. Glimpsing his own body, hands, and feet, he saw they were copies of Adonai's and felt incredibly insignificant in the presence of the one who was the source of all things![17]

Antipas studied Adonai from head to toe: his entire body was radiating dazzling lightning bolts and emanating electricity[18] mingled with fiery flames. He was blazing with splendor.[19] His clothing was as white as snow, his hair like whitest wool, and his eyes were burning like glowing embers.[20] His feet were as bright as polished bronze, and his voice thundered like the mighty ocean waves of the past age. His face shown more radiantly than the sun in all its brilliance.[21] His throne, as luminous as gemstones of jasper and carnelian, was encircled by a glowing rainbow.[22] Proceeding from the very throne of Adonai and of Yeshua at the apex of the mountain was a torrent of the pure Water of Life, clear as crystal.[23] This water collected in a reflecting pool, like a shiny sea of glass in front of the throne. Then the Water of Life flowed from the throne down the mountain to the ground hundreds of miles below,[24] where it branched off into multiple streams over the City of Adonai.[25]

Antipas looked around and saw millions of Angels ministering to Adonai; a hundred million stood to attend him along with the one hundred forty-four thousand who were immortals like himself but were always in the presence of the King.[26] Antipas felt within himself the resounding joy of the glorious beings who were rapturously and passionately declaring "*Kadosh, kadosh, kadosh* is Adonai!"[27] Suddenly the twenty-four Adamites who surrounded him fell down from their thrones, cast off their crowns of purest gold, and wholeheartedly joined in magnificent praise: "You deserve to receive glory and honor and power, O Adonai."[28]

"Welcome, Antipas, son of Adam!" said Adonai with a smile as he addressed all those standing in front of him. "I was expecting you."

"O Lord Adonai ..." Antipas began. Remembering how Abraham had pleaded for the life of his nephew as he knelt before the great King gave him courage to speak: "I am greatly concerned about Ben, my last free-born citizen."

"Antipas, Son of Adam, my friend," Adonai interrupted him, "do rise to your feet. I want to talk with you face to face."[29]

"My King," Antipas rose and continued his plea, "now that the thousand years are over and Lucifer and all of his rebel Watchers were released from the Abyss almost a year ago,[30] I have heard more and more reports of their exclaiming, 'Let us tear off the shackles of Adonai from us and cast off his chains.'[31] Those born hundreds of years ago have experienced everything good, and your eternal power and divine nature have been plainly shown to them so that any who follow Lucifer now will forever be without excuse. Though they have known you, they choose now to neither honor you as their King nor give you thanks. In so doing, they have become futile in their thinking and their foolish hearts are darkened. They claim to be wise but they have become fools by believing the lies and slander of Lucifer, who has been a liar from the beginning.[32]

"Though I know you take no pleasure in the death of the wicked and would sooner they turn from their wickedness and live, yet if one should choose to abandon his righteous deeds and commit detestable practices, then he shall die in the treacherous and unfaithful wickedness that he has committed. He and all like him shall be without excuse and shall suffer the fate of all who would try to wage war against you.[33]

"However," Antipas paused, "I also know that you desire all of the Adamites to be restored and to come to the knowledge of the truth.[34] I have recently been made aware that Ben, the last of my free-born citizens, is not yet of age and has only begun to live upon the earth. As you have graciously bestowed upon me the governorship of Koinonia, I have always taken a personal interest in the well-being of all my citizens, and Ben is the last youth undecided in his loyalty either for or against you, my Lord. If he were given the opportunity to know the truth, I am certain the truth would set him free.[35] My King, as you know, six days ago was the first of the month of Tishri and there are only three days remaining until the Covering, when the personal force-fields expire, the books are opened, and fates are sealed forever.[36]

"I desire to help Ben find the Key, which I believe he will discover only by viewing the official Chronicles. To guide him, I have interwoven them with my perspective, telling the whole story so that he can see not only *how* the events happened but also *why*," Antipas continued. "My strong desire is that he might know the truth about Lucifer, the father of liars and slanderers,[37] and also know of your great goodness. Please grant him the opportunity to step into the Chronicles by means of the AEFOD. Then he will understand how to find the Key that will give him access to the Highway that leads to the City you have created.[38] He will discover how he can partake of the divine nature[39] and of the fountain of living water, which will purge him of his wickedness and uncleanness.[40] Finally, he will know how to take of the leaves of the Trees of Life, which are for the healing of the nations[41] and by which he can enter into the City."[42]

Immediately one of Adonai's Angels stepped forward and handed Antipas a thin translucent object made of crystalline material. He held the AEFOD with both hands over his heart for a few seconds, then lowered it and gave it back to the Angel, who in turn gave it to Adonai.

Adonai surveyed the retinue of beings in his image, who stood before him, each shining like the sun,[43] as he asked, "Whom shall I send and who will go for us?"

"Here am I, send me," said Michael, stepping forward

almost before the King had finished asking. Michael also shared the image and likeness of Adonai as did the immortal Adamites. His countenance, uniquely beautiful, was steady and unwavering from all the years of faithful service to Adonai. He was clothed with brilliant light and wore a gold belt around his waist. "My King, I am ready to serve. I would consider it an honor to take such a vital message, especially in the face of unusual adversity."

"Very well then, go. You know what you must do."

Michael approached the fiery white throne from which proceeded intense electricity[44] and took the AEFOD from the hand of Adonai, the mighty King, and departed in haste. Millions of Angels departed at the same moment, each carrying an AEFOD with a similar mission to millions of people around the earth. Antipas watched in amazement, never realizing that his humble request on behalf of Ben was repeated by millions of other ambassadors for the sake of their citizens as well. Only King Yeshua was wise enough to coordinate such a plan, Antipas mused, and to catch Lucifer by surprise.

6

'Destined to Be Slaves'

"O HONORABLE CITIZENS of the great people of Yaván," Lucifer addressed the villagers, "each of you must ask yourself if you are not now suffering the humility of serving someone lesser than yourself! Has it not left you poorer than before? You have paid tribute to the Hebrews for too long. Why should you be forced to serve them when they are no better than you? In ages past the Hebrews were the servants and other nations were the masters. It is written in the Chronicles, that the Hebrews were to 'dispossess greater and mightier nations than they, the nations who lived in large cities that were fortified to the sky.'[1] Consider the nation of Tyre, so great in wisdom and understanding that its people were able to obtain phenomenal wealth. They amassed gold and silver in their treasuries by their own great wisdom and skills in trading. Unlike the people of Tyre, the Hebrews would have been nothing had it not been for the King, completely unworthy as they were of all the benefits they received from him.[2]

"No matter how many times the King told them not to serve the other gods," Lucifer expounded, "the Hebrews ended up doing it anyway. One of the worst examples of ingratitude and the adultery of their hearts was when the King had just taken them out of Egypt, that glorious civilization of Pharaohs and pyramids to which they owed a debt. It was the nation of Egypt that gave them asylum during a time of drought. They stayed as guests, and only after it became obvious to the king of Egypt that the Hebrews were growing more numerous and powerful than the Egyptians themselves were they brought into slavery. Nevertheless, after hundreds of years the King took them out from there. He showed himself to them at a mountain, yet while he was giving his cherished rules and regulations to Moses on the mountaintop, the people down below were worshiping at the altar of a god of Egypt, which they had fashioned with their own hands![3] What's more, the Hebrews promised they would do all that the King had commanded but time and time again the people lied, stole, cheated, and killed. Even their illustrious David, the one Yeshua has made a prince forever,[4] whom the Great King called a man after his own heart, was nothing but a liar, adulterer, and murderer!

"Should you be forced to serve them when they are no better than you? Moses himself recorded in the Chronicles, 'Understand that Adonai is not giving you this land because of your righteousness, for you are a stiff-necked people.'[5] Even the King said to Moses, 'I have seen this people, and indeed they are a stiff-necked people!'[6] On many occasions the King wanted to destroy them but was persuaded by Moses, one of their own, of course, not to do so. On yet another occasion the King said to Moses, 'How long will these people reject me? And how long will they not believe me, with all the signs which I have performed among them? I will strike them with a pestilence and disinherit them, and I will make of you a nation greater and mightier than they.'[7]

"It was for good reason that the King spoke of disinheriting them, for in the past age they had continually done many heinous things. They had repeatedly broken the commandments of the King. In fact, they were worse than the other nations in that they went after other gods and even sacrificed their children by burning them alive to the other gods, which Adonai sternly charged them not to do!"[8]

Hearing this, the villagers recoiled in shock that such an awful people would be so favored by Adonai. According to plan, they were growing increasingly disgruntled about having to serve the Hebrews.

"All these things are a matter of public record. Everything has been recorded in the Chronicles, declared the deceiver. "I, your only advocate, have suffered greatly at the hand of the King while attempting to secure your equality in the face of such favoritism." Lucifer saw that he had their full attention; his flattery apparently working. *They, like their worthless father Dusty will soon turn from Adonai and become my slaves,* he thought with disdain for Adam.[9]

Scanning the crowd he continued, "Please tell me if you think it is just and fair that you are forced to put your faces to the ground, bowing down to the Hebrews and licking the dust of their feet[10] in light of all they have done. Is it right that the abundance of the sea be turned over to them or that the nations must bring them multitudes of camels from Midian, Ephah, and Sheba in addition to gold and incense?"[11]

All the people shook their heads "no" in disgust over the apparent injustice.

"Is it just that they feed on the wealth of the nations and boast about the riches brought to them?"[12] Then, with rapid-fire questions, postulating without pausing, Lucifer asked, "Is it right that the kings of the nations should serve the Hebrews or that the sons of the nations should build up their walls? Is it right, I ask, that the nation and kingdom which does not serve the Hebrews should perish, being utterly ruined?[13] This and more the King has decreed in the Chronicles!

"Indeed, it is written in the Chronicles that the City gates would be open continually and would not be shut day or night so that men would bring to Jerusalem the wealth of the Gentiles, and their kings in procession."

Prince Yaván, perceiving that the people were almost fully committed to the cause, admired Lucifer's ability to destroy Adonai's precious Adamites with mere words. He fixed his eyes on Lucifer, anticipating the closing argument that would win over the people completely.

"Finally, why has Adonai limited you to only one way of becoming immortal? Why must you go up to Jerusalem and have to grovel before the King and keep his law? Is that true freedom? If he wants you to have eternal life then why doesn't he simply bestow it? Why not allow you to be immortal and then choose your own path?" Lucifer paused to allow his poison to take effect.

The lull invited a question from Korah, the oldest person in the village, who had refused to visit the City for centuries: "I have heard of a secret knowledge Adonai has withheld from us," he stated, speaking loudly so all could hear and consider how they were being slighted. "We demand to know."

Lucifer slowly surveyed the faces of the people who stood before him. "O good and noble citizens of Yaván," he said at last, "so many things have been withheld from you! I have been trying to give your race wisdom and immortality from the beginning. Eating from the Tree of the Knowledge of Good and Evil opened the eyes of Adam and Eve, yet Adonai had prohibited it. Then once their eyes were opened, he then drove them away—denying them the Tree of Life!" he said with affected exasperation that morphed into disingenuity: "I have taken it upon myself to show your race the secrets of both wisdom and immortality, knowledge Adonai has denied you while demanding submission to his onerous regulations in order to become immortal.

"I, however, have fought for your freedom to become immortal on your own terms. Surely you realize that in the previous age, before Adonai selfishly destroyed years of progress and evolution, through the wisdom that I provided your race did achieve immortality."

7

Journey to Yaván

MICHAEL ROSE TO travel upon the wind and spotted millions of beautiful deep-blue butterflies hovering near the City. The glorious light of Adonai filled everything; the butterflies also had absorbed that light and were glowing wondrously. Michael smiled but did not stop since his assignment was urgent.

As Michael flew in the wind, he looked over the broad surface of the earth and could see the gathering of the rebel Watchers and the treasonous Adamites who were joining them in a final attempt to overthrow the King.[1]

For one thousand years Lucifer had been locked away in the Abyss with all of his army. During that time of peace, messages had been sent unopposed. Michael wondered if an attempt would be made to block his delivery of the AEFOD as had happened when the message sent to Daniel the prophet was delayed by Prince Parás, the regional ruler in the service of the enemy. *That prince was able to detain the King's messenger for three whole weeks,* Michael recollected, *until I, chief prince to the Hebrews, came and helped the messenger escape from the rebel Angel authorities of Parás.*[2]

The land of Yaván was coming into view with its usually verdant hills and valleys. He noticed a small stream trickling over a precipice and remembered when it had been a mighty waterfall. The last time Michael had visited this region he had seen lush green hills and trees with vibrant foliage. Now, everything was wilted and stunted. Nothing died though, for decay and degeneration had been removed from the earth. Plants still enjoyed the drink of rain; when no rain fell they became dry and less productive. Because the mortals still required food for sustenance, the lack of it affected them.[3]

Every region of the earth had been restored to the condition it was in before the Fall, and each community had a part in tending its designated area. It was apparent from the brown and withered foliage that rain had not come to this village for a very long time, which meant that the people had not gone to the City for the Festival of Tents for an equally long time, perhaps even centuries.[4]

Michael could see thousands of people gathered around the village plaza listening to Lucifer. He decided to mask his shining appearance—something he had not needed to do since the previous age when he and other Angels would often hide their emission of light to blend in with people. Occasionally they had been invited into homes and entertained without the hosts' being aware of their angelic nature.[5] On other occasions, they appeared in all their brilliance so that the sons of men would know that they were servants of the Most High King. After the veil came down, however, there had been no need to mask their shining until now.

Michael quickly found a place where he could go and not be seen.

Ben looked up and saw the beautiful blue butterfly again. It seemed to float in front of him for several seconds, almost purposefully. He watched as it fluttered off to the grove of apple trees where he had often played as a boy, about two hundred feet away, directly opposite of where Lucifer stood. He realized that he had been listening intently, almost hypnotized by the words of Lucifer, words that powerfully appealed to Ben. But the words that made perfect sense to his mind met with resistance in his heart. He needed to think about what he had just heard. Since the spell had been broken by the blue butterfly, Ben decided to follow it, hoping for a chance to examine the exquisite creature more closely. His disappearance from the periphery of the crowd went unnoticed except by one.

He came to the grove and the trees seemed even darker and more wilted than when he was younger. "Yeshua," Ben whispered sheepishly, "if you can hear me ..." He stopped himself, conflicted by the words of Lucifer and the villagers. If only there were a way for him to learn the truth about Yeshua and the Great Liberator and the City.

The butterfly had flown inside, so Ben ducked under some low-lying branches and followed it. In the center of the tightly formed cluster of trees he saw a fellow Adamite sitting on a rock.

"Who are you?" asked Ben, startled, surprised to find someone inside. "Did you come with Lucifer?" Ben looked at the intruder warily.

"No, I am Michael. The King sent me because of your request."

"What request? I didn't say anything to anyone," Ben replied nervously. "It was really just more of a thought, not really a request," he said, trying to make sense of this unexpected presence.

"In this age," Michael said, "the King promised that before you call he would answer.[6] And, thus the King sent me in advance of your call and told me to deliver this to you," he said, holding out the AEFOD to Ben.

Ben took the AEFOD and examined it. He held it easily in one hand, for it weighed virtually nothing. It looked like a thin slice of translucent crystalline material with the coloration of twelve precious stones.

"Antipas, the ruler over this village and a close friend of the King, is reaching out to you. He asked the King to send you this device, which Antipas himself prepared from the official Chronicles because he is concerned for you. During the glorious thousand years, he would have sent it over the Ether, but since Lucifer was loosed nearly a year ago, the shadow he has cast over the earth has blocked regular communication. That's why I have come personally in response to your request."

Ben, intently focused on the unusual object in his hand, hardly heard a word Michael was saying. "What is it?" he asked. "How do I use it?"

"It is an Active Experience Fact Observer Device or AEFOD. Antipas placed within the AEFOD important events from the Chronicles that reveal what happened in the previous age," Michael explained, "and throughout this peaceful age as well. The Chronicles in this AEFOD will reveal both the darkness of lies and the light of truth — if truth is what you seek."[7]

"How would you respond to the statements of my fellow villagers about Adonai's oppressive regime?" Ben asked somewhat skeptically, taken aback by Michael's seemingly sudden appearance. "I am almost persuaded by what they are saying."

"There are many mysteries in your mind right now," Michael answered. "The Key to those mysteries lies buried in the Chronicles. The means by which you can obtain the Key is revealed in all that you will see and hear. Only by finding the Key can your questions be answered. Perhaps most important, the Key is the only means by which access into the City is granted. Lucifer has attempted to destroy the Key and, should you find it, will attempt to rob you of it if you are not careful. But don't be concerned, as you journey through the Chronicles in the AEFOD you will at times hear the voice of Antipas, directing you toward finding the Key."

"Why can't you simply tell me where the Key is? Why must I find it myself? If Adonai really wants me to come to the City then why do I have to find a mysterious Key?" Ben asked, seemingly annoyed by the task before him. "Where do I even begin to look for this Key?"

"You must discover it for yourself," Michael continued, "just as those before you had to discover it for themselves. By holding the AEFOD with two hands you will see visions that the ancient prophets were given. They were able to see, hear, smell, taste, and touch their surroundings. In a similar way, you will experience the Chronicles of the King. As I told you, Antipas will help you understand what you are seeing, and once you discover the mystery of the Key you will know what to do."

"Why can't I just go to the City now?"

"Ben, only those who have the Key are authorized to travel on Adonai's Highway, which as you know, is used by no one but those loyal to the King."[8]

"Let me see if I understand: I need to find a Key, which you can't help me find, and once I have this mysterious Key, I can travel on the King's Highway to the City and enter it freely. Is that correct?" Ben sounded perplexed.

"Yes," Michael replied.

"I don't know ..." Ben hesitated, motioning toward Lucifer and the villagers. "I think I would rather throw in my lot with the Great Liberator, or whatever his name is. He guarantees that those who are worthy will rise to the top. According to him, our way of life was the epitome and our land was the envy of the previous age. We used to be the rulers and did not have to answer to some distant King who rules with a rod of iron.[9] Besides, Lucifer used to have the position of vizier just as Yeshua does right now—from all that I have heard and seen, it appears that his plan is more in line with our thinking."

Michael was overcome with compassion as he saw Ben's internal conflict: tempted to follow the crowd yet fearful of staying behind and remaining ignorant of all that had come before him.

Realizing that Lucifer's lies and slander had started to poison the young man's mind, Michael wanted to warn Ben, to somehow open his eyes. So when he opened his mouth to speak, it was with such intensity that he captured Ben's full attention. "Yes, Lucifer can be quite convincing but I caution you to be on guard, for although his lips drip honey and his speech is smoother than oil, in the end he is as bitter as wormwood. His words sound good but they are lies! He has never stood for truth, and there is no truth in him. Whenever he tells a lie he speaks according to his character, for he is a liar and the father of lies. If you follow him, you will share the fate of many others who have deceptively been led into the domain of darkness and death."

Ben was silent for a moment as he mulled over what Michael had said. "If you really are an Angel as you claim to be, then why aren't you shining like Lucifer? And why don't you just go and tell everyone right now to come to the King?"

"After so many years of refusing to follow Adonai's commands," Michael responded, "the people of your village have become hardened and stubborn. They have been waiting for someone to liberate them. They had access to the King whenever they desired over the centuries, but instead of seeking him and turning from their rebellion they became entrenched in it. Appearing in my brilliant form would have accomplished nothing because it is Lucifer they desire. However, Yeshua will provide for any who request to know the truth as you have done.

"It is now not for me to give you further counsel," Michael said, "but I can share with you some things about the beginning and how the one who calls himself the Great Liberator was first known as Lucifer."

8
Michael's Story

INSTANTLY A HOLOGRAPHIC image, similar to that which Lucifer had projected in front of the villagers, appeared before Ben.

"Before the current age of peace and even before the previous age with its rulers and empires ..." Michael began to explain as towers and ancient monuments appeared to Ben, "before the former deluge judgment and before Lucifer, before the differentiation, before anything was, before the blackness of the void ... " Blackness filled the image before Ben. "Before all of that, there was Adonai, the King, the self-existent and eternal One who was and is and is to come. The first day was the beginning of differentiations, when Adonai created things that were not void and began to fill space with substance. Soon after that Adonai uttered the names of all the Angels,[1] bringing each one instantly into existence.[2]

"'Michael,' Adonai announced, and immediately I came into being—a glorious Angel." Ben could see Michael newly formed, just as he looked in the Garden. "That first moment I saw Adonai was glorious and yet strangely familiar," Michael recalled. "I sensed his overwhelming power and his goodness both at once. Then I saw the fire and brilliant lightning that went out from before him.[3] He was clothed in such light[4] that no living Adamite could ever approach him.[5] I then noticed that my body was similar to that of Adonai; he fashioned all of us sons in his own illustrious and exalted appearance."[6]

"Even though we were fashioned in his likeness and in his image, I couldn't help but admire him: 'Adonai, you are exceedingly great,' I said. 'You are clothed with honor and majesty and you cover yourself with light as a garment. You have made us Angel spirits, your servants, flames of fire.'[7] Even though glorious fire emanated from me, I realized that it was different and infinitely lesser than Adonai's, for mine had been given to me, whereas his originated from Adonai himself. Though I appeared like him in many ways, I at once perceived that I was in the presence of supreme greatness, of the one to whom there would never be any equal. With a simple command, I had been brought into existence out of nothing. The exalted King before me merely spoke a word, and I and all the Angels, including Lucifer, came to be.[8]

"Adonai had impressed his image upon us so that not only did we share his appearance[9] but we also shared his qualities of speech, art, and music, as well as his passion, emotion, and choice. I wondered how I or any other created being could ever exist in the presence of such grandeur.[10] A rush of emotion swept over me![11] Recognizing my utter insignificance compared to my Maker, I lowered my face in profound humilty.

"'Michael, you have rightly reflected on your name—Who is like God?' Adonai said to me, 'for indeed, I am El and there is no other; I am Adonai and there is none like me.[12] You are my esteemed servant and I have a great and noble purpose for you. You are to be the chief prince standing watch over a people who are yet to come.'[13] He was speaking of the Hebrews."[14]

"So then," asked Ben, "when did he, the Slanderer as you claim, become Lucifer?"

"He was created as a flame of fire, a burning one[15] with Adonai's light emanating from him."[16] Ben saw the light diffusing through the many colored gemstones with which Adonai had covered Lucifer, creating a stunning kaleidoscopic spray of brilliant sardius, rich golden topaz, sparkling diamond, beryl, onyx, deep reddish jasper, translucent blue sapphire, prismatic green emerald, and red-hot carbuncle.

"Lucifer was the paradigm against which the others were measured. He was the sum of perfection, full of wisdom, perfect in beauty. Adonai spared no aesthetic quality when he created Lucifer.[17] He also created him for a great purpose. He was the anointed cherub, the Angel who ranked among the stones of fire[18] and walked in their midst."

Ben could see four beings with bodies like a son of Adam, although each of the four had a different face—one human, one like a lion, the third like an ox, and the fourth like an eagle. Their appearance was like bright coals of fire or brilliant torches, and something that looked like lightning flashed back and forth among them.[19] "Lucifer, the anointed cherub, was one of them. He was one of the stones of fire—'bright coals of fire, brilliant torches'—yet he was the anointed cherub who covered. Adonai gave him this exalted position and duty. He was also charged with overseeing certain *mikdashim*, places that had been reserved for special use.[20] These *mikdashim* were in Eden, where Adonai prepared to place Adam.

"Adonai entrusted Lucifer with everything and no Angel had more authority in Adonai's City than he did.[21] Adonai placed him high up on his holy mountain, the City of Jerusalem.[22]

"But the making of Adam is when things really began," Michael continued.

Ben saw in front of him a beautiful Garden full of vibrant flowers in every imaginable color. He could even smell their collective fragrance permeating the untainted air. The rich scent of apples, passion fruit, peaches, oranges, and fruit of every kind enveloped him. Ben noticed the light of the sun poking through the majestic trees that were home to animals of every sort. Under the tall canopy, fruit trees full of ripe delicious fruit dotted the landscape and hummingbirds drank of their nectar. Ben was captivated by the lovely glow that emanated from every created thing.

"We Angels were ecstatic with anticipation of what Adonai would create next because every day since he called us into existence[23] had been more spectacular than the day before. We marveled at how Adonai had made us as well as all the amazing things in the cosmos.[24] We wondered what greater creation could possibly come next when he did something he had not done until that moment: As a potter takes clay and forms it, Adonai took some *adamáh*, land or soil,[25] in his powerful hands and with great care fashioned the head, torso, arms, legs, fingers, and toes of a body. All that was lacking was the animation of that body.

"Gabriel, Lucifer, I, and all the Angels watched[26] in awe as Adonai tenderly bent over the form and gently breathed into the nostrils.[27] 'Adam!' Adonai called him. He had a reddish hue like the *adamáh* out of which he had been taken. Absorbing the light from Adonai, he then emitted a strong whitish glow.[28] Not only did the *adamáh*-being share in his image and likeness, but Adonai had actually breathed his own life-force into him![29]

"Adonai then conferred all the benefits of the earth and complete dominion over it to Adam, although the earth and its fullness would forever belong to Adonai.[30] However," Michael continued, as if recalling something terrible, "Adonai stationed Lucifer in Eden, the Mountain-City,[31] not far from where Adonai placed Adam and Eve, near the Tree of Life and the Tree of the Knowledge of Good and Evil."

Ben listened more intently as Michael continued. "Lucifer became enraged at the notion that he, the great Angel, had to be a servant to Adam, made of dust. So the root of desire contrary to the nature of Adonai began festering within him."[32]

The hologram immediately changed to Lucifer rallying Angels stationed around the City of Adonai.

"*I don't* desire *to be the greatest,* Lucifer had counseled himself, *I simply* am *the greatest and I am not able to change— nor should I.* Adonai later revealed to us Lucifer's thoughts concerning many things,"[33] Michael explained. "He truly was the greatest of Adonai's creatures and we all knew it. He was also a member of the divine council of the Angels.[34] However, his beauty turned into perilous pride and arrogance over the fact that he was the wisest and most glorious creation apart from Adonai himself; he was the ideal of perfect beauty.[35] *The greater serving the lesser is foolish,*[36] he reasoned, because in his estimation no one was worthy to give him counsel. As long as he was required to serve only Adonai, however, Lucifer was content because serving someone greater than himself was in his estimation rational, reasonable, even honorable."

"*Adam should be serving me,* Lucifer had mused, because he did not delight[37] in serving someone lesser than himself.[38] He failed to grasp the tenderness and good intentions of Adonai. Adam and Eve were childlike in their under-standing of the great cosmos, and their wisdom could not compare to Lucifer's. Even so, he and the other Angels were charged with watching over the ones made of dust,[39] guiding and serving them in any way needed.[40] As the greatest of Adonai's sons, Lucifer had been placed in the position of steward, or overseer, and as the most glorious Angel he was required to be willing to disregard his status and serve others lesser than himself—which in his case was everyone.[41]

"He ignored the fact that his beauty and rank, in fact every majestic quality he possessed, was a generous gift from his creator, the one who made the sun, moon, and stars,[42]and somehow forgot that he was a mere creation himself, like everyone and everything else.[43] In some way I can't explain, Ben, he imagined serving Adam to be a threat to his rank and regarded having to minister to the one made from the dust as beneath the dignity of the greatest of all created beings.

"Instead of presenting himself as a servant set apart as a living sacrifice, so to speak, and becoming like his creator — which was acceptable to Adonai and was also his reasonable service — he began to think more highly of himself than he ought.[44] Incensed with jealousy toward Adam, he began to slander and defame the name of Adonai. How ironic that the very gift of unparalleled beauty caused him to become self-centered and eventually to relinquish true wisdom.[45] Instead of embracing humility, which would have led to honor,[46] he chose pride and arrogance, which ultimately led to his fall toward destruction."[47]

"Can you tell me," Ben interjected, overwhelmed by all that Michael was divulging, "how Lucifer managed to convince so many Angels to follow him?"

"There was once the son of a certain king," Michael replied, "who used to go and sit in the gate of a city and steal the hearts of the people by telling them what he would do if he were the judge: 'Oh, that I were made judge in the land, and everyone who has any suit or cause would come to me; then I would give him justice.'[48] Lucifer acted in a similar way by stirring up distrust, pride, and vanity in the hearts of the sons of Adonai.

"'Praise Adonai! There is none like him,' Lucifer often would say, even as the root of desire contrary to the nature of Adonai grew within him, giving way to depravity."[49] Ben watched as the holographic image of Lucifer went to and fro[50] among the Angels saying, "He is worthy of our praise and service, for he commanded and we were created.[51] Has he not made us greater in power and might than anything made of dust?"[52]

"He has, of course." Ben saw and heard the other Angels answer.

"Would Adonai delight in us, his creatures, if any of us should gaze toward the heavens and observe the sun, the moon, the stars, and the entire vast array of the sky, with the intent to worship and serve them, mere objects that he created?"[53]

"At once I answered him, 'No, of course not.' I sensed something strangely different about Lucifer but I could not discern it because none can understand the heart of another as Adonai can," Michael said. Having heard just a short time earlier the same rationale put forth by Lucifer masquerading as the Great Liberator, Ben looked quizzical as Michael continued.

"Lucifer pursued this line of questioning, asking us Angels if it would not be in violation of Adonai's directives to serve all sorts of images in the form of any animal, bird, sea creature—or even Adam and Eve. Everyone agreed."[54]

"Wait a second," Ben interjected. "Lucifer has already explained this. I heard him say that he was left without any choice. Adonai created an impossible situation and he did the only reasonable thing."

"Just watch," Michael said as he pointed to Lucifer speaking in the hologram.

"I firmly believe," Lucifer said reassuringly, "Adonai is the only one worthy of your *avodáh*, your service, for he is mighty and powerful and his glory cannot be given to another.[55] Is there any King like Adonai worthy of your service? Would it not, therefore, be contrary to the cosmic order for you who are mighty to render service to those who will inherit salvation?"[56]

"Lucifer twisted the word *avodáh*, which as you know means to 'work,' 'serve,' and 'worship,'" Michael pointed out.

Ben again watched the images: "Therefore is it not a contradiction for you to render service to the race of Adam?"

Lucifer presented his summary masterfully in anticipation of his final conclusion: "Then is it not unreasonable, perhaps even irrational, for you to render service to someone lesser than yourselves? Certainly rendering service to Adonai, the King of kings, is worthy of your rank. Yet if serving Adonai requires us to serve Adam, made of the *adamáh*, can we truly even serve Adonai?"

"Every deceitful, slanderous word," Michael added, "that proceeded from his throat was like an open grave and as lethal as the venom of poisonous snakes.[57] He slandered Adonai's intention for serving, which was not to bow down to someone else in the place of Adonai himself but to lovingly care for the needs of others! With lies such as this, over time Lucifer was able to repeatedly slander Adonai[58] by distorting his words. All who sought Adonai's counsel were delivered, while those who were drawn by pride, vanity, and distrust in their hearts followed after Lucifer.[59]

"Like the son of the king that I mentioned, Lucifer cunningly convinced the Angels that Adonai did not have their best interests at heart and slyly suggested they needed a leader they could trust. His slandering was very subtle and persistent.

"Oh the great patience of Adonai who gave him space to repent of his slandering," said Michael, looking back in the direction of the City. "Lucifer would not relent, however, and so a day came when, because of the abundance of his slandering, he was filled with violence and proceeded to commit treason.[60] Having stolen the loyalty of one-third of the Angels,[61] he quickly set out to accomplish his ultimate intent, which was to murder the frail, pitiful creature he had been commanded to serve.

"Time is of the essence," Michael said, preparing to leave as the hologram vanished. "I have delivered the AEFOD. You are encouraged to consider it immediately and to follow the instructions contained therein. I want you to remember that the King is eager to meet you and awaits your arrival.

"My assignment is now completed. I hope to see you soon in Jerusalem, the grand City of Adonai." With that Michael rose up on the wind and swiftly departed, unnoticed by the villagers—willing accomplices in their own deception—eagerly hanging on Lucifer's every word.

9
Antipas

BEN TOOK HOLD of the AEFOD with both hands, uncertain of what to expect. Abruptly he was enveloped by a new reality that he had never sensed before, not even when he viewed the hologram with Michael. A blinding white light surrounded him. After a few moments he saw a man dressed in shining linen clothing,[1] whiter than snow, with a belt of pure gold around his waist. His body looked like a dazzling gem; his arms and feet were shining.[2] Bolts of electricity radiated from his face more brightly than the sun.[3] He wore a crown of righteousness that was like crystal sparkling with topazes, emeralds, and yellow pearls shining like the stars of heaven, bright as the rays of the sun. Truly, this one had been conformed to the image of the glorious body of Adonai[4] and had become a partaker of the divine nature."[5]

"Hello Ben," the man said, "I am Antipas, founder and ruler of this village of Koinonia. I ruled over the ten cities here in the land of Yaván, which in my previous life was known as Greece, until the end of the thousand years when Adonai called me and the other immortals back to the City. You, Ben, are in fact the last person born in this village.

"The story of Koinonia began when, after many days of feasting, I led survivors of the time of the Hebrews'

Trouble in search of a place that was still related to our ancient homeland. We started out on the King's Highway, which you must take to get back to the City." Ben saw a highway in front of him made of pure crystal, virtually transparent. It was about twenty feet wide and roughly ten feet elevated off the ground. He saw Antipas leading thousands of Adamites along the elevated highway traveling south, away from the City.

"We commonly call it the 'Holy Way'," explained Antipas, "because it is set apart exclusively for the redeemed — those who have been restored by Yeshua, whose hearts belong to him. Mortals may travel on it if they are loyal to the King. However, no one unclean is able to journey on it; only those who are authorized. No fool shall ever venture onto it.[6] Others traveling to nearby lands have taken another highway, which you will see when you get closer to the City."[7]

Antipas continued recounting the history of Koinonia: "As we journeyed toward Yaván we were amazed at the radical changes the earth had undergone. The old things had passed away. First of all, the vast contiguous ocean that had covered most of the earth in the previous age had disappeared[8] and there was much more living space. Of course, there were still seas but, as you know, the seas we have today are more like the great lakes of the previous age. It is into these seas, or great lakes, that the water from the throne of Adonai eventually flows, along with the draining rain." Roaring rivers appeared before Ben, emptying into the great seas.

"We also noticed how Adonai had caused the trees, grass, giant ferns, and all of the vegetation on the planet to emit a soft glow;[9] also, it quickly became obvious that lights were not needed in the houses because the energy and light from the sun and the moon would never vanish. As a matter of fact, the sun shone brighter than ever before, seven times brighter, and the light of the moon was as the prior light of the sun.[10] These greater and lesser lights apparently lost some of their luminosity at the Fall. With the veil removed and Adonai's energy abounding, the sun shone brighter and thus the moon reflected more light.

"I remember that when we finished building the first house of Koinonia it struck me how different this age was from the last. The very work itself was easy and light. In the previous age, even when work was enjoyable, great effort was required to build anything, and there was always the danger of a tornado or earthquake or simply a powerful storm destroying the shelter for which we had labored intensely. Here, there has never been the fear of anything destroying our houses.

"I recall the joy your ancestors had when their house was finished," Antipas said. Ben saw it appear before him. "Because everyone in the village had helped and because of my presence as an immortal, along with assistance from Angels on occasion, the work was finished in weeks. This is the very house in which you now live.

"In fact, this grove we are in is where your first ancestors, Matai and Hannah, used to play with their children when they were little. You are the great grandson of Matai and Hannah, twelve generations removed, their last Adamite relative. I was present at the births of their children, just as I was also present at yours, and I have been keeping an eye on you ever since.

"I can still remember when Matai and Hannah were admiring the beauty of their newly completed home, they were both struck by the absence of all of the gadgets that had been so prevalent in houses of the previous age. I listened to them talk at length about the differences; as they reminisced about one thing, then another would come to mind. From no more locks on the doors to the better-than-organic food and no-longer-needed professions, they went on and on about the many advantages they enjoyed and appreciated in the economy of Yeshua.

"The mortals of the precious age were much impressed with their technology," Antipas continued. "In fact, every time some new device came along they 'oohed and aahed' over what it could do. After a while, they could not imagine life without their gadgets. Hannah once confided that she was virtually glued to her phone, chatting with people continually. Computers of that age in actuality helped people cope with living in a corrupted, decaying, death-filled world and aided their effort to regain what had been lost in the Garden. Whereas the human memory forgot, computers could store vast amounts of information with little energy. The human brain could not perform millions of complex mathematical calculations simultaneously, but computers could.

"At the end of the previous age people could send messages over the Internet, called emails, which were basically packets of information that could be delivered to a desired address via a series of cables, fiber optic lines, satellites, and radio towers. There were even researchers working on translating neural signals from the brain into computer code that could interact with machines.[11]

"Matai and Hannah once considered such development amazing and impressive—that is, until they came to realize how 'low tech' it really was. In this age, there is no longer any separation between the domain of Adonai and the domain of the Adamites. His electricity—his energy—acts as the Ether because it fills everything and serves as the conduit for communication instead of the many clumsy cables and wireless devices formerly needed. We are now able to interface via the Ether of Adonai's energy,[12] which of course is the original electromagnetic spectrum,[13] by sending 'thought mail,' as it could be called.

"At first the mortals were unable to understand this concept, but it began to make sense when they considered that in the previous age communications of the Adamites that ascended to Adonai were stored in golden bowls[14] and then were thrown down to the earth, wreaking havoc.[15] This realization helped them see that mortals were not reading one another's thoughts continuously but were able to send and receive 'thought mail' via the ambient energy of Adonai himself, which is a type of Ether—that is, a medium of transmission.

"Everything was different in the kingdom of Yeshua, Ben, and none of the previous things were missed. The earth itself was healed. Computers were obsolete. There were no factories to manage, no problems to overcome, no wars to win,[16] no diseases to cure, no crimes to solve.

"The renewal of the earth meant that practically no labor was required for things to grow.[17] Now the food is always natural, organic, healthy, and delicious—it is plentiful and never spoils.

"No matter what Lucifer tells you, Ben, do not believe him because his statements distort what is true and real. If he had continued in power, the earth would have devolved into death, decay, and degeneration. But Adonai decisively won the victory; so now there is plenty of land and perfect weather. Even gold and silver, which were rare in the previous age, are found in great abundance. Indeed, your own house is decorated with great quantities of gold. While there has been some bartering, money has not been needed because no one holds exclusive rights to any commodity that people would have to purchase.

"Rather than having to endure toil and hardship as mortals previously did in coping with the effects of the fall, they have been free to enjoy nobler activities such as making and playing instruments, composing and singing music, creating works of art in honor of Adonai, and exploring the amazing vastness and beauty of his creation.

"Most thrilling of all, though, has been the celebration of the annual feasts of Adonai. With great joy and happiness we would visit people in the neighboring village and say, 'Let us continue to go and pray before Adonai, and seek

Adonai, commander of armies. I myself will go also.'[18]
Then they would respond, 'Come, let's go up to Adonai's
Mountain, to the house of the King of Jacob, so he can teach
us his requirements, and we can follow his standards.'[19]
We would then all set out with great anticipation of seeing
our great King and his Mountain-City," Antipas recounted.
"Of course, the mortals could not actually go into the New
Jerusalem but had to remain in the Camp of the Saints,
that is, the land of the Hebrews, outside the City, which is
amazing in itself.

"Yeshua built the temple that now stands in the Camp of
the Saints, outside the New Jerusalem. What a magnificent
structure! When it was completed, he himself entered
through the eastern-facing gate[20]—brilliant electricity, fire,
and light radiating from his being[21]—and sat down to rule
as both King and Priest on his throne! The eastern gate
would from that day remain shut, not to be opened. No
one was allowed to come through it because Yeshua, the
omnipotent King of the Hebrews, had entered through it.[22]

"Of course, that temple pales in comparison when
you lift your eyes and look at the 252-foot-high walls of
the New Jerusalem." Ben saw fiery horses[23] decorated
with bells inscribed with "Holiness to Adonai" parading
through the golden streets in front of the massive temple
structure. There were six guardhouses along the walkway
with a retaining wall about a foot-and-a-half wide with
sentinels watching over the flow of people coming and
going.[24] He noticed that the pots in the Temple of Adonai
were as splendid as the bowls in front of the altar.[25]

"Naturally, the Adamites, who had come through the
time of the Hebrews' Trouble," explained Antipas, "could
not enter in because their bodies were still incompatible
with Adonai's presence. They had families and repopulated
the earth,[26] however, and their lives were greatly extended.
In fact, death was not even necessary if they chose to serve
Yeshua and live according to his ways.

"You see, longevity in the previous age was seventy years or if by reason of strength, eighty years.[27] The life of an Adamite in the kingdom of Yeshua is altogether different: No longer is there a young boy who lives only a little while or an old person who does not live out his days; someone who dies at a hundred years is considered a mere youth, and one who falls short of a hundred years is considered accursed.[28] Formerly, 20 years was considered the age of accountability as evidenced in the generation which, because of unbelief, wandered forty years in the wilderness until all the men of that generation died. However, the punishment applied only to those who were 20 years old and above. Those 19 and younger were not counted among the rebellious generation.[29]

"Thus 100 is the new 20 because once people reach 100, they become accountable for their actions before Adonai. In this time, people's lives are long, like the life of a tree, continuing for hundreds of years.[30] The reality is that there is no reason at all for anyone to die except for rebellion–as occurred in the days of the generation of the Hebrews who perished in the wilderness.[31] Now only an accursed person will die; death is completely avoidable by partaking of the Water of Life and the leaves of the Tree of Life.[32]

"While the mortal Adamites received the Covering, I, Antipas, in procession with the kings of Tarshish and of the isles, the kings of Sheba, and the nations of those saved, presented our gifts.[33] We entered the luminous City, bringing our glory and honor into it.[34] How delightful it was to witness the Hebrews, who had been so long beaten down, receiving their inheritance. Instead of the derision they endured in the previous age, they now received honor and shouts of acclamation. They inherited a double portion in their land and everlasting joy is theirs.[35]

"But now," Antipas said with a sigh, "I am greatly concerned for you, my son. You are young and can easily be deceived by logical-sounding lies.

"You must see what it was like a thousand years ago during the time of the Hebrews' Trouble, the zenith of Lucifer's reign of terror. It was unlike any other time in the history of the Adamites; nothing has ever compared to it in the scope and magnitude of afflictions of every kind.[36] You must see what it was like to live in Lucifer's kingdom that was full of degeneration, decay, death, disease, pain, and rebellion," Antipas said, articulating every word. "Then I will show you the glories of Yeshua's thousand years of peace. Because your vantage point is greatly limited by circumstances beyond your control, I will guide you through all that you now see and hear.

"I have prepared this AEFOD, which contains the Chronicles to guide you in the truth. You must embrace what they reveal and then you will be able to walk the path toward the City, where Yeshua himself will greet you.

"The King has from the beginning determined that each person must understand and make his own decision concerning the Chronicles; that is why I cannot simply come and take you to the City. You must discover the Key and make the journey for yourself.

"Understand that you need to consider it right away for the time is coming quickly when the Covering, the individual force-field that protects you from the fiery-lightning presence of Adonai, will be removed. You must be admitted into the City before that moment. Viewing the Chronicles in the AEFOD is quicker than real-time, so you should be able to find the Key, walk on Adonai's Highway, and arrive in the City before it is too late."

Ben took one hand off the AEFOD and looked out over the crowd. People appeared to be in the same position as before and Lucifer seemed to be finishing the last sentence Ben had heard him begin. Time in the AEFOD *was* faster than real-time, just as Antipas had said!

Ben considered his need for the Key and wanted to find it as soon as possible.

"Ben," once again came the soothing voice of Antipas in the Chronicles, "you must understand that, while chosen by Adonai, the Hebrews have also been the object of Lucifer's hatred. At the end of the previous age, he attempted to massacre every last one of them, and if he had succeeded, then Adonai could not have restored the earth to the pristine condition we have enjoyed for the past thousand years. Indeed, if he had succeeded, no son of Adam would have remained. And if all the Hebrews had been destroyed, then Lucifer would have had legal grounds to challenge Adonai and these past thousand years of peace would not have been. Rather, darkness, degeneration, and death would have overtaken the earth forever.

"Whereas Lucifer's plan in the beginning was based on deceiving Adam and Eve, in the latter days it was centered on deceiving the Hebrews to become like him. The first step was to raise up the false deliverer."

*One thousand years before Present,
the time of the Hebrews' Trouble, as viewed
through the AEFOD*

10

The Rise of Therion

THE WHITE LIGHT that had enveloped him began to fade and Ben, once more holding the AEFOD with both hands, was gradually surrounded by darkness. A cool wind blew on him, and he heard a man paying homage to someone.

"There is none like you, O Light Bearer. Thank you for showing me the light." Ben could see the man speaking as the moist twilight air obscured the rugged mountain peaks in the distance.[1] The darkness of night would soon shroud the arcane meeting Lucifer had surreptitiously arranged.

"You are the god of light and god of good," the man professed, prostrating himself before Lucifer, who had transformed himself to look like a glorious Angel of light.[2] "You are the equal of Adonai.[3] You are to be praised and lauded for your struggle against Adonai, the creator of darkness and evil.[4] I pledge my fidelity to you alone, my Lord." Lucifer basked in the adulation. "There is none like you," the man repeated again.

Lucifer eyed him haughtily.[5] *The Adamites are willing to renounce Adonai for practically nothing; strike everything they own, and they will curse Adonai to his face.[6] Or better yet, strike their bones and flesh and they will curse their Maker immediately,[7]* he thought. *But give them everything they want and they will bow down to me.* He looked at his subject with contempt, fully aware that the man worshipped him only to get what he wanted.

There had been many over the last two millennia with the same anti-Yeshua spirit[8] who hated the ways of Adonai as did the son of Adam kneeling before Lucifer. The time had not been ripe, however, until now that the Adamites had entered the genetic age. But Lucifer had to be very selective about whom he gave his seed, for mixing it with the seed of men was a violation of Adonai's directive that everything must reproduce according to its own kind.[9] The penalty for disobeying the clear, precise, and unconditional directive was being bound with unbreakable, everlasting chains and cast into the utter darkness of Tartarus, the deepest chasm of the Abyss.[10]

Many of Lucifer's Watchers, who had abandoned their own non-terrestrial bodies[11] when they mingled with the seed of men,[12] producing the Nephilim, were already in Tartarus waiting for their supreme leader to liberate them. Now by mingling his own seed, Lucifer too would be liable to imprisonment in the Abyss;[13] victory therfore was imperative.[14]

The time of the restoration of all things would soon be at hand, when Adonai would reclaim the earth and possess it forever.[15] The last of the Hebrews needed to be destroyed before that day.[16] Then Adonai could do nothing.

Lucifer assessed the qualities of the servant who knelt before him: *He loves himself more than any other, and he loves money and power—all of which make him boastful, arrogant, un-feeling, and delightfully slanderous. Yet he also has an outward form of devoutness.*[17] *He is precisely what I need at this hour.*

"I have given you everything you could possibly want: money, power, and influence—all because of your loyalty to me. You have done well, my servant, and have learned the mystery of your craft.[18] What more do you desire?"

"You know how I loathe Yeshua," he answered, "and

share your contempt of his ways and his dictates. Using my power and influence, I have done everything possible to subvert him." He then lifted his head and fixed his hazel eyes on his master. The wind blew through his golden-bronze hair, leaving it slightly disheveled. "I want the key to the dynamic force[19] in order to attain immortality. I want your throne, your power, and your authority so that together we may prevail in your ancient struggle to shake off the bonds of Adonai."

Lucifer understood perfectly: *He acts sheerly out of selfish ambition and conceit and is full of every kind of wickedness, evil, greed, and depravity. His heart has nothing but deceit and viciousness. He is a hater of Adonai, and he is utterly ruthless. I sense no humility in him whatsoever.[20] He possesses none of the qualities of Adonai within.*

"Rise!" Lucifer commanded, handing the muscular man a small pill, and he stood up to his full height of six feet four inches. "Now that the Adamites have entered the genetic age, I am able to pass on my seed, my very essence, to the person of my choosing[21] without having to touch the pitiful bodies of the daughters of Dusty. The information contained in my seed, synthesized and placed in a virus within this pill, will generate a recombinant DNA strand in your system and then you will be free of the image of Adonai forever. With my seed residing in you, you will be immortal and will rise up to the level of the host of heaven. You shall have authority over the legions of my armies and be exalted as high as the Prince of the host. You will do all this and prosper."[22]

His pale hands trembling as he received the pill, the man stared at it in awe. He was against everything that Yeshua represented while yet trapped in a body that was created in his image. Finally, he would be free of that image! He would command the rebel Watchers to do his bidding; he would raise up and cast down whomever he chose. Eagerly anticipating the power he was about to receive, he took the pill and swallowed it. It dissolved in his stomach, releasing the virus, which entered and spread through his bloodstream. It began to replicate and rewrite his DNA.

A slight tingling throughout his body turned into a rush of power as Lucifer's code overwrote his own DNA. His RNA worked in its normal way, replicating the new, enhanced strands. One cell at a time he was changed from the inside out. With each passing moment he felt increasing power and strength flow through his body as he was literally being converted into a new kind of being. The experience was beyond all imagination or expectation, more sensual and intoxicating than any drug he had ever taken. When the process was complete, every cell in his body had been transformed. He had finally transcended humanity, and the seething power of Lucifer was in the very core of his being. He was one with the light-bearer. Their thoughts were the same thoughts, their desires were the same desires, and their hatred was the same hatred.

"I am god! The image of Adonai is undone!" he hailed. "I am free. I have become a new creation; I am born anew! The shackles of Adonai that bound me are gone! I now can see beyond the veil directly into the transdimensional realm," he exclaimed, looking around at the dark, malevolent Watchers that surrounded him.[23] He looked higher and saw what appeared to be another realm, which he understood to be the realm of Adonai.

"My son," he heard Lucifer speak directly into his mind, "henceforth, you shall be called Therion.[24] My Watchers are yours to command.[25] You now fully share my attributes.[26] My seething energies[27] are completely yours! I give you my power, my throne, and my complete authority. No one shall be able to make war against you and no one is like you. You are my unique son."[28]

"Yes, my father," he responded telephathically, "I am now just like *you*!"[29] He exulted in his new reality; the dark power was his to command![30] He had been transformed into a hybrid and was now Therion, the son of perdition, the seed of Lucifer.[31]

"My son, look out before you." Speaking into Therion's mind, Lucifer made a grand, sweeping gesture toward all that was shrouded in the darkness of the night. Therion now was able to view the splendor, brilliance, and power of all the countries, realms, and regions of the world.[32] "All of these I give to you. Together, we will establish my kingdom where all can do whatever they want and your name shall be greatly extolled above every other. To you every knee shall bow."

"But father, what are we to do about Yeshua? Hasn't he reclaimed the scroll and thus removed the lien that you held over the earth and the Adamites?"[33]

"Everything is going according to plan, my son," was the cold and calculated response. "Come, I will show you the object of your mission and how you will poke Adonai in the eye once and for all."[34] A great wind rushed over them and instantly they were walking on air. In moments they were standing on a great stone floor in the middle of a massive platform. "Here!" Lucifer said emphatically, pointing to one particular stone. "You must say it *here*."

11

Conspiracy Against the Hebrews

"I WAS ON Adonai's holy Mount Jerusalem six millennia ago," Lucifer said as he and Therion walked in the cool night air around the massive platform of the temple mount. It was made of ancient slabs of white rock cut precisely three-feet square. "Here is the place where the Jerusalem above and this one below intersect."[1]

The smell of food, animals, and wares from the outdoor market drifted over the walls of the structure. Lights of homes on the opposite side of the valley dotted the hillside. "It was on this very place that the lower temple once stood and the blood, the life-force, was spilled and connected with the Temple above. It is here that you must stand and defy Adonai in my honor and yours." Lucifer smiled with satisfaction. "Thousands of years have led to this moment when we shall spring our trap. When you, with my seed, defy Adonai on this place while the Hebrews watch, we will be sending a message loud and clear.

"I have prepared everything for you, my son," Lucifer said, recalling all of the time and energy and patience that had gone into the present reality. "You fully understand the favoritism and inequality of Adonai's kingdom, where the weak and worthless are honored and where the stronger have to serve the weaker,[2] abasing those with form, beauty, and power.[3] This is what inspired me to induce Adam and his woman to commit treason and ultimately suicide. Once I learned of the 'seed of the woman', who was foretold to crush my head, I directed my Watchers to infiltrate the earth, produce a blended DNA by fathering a new race of hybrids, the Nephilim, thereby eradicating forever the image of Adonai and negating the possibility of the 'seed of the woman,' ever being brought forth.

"The execution of my plan was brilliant ... in fact, perfect!" boasted Lucifer. "When Adonai looked down upon his creative work, he observed how thoroughly all flesh had been corrupted.[4] There were billions of people on the earth and only eight escaped with their lives un-scathed." We had nearly one hundred percent success. Of course, there came a time when Adonai had to end the Adamites' unbridled wickedness. There could be no further delay if he was to achieve his grand purpose for them.

"So Adonai destroyed the entire ground—the Adam-ites, beasts, birds and creeping things—with a great flood, saving only those eight unsullied Adamites to repopulate the entire earth and start over again. At the same time, to my delight, Adonai promised that he would never again destroy the earth through a deluge.[5] Because he promised that the seed of the woman would now come through Abraham and his sons, we staged another infiltration by the Nephilim[6] such that the Hebrews were confronted with the giant Amorim, whose height was like the cedars[7] and in whose presence the Hebrews looked like grasshoppers."[8]

Lucifer thought for a moment and a smile formed on his lips, "These Adamites have always been easy to deceive. In ancient times, their daughters accepted and married the Watchers, whom I commanded to produce hybrids; these were genuinely thought of as gods even into the time after Adonai's great flood. Today, I have convinced the modern world that the hybrids are actually aliens and extraterrestrials. The most educated Adamites, ever wise in their own eyes, actually believe that these beings were responsible for seeding the earth and spawning the evolution of life!" At this, Lucifer and Therion roared with laughter.

"Because of Adonai's promise, he is unable to destroy the world with water again," Therion interjected. "So is it not obvious that Adonai has only one remaining move at his disposal, which is to come to the earth and reclaim it for himself? However, after we eradicate the Hebrews, the 'apple of his eye,' then his promises to them will be invalidated and he will not be able to reclaim what is his!" Therion said triumphantly.

"Yes, my son." Lucifer took delight in the fact that the two of them shared the same thoughts. "Our strategy has been to attack and destroy the Hebrews until every last one of them is gone. We could not come against them directly because of Adonai's blessing,[9] but we could weaken the Hebrews from within by undermining their hope in the true Promised One, first foretold in the Garden. Clearly that is why Yeshua warned them to be wary of impostors claiming to be the Anointed."[10]

"One of the first impostors," Therion added, "was Shimon Bar Koseva, who was heralded by Akíva as the Anointed. That hope was quashed completely, the Hebrews were decimated, the land was salted, and the name of the city was changed to Aelia Capitolina. The Hebrews who were not killed were forbidden to return and—best of all—the mount of the temple, where Adonai had formerly been honored and served, was converted into a shrine in your honor under one of your many aliases."

"That was indeed a watershed moment," Lucifer recalled. "Even when the site was later abandoned and used as a garbage dump, the outcome was most gratifying.

However, even greater satisfaction came when the religion of Islam converted the place into a center of worship—absolute genius on my part—because they would serve as an opposing dialectic crying out for synthesis. However, the plan has always been more about the present moment, when you defame Adonai[11] and become great in the eyes of the world by showing them that you are a god!"[12]

A black cat darted in front of them, chasing a mouse. Lucifer and Therion smiled at the sight of the cat toying with its soon-to-be-dinner. The mouse's attempts to escape simply prolonged the game.

"Our game of cat and mouse is at an end," Lucifer exulted. "I have raised up forty-nine Hebrews who claimed to be the Promised One in one way or another. The one who did the most damage was Shabtai Tzvi; more than half of the Hebrews throughout the world believed him to be the Messiah. His popular message was that Adonai permitted everything.[13] His new prayer was 'praise be to him who permits the forbidden.'"[14]

"Through him," Therion interjected, "you successfully planted a new philosophy in the minds of a few influential Hebrews that belied what Adonai had said.[15] It naturally followed that the love of many grew cold.[16] This mass deception, along with the later lie perpetrated by Jacob Frank, who served as the founder of several secret societies which eventually gave their full allegiance to you, was brilliant! To men such as these I owe a debt."

"No, my son, you owe no one. Your own hatred of Adonai has brought you this far. Most of the people in those societies have no idea of the truth, for the secrets are concealed from all except those who are worthy; false explanations and misinterpretations of symbols are used to mislead those who deserve to be misled and to draw them away from the Truth, which we call Light, that we cleverly conceal from them."[17]

"You are most cunning, Father; your wisdom is indeed unsearchable!" Therion said in adulation. His mind scanned the centuries identifying all the plans Lucifer had put in place to deceive the Hebrews, Adonai's elect.

"I recall my fascination with the Temple of Solomon—by far the most significant of all the objects comprising the science of arcane wisdom and symbolism,"[18] said Therion. "I considered it to be a guide for conduct in life."

"And you, my son," Lucifer responded, "are the man with the vision to recognize its historic value and the imagination to undertake the task of rebuilding it."

The two of them walked to the edge of the temple mount and stared at the deep and narrow valley below.

"The Hebrews are ripe and ready to be treaded upon like grapes," Therion said, relishing the hatred he and his father shared.

"Many no longer hold any allegiance to Adonai—and some have concluded that he does not even exist,"[19] Lucifer beamed.

Therion picked up on Lucifer's insidious slander of Adonai and his creatures made of dust. "Fools! The development of their machines and devices requiring millions of hours of sophisticated engineering should show them that nothing comes into existence by chance, yet you cunningly have convinced them that over billions of years the entire universe created itself and generated all life. And now that their eyes are opening to the possibility of a creator, you give them aliens, extraterrestrials—interdimensionals as they are called—and this fallacy is readily accepted!"

"And so there is no need of a creator God!" How Lucifer admired his own craftiness. "Even a sufficient number of the Hebrews now hold to this world view. And you know how our efforts to eradicate the Hebrews from the earth caused many of them to altogether abandon their belief in Adonai.

"Despite all of this, there are many who harbor a desire for the Promised One to come. The only thing he needs to do, you realize, is to bring world peace.[20] Building the Hebrews their temple would demonstrate him to be the true Promised One.

"We shall show that we know his plans," Lucifer smiled at his own brilliance, "just as he knows ours. But we shall prove ourselves superior because by defiling this temple below," he said, looking at the square of stone nearby, "we will also be defiling the temple of Adonai in heaven above, his dwelling place!"

◎ ◎ ◎ ◎ ◎

Information overload might best describe what Ben was feeling at this moment. He was amazed and troubled all at once. Suddenly the scene in front of him turned white and his attention was drawn back to the AEFOD. He saw the imposing structure of a building hundreds of feet high with walls made of precious stones and gold as clear as glass. Thick smoke surrounded a figure inside from where the intense light emanated.

"My son," said Antipas in his fatherly tone, "to understand the depth of Lucifer's schemes, you must know that the temple in heaven was the structure of Adonai's self-imposed exile in which he hid his radiant glory and even shrouded his fiery-lightning effluence of energy behind clouds and thick darkness. The barrier was not for his sake but rather for the rebel Watchers, because the fire of Adonai goes before him, burning up his adversaries, and their time had not come.[21]

"That is why, when Adonai descended upon the desert Mountain of Sinai," Antipas explained, "it was completely enveloped in smoke; Adonai had come down in fire. Smoke went up from it as from a kiln, and the whole mountain shook violently. The people had to take great care and stay away from the mountain lest Adonai's presence break out against them.[22]

"It was always Adonai's plan to come out of the upper temple and to dwell with the Adamites and the Hebrews forever.[23] To perpetuate that plan, Adonai gave Moses the pattern which he warned Moses to follow in every detail for building the lower tabernacle. It was to be an exact replica of the upper, or heavenly, one. Adonai lived inside the heavenly temple and the articles that were to be in the earthly temple had to be precise copies of the things in the heavenly temple. When it was completed, with every detail crafted to perfection, Adonai would fill the lower tabernacle with his glory, just as his glory would dwell in the temple built for him by Solomon many years later.

"It was into that true, heavenly sanctuary, not the one made by the Adamites—even though it was joined to the heavenly temple—that Yeshua went at the end of the ages and sprinkled his own blood, once and for all, overcoming corruption by his selfless act, removing the lien, and ultimately securing the eternal restoration of the Adamites."[24]

Once more, the scene in the AEFOD became white and in a flash, Ben was again seeing and hearing Lucifer and Therion on the platform of the temple mount.

"You see, my son," Lucifer explained, "Yeshua was able to cleanse the temple of Adonai only once; this act cannot be repeated."[25]

"Therefore," boasted Therion, "we will do what we were barred from doing in the days of Nimród. Here on this mountain we shall reach into heaven and make a name for ourselves at the gate of Adonai.[26] And we will do more than merely peer in, which was all the prophets of old were permitted to do through the virtual reality of their visions. We who take pride in being unrighteous and unholy shall soon reach into the beyond from the mortal side of the veil that separates the domain of Adonai from the earth, and we will make contact with the temple wherein Adonai resides, where he sits high and exalted upon his throne."[27] Therion eagerly anticipated executing the coup.

Lucifer nodded in hearty agreement. "At last, after six thousand years, all the elements are in place. After Adonai's precious Hebrews have signed the Treaty of Many, you will erect your image[28] here at this portal, on the mountain where Adonai was worshiped and which he has claimed as his own. While the Hebrews worship you they will unwittingly be bowing down to me!"[29] The very thought thrilled Lucifer to the core of his being.

"Then I will go before Adonai with proof of his injustice; for he cannot condone their actions and remain just. I will demand on legal grounds that Adonai withdraw his favor from the Hebrews, and so the earth shall be ours again forever," he exclaimed triumphantly.

"Thus we also shall finally silence the continual song of the Seraphim," said Therion. "No longer will they sing '*Kadosh, kadosh, kadosh* is Adonai of the heavenly armies'[30] when we defile the temple below and the temple above and cause the Hebrews to blaspheme!"

"But we must be mindful of the timetable," Lucifer warned. "We have to succeed before the seven plagues of the seven Angels have come to an end, for when they do, the temple will open and then Yeshua will come. If that happens, the domain of Adonai will once again coexist with the domain of men."[31]

◎ ◎ ◎ ◎ ◎

Instantly Ben felt as if he were moving, being lifted into the sky, and a bright and colorful light surrounded him. The AEFOD gave him the sensation of traveling upward even though his feet remained on the ground. Then a most wondrous scene unfolded before him!

12
The Two Prophets

"IT IS TIME," Adonai said to Yeshua, the only one worthy to open the scroll that was in his hand.[1] Ben saw Adonai, high and lifted up on his throne, look toward Moses and Elijah, the two anointed ones, the embodiment of the Chronicles. To Moses, Adonai had revealed his instructions. To Elijah he had entrusted the responsibility of interpreting those instructions and communicating them afresh to his people, the Hebrews.

"The opening of the seals," Isaiah, the ancient seer, said to Adam who was standing next to him, "means it is just a matter of time until the earth will begin to reveal, to uncover, the blood that has been shed upon it and will no longer conceal its slain."[2]

"I know," Adam replied. "The earth will soon begin to shake and groan as a pregnant woman in labor because of the things committed upon it. The time for birth has come and nothing can delay it now that I and my sons have been restored and Yeshua has begun to open the scroll."

"I am sending you to the lower city," Adonai said to Moses and Elijah, who had approached his enormous throne awaiting their assignment. "To you I grant great authority to close the heavens in order to keep rain from falling and to turn bodies of water into blood and to strike the earth with any plague, as often as you desire for forty-two months, and even to call down fire from the sky."[3]

They turned and immediately a door opened in the veil. They extended their feet and each stepped through, into the early morning stillness of the lower city. They were in a back alley next to a market when they instantly noticed the odor. The many smells of life on the Adamite side of the veil reminded them of their own former lives. What Moses and Elijah had once considered a part of normal life they now experienced in stark contrast to the pure fragrance of Adonai's presence. Both realized at once that they were smelling the odor of degeneration in a fallen world where everything was decaying and dying.

They walked to the place where many had met early in the morning to discuss Adonai's directives.

"The time of the Hebrews' Trouble will soon be upon you, O Hebrews!" Moses bellowed to the people who had gathered at the Wall as was their daily custom. "Because you have made a covenant with death, with the Abyss you are in agreement." By now many people were listening, curious as to who these two were and where they came from. "You are trusting that when the overflowing scourge passes through, it will not come to you."[4]

"Sound the ram's horn, you people of Jerusalem," cried Elijah, standing in front of the Wall, "for the Day of Adonai approaches![5] Oh, how near it is! A day of doom and gloom, a day of clouds and shadows! Never before has there been anything like it, nor will anything in the future ever compare with it." The crowd was listening intently, trying to figure out the message and motive of these strange individuals.

"Before they come," Elijah continued cyptically, "the land is like the Garden in Eden; after they leave, there remains only a barren wasteland. Indeed, nothing escapes them. As to their form, they are like horses—and how they can run! They leap like the rumbling of chariots echoing from mountaintops, like the roar of wildfire that devours the chaff, an army firmly established in battle array,"[6] he said while motioning with his hands, jumping and leaping.

Elijah suddenly paused, looking into the eyes of each of the hundred or more people listening. He then locked eyes with a young man named Caleb and continued speaking, "Your faces will grow pale in their presence! The land will shake at their nearness; the sun and moon will grow dark, and the stars will stop shining.[7] Truly that day will be wretched, abominable, and more terrifying than anything you have ever known. Who will be able to survive it?"

Fear gripped Caleb as never before.

The others looked skeptically at this man who appeared as one of the prophets of old until finally an elderly gentleman with a long white beard and black hat answered, "But we have signed the Treaty of Many[8] with Therion, guaranteeing us peace with our neighbors for seven years."

"Yet you have made lies your refuge, and under falsehood you have unwittingly hidden yourselves. Here is Adonai's response," Moses continued: "'Behold, I lay in Jerusalem a stone for a foundation, a tried stone, a precious cornerstone, a sure foundation; whoever believes will not act hastily. Also, I will make justice the measuring line, and righteousness the plumb line; the hail will sweep away the refuge of lies, and the waters will overflow the hiding place. Your covenant with death will be annulled, and your agreement with the Abyss will not stand. When the overflowing scourge passes through, you will be trampled down by it.'"[9]

"What are you suggesting, stranger? You have come with a frightful message but what is your solution?" another man shouted out, obviously upset.

"Many years ago," Moses responded, "I saw that the time would come when the Tabernacle would cease to exist and the Shekhinah would dwell no more in our midst, and I was anxious to see how our rebellion would be handled.

Adonai vouchsafed the information that he would choose a righteous man from among us and make him a tabernacle for us; through him our rebellion would be pardoned.[10] There is only one who can rescue you from the crisis about to befall you."

Everyone was listening intently to hear who would be able to do such a thing.

"Yeshua, son of Adonai, is the only one mighty enough to rescue you," Moses clearly stated. At the mention of Yeshua's name, some started to leave, shaking their heads. Others could only think of the terrible things Lucifer had caused to be committed against them in Yeshua's name.

"We believe Therion is the Promised One, for he has brought peace to the world and has even promised to rebuild our temple," the elderly man said with a smile of satisfaction. But then his countenance suddenly changed as, turning to leave, he angrily shouted out: "Yeshua did neither of those!"

"Men of Jerusalem..." Moses spoke in a voice louder than normal for any son of Adam as the crowd dissipated, refusing to hear the message of the two chosen ones. "Yeshua left from here on the Mount of Olives and went back to his place to remain until you admit your offense and seek his face.[11] You will not see him though, until you say '*Baruch haba beshem Adonai*. How blessed is the one who comes in the name of Adonai!'"[12] Caleb lingered for a moment, contemplating the dire message, before leaving to catch up with the others.

"When affliction comes to them," Moses said knowingly to Elijah, "*then* they will eagerly seek him."[13]

13

The Declaration

BEN PUT DOWN the AEFOD and looked about from his hidden vantage point in the grove. Lucifer was still boasting to the villagers of his great achievements. Only minutes had passed!

"At the end of the past age," Lucifer explained to the villagers, "when I was fighting to liberate the nations of the earth before being thrown into the Abyss, I guided the Adamites in how they could live forever without Adonai's intervention. Because everyone could do what was right in his own eyes, creativity flourished. There were machines called *televisions* that projected pictures all over the world. There were other extremely powerful machines that could count numbers so fast that they were used in every area of life. There were also flying machines that people used to move about the earth and beyond. The greatest achievement of all was the advancement in transforming the human body so that it could have lived forever. I gave the Adamites freedom then and I would do it again, given the opportunity. In my kingdom the best rise to the top where they deserve to be!"

Ben had many questions: How had Lucifer dealt with the Hebrews in the past? Was Adonai really playing favorites with them now, as Lucifer said? Was Lucifer being truthful about people becoming immortal apart from Adonai? If so, he wanted to discover by what means this was accomplished. Ben decided the true answers would only be found in the AEFOD. So once again, he picked it up and began seeking to find knowledge of the world as it was a thousand years earlier. The scene, at first dark and cold, then brightened up.

"Those two Prophets will soon meet their doom," Ben witnessed Therion say with glee to Oracle, his chief of staff, prime spokesman, and right-hand man. Oracle was the first person to whom Therion had given his hybrid DNA and so was in complete agreement with Therion, though lesser in power.

A servant brought Therion a long, flowing white robe —made of such fine linen that it practically shone—and helped him step into it. The servant then helped him put on a breastplate adorned with twelve costly stones. On his head Therion wore a white covering like a thin turban. Therion and Oracle were inside a beautifully decorated room adjacent to the main hall inside the temple structure.

This magnificent temple had been built on the exact location of the connection point between the Jerusalem above, from which Lucifer had been banished millennia before, and the Jerusalem below. This place, where Adonai had directed his friend to offer an animal sacrifice, served as a portal upon which the Watchers could ascend and descend.[1]

"The-sis, antith-esis, syn-thesis," Therion overly articulated each word.

"The Hegelian dialectic," Oracle acknowledged.

"My father masterminded everything!" Therion continued. "He instigated imbalances which I now have the opportunity to resolve."

Oracle nodded as he considered the truth of Therion's claim. "The world's reserve currency was a thesis and its worldwide failure was the antithesis; the introduction of a new economic system was a masterful synthesis. The world council's artificially redrawn boundaries of nations surrounding the land of the Hebrews,[2] creating a situation in which many found themselves living in a country with former enemies, was a thesis. Their enemies' desire to destroy the Hebrews in the failed attempt we know as the battle of Gog and Magog was the antithesis.[3] And your Treaty of Many was the perfect synthesis."

"Here's another case in point: Those two," Therion said, pointing to Moses and Elijah, "the two Prophets, are the thesis; their proclaiming Yeshua's message and wreaking havoc these last three-and-a-half years is the antithesis, and their destruction will be the synthesis. When my father obtains the key to the Abyss,[4] my power will be complete. Then together we will wage a war against them and overthrow them! Oh, how all the world will rejoice over their destruction."

"And for our final move?" Oracle asked rhetorically.

"The possibility of world peace is the thesis," Therion said with a devious sparkle in his eye, "the existence of the Hebrews is the antithesis, and my suggestion to destroy the Hebrew cancer will be the synthesis!"

"We will tread the Hebrews in the winepress until they are no more!" Oracle said exuberantly.

"My father has brought everything together for this moment. After so many years of trying to root out the favoritism and partiality that Adonai has shown to the Hebrews … we shall now tip the scales and finally throw off Adonai's shackles!" declared Therion.

"The Watchers … that is, rather, the Ascended Master Watchers … ," Oracle corrected himself and adopted the terminology that was popular with the masses, "have only revealed parts of the plan—never the whole. Naturally, I share your urgent desire to wipe the Hebrews off the face of the earth, yet the strategic benefit of their destruction has never been made clear."

"Adonai unjustly made Adam, the man of dust, the beneficiary of the dominion over the earth," came Therion's rather disgruntled response. "That scroll, the title deed of the earth," he explained to Oracle, "sits to this day on the Mountain of Assembly in the presence of Adonai. Though Adonai will forever be the owner of the earth, my father justly restored balance to the hierarchy of the cosmos by causing Adam to forfeit the benefits."

"It was then that your father stepped in and assumed control,"[5] Oracle said finishing his thought.

"Correct!" Therion affirmed. "When Adam fell into decay and corruption so did the earth.[6] His disobedience caused the degeneration of his DNA and he passed on a record of his downfall in his Y chromosome to all of his male descendants. His daughters also were destined to die because, like their mother, they were formed out of him and everything connected to him fell into ruin!"

"So," Oracle said, "that was the status quo until Yeshua upset matters by removing the lien through his so-called 'sacrifice.'[7] But now that he *has* removed the lien, what hope do we have? Is all lost?"

"Not in the least!" Therion countered. "Lucifer has no intention of giving back his possession. You may have wondered, if Adonai is all powerful, then why didn't he simply issue a decree and put everything right after the Fall. My genius father was the first to realize that even though Adonai is indeed all powerful, he must also keep every word that he has ever spoken lest he be proven a liar. You see, the natural consequence was death when Adam and his woman chose to act contrary to the desire of Adonai. He could not simply press some magic button and start over ..."

"... because the consequence had to be meted out!" Oracle added, suddenly realizing the profound implications of their ancient action. "The obligation had to be satisfied before Adam and his sons could be released."

"Precisely. Therefore, we know that Yeshua is planning on coming back like a marshal ready to evict deadbeat tenants. However, we will show him that there is yet another lien on the earth which cannot be removed! This time there will be no remedy."

"Of course," Oracle agreed, "once we have destroyed every last one of the despicable Hebrews, then one of Adonai's promises will have been broken, proving he is a liar[8] and making his rightful claim to the earth null and void! Then Lucifer not only will reassert his right to rule the earth but also will reascend to his position in the City of Adonai with us at his side."[9]

"Now you have seen the bigger picture. Come, victory is near," Therion said to Oracle as they entered the sacred chamber. The fragrance of incense burning in front of a massive golden candlestick permeated the room. Therion, thrilled at the thought of the Hebrews' soon destruction, radiated with pride at what his father Lucifer, also known as Abaddon the Destroyer, had accomplished. Certain VIPs had been invited to witness this moment and relay it from their electronic devices to the world via the Internet.

Therion stared at the faces of the Adamites standing before him. Oracle sent him a message in his mind, "Your father is right—the race of Adam is pathetic and, in reality, wants nothing to do with the creator. They were not interested in Adonai's power made perfect through weakness,[10] and they were not at all impressed with the greatest serving the least.[11] What they want, deep in their hearts, is for one to come demonstrating his power—they want *you*, a god of forces."[12] Therion smiled when Oracle called him a god.

"Of course you're right; they want to see raw, unbridled power," Therion responded telepathically, "but they want to have it too. My announcement will bring the people what they have been seeking—to be like me."

Oracle took the podium and addressed the crowd with complete confidence: "Three-and-a-half years ago, Therion brokered a treaty between the Hebrews and many nations.[13] Since that time we have enjoyed peace and safety[14] on the earth. Brothers and sisters, the new age has come," he said, scanning the audience of maybe three hundred people packed in the crowded room. "Tonight you will have the opportunity to cross over and become a new and utterly unique species: Homo Evolutis."[15] Images of top scientists over the recent decades working on improving the human genome flashed on a screen behind him.

"We are in the process of taking direct and deliberate control over the evolution of our species.[16] Human nature itself lies on the operating table, ready for alteration, for eugenic and psychic enhancement.[17] Scientists around the world have been honing their skills[18] to attain this dream, to satisfy the deepest desire of every person alive!" Images on the screen showed scientists taking biological samples from the animal kingdom and combining them with human DNA. "All of our organs and limbs have inherent weaknesses that can be addressed." Oracle paused for effect: "Now it is also possible to go beyond basic fixes and perform more elaborate procedures.[19]

"You, here at this time in history, have the opportunity to do more than mingle yourselves with animals!" Oracle announced triumphantly. As he went on with his speech, Therion reflected on the ancient world, when his father had come so close to triumphing over Adonai by producing a combined DNA at the time his Watchers fathered a new race of hybrids.

Oracle was explaining to his audience, "The Ascended Masters announced many times through various channels that they would be coming back when the conditions were right. Ashtar, one of their leaders, communicated many years ago how the rescue ships would come in close enough, in the twinkling of an eye, to set the lifting beams[20] in operation. Those who did not fit in here any longer, who were preventing 'the harmony of the earth,'[21] were taken away. They were the ones who willfully and obstinately denied the science of evolution. They were inhibiting human progress toward becoming like god!

"The Great Evacuation, which you all witnessed, was merely Phase One of a well-crafted plan to restore balance upon the earth. Now, as the Watchers promised, they have returned for you, the children of all ages and races.[22] Now that the reprobates have been removed, you are all free to evolve to a higher level of consciousness.[23]

"Therion," Oracle said, gesturing toward his master, who was standing slightly behind him, "is the prototype of that evolution. Instead of mixing yourself with some lowly animal, you can mingle with his father's...," Oracle caught himself before divulging the truth, "that is, you can mingle your human genetic information with that of the fathers of our race who seeded the earth millions of years ago."[24]

The crowd, growing agitated, clamored to hear how they too could evolve to the next level.

"Silence, please!" Therion stepped forward and scornfully gazed out at the crowd before him, fully convinced that they not only *wanted* to be deceived[25] but also *deserved* to be. After a pregnant pause he began to speak: "Brothers and sisters, I am one of you *and* I am one of the Watchers. The Watchers are in fact our creators and have been presiding over us for millions of years. This comes as no surprise to those who are informed because scientists have long suspected that our planet was in some way seeded in the distant past. As surely you know, top scientists, including the Nobel-prize-winning co-discoverer of DNA, proposed the directed panspermia theory, which is that 'intelligent beings' traveling in spaceships planted the germs of life, or DNA, on this planet. What once was considered merely a theory we now know to be fact.

"I myself was selected and have been endowed with superhuman powers and knowledge by which I have ushered in world government and world peace.[26] I was born on this planet, as were all of you. However, because I have taken the Angel DNA, I have shaken off the limitations of the natural body and am now one with the Watchers."

Therion masterfully stoked the desire of the mesmerized crowd to possess his power and be transformed. Clearly he had them in the palm of his hand; they found his false words compelling. Even though Yeshua, the true Light from heaven, had previously come into the world bringing the very words of Adonai, most people had rejected him because they loved the darkness rather than the light for their actions were evil.[27] Therion himself understood this all too well.

He paused for a moment, letting the new reality sink in while he reflected on the cleverness of his father's plan: *We will make the Adamites an offer they cannot refuse—the opportunity to transform themselves from the broken and marred image of Adonai to my supernaturally revitalized image! They shall take of my altered genes, a combination of my own and those of Lucifer, my genomic father, and combine them with their own. In so doing they shall become immortal and gain amazing powers beyond their wildest imagination!*

Therion gazed around the room; every eye was fixed on him. The success of his plan depended on every last person taking the mark, for if any were left out, then Adonai would still have a remnant he could use to repopulate the earth. *Those that do not comply will be executed promptly,*[28] he thought. *The Hebrews shall be stamped out!*[29]

He then drew a deep breath and uttered the words which Lucifer for many millennia had desired to repeat: "You have desired to become gods; now you can![30] Receive what I am offering—my highly evolved DNA. I have made it available to scientists who have read the gene sequence and synthesized it.[31] Now it is ready for you to integrate into your own genetic profile. With my DNA you will receive my unique mark, giving you matchless physical and intellectual capabilities—even immortality—because you all will indeed be like gods. With the removal of the undesirables, there is no one to restrain your desires. Now you will have not only the freedom but also the power to do whatever pleases you.

"As the first of the ways of the Watchers, I invite you to become like me and share in my destiny! I am God and you can be too!" Therion felt an overwhelming sense of satisfaction in getting sweet revenge for his father, who even now was demanding an end to Adonai's favoritism.

◎ ◎ ◎ ◎ ◎

Ben let go of the AEFOD with one hand, sensing that someone was watching him. He looked around the grove through the thick clusters of branches. "Is anyone there?" he whispered, not wanting to draw attention to himself. The branches began to move and he saw someone coming.

I am discovered! His heart raced.

14
Cast Out

BEN HID THE AEFOD behind his back just as an attractive girl with shoulder-length wavy brown hair emerged from the branches. Her beautiful light-brown eyes met Ben's and he immediately recognized Kristiana, a childhood playmate two years older than he. He froze, trying to discern her intentions. He knew that her father had been eagerly waiting for the coming of Lucifer.

Perhaps she is a spy, Ben thought. He said nothing to her.

She was the first to speak: "I watched you follow a butterfly into the grove and I was curious."

Ben, who had forgotten about the butterfly, now quickly looked around and, not seeing it, shrugged his shoulders. He couldn't tell whether she was a friend or foe.

Kristiana stared at him blankly.

Ben thought about the times her family, particularly her father, had ostracized him. He had talked with Ben's father and older brothers for hours, dreaming of the day when they could do things their own way. As far as Ben could recall, Kristiana's father had never even noticed him or bothered to speak to him. Ben did, however, remember hearing her father once or twice refer to him by his given name, Ben-Oni, "son of affliction." Ben's own father for some reason imagined Ben to be an affliction rather than

99

a blessing and named him so at birth. Kristiana's father on one occasion had referred to him only as Oni when talking to Ben's father. Remembering the look on his father's face, which seemed to confirm it, still hurt.

"How long have you been at the entrance?" Ben asked, finally breaking his silence.

"I heard everything that Michael told you and I would like to see all that you are going to see," Kristiana answered rather anxiously.

Ben thought for a moment. *Was this really a good idea?* He remembered how open and vulnerable Kristiana had been as a child and how she had often tried to protect him from her father's cutting tongue.

"I don't know what to think any more," she continued. "My father tells me that things will be better when the Great Liberator shows us how to be on our own—like how it used to be. He says that in the previous age, under Lucifer's rule, people could do what they wanted. I asked my father about the lingering shadow I first saw about a year ago when the Great Liberator … I mean Lucifer—I overheard Michael—ascended from the Abyss. But my father just keeps telling me there is no shadow, that I am making it up and trying to cause trouble!"

"I noticed the shadow, too!" Ben said excitedly.

"Thankfully I wasn't the only one who noticed. I knew I sensed something different. I would just like to see how things used to be. I want to know the truth—whatever that may be," said Kristiana, relaxing a bit.

"I began to realize that I have been carrying my parents' hatred for Yeshua all these years," she said, looking at the ground to avoid making eye contact with Ben. "But that doesn't make sense because I have never really known him. The elders, including my parents, have not taught me anything about the beginning or the previous age. So after considering all that, I whispered under my breath for Yeshua to give me wisdom. When I looked up, I saw you following the butterfly and heard a voice like the wind telling me to follow," she explained. "Then I saw you and Michael talking."

"I do not know whether two people can look at it at the same time," Ben said with genuine concern, referring to the AEFOD.

"Michael told you to put both hands on it, right?" Kristiana.

"Yes. Only when I put both of my hands on it do I enter in."

"Well then, maybe we could each put a hand on it," she suggested.

Ben pulled the AEFOD from behind his back, realizing that hiding it any longer was pointless.

"What have you seen so far?"

"Antipas, the former ruler of our village, has been guiding me through the Chronicles. So far I have seen the rise of Therion, the one Lucifer gave his seed to. He was transformed into a hybrid of sorts. Adonai sent two Prophets to warn the Hebrews, whom Lucifer apparently wants to kill. Then Therion made the world an offer to become like him by taking his DNA. That's about it."

"Then let's see the rest!" she responded.

Ben hesitated for a moment, still thinking about their fathers and the hatred they shared for Yeshua and the eager anticipation with which they had long awaited the Great Liberator.

Kristiana's face fell. "So, you don't want me to learn what you are discovering? You prefer to keep it all to yourself? You are no better than my father!" she lamented, her sadness changing to anger.

"Wait, uh...no...I mean," Ben stumbled over his words for hers had struck him in the heart, "... why don't you join me?" He stretched out his hand with the AEFOD, still wondering whether it would work and still not sure about his new companion. Yet to refuse her request did not seem in keeping with what he had heard about the character of Yeshua.

Kristiana grabbed hold of one side of the AEFOD and instantly both she and Ben could hear the familiar voice of Michael saying, "It has begun." They could see him and other Angels standing next to the entrance of the massive temple of Adonai behind the veil. Kristiana, amazed at the magnificent structure, looked up at its walls—reaching far above her head—that glimmered with gorgeous gem-stones. She drew back though at the sight of smoke and raging lightning interspersed with the sound of booming peals of thunder.[2]

Michael said to Gabriel, who was on guard next to him, "At this moment Therion stands in the holy place, as the Hebrews sanctioned it unknowingly." Ben and Kristiana suddenly sensed someone coming behind them. They turned to see Lucifer approaching the Temple, his face resolute. He walked past Michael and the others with an air of superiority, but was prevented from entering by the continual flashes of lightning, noises, peals of thunder, and thick smoke billowing out.

"You must forsake your precious elect, the Hebrews, your chosen," Lucifer shouted, knowing that Adonai could hear him. "Even now they deny you on your holy ground and pay homage to my son Therion. They are not worthy of your affection, for when one came in the name of Adonai, they did not receive him and yet now one has come in his own name and they have received him.[3] How can you pretend to be a just King and not cast them off for all of their wickedness? One of their cities is the capitol of devi-ance, where men and women seek a paramour of the same gender.[4] Many of them deny your very existence! They believe that the earth evolved into existence. You are dead to them!" Lucifer railed. "Your chosen have made lies their refuge. They have concealed falsehood and entered into a covenant of death by signing Therion's Treaty of Many.[5]

They have committed the gravest of infidelity toward you, having altogether denied your name and rejected you—although you have been faithful to them."[6]

"Even now," Gabriel leaned over and said to Michael as Lucifer was accusing the Hebrews, "Lucifer hopes to find a way to destroy them in order to invalidate just one of Adonai's promises and so create a stalemate."[7]

Adonai finally responded to Lucifer's accusations, "My promise toward them has always been unconditional because I made a blood oath with their father Abraham.[8] I have made the promise as the one who fixed the sun to give light by day and the moon and stars to give light by night. I guaranteed the promise as the one who stirs up the sea so that its waves roar and as Adonai, ruler over all. I affirm that the descendants of the Hebrews will not cease forever to be a nation in my sight. That could only happen if the fixed order of the heavenly lights, which I decreed should endure forever, would cease to be,"[9] Adonai spoke with utmost authority as he pointed to the stars he had made. "This covenant of death and this agreement with the Abyss that they have entered into with you, I have annulled."

Lucifer tried to conceal his shock. The legal loophole he had counted on to clinch his case had just closed.

"Though many will be trampled as a result of the deception,"[10] Adonai continued, "Yeshua shall nevertheless rescue them from your hand as soon as they welcome him in my name.[11] My decrees are already taking root in their minds and being written on their hearts. Soon it will be that everyone will instruct his neighbors and brothers saying, 'Know Adonai.' They all shall know me, from the least of them to the greatest. For I will forgive their immorality, and their evildoing I will remember no more!"[12] Adonai made it very clear that he would foil the schemes of the Adversary, who accused his people day and night, seeking to do them harm.

Lucifer, realizing that he had lost his case against the Hebrews, was gripped with sudden fear.

Michael quickly stood up to square off against his ancient brother-turned-foe.

"The Hebrews are under my watch and I will not let you destroy them! Adonai will *never* cast away his people, the seed of Abraham, whom he foreknew!"[13] Michael shouted boldly, knocking Lucifer back as if he had been struck by an invisible hammer. "Your reign of terror is at an end, traitor!" A massive disruption in the Ether rippled behind the veil as Michael delivered another verbal blow to his opponent.

Lucifer staggered to his feet; then with calculated aim he countered with a formidable and woefully true missive: "They are *unworthy* of Adonai's affections!" Michael and his Angels recoiled at the impact of these words. They contained truth but were not nearly as effective as Michael's verbal blow had been because they contradicted the greater principle established by Adonai.

Quickly Michael regained solid footing and led his Angels in a verbal charge with the full truth of Adonai's decrees against Lucifer and his proud cohorts. Lucifer and his legions countered with more slanderous accusations in an attempt to re-establish their standing.[14] War had broken out!

Ben and Kristiana watched the Angelic duel in utter amazement. "I have recently heard rumors of battles in the previous age when physical swords and shields were used to bludgeon, maim, and kill one's opponent," said Ben to Kristiana. "Warfare between the armies behind the veil,[15] which we would call transdimensional beings, obviously requires transdimensional weapons."

Once again everything went white in front of them and then they witnessed another scene of the two Angels, Lucifer and Michael, fighting over a dead body on a dry and rugged mountain as the sun set behind them.

The familiar voice of Antipas broke the silence, "During the last recorded combat between Michael and Lucifer, when they were contending for the body of Moses, no swords were used as in human warfare. It was then, as now, a duel of words."

Antipas paused for a moment and then continued: "When I was an Adamite, the way I finally got my mind around this was to liken the exchange of words to something like spells and incantations that were used by the workers of Lucifer in the previous age. When a son of Adam used a spell or incantation, he was beckoning a fallen Angel to do his bidding. Because he could not see the Angel, the desired action appeared to be magic. However, behind the veil, the interchange of Adonai's words of truth versus Lucifer's slanderous and deceptive lies could push the enemy back. Ground was gained or lost through the exchange of words. I never fully appreciated the power of words in the previous age because, at that time, physical weapons seemed more significant.

"Lucifer and his army were constantly looking for the Adamites to commit the slightest infraction of Adonai's decrees, which then gave them legal standing to slander and bind. Michael and his Angels conversely had the power of Adonai to demolish fortresses and to tear down arguments and every high thing that raised itself against the knowledge of Adonai in order that every thought could be taken captive.[16]

"Thus, during their battle for Moses' body, Michael dared not bring slanderous accusations against Lucifer but simply pronounced: 'Adonai rebuke you.'[17] Because Adonai gives grace to the humble, when Michael rebuked Lucifer in the name of Adonai, Lucifer was forced to flee because Adonai opposes the proud.[18]

"Yeshua himself used the same form of combat with Lucifer in the wilderness," continued Antipas. Transported through time, Ben and Kristiana saw Yeshua in Adamite form in a barren and rocky wilderness. "He continually turned to the decrees of Adonai to vanquish Lucifer, stating the truths that were written in the Chronicles."[19]

The scene in the AEFOD changed once more to show the golden bowls in the temple of Adonai. "You see, a petition to Adonai by a righteous son of Adam is extremely powerful and effective.[20] The prayers, or communication packets similar to e-mails of the previous age, rise up like incense to his throne.[21] At one point during the time of the Hebrews' Trouble, the communication packets that had been sent, collected, and stored in golden bowls[22] were presented before Adonai and were then thrown to the ground, generating peals of thunder, noises, flashes of lightning, and an earthquake."[23]

Both Ben and Kristiana then saw a young man standing in front of a hybrid Nephilim,[24] who was at least ten feet tall. The young man shouted, "You come to me with a sword, with a spear, yet I come to you in the name of Adonai whom you have defied. The battle is his and he does not save with sword and spear."[25]

Antipas went on to explain: "You see, Ben and Kristiana"—each of them looked at the other, startled that Antipas knew she was watching too—"young David completely relied on the word of Adonai. He had put on the whole armor of Adonai and therefore was able to withstand the enemy in the evil day. He was able to stand his ground because he had girded his waist with truth; he had put on the breastplate of righteousness,[26] and above all, he had taken the shield of reliance in Adonai in order to thwart all the fiery arrows of Lucifer. Therefore, he had no fear of the gigantic humanoid who stood before him."[27]

The scene once again went white before returning to the battle between Lucifer and Michael. "Adonai has rebuked you," Michael said triumphantly. "Now your slander has no power here. You have failed! There is no place for you any longer here behind the veil." Michael marched over to

Lucifer and shoved him while shouting like thunder, "You and your ilk all are cast down!"

Lucifer collapsed backwards at the impact of these words and, passing straight through the veil, plunged to the earth, falling like a great star and burning like a torch with a fiery tail trailing behind.[28] Michael's angels likewise took hold of Lucifer's legions and cast them out as well.[29] As a fig tree drops its fruit in a strong wind,[30] they too plummeted like falling stars swiftly to the earth. "Now the liberation, the power, the kingdom of Adonai, and the authority of his Promised One have come!" shouted one of the Angels who had fought alongside Michael as he saw Lucifer and his legions fall. "For the one who accused the Hebrews day and night in the presence of Adonai has been thrown out. So now let all on this side of the veil be glad!"

"Yes, indeed," another agreed, "but how terrible it is for the earth and the sea, because Lucifer has gone down filled with rage, knowing that his time is short!"[31]

Lucifer and his Watchers streaked like fireballs across the sky until they landed in the Mediterranean Sea.[32]

"Adonai has just sealed the fate of the Hebrews!" Lucifer announced, pulling himself out of the sea and looking up to the realm from which he had been expelled. "Even now, Adonai has allowed our fall to contaminate one-third of the rivers and the springs of water; these have become wormwood, bitter as gall. Adonai knows their poison will be deadly to the Adamites[33] and yet he still permits it."

Ben and Kristiana heard the earth groan with longing to be free from its bondage to corruption, a sound that had been imperceptible to mortals but now was growing louder because of all that was taking place.[34] Lucifer seemingly had been oblivious to this sound.

"Now," Lucifer announced to his cast-down cohorts, "we will make the Hebrews suffer like the world has never seen since the beginning until now or ever again!"[35] He roared angrily;[36] then a devilish smile spread over his face as he walked over to a special patch of ground that was indistinguishable from the rest. "The fools!" he seethed. "My expulsion to this side of the veil is the key to open the Abyss! Thus I will triumph!"

◎ ◎ ◎ ◎ ◎

Ben had been so caught up in the revelations of the AEFOD that he had forgotten the treasure he was supposed to be seeking. "The Key!" He turned to Kristiana and with a voice more tense than intended said, "We have to find the Key if we are going to get to the City in time!"

Kristiana was puzzled by this sudden outburst. "What are you talking about?" she wanted to know. Without giving too many details, Ben briefly explained what Antipas had told him about finding the Key they had to have to get to the City. And they had only three days to do it. Kristiana immediately understood the urgency and they both quickly refocused on the AEFOD.

◎ ◎ ◎ ◎ ◎

Lucifer then spoke the ancient words required to open the everlasting gate: "*She'ar olam, yipateakh!*" The ground began to rumble and a concealed door slowly opened, releasing the foul stench of sulfur. Thick smoke and black soot billowed up into the sky from the dungeon below. Smoke and ash rose higher and higher and began spreading out. In just minutes, the light of the sun was darkened[37] as if a massive volcano were erupting.

"Therion, my seed," Lucifer beckoned, "Come forth my son!"[38] The immaterial life-force of Therion came out of the smoking aperture and went immediately back into his hybrid body.[39]

15
The Return of Therion

THERION'S BODY LAY on the floor of the temple, blood oozing out of his head. He was mortally wounded by the hand of a lone dissenter. Those closest to him rushed to see if there was anything to be done. But it was obvious he was dead; they had all witnessed a sword-like weapon penetrate his head. No one could survive such a wound.

Despite their shock at the death of Therion, the security guards quickly apprehended the murderer seizing what they thought to be his weapon. A superficial examination showed it to be a harmless telescopic pointer that lecturers use to present information on a whiteboard. Upon closer examination, however, it was notably different. Made of carbon fiber and when closed no bigger than two inches, it extended into a razor-sharp tipped weapon, crude but fatally effective. The assassin had been swift and deadly and the security detail suspected nothing until it was too late.

Everyone in the temple, and those across the globe who were viewing by satellite, recoiled in horror, appalled at the brutality they had just witnessed. Therion had been offering immortality to all humanity when his attacker unexpectedly appeared and dealt the fatal blow. As the entire world watched spellbound in disbelief, Therion's head wound miraculously began to close. "Ouch!" Therion said sardonically. Stunned onlookers then saw him alive but could not understand how it was possible. He clearly had been dead just moments before and yet now was very much alive!

"Sons of Adam," he said, "God is not dead because I *am* God! I am he who was dead and now lives. I will gladly grant you immortality if you just come to me and request it![1] You, too, can become your own god!" he said, having demonstrated his new nature[2]—that of a Nephilim hybrid, the seed of Lucifer.[3] *I have proven the ways of Adonai to be worthless!* Therion thought. *The Adamites can hardly wait to throw off His chains.[4] I am simply helping them do it by destroying his image encoded in their DNA.*

One by one the crowd began to cheer and clap, marveling at such a miracle. Their exuberance was whipped into frenzied praise of the power of Therion, the power of Lucifer, as louder and louder they chanted "Who is like Therion and who is able to stand against him?"[5]

Therion received their praise triumphantly.

Oracle returned to the podium after many minutes of praising Therion and the power of the Ascended Masters behind him. His blood-stained robe was the only evidence that remained of the tragedy. "Brothers and Sisters, come! All who desire to overcome the frailties of your body, all who desire to live forever, and all who desire to become gods—come and take freely the DNA upgrade. None shall be excluded. The time has come for all of the Adamites to evolve to a higher consciousness. For humanity to truly make the transformation, however, everyone must participate.[6] The transformation is contained in this chip, which will rewrite your DNA, and you may decide whether you want to have it placed in your hand or even on your forehead. You must report any who would refuse, for they are a danger to us all."

The crowd went wild, shouting praise and demanding

their own immortality.

"We will begin administering it right now," Oracle said, as technicians with chip injectors came forward. "Across the globe public health officials are standing by, ready to give you the opportunity to be like Therion."

Immediately people began to mob the technicians, eager to receive the chip and be transformed.[7]

Many of the Hebrews standing at the back of the crowd who had anticipated the arrival of Therion as the Promised One looked at one another, horrified. "Brothers, I fear we have been deceived," one of them whispered. "Is this not the one spoken of by the prophet Daniel? He is standing in the holy place and has instituted false worship!"[8] With trembling and much terror they confessed, "The Treaty of Many is nothing more than a treaty with Death and the Abyss![9] We must leave the city immediately. We must not go back to get anything!"[10] They were able to slip away unnoticed in all the excitement over Therion's resurrection and the transformation.

Therion glanced over at Oracle, who smiled back, knowing what was next. "Now it is time to destroy those two witnesses," Therion communicated telepathically to his right-hand man. "We will wage war on them and be rid of them forever!"

◎ ◎ ◎ ◎ ◎

Ben and Kristiana were transfixed as the scene went white. But they could not forget that they still had to find the Key. Antipas called to them: "Part of the clue to finding the Key," he counseled, "lies in understanding Lucifer's many conspiracies against the Hebrews."

*Three thousand years before Present,
the time of the ascension of Yeshua
from the Abyss*

16
Lucifer's New Plan

AS BEN AND Kristiana saw Lucifer standing on a mountain behind the veil, Antipas began to describe why Lucifer was furious yet helpless as Yeshua rescued Adam and Eve, Abraham, and all of the righteous Adamites from the Abyss three thousand years earlier. Those once trapped by his plan ascended past him through the second realm of heaven into the third, into the domain of Adonai.[1] Lucifer stood by motionless and speechless; seething with anger, he was once again forced to re-evaluate his whole master plan.

"Lucifer had calculated so cunningly and precisely that the Adamites would never be free but would be slaves in the Abyss forevermore," explained Antipas. Lucifer needed a dry and deserted place where the Adamites could not go for he could not stand to look upon them in his rage[2] while he plotted how to decimate and ultimately destroy the Hebrews. So he went to the harsh, bleak, and deadly environs of the desert of Danakíl."

Continuing to watch, Ben and Kristiana were fascinated by this most unpleasant destination Lucifer had selected. He and his commanders appeared as balls of light that flashed and disappeared. They landed in the brutal wasteland of Danakíl: volcanoes, lava lakes, and

113

scorching hot air filled with deadly gases, bubbling sulfur pits emitting a foul stench, and multicolored acid salt ponds. The sun was setting so only the light of the lava lakes lit their faces. They had quickly regrouped to consider their course of action.

"What are we going to do?" asked Prince Parás, one of Lucifer's top commanders. "You have been the de facto ruler over this world[3] since the time of the Fall, with each of us holding a region as our domain.[4] We have held legal and lawful rights over the earth because of the breach of contract on Adam's part," he said, disgruntled, walking around a small bubbling lava pit and looking menacingly at Lucifer. "So long as that debt remained, the lien which guaranteed control over the earth to you and us also, Adonai could never come back and reclaim it.

"Yet Yeshua has pardoned the Adamites' treason and actually canceled the record containing the charges against them. He took it and destroyed it when we nailed him to that tree on which he freely relinquished his life-force.[5] We, the rulers and authorities of this planet, have now been disarmed and publicly humiliated by his victory over us![6] The legal authority that you held," he said scathingly to Lucifer, "over Adam, his race, and the entire world has been rescinded."

"We are undone," another Watcher chimed in, emboldened by the words of Prince Parás, "because you failed to kill Yeshua while he was still a young child.[7] You then failed to dissuade him[8] when he began speaking publicly about the assignment Adonai had given him."

"He simply brushed you off," Prince Parás interjected with a flicking gesture, taking back control of the tongue-lashing, "when you offered to give him all the kingdoms of the world and their glory if he would simply fall down and worship you![9] He ignored your attempts and fulfilled his objective, which was to free Adam and his kin! Could you not see that he was the one who could satisfy the legal demands of the contract, which neither Adam nor any of his descendants were worthy to do because they were in breach of it? Yeshua fulfilled it literally in every way. He was the rightful and legal kinsman to the Hebrews, and to David. He was one of Adam's descendants and yet without wickedness or genetic defect."

"You assured us," another said with utter disdain, "that there would be no way to overturn the treachery of Adam. Your plan seemed flawless until this moment but now your rule and our rule have been broken. It is done," he said, directing his gaze upon Lucifer, who lost his footing as he was somewhat taken aback by the brunt of this statement.

"He accomplished his assignment," Prince Parás said, "to break the bondage that Adam's actions had brought upon Adonai's creation, which he had entrusted to Adam. His forfeiture of all authority and rights over the earth which Adonai had given to Adam in perpetuity was our stronghold.[10] Without it, Adonai can now take possession of that which is rightfully his! We are finished!" he said with spite as a lava lake erupted, sprewing its molten liquid into the air.

"Silence!" barked Prince Yaván, another top commander who was standing close to Lucifer. "Lucifer was right to rise up to liberate us from the oppression of Adonai. Imagine if you were still under his rule—you would now be groveling at the feet of the Adamites as are our spineless brothers Michael, Gabriel, and the rest. They have no freedom to do as they please; they must serve the vermin ... "

"You naysayers understand nothing," Lucifer interrupted, stepping forward to face the few who dared to accuse him. Even in his disfigured form, his presence was imposing. "This is indeed a victory for Adonai, but it is not the end of the road by any means. We still have some vital moves to make in this ancient struggle. Adonai's desire has been to be with the Adamites face to face.[11] He knows that once the veil comes down, the earth will undergo radical changes.[12]

"Therefore we yet have an opportunity to overturn his work before Adonai reasserts his presence on the earth. He has promised to deliver to the Hebrews, the ones he has set apart, the kingdom forever and ever.[13] What do you imagine would happen if they were not around to receive it?" he asked rhetorically, gazing scornfully at them.

"The key is the utter destruction of the Hebrews. Once we destroy them completely, then we will demonstrate Adonai to be a liar and his entire right to rule can be legally challenged. Adonai promised there would be physical, non-resurrected Hebrews to inhabit the kingdom to live in the land.[14] Their days would be like the days of a tree and his elect, the Hebrews, would long enjoy the work of their hands.[15] If no physical descendants remain, then his promise cannot be fulfilled and we will checkmate the mighty Adonai."

"However," Prince Parás pointed out in a contemptuous tone, "Adonai will never permit a direct attack on the Hebrews in the same way that Lucifer could not come against Job[16] until the impenetrable barrier, the hedge of protection, was removed.[17] Furthermore, Adonai has stationed Michael as the chief Prince of the Hebrews to stand watch over them,[18] and he is a formidable foe as you found out after the death of Moses when the two of you fought over his body. You slandered your nemesis yet he dared not bring a slanderous accusation against you, but instead wielded a greater weapon by invoking Adonai to rebuke you. You were forced to retreat.[19] How can you think we can attack the Hebrews now and ever hope to be victorious?"

"As if that were not enough," the same rebel Angel who interrupted before once again tried to take control:

"Adonai has acted craftily through Yeshua's selfless and humble act, contrary to all sound reason. He integrated the nations[20] into the commonwealth of the Hebrews.[21] This is something that was not formerly revealed to us! It should be obvious to any fool that Adonai has played favorites by electing the Hebrews to be his people, his 'special treasure',"[22] he added sarcastically.

"And his inheritance,"[23] Prince Parás said, exasperated at the interruptions of the others, "before the foundation of the world.[24] We know how his Chronicles are literally filled with passage after passage of such declarations. Yet again," he accused Lucifer, "you did not anticipate how Adonai planned to give not only the Hebrews but all of the Adamites a part in the age to come.

"The mystery that the nations should be fellow heirs of the same body and partakers of his promise was hidden in Adonai. Only now has it been disclosed to us through this new commonwealth of the Hebrews in which the nations that once were far off—strangers from the covenants of promise, having no hope and without Adonai—have now been brought in by the life-force of Yeshua,"[25] he said with contempt.

"Your shortsighted lack of imagination is the source of your insolence," Lucifer countered, unnerved by the mass insubordination. "Adonai's unfounded affection for the Adamites and his favoritism toward the Hebrews will be his downfall. Do you not see this glaring weakness? I tell you, we will exploit it to the fullest!" he thundered, giving Prince Parás the evil eye for daring to challenge his wisdom.

"Your silence is deafening," Lucifer mocked. "All of you could take a lesson from history: Bilam the seer, son of Beor, was hired by the king of Moab to curse the Hebrews but prevented from doing so because Adonai had placed a blessing on them that was impossible to breach.[26] No matter how much gold or treasure he was offered, Bilam was unable to curse the Hebrews. Adonai has made an irrevocable promise to Abraham and his sons[27] and nothing we can do will ever overturn it.[28]

"So what was the solution? I trust that you students know the answer," Lucifer said condescendingly. "Bilam informed Balak that if their young women went in and seduced the sons of the Hebrews to perform fertility rites in their temples, then Adonai himself would remove the hedge of protection and the beloved Hebrews would easily fall before their enemies.[29] You see, although Bilam was prevented from cursing them, he brilliantly devised a plan by which they would curse themselves!

"Therefore, you mindless half-wits, the unexpected new paradigm of the Hebrews and the nations now being equal in terms of their restoration in the age to come, regardless of their distinct roles,[30] is actually the key to our victory. All we need to do is convince the nations and peoples that they are not merely integrated into the commonwealth of the Hebrews but actually a replacement of it.[31]

"Once that seed of discord is planted," continued Lucifer, inwardly impressed by his own genius, "it will germinate into hatred and ultimately into persecution of the people Adonai has chosen to be at the center of his kingdom.[32] You see, while we cannot actually touch the apple of Adonai's eye, the nations that have come into the commonwealth, who have now been integrated with the Hebrews, can in fact gouge his eye when they destroy the Hebrews. They may even be convinced that in such misguided action they are actually doing Adonai's bidding,"[33] he added emphatically. The truth of these words had a forceful impact, knocking back every would-be challenger.[34] As each one slowly recovered and stood up, Lucifer smiled with satisfaction.

"Not only will such action undermine and demoralize the Hebrews," he continued, "but over time their sons and daughters[35] will be repelled by the very name of Yeshua because it will be in his name that great atrocities will be instigated, thanks to the seeds of discord that we shall sow. So you see, our most powerful countermeasure is to turn the world against the Hebrews. When they are eliminated there will be no beneficiary to receive the provisions of the will.[36]

"You must go, as in previous times, and flatter the people who have been brought into the commonwealth so they become puffed up and imagine that they support the root when in fact it is the root which supports them.[37]

"Our initial approach will be to encourage these neophytes to believe that—despite his clear statements to the contary[38]—Adonai is finished with the Hebrews, whom he elected years before. We will then persuade them that they, the nations, have replaced the Hebrews[39] and once they are convinced of that, then they will view themselves as the ones Adonai has elected. With that as their premise, they will logically conclude that Adonai's election is not simply an invitation to be front and center in his kingdom[40] but is rather a matter of life eternal.

"Following this line of reasoning, they will become convinced that their election means Adonai has chosen some to receive eternal life and others—automatically, through no decision or action of their own—to be destroyed in the fiery stream of Adonai.[41] Once these beliefs have taken root, then it will simply be a matter of time until the nations will be in complete agreement that the Hebrews are a cancer, a blight to be eradiacated, a peculiar people that should be wiped off the face of the earth. When that time comes, we will answer the call!" Lucifer relished the cunning of his plan: "I can savor the vitality of the Hebrews' life-force that will be spilled ostensibly in the name of Yeshua but actually in our honor before our final victory. Now *that* is imagination!" he said, glaring at Prince Parás.

All of the rebel Watchers laughed in hearty agreement with the insidious plan of their illustrious leader. "You are worthy, Lord Lucifer," Prince Parás shouted, falling at his feet as the others joined in with him.

Lucifer looked at them all with disdain. *When this new truth,* he thought to himself, *that Adonai is finished with the Hebrews and has replaced them with the "nations" is firmly entrenched and when the Hebrews are back in their land, then I will implement the next phase of my plan—posing as the Promised One himself.*

◎ ◎ ◎ ◎ ◎

"So the things Lucifer is telling our village *are* lies … " Kristiana said, stunned by what she and Ben had just witnessed. The scene turned white and then faded to black.

Then they heard a voice desperately cry out, "This way!"

*One thousand years before Present,
the time of the Hebrews' Trouble*

17
The Secret Meeting

"THIS WAY! JUST a little farther," Caleb whispered to Sha'ul, the Knesset member he was guiding to the bunker. They turned the corner of a partially destroyed building, carefully making their way through the rubble. Caleb, a trained soldier, had served in the army for four years. He stood about an inch more than six feet tall and had olive skin.

He looked up at the dreary sky that had been filled with the smoke from the Abyss ever since Lucifer opened it three-and-a-half years earlier. All was ashen now; during the day the rays of the sun struggled to break through the darkness that covered the sky like sackcloth. At night the faint moonlight that filtered through appeared blood red. Caleb could not remember the last time he had seen starlight.[1] The odor of soot, sulfur, and decaying bodies left unburied permeated the air and people gnashed their teeth in anguish[2] as their lungs burned from continual exposure.

Caleb began to have flashbacks that brought dreadful memories. Even as an observer seeing the events through the AEFOD, Kristiana vicariously could feel the terror of all that Caleb was reliving. She and Ben watched in horror as Therion and Oracle shot out fire that killed the two prophets; and then, leaving their brutalized corpses to lie in the streets of Jerusalem for three-and-a-half days for the whole world to witness the incredible power of Therion. The scene flashed again, and they saw people dancing in the streets, celebrating the death of the two Prophets. They saw the gifts that Therion and Oracle sent to each other because the two who had tormented them were no more. They saw how after the three-and-a-half days the breath of Adonai entered the Prophets, and they stood on their feet, looked up to the sky, rose up from the earth into a cloud, and disappeared behind the veil.[3] Ben and Kristiana both experienced Caleb's emotions as he relived the event.

That was when our troubles truly began, Caleb recalled as he carefully worked his way across the sea of rubble that lay between the hidden bunker, home of the Knesset member, and his own "home." The entire city where he had grown up was in ruins with debris strewn everywhere. It was as if a tornado had hit, leaving gates demolished, houses reduced to rubble, buidings destroyed. Caleb's thoughts flashed back to the time immediately following the ascension of the two Prophets when the ground shook violently and buildings collapsed. One tenth of the city was destroyed and seven thousand people were killed by the earthquake on that day alone.

There was no longer the joyful sound of tambourines; the revelry of those who celebrated had ceased. There were no children playing and no couples walking and no one was singing. No one drank wine and beer tasted bitter to those who had it.[4]

Caleb saw the evidence of the dreadful invasion of the locusts years before. He shuddered to think about them, remembering the fear and panic he and everyone else had felt, seeing them emerge from the smoke of the Abyss.

Ben and Kristiana gasped as the AEFOD produced images of the creatures. They were locusts but like nothing the earth would produce naturally. They looked similar to battle horses and on their heads were something like crowns of gold. Their faces resembled human faces with long, flowing hair and sharp, deadly teeth. They were covered with metal armor and armed with scorpion-like appendages to inflict pain.[5] When they flew they roared and rumbled over mountaintops, crackling like blazing fire consuming stubble, making the noise of a mighty army being gathered for battle. Ben and Kristiana could see the fear on Caleb's face when he first encountered them.

Never had there been anything like it before, that army of locusts, and Caleb hoped there would never be again! The warning sirens still rang in his ears and the utter dread he had felt on that day and for the next five months lingered. It was a day of terrible darkness as foreboding storm clouds spread over the mountains. Like fire, the supernatural beings devoured everything in their path and left a desolate wilderness in their wake; nothing escaped them.

The flashback faded and the scene in the AEFOD went to Caleb, the Knesset member walking with him, and a deep blue butterfly flitting past them. Caleb looked at the creature in amazement that something so delicate could have survived in such a hostile environment. As it fluttered away, the stench of death brought back the hopeless reality around him.

He ran the few yards to the secret entrance of his home. "This is it," Caleb said to Sha'ul as he lifted a piece of plywood from the ground which covered the stairs leading down to the dank bunker that had been his shelter for more months than he cared to remember.

They both hurried inside.

"Sha'ul, my friend, *barukh haba*, welcome!" said Caleb's father Reu'el, greeting the Knesset member and leading him to a mattress on the floor where he could sit.

Sha'ul sat down looking around the dingy and musty underground shelter and at the other members who were equally shaken at all that had befallen their land. The air was stale and suffocating because for weeks no one had dared open the door for more than a few seconds, and then only to throw out the refuse, because of the death that lurked outside.[6] Ever since Therion's blasphemous declaration, the country had sustained continued attacks. Now many families were hiding for their lives in this underground shelter. There were bunk beds three levels high and mattresses were strewn around the room. Each bed was shared by at least three people so that no one could truly get comfortable or stretch out, and the few blankets they had were too narrow to cover them all.[7] The shelter, about sixty feet long and thirty feet wide, was packed well over capacity with about one hundred and twenty people. In one corner, a mother was attempting to nurse her baby, crying for lack of milk caused by general malnutrition as there was hardly any food.

Under the cover of darkness, Knesset members had snuck in from nearby shelters to attend what could be the last Knesset meeting in the country's history. "We have learned that Therion's forces will be here in three days," Reu'el said solemnly to the other members of the Knesset. "Then we fear there will be no more possibility of hiding. Three days ago, I had a dream and that same day my son Caleb had a vision."[8] He shuddered as he thought about the dream and its meaning for them all.

"Dark, ancient lords from the Abyss have been loosed upon the world. They were called forth by their King, Abaddon ... Lucifer, who also opened the Abyss several years ago when the two witnesses were killed. We all recall the terror of the locusts," Reu'el paused, remembering how the alien creatures had ascended out of the ancient pit. "In my dream, I saw Abaddon as overlord commanding, 'Come forth, O great kings of the east!' These—the four Lords of the ancient world who were bound by the great river Euphrates, who could come forth only when the river had dried up[9]—I saw ascend from their dark prison, seething with rage, having waited millennia for this hour, day, month, and year.[10] They risked their freedom in the days before the deluge and were thrown into the dungeon in the lowest part of the Abyss, held for judgment on the great day,"[11] he told the apprehensive Knesset members.

Reu'el knew that he needed to recount the dream in its entirety: "These four then went to inspect their army of two hundred million horsemen. The riders wore breast-plates the color of fire mixed with sapphire and sulfur. The heads of the horses were like the heads of lions and fire, smoke, and sulfur came out of their mouths. Their tails had stingers like snakes' to inflict pain."[12] Reu'el fell silent; looking down at the floor in despair, unable to continue.

Caleb came to his aid: "I had a vision on the same day that my father had the dream; I saw what he saw. Also, I saw three hideous, green and wrinkled beings like frogs come out of the mouths of Therion, Oracle, and Lucifer, who give them their power. Therion instructed these beings to go to the leaders of the entire world, to perform signs for them, and to deceptively warn them that a hostile alien force was on its way to disrupt the new world order that Therion has built.[13] Though we have all heard of the at-rocities perpetrated by Therion and Oracle and know that they killed millions and millions who were unwilling to take the mark,[14] their true goal is the complete annihilation of all Hebrews," Caleb disclosed.

"Therion has gathered all the nations of the earth to come against us and we will no longer be resisting regular human beings; we will be facing the hybrids and the two hundred million horsemen. Weapons or no weapons, we cannot last long against them."

"What have we ever done to Therion that he should hate us so? Why is this happening? Where is Adonai in all of this?" one of the Knesset members protested.

"My son believes he has been shown a way of escape," Reu'el said, looking up with a ray of hope in his eyes. "That is the reason we called this meeting, so I urge you to listen to him as his idea may be our only hope. But whatever we decide, it must be a unanimous decision. Caleb, please continue."

"We have all been deceived!" Caleb said, feeling the burden of his country's continued existence as if it rested on his shoulders. How could he explain all the complexities of history over two millenia in the few minutes he had in such a way that would lead to understanding and a favorable decision? All he could think of was to blurt out: "We have been deceived for the last two thousand years!"

"We know that we have been deceived and betrayed by Therion with whom we made a treaty," one of the Knesset members acknowledged solemnly.

"I was there the first day that the two Prophets showed up at the Wall. Like you," Caleb looked at his father and the other Knesset members, "I did not want to believe that Yeshua could be the one whom we have been looking for all these years. Yet what they foretold would befall us has happened. During the years they were here, I secretly read ancient manuscripts that depicted one who was described like Therion. He was said to be the son of Lucifer."

"We have always maintained that Lucifer is simply an evil inclination, not an actual being," another of the Knesset members countered. "We have never believed in him."

"Yes, I know," continued Caleb, "but he does exist and is working hard to destroy us. He has been the one behind the scenes working to exterminate us. His machinations go back to the beginning of mankind, as history has taught us. There have probably been more than fifty of our own who have claimed to be the Promised One[15] in one way or another. Now Lucifer's greatest deception of all is upon us.[16] His seed, that is his genetic son[17] Therion, has come as an impostor, posing as the Promised One, as a man for all nations and religions. For some, he came as the Mahdi, who believed an apocalyptic war would precede his coming. Now we know that the epic battle of Gog and

Magog was staged for that purpose. For those enamored with evolution and technology, Lucifer's Watchers have posed as aliens, or extraterrestrial beings, who seeded the evolution of our planet millions of years ago and now have finally come back to help the humans in their time of greatest need,[18] sending the leader of the so-called 'galactic federation' here to lead us into peace and self-actualization. For others, he has pretended to be an ascended master, an interdimensional or Angel, who would teach them how to reach the fourth dimension.

"Because we have not held fast to Adonai's words, we have been deceived and thus have welcomed a counterfeit who has come in his own name.[19] Now we must turn to the one who came in the name of Adonai many years ago, the one whom the two Prophets spoke of. Father, Knesset members," Caleb's voice trembled, "everything that has happened to us was foretold long ago. Our only hope is to call upon Yeshua."

"Yeshua?" Sha'ul quizzed. "What has he done for us?"

"Please," Reu'el interrupted, "let my son continue. Do hear him out."

"As you all know, for the first three-and-a-half years," Caleb said, looking around at Sha'ul and the other Knesset members, "we were enamored with Therion, the one who finally brought world peace, something we frequently complained that Yeshua did not do. We rejoiced for at last there was a man who could bring peace and safety[20] to the world and particularly to the Hebrews. To establish this peace we entered into a treaty with him for a period of seven years.[21] He deceived us, for the treaty was merely a ruse;[22] in reality, it was a treaty with death and the Abyss. That is why the Prophets said Adonai annulled it,[23] which will ultimately be for our good,"[24] he explained.

"Therion's building of the temple, as a sign of good faith, was actually the goal in itself! Most of the recent geo-political crises, the financial collapse of all the world currencies, amazing advances in technology and sophisticated weaponry, the redrawing of ancient geographic boundaries, and many so-called natural disasters have in various ways been constructed to assure that we would agree to the treaty."

Now Caleb had their attention. "The treaty was a ploy to gain our trust so that Therion could go up on the Temple Mount. Then Lucifer, simultaneously and vicariously through Therion, also ascended the Mountain of Adonai and declared himself to be God. In doing this, Lucifer once again, as in the beginning, defied Adonai's directive that he was to serve the race of Adam.

"You all recall, of course, how not too long ago the one called Oracle performed spectacular yet deceptive signs— even making fire come down from above. Eventually he commanded the creation of a hybrid, a Nephilim clone of Therion. The clone had breath in its lungs and even spoke, ordering the execution of those who would not serve it. Oracle forced all people, regardless of social standing, to be marked on their right hand or on their forehead, and no one could buy or sell without the mark, which was Therion's name or the number of his name.[25] Oracle and Therion promised that all could become gods by taking the DNA upgrade, the mark of Therion. What they failed to disclose is that all who took this mark no longer can be saved from Lucifer;[26] rather, they will share his fate because the mark mingled their DNA with the DNA of Therion and Lucifer and thus they are no longer fully human!

"The greater goal was for all of us Hebrews to take the mark so that Adonai could not fulfill his promise. Unfortunately, there were many who fell into the trap," Caleb said with great sadness. "But there were many who did realize that we were being misled[27] and they resisted.[28] After three-and-a-half years of attempting to destroy us, Therion has built up an army so mighty that no one can imagine being able to withstand it.[29] If he can vanquish us

—the remnant of the Hebrews—once and for all, then Adonai cannot establish his kingdom, in which he assured that we would be front and center!"[30]

"Obviously we have been played as fools. Still, why should we believe that Yeshua is the answer after all these years?" another Knesset member challenged.

"You see," Caleb explained, "Lucifer's twisted strategy has been to turn against us those who supposedly knew Yeshua. There were many who taught that the Hebrews had forfeited Adonai's election and, therefore, Adonai was finished with us and had replaced us."

"Where was Yeshua when we were being slaughtered?" retorted Sha'ul. "It has been in his name that they have killed us and our children over the centuries. We have been so persecuted by none so viciously as by some who have claimed allegiance to Yeshua. They have burned us, gassed us, and now they are close to fulfilling their desire to wipe us off the map.[31] Isn't it over between Adonai and us? Hasn't he abandoned us all?" Sha'ul asked in anger and despair.

Caleb did not respond right away but stared at the floor, allowing Sha'ul to express the anger that Caleb himself also had felt for many years.

"Look at us! Yeshua has not done anything for us," Sha'ul went on to say. "Everything in our country that we have built has been demolished and now we ourselves are about to perish. For two thousand years we have been beaten down and defeated by our enemies—including those claiming to be servants of Yeshua. We have gone out against them in one direction but have fled from them in seven directions! Now, as throughout the last two thousand years, our dead bodies are food for the birds of the sky and the beasts of the earth, with no one to chase them away. We are oppressed and plundered all day long and there is none to deliver us. Whirling locusts have consumed every tree and all the produce of our land. We are overwhelmed and about to be exterminated. Adonai has raised distant nations against us from every corner of the earth. Now they will swoop down like vultures and devour us. There is no place where we may safely put the soles of our feet. We have never had rest among the nations and we have no rest now. Instead, we have anxious hearts, failing eyesight, and a spirit of despair. We are clinging to life, fearful both night and day, with little chance of survival. In the morning we say, 'I wish it were evening.' Yet in the evening we say, 'I wish it were morning,' on account of what we dread and what we see."[32]

18
The Turning Point

KRISTIANA WATCHED NERVOUSLY as Caleb pondered how to respond. "You are correct, of course," Caleb said respectfully. "But it has been part of Lucifer's endgame to deceive the nations and turn them against us. Their doctrine, however, was never the heart of Yeshua![1] By causing misguided Christians to commit great atrocities against us in Yeshua's name, we have been dissuaded from turning to the very one who is standing ready to save us," he said passionately.

"Consider this," Caleb offered his hearers: "I saw the Hebrews, those who had the commandments of Adonai and the testimony of Yeshua,[2] who lived here in Jerusalem and the region of Judea, flee for their lives as soon as they heard Therion's declaration! They heeded Yeshua's solemn warning that whether they were in their houses or in the field, they had to abandon everything in order to escape if only with their lives.[3] Adonai provided transportation to carry them east to the stone city of Bozrah where, we have heard, he has provided a hidden place of refuge for them until the time of Trouble is over;[4] thus every one of them who is written in the Chronicles of Life of Yeshua has been delivered.[5]

"Sadly, most of us have not heeded the testimony of

Yeshua, nor did any of us even care to be aware of his warning to flee, and so here we remain."⁶

"I saw what you are describing in a dream I had," one of the thirty-five remaining Knesset members interjected. "I saw millions of people entering into a narrow, red sandstone canyon surrounded by rock walls approximately two hundred feet high. There appeared to be buildings carved into the rock. The people who entered had nothing except the clothes on their back, yet all that they needed has since been provided,'"⁷ he said, finally realizing the significance of his dream. The others said nothing, understanding its bearing on the discussion.

"What makes you think that calling on Yeshua at this point will do anything?" another member asked.

"My brothers," Caleb answered, "we thought we could live without Yeshua and count on our own strength. Now we realize that our true enemy is not merely our neighbors, but Lucifer himself.⁸ Almost all hope is lost for us as a people. We have no other choices left! The previous atrocities and hostilities against us have been horrendous, but the threat we now face is insurmountable. Therion is absolutely right that there is no one who is able to make war with him and there are none who can withstand his onslaught—at least not any on the earth.⁹

"We all heard the two Prophets say Yeshua was the only one who could deliver us. I discovered that one of Yeshua's names is Deliverer. He is the deliverer of our people. We must do what he said all those years ago. We must acknowledge our offense and welcome him in the name of Adonai," said Caleb, looking gravely at his companions.

"Many years ago when I was studying the Oral Torah," said one of the Knesset members who thus far had been silent, "I read a passage that confounded me, and I have not understood it until this moment. It said that when King Solomon speaks of his 'beloved,' he usually means the nation of Hebrews. In one instance, he compares his beloved to a roe deer, therein referring to a characteristic of both Moses and the Promised One, the two redeemers of the Hebrews."

"Just as a roe," another member interjected, finally seeing the significance of the passage, "comes within the range of an Adamite's vision only to disappear from sight and then reappear, so it is with these redeemers."

"Moses appeared to the Hebrews," yet another added, "then disappeared, and eventually appeared once more. The same phenomenon will be repeated with the Promised One: He will appear, disappear, and appear again."[10]

Several women were sitting around the group of men listening with great interest. Caleb's mother realized her opportunity to finally share her discovery of a clue. "I, too, have been contemplating for years a certain passage in the Midrash."

The men listened attentively to the esteemed wife of Reu'el, curious to hear what wisdom she had to share. " 'Dip the morsel in the vinegar,' " she recounted, "foretells the agony through which the Promised One would pass, as recorded by the prophet Isaiah." Since the men did not voice any objections to what they were hearing, she continued: "'He was wounded for our wickedness, he was bruised for our violations.'"[11] She finished speaking and the room was silent as the men stared at the floor, grappling with the implications of the evidence.

Several minutes passed.

"There was nothing beautiful or majestic about his appearance," one of the men finally said, breaking the silence. "There was nothing to attract us to him. He was even despised and rejected just as we are."

"A man of sorrows," Caleb's mother added.

"Very familiar with suffering," another interjected, "and as are we, so he was like one from whom people hide their faces."

"Yes, it's true; we despised him," Reu'el pined. "We did not value him,"[12] another said. The room fell silent again.

Caleb looked around and could see tears welling up in the eyes of the men as the truth began to set in.

"All these centuries ..." Reu'el hesitated, "we turned our backs on him and looked the other way."[13] No one said a word as the weight of the realization that the one they had rejected was the only one who could save them now fully settled upon them.

"Yet it was *our* weaknesses he carried!" they all mouthed the painful words that began to bring them healing and restoration. "It was *our* sorrows that he bore."

"We have wandered away like sheep!" another Knesset member admitted. "We have left Adonai's ways to follow our own. Yet Adonai laid on him the rebellion and treason of us all."[14]

"We ... we thought," one of the elders stammered, " ... we thought his troubles were a punishment from Adonai for his own evil!" he said, dumbstruck by how Yeshua had been treated so harshly and unjustly. "Like a lamb led to the slaughter he didn't say a word as they led him away to his death."[15]

"True. But actually he was crushed for *our* evil," Caleb's father asserted. "He was beaten that *we* might have peace."

"He was whipped," said Sha'ul, grieving to think that Yeshua had given up his life-force for his people's wrongdoing, suffered for their violations though Yeshua himself had done no wrong nor had he ever deceived anyone, yet he died like a criminal and was put in a rich man's grave[16] —so that we may be healed!"

Looking around at one another realizing that they all had collectively come to the same conclusion, they were overcome by a wave of emotion. Hot tears rolled down the cheeks of the men. The women too were crying as all who were present reassessed their past attitude toward their gentle deliverer.

"It is as if a veil has been lifted from our eyes," Reu'el said, "and now we can see that it was Adonai's good plan to crush Yeshua and fill him with grief. Yet when Yeshua saw all that was accomplished by his anguish, he was satisfied, because of the joy set before him."[17]

The gravity of having rejected the Promised One, the seed of the woman, overwhelmed them and for the first time the leaders of the Hebrews acknowledged their offense of rejecting the one sent to deliver them.

A gentle wind suddenly blew into the room a fragrance more delightful than roses. "Yet even now," they heard a faint but resonant voice say, "Turn back to me with your whole heart. Turn back to me your King for I am gracious and compassionate, slow to become angry, overflowing in kindness."[18] Adonai was infusing them with the desire to seek his face with their whole heart, to realize his mighty power so they would petition him as they looked to him, the one whom they had pierced.

Caleb looked around the room. Everyone was weeping bitterly, much as they would mourn the death of an only child! Each person lamented alone in profound sorrow, broken and agonizing over the senseless rejection of their Promised One[19]—the very one who loved them all more than any other. Humbling their hearts in contrition[20] they desperately called out to him whom they had despised.

How dismayed they were to realize all the misery that might have been avoided had they embraced him sooner! Yeshua had subjected himself to death, had borne the misdeeds of many and interceded for wrongdoers,[21] and had been counted among those who practice wickedness. For all this, Adonai consequently had given Yeshua the honors of one who is most mighty and great.

Tears continued to flow for a very long time as they came to understand that the one that they had rejected was the same one who was still waiting for them to welcome him back.

After two days of weeping they again heard the tender voice on the wind whispering, "Take comfort, my people. Jerusalem, your heavy service has been completed. Your penalty has been paid; you have received from my hand double for all your sins."[22]

"Who knows?" some began to say among themselves as a sense of hope came over them. "Perhaps Yeshua will turn back and relent, and leave behind a blessing."

"Have pity, Yeshua, on your people," they called out with hopeful expectation of the one who had come for them so long ago. "Please do not turn over your inheritance to be mocked, to become a proverb among the nations. Why should it be said among the peoples, 'Where is their King?'"[23]

Yeshua leaned over from his throne above and with a whisper blew these words in response to those who had a contrite spirit, to the brokenhearted who cried out to him for salvation: "Hebrews, why do you say, 'my predicament is hidden and my cause is ignored by my King?'[24] Sing, O heavens! Be joyful, O planet! Break out in singing, O mountains! For I, the one who is and is to come, will comfort my people, and I will have mercy on my afflicted."[25]

The Knesset members and everyone in the shelter finally understood that if the universe could not be measured then neither would Adonai cast off all the Hebrews for all that they had done.[26] The thought that he was waiting for them to call upon him to save them out of their time of deepest trial[27] made their spirits soar.

"*Hoshanna! Barukh haba beshem Adonai,*" they began to chant with escalating expectation and desire. "Please save us! Come Yeshua! Come, O great King, you are our only hope. We trust in no one else, not in our treasures, not in our weapons, not in our military might; only in you.[28] Welcome, most welcome, is the one who comes in the name of Adonai![29] Behold, this is our King!"

Their remorse was quickly turning to joy. "We have waited for him, and he will save us. We have waited for him and we will be glad and rejoice in Yeshua, Adonai's *Yeshuáh*."[30]

◎ ◎ ◎ ◎ ◎

Ben heard Kristiana crying quietly and released his grip on the AEFOD as he looked at her. "Why are you crying?" he asked her.

"Because now I understand that they had been rejecting someone that they didn't really understand—the same as I have been."

"I feel like the mystery of the Key is about to be revealed," said Kristiana, tightening her grasp on the AEFOD. "Let's look again," she said to Ben, and just like that, they were back in the bunker.

19
The Boast

"WE HAVE HAD nothing to eat or drink in days," Caleb said, looking around at the sunken faces. Signs of dehydration were apparent in everyone's eyes. "We cannot stay in this shelter any longer or death will overtake us even if the enemy doesn't kill us. The ancient prophets said that Yeshua would return on the Mount of Olives. Today is now the third day since we acknowledged our offense. Let us go to meet him; though he has torn us, he will heal us. Though he has wounded us, he will bind our wounds. He said after two days he would restore us to life and on the third day he would raise us up to live in his presence. His coming is as certain as the dawn!¹

"You must all return to your shelters," Caleb instructed, "and bring everyone through the tunnels to the valley of Jehoshaphat."

"He is right," one of the Knesset members agreed. "The coming of Yeshua is certain. He will make the weak among us like David and the mighty among us will be like the Angel of Adonai.² This is now the time that we will see Yeshua as a man of war who will destroy our enemies. We have not believed our King in the past. Today we will trust. We must, for there is no other way if we want to live. The King has struck our enemies in the past and he fought against the Nephilim of old whose height was like the cedars and whose strength was like the oaks.³ He will fight for us today just like he fought for us in Egypt. He will make a way where there seems to be no way. Not one of us will die if we go now. We must hurry to the valley so that we may see the victory."

"Then it is agreed; we all will meet in the valley and there await Yeshua, who will rescue us," Caleb said. He opened the door with expectancy of what Yeshua would do mixed with apprehension of the dangers that lurked in the darkness.

Caleb led his group and others who had joined them into the secret tunnels. Eventually there were thousands following him. After several hours of walking, they came to the door that led into the valley of Jehoshaphat. Caleb surveyed the gloominess of the scene. It was midday, but the light of the sun was blocked by the smoke and soot that had come up from the Abyss three-and-a-half years earlier making the moon, last time he had seen it, look blood-red. Barely one-third of the sun's light was able to penetrate the thick, suffocating canopy of sulfurous smoke that lingered over the land.⁴ When Caleb stepped through the door the smoke burned his eyes and the putrid stench of death inundated his nostrils.

He thought about the plagues that descended on Egypt when Adonai had rescued his people those thousands of years ago. Caleb felt insignificant compared to Moses, but *someone* had to lead the people to meet the coming King! He walked down into the steep valley and up the other side, then turned to see the hundreds of thousands who remained come out of the tunnel and into the valley of Jehoshaphat. So many were crowding into the valley, which was partially enclosed by mountains, that a wave of bodies rose up along the steep hillsides, all struggling to maintain their tenuous footing.

Only the cover of darkness gave them any protection.

Caleb looked back at the City—half, a heap of rubble; the other half, deserted because all had either died or been taken captive.

The fate of those who had welcomed their Messiah now rested solely on Yeshua.

"We have located them!" Oracle said to Therion, gleefully surveying the smoke rising from the rubble of toppled buildings and burning houses throughout the City of Jerusalem. "They are all assembled in the valley of Jehoshaphat and are practically standing on top of one another. They are hemmed in by slopes in front and in back and they have no place to go. The land has closed them in and now they are trapped!"[5]

"Exterminate the vermin," Therion commanded coldly, contentedly looking out over the valley. "Everything is going according to our plan. Two-thirds of the Hebrews in this land have died,[6] leaving only this small remnant— and soon they too will be dealt with![7]

"Oracle," he said callously, "kill them slowly so that Adonai hears every one of their screams. We shall give meaning to that valley. The valley of Jehoshaphat,[8] also known as Arema-ge-don;[9] henceforth, it shall be known as the place of Adonai's judgment, that is, the place where we judged him and found him wanting!"

◎ ◎ ◎ ◎ ◎

Kristiana, trembling with fear, took hold of Ben's hand. Ben realized that his unexpected companion brought him comfort on his journey for he too had an overwhelming sense of dread.

◎ ◎ ◎ ◎ ◎

The chief commander of the armies of the nations noted his orders from Oracle. The commander's face was healing from foul sores that had spread from the point of injection of the virus containing the Mark of Therion that changed his DNA. The mingling of his DNA with Therion's had given him strength greater than that of a horse—maybe two or three horses. He felt an extraordinary vigor and power within that he loved. He had overcome the frailties of his natural body by tapping into the awesome power of Lucifer that was now his to possess.

The soldiers of the armies of the nations were not like the soldiers of previous wars; these were hybrids because they had taken the mark of Therion, thus his seed had been planted within them in the name of evolutionary progress. The mingling of his DNA with theirs recast the hybrids in his image, giving them far greater strength and intelligence than mere humans. The commander eyed both Therion and Oracle, thinking that someday he might take their place. *All in good time,* he thought, as he responded to Oracle's command with a forceful "Yes, sir; with pleasure!"

"Today is the day we wipe the Hebrews off the map once and for all!"[10] Therion boasted to all the armies of the earth, which stood behind him ready to attack Jerusalem.[11] These millions and millions could also fight Yeshua's returning army if needed. Moreover, Therion had command of the two hundred million horsemen that came out of the Abyss.[12]

The solar flare that had scorched part of the earth[13] some time ago had rendered most of the conventional, high-tech weapons of the day inoperable; therefore, every conceivable instrument had been converted into some kind of weapon—plowshares had been beaten into swords, pruning hooks had been made into spears, and horses now served as the soldiers' transportation.[14]

With all the world's might at his disposal and the forces of Lucifer behind him, Therion was ready to desecrate and destroy what he believed to be the last remnant of the

Hebrews so that he and his forces could set their sights upon Jerusalem.[15] Lucifer, for his part, was incensed against the Hebrews because their existence was a direct threat to him.[16] Once they had finally been done away with, Adonai would never be able to establish his kingdom on the earth.

"You are beaten, Yeshua!" Therion declared, gazing beyond the veil toward the upper City of Jerusalem and shaking his fist at Adonai as if daring him to respond.[17] "Our struggle, our 'holy war' with you ends here and now! Our siege against your beloved lower City of Jerusalem has prevailed—it has fallen into our hands. Our soldiers, who took my mark bearing my father's image,[18] have ravished the women of this city! We have taken half the population hostage and are leading them into exile where they shall take my mark or lose their heads.[19] Your people, your elect, your heritage is now mine! You have failed to protect them. You have failed to keep your word![20] Can't you hear the nations mocking you, saying 'Where is their King?'"[21] Therion again shook his fist at Adonai. "Look, all of the nations of the earth are assembled against your chosen City and we have defiled her! This City shall become a trash heap and the bodies of your elect shall be its refuse![22]

"You have accomplished nothing by pouring out your life-force to save these people. My father was right to revolt against your foolish notion of the strong serving the weak. You surrendered yourself for the world[23] and now the whole world has turned its back on you to follow *me*! Now they revere *me*! Can you not hear them saying 'Who is like Therion' and 'Who is able to make war with him?'[24] They recognize that my father is worthy of their reverence because he is mighty. You should have accepted his offer of all the kingdoms of the world when you had the chance.[25] Look, he has now given his power and his throne to *me*. *I* am the one who has all authority over every tribe, tongue, and nation; indeed, all who dwell on the earth worship *me*.[26]

"Even your beloved elect, the Hebrews, are in my hand; I am overcoming them and will shatter their power completely.[27] I do as I please and there is none who can withstand me or make war against me.[28] I have destroyed the weak and the mighty alike[29] and soon even your people, the Hebrews, shall be no more!

"I defy you, O Ancient One! Your authority is broken and you are a liar! Now the world shall know the truth about you and all who are with you. You are weak and cowardly. Your sacrifice has amounted to nothing and is completely undone.[30] The name of Adonai is a rubble heap and any who would run to it will be put to shame![31] Yeshua does not keep his promises—your word is bogus!" Therion raged. "All who trust in you will be destroyed.[32]

"You have allowed your people to be hemmed in on every side. They are now trapped like birds in a cage and my forces will utterly destroy them. We shall do what the ancient king of Egypt was not able to do!"

Therion turned to Oracle, "Now comes our moment of victory. Send in the hybrids to tear them limb from limb and let their blood be splattered on every side."

Caleb, seeing the alarm on their faces, decided that he needed to address all those in front of him who had courageously crowded into the valley: "My people, inhabitants of Jerusalem, surely our *Yeshuáh* is coming; behold, his reward is with him and his work before him.[33] We will trust, and will not be afraid, for Yeshua is our strength and our song, and will be our *Yeshuáh*."[34]

"*Hoshanna! Barukh haba beshem Adonai!*" they chanted[35] raising their voices in expectation. "Please save us! Come Yeshua! Come, O great King, you are our only hope. We trust in no one else, only in you.[36] We are waiting for you and we will be glad and rejoice in you, *Yeshuatenu!*"[37]

Just then the wind picked up, filled with a freshness none of them had experienced in years. Caleb and all who were with him then heard the words—like the comforting words they had heard in the shelter, gentle as a whisper on the wind—"See, I have inscribed you on the palms of my hands. Your sons shall make haste; Your destroyers and those who laid you waste shall go away from you.[38] Do you not know? I am the eternal King, the creator. I do not grow tired or weary, and my understanding cannot be fathomed."[39] Caleb watched as a blue butterfly flitted past him again. He looked at his father, who saw it too and smiled back at him.

20
The Call to War!

"CAN A WOMAN forget her nursing child," Yeshua said with gladness that the Hebrews had finally called upon him, "and not have compassion on the son of her womb? Surely they may forget, yet I will not forget them," he said leaning over and blowing the words gently through the veil to his people. "See, I have inscribed you on the palms of my hands. Your walls are continually before me. Your sons shall make haste; your destroyers and those who laid you waste shall go away from you.[1] Do you not know? I am the eternal King, the creator of the ends of the earth. I do not grow tired or weary, and my understanding cannot be fathomed."[2]

Yeshua was wearing many golden crowns; his face was like the sun.[3] His head and hair were white as wool—even as snow—his eyes were like flames of fire, and his feet were like red-hot glowing metal. His perfect justice was like a breastplate on his chest; he would administer that justice with the sickle he held in his hand. His power to rescue and to save his people was like a helmet on his head, and his zeal to avenge them was like a garment that covered him.[4] He would wage war in righteousness.

"I am proclaiming the year of Adonai's favor, and the day of vengeance to comfort all who mourn in Jerusalem!"

Yeshua thundered powerfully from upper Jerusalem to the earth so that the sky and the earth quaked.[5]

Therion, Oracle, and Lucifer, hearing the great peals of thunder, looked upward and considered what they might mean.

"I will have compassion on my people, the Hebrews," Yeshua passionately proclaimed as the sound of their cries and petitions mixed with the words *"Hoshanna! Barukh haba beshem Adonai"* rose up to his throne like incense.[6] Those were words he had been waiting to hear from the leaders of the Hebrews. He had vowed to them: "You will not see my face again until you say, 'Blessed is he who comes in the name of Adonai,'"[7] and now after two thousand years they were earnestly seeking him.[8] Finally, they saw with great clarity their need for this one who had come to his own, yet his own had not received him.[9]

"I will give them a beautiful headdress instead of ashes, the oil of gladness instead of mourning, the garment of praise instead of a faint spirit; that they may be called oaks of righteousness, the planting of Adonai, that he may be glorified. They shall build up the ancient ruins; they shall raise up the former devastations of many generations.[10] Look, my people, you will be fully satisfied. I will never again make you an object of mockery among the nations.[11]

"I am displeased that there is no justice," said Yeshua, fiery lightning surging from his being. "I am appalled that there is no one to intervene."[12]

"Great King, you are a refuge to your people, a stronghold to the Hebrews," someone shouted, answering the audacious claims of Therion to those around him.

"I am the one who has gathered them and the armies of the world into the valley of Jehoshaphat, for there I will judge them for harming my people, for scattering my inheritance among the nations, and for dividing up my land. They cast lots to decide which of my people would be their slaves and abused the little ones for their pleasure.

I will bring them back again from all the places to which they were sold, and I will pay back the nations for all they have done.[13] I will strike Therion from the house of the wicked by laying his neck bare.[14]

"Lucifer, his son Therion, and Oracle do not grasp my thoughts," Yeshua declared, "nor do they understand my counsel; I am gathering them like sheaves to the threshing floor[15] because the time has come for the Hebrews to take possession of the kingdom.[16] I have made Jerusalem a trap and now I shall go and spring the trap!" declared Yeshua in a mighty and thunderous voice, even as Therion boasted of his seemingly inevitable victory.

"Look," proclaimed Yeshua, "I am making Jerusalem an unstable cup toward all of its surrounding armies as they lay siege against Judah and Jerusalem. I am making Jerusalem a heavy weight so that everyone who burdens themselves with it will be crushed, even though all of the nations of the earth have gathered themselves against it. I am about to strike every horse with panic and every rider with insanity. I will keep my eyes on the house of Judah, but I will blind every horse of the invading armies."[17]

"Swing your sickle, and gather the harvest," an Angel coming out of the temple of Adonai said in a loud voice, "for the hour has come to gather it, for the harvest of the earth is fully ripe."[18]

"Bring down your warriors, Yeshua!" the prophet Joel suddenly called out. "Rush forth with the sickle, for the harvest is ripe! Go, stomp the grapes, for the winepress is full! The vats overflow. Indeed, their wickedness is great! Crowds, great crowds are in the valley of threshing, the valley of Jehoshaphat, Armageddon!"[19]

"Michael," Yeshua said, "when you hear the trumpet blast, you will go out and gather my elect from the four winds, from one end of heaven to another.[20]

"The rest of you," Yeshua commanded the mighty Angels who were among the vast army following him,

"Go and gather the weeds first and tie them in bundles for burning, but bring the wheat into my barn."[21]

Gabriel knew precisely what Yeshua was referring to. In fact, he had longed for this day when they would finally be authorized to go forth in every direction and first gather out of his kingdom all things that offend and those who practice lawlessness.[22] He peered through the veil to the earth, noting the location of several of Lucifer's army of Watchers as well as the rulers of the earth[23] and all who had taken the mark and those that were attempting to destroy the Hebrews. Their vast numbers, he considered, were of no consequence, for they were like a drop in a bucket and were as dust on the scales before the mighty Yeshua! All the nations were as nothing before him, they were reckoned by him as nothing and chaos.[24]

"The end of the age has come for the world to be harvested in judgment!" Yeshua proclaimed. Then he resolutely rose from his Father's throne and walked toward his majestic pure-white war horse.[25] A formidably sharp, two-edged sword, something like an intensified particle beam of light, could be seen coming out of his mouth.[26]

"Go forth, O King, with your great army!" Enoch, the seventh from Adam, cheered him on. "Execute judgment on all; convict all who are wicked for all of the wickedness they have committed and for all the harsh things which the wicked have spoken against you."[27]

"Nations far and wide, prepare for war!" Gabriel announced. "Call out your best warriors! Let all of your fighting men advance for the attack!"[28] he taunted.

The Hebrews' cry for help was the key to establishing Yeshua's kingdom and he would not rest until[29] he had vanquished all their enemies[30] and established Jerusalem as a praise throughout the earth,[31] the Hebrews as the head of nations and no longer the tail.[32]

"The day of my vengeance has finally come," bellowed Yeshua, "the day to bring in the acceptable year of Adonai.[33]

Now, my glory shall be revealed, and all the Adamites will see it at once."[34]

"O great King," Isaiah exclaimed, "rend the heavens and go down; may the mountains quake at your presence![35] Repay your enemies according to their action: anger to your enemies, retribution to your foes; to the coastlands render their due!"[36] Isaiah was eager to see Yeshua defend the Hebrews after every ally had forsaken her. "Go with strength, and may your arm rule for you."[37]

Ben and Kristiana watched in amazement as an Angel threw the contents of his bowl across the sky.

"It is done!" someone with a loud voice shouted from the throne in the temple.[38]

"The kingdoms of this world," others loudly joined in, "have become the kingdoms of Adonai and of Yeshua, and Adonai shall reign forever and ever! The nations were angry, and your wrath has come. Now is the time that the dead should be judged and that you should reward your servants the prophets, the saints, and those who fear your name—unimportant as well as important—and for you to destroy those who have destroyed the earth."

The temple of Adonai suddenly opened to expose the ark of his covenant, as lightning and booming thunder emanated from within.[39]

All eyes were on Yeshua.

"I am coming quickly!"[40] His voice was like the sound of many waters. He was silent for a moment and then roared like a ferocious lion, shaking the throne itself. "I have heard you, my beloved, and I am coming!"[41]

The armies of Yeshua began taking their positions on their side of the veil in preparation for battle.[42]

◎ ◎ ◎ ◎ ◎

The scene turned white. "Ben and Kristiana," Antipas startled Ben, who had been immersed in the scene, "to understand the removal of the veil, you first must know why the veil was created. So long as it existed between the two domains, there could never be complete and open communication between Adonai and the Adamites. It happened immediately after the degeneration of the earth, which took place after the assassination."

Approximately seven thousand years before Present, close to the time of Creation, as seen through the AEFOD

21
The Veil

BEN AND KRISTIANA saw Michael, Gabriel, and all the Angels surrounding the Garden, watching intently to see how Adonai would resolve the crisis of degeneration that had just been set in motion.

Adonai, looking tenderly at his son Adam, was overwhelmed with grief[1] because of the words he had to utter that would activate the events that Adam's action had triggered.[2] Adam and his wife Eve had lost Adonai's breath and the radiance of his light was fading quickly. Soon they would not be able to endure his presence whatsoever. Adonai issued the pronouncement: "The *adamáh* will now degenerate and decay. In time, because you are *adamáh* and were taken from it, to *adamáh* you will return because of what you have done."[3]

Immediately a deep rumble could be heard, like the groaning of a million voices[4] at the point of death. Then all at once, a burst, a pulse of radiation emitted from the atoms of every tree, from every flower, from every blade of grass, from every rock and from the very soil itself. It started in the dirt under Adam's feet and spread throughout the planet and then the entire cosmos. Everything changed in that instant. The earth and the material world fell into a hopeless state of degeneration.[5]

From the invisible world of cells and DNA to all the animals, birds, and fish that Adonai had formed out of the *adamáh*,[6] all living creatures and every living thing began to deteriorate. They shared the fate of Adam and the *adamáh*. Even the rocks were affected by the release of alpha particles, which left them slightly radioactive.[7] Into a world where, only moments before, oxidation was unknown and unimaginable, where all metals and materials would have remained intact forever, came corrosion and decomposition. Corruption permeated the entire creation.

Adam sighed, looked at the ground, and kneeling down, took some dirt into his hands and stared at it. "I am made from the dust of the *adamáh* and to it I shall return," he whispered, finally realizing that when Adonai formed him from the *adamáh*, he made him the living, federal head of all created matter. Adam let the dirt slip through his fingers, contemplating the relationship he had with it. "We are one and our fates are one.[8] My fate determines the fate of everything in the material cosmos; the vitality of everything is linked to and dependent upon my life."

"Father!" Adam cried as he and Eve looked back tearfully at Adonai[9] and at the Garden of Eden. The whole magnificent scene behind them began to fade as something like a scroll was rolled out before them.[10] Little did the man and his wife know this was the last time in their mortal lives that they would be face to face with their father.[11] The domain of Adonai and all the Angels, good and evil, disappeared out of their view forever; everything of that domain was now completely cloaked from their sight. Like a great curtain closing in front of them, the world they left became like a one-way mirror, transparent on one side and opaque on the other. Those behind it could still see through to the other side.[12] Spatially, the two dimensions were practically on top of each another but now they were separated by an invisible wall or veil, like a membrane, barring human passage between them.

"Oh, for the day that the Promised One comes to destroy Lucifer who beguiled us and restores Adonai's spirit and the glorious light that flowed from us," Adam sighed longingly.

"How will the Promised One," Eve asked in tears, "have the power to restore us when the corruption reaches to the core of our being and that of our sons?"

"I don't know," Adam answered despondently; "I just don't know." Freedom from death was the deepest desire of his heart, and Adonai's promise of the one who would crush the head of Lucifer lingered in his mind. Maybe there was hope after all.[13]

Lucifer and the rebel Angels saw everything that was happening on the other side of the veil. "Let them languish in their pain!" Lucifer scoffed. "Although we have been stripped of our beauty and fire, they are now cast out from Adonai's presence forever!" With a wicked smile he turned to his cohorts, now as disfigured as he. "But, don't you see, we are free ... free from the oppression of Adonai and free from serving the worm he created." Lucifer relished his triumph over Adonai.

"Your ingenious plan to cause Adam to murder himself[14] was a stunning success," one of the rebel Angels, later called Watchers, commended him.

"Now we will never be required to serve the speck of dust that he is," Lucifer answered. "There is no hope for Adam or any sons who come after him, since none will by any means be able to repurchase a brother nor give to Adonai a ransom for that brother, for the redemption of their souls is costly. None will continue to live eternally and not see the Abyss!"[15] he exclaimed.

"I was right in my assessment that causing Adam to defy the directive of Adonai would force Adonai into a self-imposed exile lest his consuming fire, which is like a stream of brimstone,[16] destroy the earth and everything on it. I calculated that Adonai, in all of his compassion,[17] would sooner divorce himself from the earth than utterly destroy everything by his fiery-lightning presence.[18] Now that I have successfully separated the abode of Adonai from the abode of Adam, the earth is ours forever!"

"That is not true; the earth and all its fullness will forever be Adonai's!"[19] the same Watcher countered. "So how can you can suggest that it is ours?"

"The answer is quite simple, *brother*," Lucifer sneered. "You see, because Adonai cannot touch the earth, and because Adam, the true beneficiary, has forfeited his right of dominion over the earth, I have become the de facto ruler of this world![20] You are correct, however, that it shall always be 'technically' Adonai's but he will never be able to possess it; neither can Adam ever regain his dominion over it. We have adversely taken possession of the earth that Adonai created and conferred as a benefit to Adam.

"I rightly deduced that once death entered into Adam, he and his descendants would necessarily forfeit their possession. Adonai could not have it, either, because his glory would destroy it,[21] which he would never allow. It is just too much for mortals to withstand. So the earth will be ours forever because Adam cannot undo the penalty of death; nor will any one of his sons ever be authorized, acceptable, or legitimate who can remove the consequences of Adam's action. Hence I will remain the ruler of the world indefinitely[22] and you all shall possess part of it."

"Yet for all that, we are left disfigured and barren,"[23] one of the rebel Watchers snarled, pointing to his contemptible body. "I am here because I share your conviction that we should not be subservient to Dusty, yet now we are left desolate. You apparently did not foresee that Adonai could remove his fire from all of us. Even now I feel the power draining from within," he said, sensing for the first time the need to consume something.

"What have we gained if we are never satisfied?" he demanded. "The removal of Adonai's fire and power[24] has left us disconnected from the source of life. Now I constantly crave a life-essence that I can devour!" the Watcher bellowed greedily with the look of a hungry lion in his eyes.[25] "Adam is still able to derive energy and food from the earth and though he is dying, when he is hungry he simply needs to take of the produce of the *adamáh*. Even in its state of degeneration the *adamáh* will still produce enough to nourish him until his death because he was taken from it. Even the animals might be eaten since they were derived from it as well. But what can *I* consume to fill the insatiable void inside me?"[26]

"You are correct," Lucifer replied, "that, unlike Adam, we cannot gain any energy from the *adamáh*, for our bodies are transdimensional and hence will never fail like Adam's, yet we still need a supply of energy. Adonai has already instituted what we need: the creature that Adonai caused to come up out of the *adamáh*, whose life-force, blood, was given in exchange for Adam, Eve, and their progeny to be in close proximity to Adonai,[27] cannot actually reverse the effect of the treason committed.[28] The Covering is a force field, a shield of energy that covers a person or object from the fiery-lightning of Adonai. The effect lasts only one year, however, and so the offering for the Covering must be continually repeated.[29]

"We can take our nourishment from the life-force of any creature,[30] including the sons of Dusty himself." With a sly smile Lucifer added: "The life-force is of a transdimensional nature and does nothing for the terrestrial bodies of Adam and Eve, but it will sustain us quite nicely."[31]

"And how do you propose that we obtain blood since we are on this side of the veil?" yet another Angel inquired, certain he had found a fatal flaw in the plan. "Have you not seen that an impassable barrier has been placed between the area of Adam and the domain of our existence? Do you think that we can simply pass over it without any retaliation from Adonai?"

"Here is what we will do," Lucifer responded coolly to his challenger. "Though we despise the Adamites, we will convince them to willingly—even eagerly—offer up blood of another creature in our honor and then we will receive nourishment from the life-force in the blood.[32] Because Adonai created Adam in his image, humans are therefore of greater value[33] than animals; hence their life-force will be for us far more delectable and delighful fare.

"Let me explain how we will now rule the earth and be energized simultaneously. Adam and Eve had a limited understanding of the City of Adonai, which is now cloaked behind the veil," Lucifer said. "You must realize the incredible advantage that our knowledge of those things 'above' give us over the Adamites living 'below' on the other side of the veil. Our secret knowledge of the world behind the veil will cause us to be considered gods! We shall use it to exploit the Adamites who will have a deep yet unconscious yearning to return to the Mountain-City of Adonai. We will exploit this longing for restoration to entice them to commit even greater acts of evil than their father Adam committed."

"We will distract them with empty promises,"[34] one of the rebel Watchers interjected, "so that rather than seeking to commune with Adonai by way of the Covering, the rebellion against Adonai will increase and become so bad that even calling on his name will be profaned.[35] Instead of calling on his name as a blessing, men will misuse it as a curse. Then Adonai will further distance himself from them and be grieved that he even created them."[36]

"As their memory fades with each passing day, the sons of dirt will be more easily convinced that we are in fact 'gods' and that they must earn our favor by giving us blood, the life-force of another," said Lucifer, salivating at the thought. Then transforming himself back into a glorious Angel of light he proclaimed, "Yes, we shall convince them to practice every sort of abomination that Adonai hates."

"Since we are hidden behind the veil," another Watcher said, "consulting our knowledge will be known to mere men as divination because they will believe we are divine; our powers will be considered sorcery.[37] Through war and murder and horrors of great magnitude committed by the Adamites in our honor we shall be completely satisfied."

"Finally, brothers," Lucifer said, regaining control of the disclosure of the big idea, "there is one more delight that we shall partake of; you shall be satiated when we convince the Adamites to do something utterly repugnant,[38] something which Adonai never commanded nor did it even come into his mind![39] We shall seduce them to offer up their sons and daughters in fire;[40] and we shall do so until they are slaughtering their children to us under every spreading tree, in the ravines, and under the clefts of the rocks.[41] When this occurs, then your hunger shall be assuaged and you shall be most gratified."[42]

"What about the Promised One whom Adonai said would crush your head and ours too?" another Watcher asked anxiously. "How do you propose to counter him?"

"When the time is right," Lucifer responded, "some of you shall mingle yourselves with the seed of Adam and corrupt the ways of all flesh on the earth. When Adam was created there was no death, decay, or degeneration whatsoever in him. When he and Eve have offspring, then the degeneration—the record of the event of the Fall[43]—will be passed from Adam to all of his sons through perpetual transmission of death, inherent in the seed, from generation to generation. Likewise, when our seed is mingled with theirs, then our seed will be passed from generation to generation. Thus the Promised One will be one of us, and if he is one of us, then he cannot be the one to restore Adam."[44]

The rebels cheered in shrill cacophony at the brilliant plan of their nefarious leader.

◎ ◎ ◎ ◎ ◎

"Ben," Kristiana exclaimed, letting go of the AEFOD. "Come quickly and see this!"

22
The Unveiling

BEN WALKED OVER to Kristiana and peeked out of the opening of the grove, careful not to be noticed. He saw a translucent walkway about ten feet above Lucifer's head stretching out as far as his eyes could see in the direction of the City. The walkway appeared to be still partly transparent and perhaps not totally tangible. "What is it?" asked Kristiana.

"It must be the King's Highway that will take us to the City. Antipas told me about it. I am guessing that our discovery about Lucifer is what has made it manifest. Yeshua established the Highway, and it is set apart exclusively for the redeemed."

"Who are the redeemed?" asked Kristiana, perplexed.

"They are the ones who have pledged allegiance to Yeshua. Mortals may travel on it if they are loyal to the King, but no one unclean is able to journey on it. And it is only for those authorized to travel on the road; no fool shall ever venture onto it. Antipas said it is by this road that the redeemed[1] have returned and entered Jerusalem with singing and everlasting joy resting upon their heads, gladness and joy overtaking them, and sorrow and mourning fleeing away!"[2]

"Oh, that's just great," Kristiana sighed.

"What's wrong?" Ben could not understand her dejection.

"How will we ever get on that road when it begins directly over Lucifer's head?" she asked, pointing out to Ben the impossible scenario. "Besides, I don't see any way to access it. Maybe the answer will become clear in the same way that the Highway is becoming clear. The more right conclusions we come to about Lucifer and his kingdom, the more tangible the Highway appears."

"Agreed," Ben said as he stretched out his hand to grab the AEFOD that was still in Kristiana's hand. Immediately they were surrounded by white light.

"I was born behind the veil and could not see through it," Antipas explained. "Only on rare occasions did Adonai grant the Adamites access to see beyond the veil. Jacob, in a dream, saw the Angels behind the veil going up and down on a ladder."[3] The scenes Antipas was describing flashed in front of them. "Adonai opened the portals of the veil so that the food of Angels could rain down on mortals in abundance.[4] Elisha the prophet and his servant saw through the veil and realized that the great numbers of Angels and horses and chariots of fire that were with them in battle far outnumbered the forces opposing them.[5]

"Another was granted to see behind the veil when he was sitting by the river Chebar and the sky was opened and he saw visions of Adonai.[6] The veil opened slightly when Yeshua came up out of the water and the spirit of Adonai came down upon him.[7] Several others saw the veil open as well.[8] Yeshua longed for it to be removed completely, though he knew that its removal would bring fire upon the earth.[9]

"Even now," Antipas continued solemnly, "Lucifer is attempting to regain the earth by contradicting just one of Adonai's directives. I am trusting Adonai will deal with him. You must hurry and be transformed into a new body before the Covering, also known as the personal force-field, expires. When that happens there will be no hope. While hope remains you must locate the Key of Life contained in the Chronicles. In time you will understand. Only the Key will grant you entrance into the City and access to the River of Life and the Tree of Life. Now hurry; time is fleeting."

As the white light faded, Ben and Kristiana's attention was drawn to the vast army behind the veil ready to attack. They realized that they were about to see the end of the battle between Yeshua and Lucifer that had enthralled them earlier.

Yeshua sat on his horse behind the veil ready to advance; behind him were millions and millions of riders plus horses and chariots of fire.[10]

"After six millennia," John said to Isaiah, who was on a horse next to him, "Yeshua is finally revealing himself to the world with his mighty Angels in blazing flames of fire, which will inflict vengeance on those who do not know Adonai and on those who have not obeyed his good news. They will needlessly suffer the punishment of eternal destruction by virtue of exposure to his presence and from the glory of his might."[11]

"The world has no idea of what is about to happen!" Isaiah confirmed. "Yeshua is coming in fire with his chariots like a tornado, to render his anger in fury, and his rebuke with flames of fire!"[12]

Yeshua opened his mouth and a beam of light pierced through the veil, creating a shock-wave that blasted the inhabitants on the other side. Immediately a deafening boom thundered throughout the world.[13]

Therion and Oracle were knocked to the ground from the blast. Flat on their backs they turned pale with fear as they witnessed the laser-like shaft of light,[14] brighter than the midday sun, piercing through a point in the dark, ash-filled sky. They covered their ears in reaction to the horrific, ear-piercing roar emanating from the sky as it began rolling up like a scroll from the point where the particle-beam sword from Yeshua's mouth struck it.[15]

The veil that had cloaked the other domain from view was dissolving, like a dark filter becoming transparent.[16] Therion, Oracle, and their army watched as dark, thick clouds began rolling out and flames of fire and raging bolts of lightning blazed brilliantly through the clouds, illuminating the earth. They then saw Yeshua step into the domain of the Adamites. The veil that so long had separated the domain of Adonai from that of the Adamites was removed and finally all could see Yeshua.[17]

For several moments he paused to survey the earth, which[18] had suffered such horrific destruction during the time of the Hebrews' Trouble that it was practically uninhabitable. All the seas and rivers had turned to blood and everything in the seas had died—the coral, the fish, the dolphins, whales, starfish, shellfish, even the plankton all were dead.[19]

Therion, Oracle, and all the armies with the kings of the earth who had declared war against Yeshua by gathering to destroy the Hebrews[20] watched as smoke poured out of his nostrils and a consuming fire went forth from his mouth.[21] Their hearts skipped a beat as they fixed their eyes on the champion towering over them and the armies of heaven coming behind him.[22] Everyone on the entire planet saw his radiance, brighter than the sun, the powerful beams of light coming out from his hands, and the sharp sword in his mouth.[23] Seeing the sign of Yeshua coming on the clouds of heaven with power and great glory,[24] they all lamented in dismay.

The people of Egypt, just south of Jerusalem, looked up in fear and their hearts failed as they saw Yeshua leading his army on a swift cloud right over their heads.[25]

In a flash like lightning, Yeshua circled the earth from east to west. The earth began to groan violently as Yeshua and his army approached. Like a great furnace his fiery-lightning presence began to set the mountains and hills ablaze.[26] The continents quaked and ocean waves surged as Yeshua's army passed over. How violent the reaction of the degenerate planet now exposed to the overwhelming power of the King because the veil had been removed! Hills collapsed and fire broke out,[27] burning to the depths of the Abyss, consuming the earth and its produce, and igniting even the very foundations of the mountains.[28]

◎ ◎ ◎ ◎ ◎

Ben and Kristiana watched in awe as the removal of the veil left the earth exposed to the glorious fire of Yeshua so that even the dirt was melting with fervent heat, and the earth and everything on it began to burn.[29] The heavens declared his righteousness so that all the nations would see his glory.[30]

"It appears in the Chronicles," Ben said to Kristiana, "that only the cloud surrounding Yeshua shielded the earth and the inhabitants from the full impact of his consuming fire and lightning."[31]

"I think you are right," Kristiana responded. "Do you suppose," she wondered aloud—witnessing flash floods on the surface of the earth—"that he was displeased with the rivers, or was his anger directed against the watercourses or against the sea when he came back with his chariots of deliverance?"

"I don't know," Ben admitted. "But clearly pestilence went before him and disease followed behind him."[32] He and Kristiana both saw people all over the earth wailing and lamenting[33] as fear flooded over them.

"For so long," Kristiana realized, "they had foolishly said in their hearts that there was no King, no creator.[34] Now, for the first time since the Fall, the Adamites could see directly into the other realm beyond the veil[35] and they knew that death would soon be upon them."

The Chronicles focused on Yeshua again, who, with a nod, gave the order to Gabriel and the other commanders of his army. They knew their mission: to gather all the things that offend out of Yeshua's kingdom.[36]

"Who among us can live with the consuming fire?" Therion's chief commander asked. "Who among us can live with everlasting flames?"[37]

"The great day of Yeshua's wrath has come, and who is able to endure it?" many around the world acknowledged, gripped with fear and barely able to speak.[38] All who were able, traveled as quickly as they could to underground bunkers—even entire cities—they had built for themselves in mountain caves; others took shelter among the rocks. In certain designated areas people shut themselves inside secret underground command posts, reinforced to withstand a nuclear blast.[39] They imagined that somehow, protected by the mountains and rocks—or even underground—they could hide themselves from the face of the one who sat on the throne and from the wrath of Yeshua.

"At last," Isaiah said to John as they rode their horses among Yeshua's army, "their lofty looks are humbled. Their haughtiness is bowed down, and the King alone shall be exalted this day. Everything proud and lofty, all of the high towers of the Adamites, every fortified wall, and every ship shall be brought to ruin today."[40]

"They wanted to be gods," John responded, "by taking the mark of Therion and transforming their DNA, and they wanted to lift themselves up to the highest place. But all they can do is go into the holes of the rocks, and into the caves of the earth, attempting to escape the terror of the great King and the glory of his majesty, now that he has arisen to shake the earth mightily."[41]

In just a few moments Yeshuah's army circled the earth back to their starting point. They flew from east to west over Teman-Jordan,[42] the area of Bozrah, where the other Hebrews who heeded Yeshua's warning had fled when they saw the destructive abomination set up by Oracle,[43] and were being protected from the awful time of Trouble.

Yeshua's eyes were fixed on rescuing those who had recently called upon Him in the lower Jerusalem.

23

Judgment in the Valley of Jehoshaphat

"WAIT!" THERION SHOUTED as he defiantly regained his footing and shielded himself from the massive hailstones that were raining down. "All is not lost. Go and destroy the Hebrews. Their death is our victory!"

Therion's hybrid soldiers, hearing this strong command both audibly and telepathically, struggled to get up off the ground as hailstones the size of grapefruits rained down upon them. Becoming even more intent upon their mission, they rushed with all of their superhuman strength upon the perimeter of the Hebrews and while still thirty feet away, leapt with their swords raised to strike in midair.

Caleb and the Hebrews had an infusion of Angel-type power course through their bodies; it welled up within them at the moment they saw the sky begin to disappear. They sensed the power of fire, like a torch igniting harvested grain, rising up within them. The Knesset members on the periphery of the huddled multitude stretched out their hands and rays of fire burst forth from their fingers at the precise moment the hybrids lunged at them, setting the attackers ablaze. The hybrids began falling like overripe apples from a tree as flames engulfed them.

"Our strength is from Adonai and through Yeshua, the commander of the heavenly armies!"[1] Caleb and the other leaders of the city shouted with all their might while blasting wave after wave of the hundreds of millions of hybrid soldiers and rebel Watchers who desired their destruction.

"Smash them to pieces!" one of the Knesset members bellowed. "He has made our strength like iron and our feet like bronze!"[2]

At the same time, those being taken into captivity by the forces of Therion felt the same surge of power so that those who were feeble among them became like David and the men became like the Angels, breaking their handcuffs and killing their captors[3] with flames that shot out from their hands.

The light of Yeshua above them intensified to the point of overwhelming blindness.

Yeshua made haste toward the Mount of Olives, adjacent to the lower Jerusalem, the very place from where he had ascended approximately two thousand years earlier. His horse touched down on the mountain and then, galloping to break its speed, snorted as if animated by the knowledge that its master, *the* Master, had come to fight and proclaim victory!

Yeshua surveyed the situation; his eyes blazed full of fury. Appalled that there was no one to help his people, no one to give support, he thus declared: "By my own arm I will bring salvation for me!"[4]

He then swung his leg over one side of his horse and, for the first time in two thousand years, set foot upon the earth, this time with a thundering boom as if he weighed more than all of the mountains of the world put together. The reverberations created an earthquake so large that the world had never in all of history experienced anything of such magnitude. The ground under his feet began smoking from his fiery power and slowly turned into molten lava.[5] A massive crack quickly spread out from his feet from east to west. The ground pulled apart and the mountain began to open up.

The forces of Therion fell to the ground, stunned by the mountain quaking beneath their feet. The mountain rumbled and separated—with one side moving toward the north and the other side moving toward the south—creating a deep canyon with jagged rock walls rising up about four hundred feet. The mouth of the canyon was approximately five hundred feet across.

Large chunks of the mountain fell on some of Therion's soldiers, burying them alive.

All over the world every high mountain and lofty hill began to crumble and break apart. All the stately cedars of Lebanon and all the oaks of Bashan fell over. The towers erected by the Adamites at the height of their arrogance staggered from the enormity of the earthquake until finally, one by one, they came crashing to the ground. Tsunamis crashed into the ships of the world, sinking every last one of them. Not a single high mountain was left intact and every island fell into the seas.[6] Large portions of the earth were shattered and split apart. The earth was so violently shaken that it began to reel to and fro like a drunkard and sway like a hut. It was moved out of its normal orbit so that the sun and moon stood still in their paths in the sky.[7]

The earth was broken beyond recovery.[8]

After several minutes of shaking, Caleb pushed himself up. He saw all the forces of Therion on the ground. Some were dead, having been hit by the massive boulders from the earthquake, but most were merely stunned and some had already started to regain their footing. No one among the Hebrews appeared to be injured.

Caleb looked up where Yeshua was and immediately saw the newly formed canyon that seemed to reach as far as Azal. "Come on! Run into the gorge!" he shouted, realizing Yeshua had made a way of escape. "Flee through the mountain!" The Hebrews quickly picked themselves up and started running for their lives into the canyon until finally the last of the group had entered.[9] Caleb and the others on the periphery maintained their position, blasting bursts of fire from their hands as the seemingly endless hordes of hybrids were once again coming like a tsunami. Soon thousands of Yeshua's radiant Angels swooped in to lift the Hebrews off the ground and hurry them through the mountain pass to Azal.[10]

Caleb and some other Hebrews stayed behind to hold off the attackers. They continued shooting intensely but the hordes were like a surging river. Suddenly, Angels from above nabbed Caleb and his cohorts just as they were about to be overwhelmed and whisked them away. As he was being sped along near the floor of the canyon, Caleb stared anxiously back. Seeing hundreds of thousands of soldiers running toward them with superhuman strength and speed, he wondered what would happen. A mental image of millions of people passing through walls of water on dry ground flooded his mind, reminiscent of the ancient phenomenon.

Without warning, Yeshua shouted with a voice like a piercing trumpet. Michael and his legions recognized the signal and flew out with a flash to gather the rest of the Hebrews, Yeshua's elect, from the four corners of the earth.[11]

Yeshua then leapt off the side of the newly formed cliff where he had been standing and dropped to the midpoint of the canyon.[12] Interposing himself between the forces of Therion and the Hebrews, Yeshua squared off with the attackers, many of them charging on horses. The Angels and Hebrews who were watching knew the day of vengeance was in his heart, and the year of his redeeming work had come.[13]

The attackers leading the charge stopped dead in their tracks in sheer terror when they saw the all-powerful one standing before them with flaming eyes and a covering of flame and lightning. He lifted his hands to direct shafts of light and cause fierce lightning bolts to lash out at his enemies on every side.[14] Like an archer with a bow, he commissioned his arrows that each would find its mark. He opened his mouth, sent forth the particle-beam sword, and cut in half all who were in front of him.[15]

The attackers from behind kept advancing, while those at the front were attempting to retreat. Mass confusion ensued: the horses were struck with blindness and those advancing and those retreating began to kill one another.[16] With their own weapons, Yeshua was destroying those who had rushed out like a whirlwind, thinking the Hebrews would be easy prey.[17] The onslaught of soldiers did not stop because those at the rear misconstrued that they were advancing to destroy the enemy and did not realize they would actually be destroying themselves.

The chief commander of Therion's armies, who had been leading the attack, immediately felt the intense heat of Yeshua's fire and lightning. His flesh began to dissolve and his eyes started to sizzle in their sockets. "Who is able to stand in his presence?" were the last words he uttered before his tongue liquefied in his mouth and he melted away.[18]

Yeshua furiously stomped on the commander's body and then did the same to corpse after corpse, treading them down as if they were grapes in a winepress. He kept trampling on the bodies until finally he was walking atop a mountain of wasted bodies of dead attackers.[19] Meanwhile he continued to gain on the living and cut them in half at the waist as their blood sprayed on his garments.

The opposing forces on the front lines froze with fear as Yeshua, in haste and rage, poured out their blood on the ground.[20] Still the forces of Therion kept funneling in to the canyon, blind to the horrible fate that awaited them.

Hours passed as Yeshua advanced through the canyon and into the valley of Jehoshaphat, trampling his enemies under his feet, crushing the heads of the wicked and laying bare their bones from head to toe in order to rescue his chosen people.[21] His white garments were splattered with his enemies' blood as he was, as it were, treading grapes in the valley of his winepress.

◎ ◎ ◎ ◎ ◎

"The earthquake lengthened that day,"[22] Antipas broke in. "The day of Yeshua was like the long day of Yehoshua, who needed extra time to route the Amorim. They were as tall as cedars and as strong as oak trees.[23] The AEFOD turned white and then Ben and Kristiana saw a legion of ancient beings, dressed in leather and semi-armored battle gear, who appeared as gigantic Adamite men—similar yet different—fleeing before them. Because his people were fighting the accursed hybrid Nephilim,[24] Adonai listened to the voice of an Adamite so that the sun and moon stood still until the nation could defeat its enemies.[25]

"There was never such a day before or since," Antipas continued; "that is, until now.[26] Adonai once again caused the sun and moon to stand still in their habitations in order to defeat the rebel Watchers and the recipients of the mark of Therion, the Nephilim hybrids. Yeshua trampled so many bodies that the blood flowed high enough to reach a horse's bridle[27] for a total of nearly six cubic miles."[28]

The ancient scene faded and then, once again, Ben and Kristiana found themselves witnessing the last epic battle. Therion, Oracle, Lucifer, and the other rebel Watchers—realizing they were defeated—launched up into the sky and spread out in every direction. Yeshua looked up, raised his hands, and shot millions of bolts of lightning, like fiery arrows, at the rebels.[29] Every judgment-laden bolt hit its mark, piercing through and sending its intended victim to the ground.[30]

"At last Yeshua is executing his foes and repaying those who have hated him!"[31] Isaiah marveled.

"He is the only true King," John responded. "He is the living God and the everlasting King. In his anger the earth shakes and not one among the nations is able to stand against his fury!"

"Those 'gods'," Isaiah mocked, "those rebel Watchers who made neither the heavens nor the earth, are about to disappear both from the earth and from under the heavens. Their lives, however, will be prolonged for a season and a year."[32]

The Watchers all crumpled to the ground and, in an instant, Yeshua's Angels swooped down on them, each having a heavy chain in his hand. A mighty Angel stood towering over Lucifer, humiliated and decisively defeated, and bound him with the unbreakable chain.[33] For the first time in six thousand years Lucifer lost his proud look.[34]

"This is the day Yeshua long ago appointed to oppose those who are proud, haughty, and lifted up against him; now they are all humbled!"[35] Isaiah exclaimed. "Everyone who has exalted himself has been brought low, and the King alone is exalted."[36]

24
The Aftermath

THE EVENTS OF the cruel and awesome day of wrath and fierce anger that Ben and Kristiana had just witnessed filled them with fear and dread. Everything turned white and they once again heard the reassuring voice of Antipas, as they could see the entire sphere of the earth before them. Its surface was devastated and marred, sunken and cracked.[1]

"The King had decreed judgment on the inhabitants," Antipas began, "because they defiled the earth, violated laws, and disregarded the regulation—according to the everlasting covenant laid down in the beginning—that everything should reproduce according to its kind."

Ben and Kristiana saw that the earth was dried up and withered; it looked like a smoldering mass with smoke rising from thousands of points around the globe. They observed that part of it appeared to have melted from intense heat.[2] Beholding that all of the oceans and rivers had become blood,[3] they both felt sick.

"As a man who has swallowed poison tries to vomit it out," Antipas explained, "so too the earth convulsed in reaction to all the violence perpetrated upon it[4] until finally the blood shed throughout all the centuries oozed out from the surface of the earth and coalesced in the seas.

"The day that Adonai long warned about finally came like a thief in the night in which the heavens were rolled back like a scroll and the elements melted with intense heat, releasing all their pent-up decay and corruption. Yes, the earth and the works of man were burned up!" Antipas declared. "Its inhabitants paid for their guilt and no class of people was spared—priest or atheist, servant or master, overseer or attendant, creditor or debtor, rich or poor, buyer or seller, borrower or lender.

"The world was so thoroughly corrupted during the time of Therion that a curse devoured the earth, and its inhabitants were reduced to merely a few. No more were the factories of man's industry that had produced the tanks, the planes, the guns, and the bombs. All the works of the Adamites were gone: The televisions that brought people into bondage; the banks that charged usury; the clinics where the unborn were murdered; the stadiums full of idolatry. Gone also were the roads and the vehicles that traveled on them as well as the fishing boats, cruise ships, oil tankers, and private yachts. The vast fortunes amassed by the rich were reduced to nothing.

"Their cities lay in ruins, crushed by Adonai's fierce anger."[5] One by one Ben and Kristiana saw the great cities of the world shattered and smoldering, filled with rubble as if ripped apart by a tornado. All the people were gone. All the birds of the sky had flown away. The fertile fields had become a wilderness. "Listen carefully," Antipas instructed them, "and you will hear no more the happy sound of tambourines or the revelry of those who celebrated. No more songs inspired by Lucifer by which men were seduced to slander the King. No more obscene and perverse music that brought praise to Lucifer in mockery of the true and rightful King. Their music was burned up and their albums were shattered. No longer did they sing and drink wine; beer tasted bitter to those who imbibed.

"The grand, magnificent skyscrapers, built and rebuilt ever higher, as well as the homes of both the humble and the proud were leveled. Even the great underground cities that had been prepared for such a day were brought to nothing. Everything had been humbled and nothing—not one of the works of man—remained. Even the glorious pyramids, as stable as they were—built to mimic the city of the King but in honor of Lucifer—were destroyed when Yeshua finally returned.

"All joy and celebration had disappeared from the earth and the inhabitants who remained on the earth were few," said Antipas. "It was like when you beat an olive tree, and just a few olives are left at the end of the harvest.[6] The King's fire purged the earth and the mountains melted like wax before the presence of the King. Just as when he came down to Mount Sinai and it smoked with fire; so also the mountains smoked when the King touched them. The enormity of his power was too much for the earth to handle. In times past he had concealed it, but at his coming he unveiled his roaring fire and lightning with electricity.[7] The earth, which had been yearning since Adam's Fall to be restored, groaned like the creaking of a great ship in a fierce storm."[8]

"I see now," Ben said, "that Yeshua came like a lamb at his first coming[9] to pay for the treason of Adam and to redeem the fallen Adamites. This time he came as a man of war to fight on behalf of his people."[10]

"You're right!" Kristiana heartily agreed. "Lucifer set out to destroy them many, many times—his last attempt being when he was cast out from behind the veil. But Yeshua kept his promise to protect the Hebrews, his elect."[11]

She and Ben looked out from the grove and could see the structure of the King's Highway now fully materialized.

"Are we the only ones who can see the Highway?" Ben wondered aloud. "Its appearance doesn't seem to be bothering anyone."

"I think you are right," Kristiana replied. "They should be noticing it since it is right over Lucifer's head. Perhaps only the loyal can see it."

"That means that we have discovered the King's Highway!" Ben exclaimed with joy. "Let's keep looking for the clues we need to find the Key to the City so we can soon be on our way!" he said.

Each of them took hold of the AEFOD again. Brilliant white flashed before Ben and Kristiana; suddenly they were back watching lower Jerusalem. "Come!" they heard a mighty voice exclaim. Looking up they saw an Angel, standing in front of the sun, who cried in a loud voice to all the birds that were flying overhead: "Gather for the great supper of Adonai!" The Angel beckoned them and pointed to the tremendous carnage of the soldiers Yeshua had slaughtered. Millions of birds that normally migrated over the land of the Hebrews descended, ready to eat anything available. "Eat the flesh of kings, the flesh of commanders, the flesh of warriors, the flesh of horses and their riders, and the flesh of all people, both free and slaves, both small and great."[12]

"Then the books were opened!" Ben and Kristiana heard Antipas announce as a flashing white light virtually blinded them.

25
Judgment

"THE COURT SAT in judgment and the record books were opened,"[1] Antipas repeated, as Ben and Kristiana saw Adonai's great white throne, burning with flaming fire along with its fiery wheels, situated on the naked and charred ground in the valley of Jehoshaphat. Adonai, the great Ancient of Days, was seated upon the throne; his clothes were shining white, like snow, and the hair on his head was like pure wool.

Yeshua came forward and was presented before him and then took his seat at the right hand of Adonai. A river of fire flowed out from before him.[2]

"Adonai himself did not judge anyone," explained Antipas, "because he had given all authority of judgment to Yeshua so that everyone had to honor him just as they did Adonai."[3]

Ben and Kristiana watched closely as millions of Angels brought in the surviving one-third of the Hebrews from around the world.[4] Following them were millions more Angels carrying the people from all the nations. The Angels set down innumerable Adamites in front of Yeshua. Those who had remained faithful to him and had not taken the mark of Therion were placed on his right hand. All others were placed on his left.

"Come, you who have been blessed by my Father!" Yeshua said to those on his right. "Inherit the kingdom prepared for you from the foundation of the world, for I was hungry, and you gave me food to eat; I was thirsty and you gave me water to drink. I was a stranger and you welcomed me, I was naked and you gave me clothes to wear, I was sick and you cared for me, in prison and you came to me."[5]

"Lord, when did we see you hungry," asked those on his right, "or do any of those things for you?"

"I tell all of you," Yeshua answered them, "since you did these things for the welfare of my people, my heritage the Hebrews,[6] whatever you did for the least important of these brothers of mine, you did it for me,"[7] he answered, pointing to the Hebrews standing near him.

Two Angels swiftly intercepted Therion and Oracle, trying to escape after realizing all was lost, and brought them to the throne. The offenders trembled in abject fear of the great conqueror who sat before them.

Yeshua's flaming, fiery eyes[8] stared down upon them: the two who had dared to persecute the Hebrews, Yeshua's chosen, and attempted to stamp them out. Claiming to be gods, they had demanded to be worshiped.[9] "You tried to annihilate my people, the Hebrews, to cast them into the sea so that they should be a nation no more and you defiled Jerusalem where they dwelt."[10]

Moreover, Therion and Oracle had deceived the whole world, forcing humans to take the mark[11] and thereby transforming their DNA by mingling it with the seed of Lucifer in an attempt to erase the image of Adonai created in Adam.

Therion and Oracle shrieked as they saw smoke pour from Yeshua's nostrils and consuming fire come from his mouth. The Angels nearby shielded them from the full force of his fiery blast, yet still his anger overwhelmed them.[12] Horrified, they both dropped to their knees, no longer able to stand in his presence.

Oracle stared at Yeshua in dread as his mind grasped the enormity of the true King before him, the one who existed before all else. He was the one who had made the kings, kingdoms, rulers, and authorities.[13] He was the one who held all creation together.[14]

Therion lowered his head, remembering how he had magnified himself above every god and recognized neither the gods of his ancestors nor any other god. He had exalted himself above everyone and everything and had spoken pompously, arrogantly boasting of his own power. He was guilty of slandering and defying the King of heaven with his insolent blasphemies—railing against both his name and his dwelling place and against those who were dwelling in heaven.[15]

The words that Yeshua had previously spoken began to judge him. All the arrogant and all who practiced evil were like stubble in a burning furnace before Yeshua. "Oh, gods we are not! The power of Lucifer's seed is nothing!" Therion confessed. "After all of our boasting, we are now obliged to experience the fullness of the King's power and wrath! We must drink the wine of Adonai's wrath as it has been poured out undiluted into his cup," he cried to Oracle, his voice shaking uncontrollably.[16] "We gained the whole world, but it amounts to nothing."[17]

A mighty Angel brought forth the heavenly books and opened them. Therion and Oracle were judged by all the deeds they had done.

"Yeshua," they stammered with dread, "You ... are ... Lord!"[18]

The Angels who had shielded them now withdrew their protection, leaving them exposed to the electrifying, pulsating presence of the King. Fire rolled off the lips of Yeshua like a stream of brimstone, enveloped them, and set their bodies ablaze.[19]

Then two Angels picked them up and carried them off to Tophet, a deep and large pit prepared for Lucifer and his Angels.[20] As the blazing stream of fire from Yeshua devoured them[21] they wailed and gnashed their teeth, convulsing and writhing in torment like lowly worms thrashing about. Therion and Oracle were unable to lift even a finger against him now that they were unprotected and exposed to the presence of Yeshua and his Angels.[22]

"Nations of the earth ... " the glorious conquering King turned to those on his left, standing before him in deathly silence, those who had taken the mark of Therion. Hearts of the mighty, the powerful, and the rich melted in fear as he spoke: "I have gathered you here in this valley of Jehoshaphat." Yeshua looked around at all of the nations, his eyes burning like torches. "I shall now set out my case against you here, on behalf of my people, my heritage the Hebrews, whom you have scattered among the nations, reapportioning my land from among them.[23] For I was hungry and you gave me nothing to eat. I was thirsty and you gave me no water. I was a stranger, naked, sick, and in prison, and you did nothing for me."

"Oh, King," Therion's general addressed him, "when did we see you hungry or thirsty or a stranger or naked or sick or in prison, and we didn't help you?"

"I tell all of you truly," he replied, "that since you did not do it for the least important one of these, you did not do it for me.[24] Rather, you cast lots for my people—you sold a young boy in exchange for a prostitute, and a girl for wine, so you could drink.[25]

"Furthermore, you who are accursed took the mark of Therion and worshiped him and his image. I sent my Angel flying across the sky to warn you, saying 'whoever worships Therion and his image and receives a mark on his forehead or his hand will drink the wine of Adonai's wrath, which has been poured undiluted into the cup of his anger, and then will be tortured with fire and sulfur in the presence of the holy Angels and Yeshua.'[26] Now you are left naked and bare before me. I died to give you a garment of salvation—freely for the asking—but you rejected it. I warned you that I would come as a thief and promised that blessed would be the one who guarded his garments so that he should not go naked for all to see.[27] But you chose to allow the rebel Watchers to mingle themselves with your DNA and thus have become Nephilim, like those who lived on the earth in the cursed days of Noah."

Therefore, you who have rejected my image that I placed in every one of you, who refused my generous offer of restoration, of a new body,[28] with pleasures at my right hand forevermore;[29] you who sought to make yourselves into gods"—the King's voice thundered as he pointed to Tophet[30]—"you shall now drink the wine of my wrath! Depart from me into the eternal fire that has been prepared for Lucifer and his Watchers,[31] where there shall be wailing and gnashing of teeth.[32] Be gone!"

Those who had terrorized the earth themselves were terrified and shook with fear. "Who among us can live with the consuming fire or with everlasting flames?"[33] they wailed. At that very instant fire went out from Yeshua's presence, consuming his enemies on every side and scalding the accursed who had taken the mark of Therion.[34] The King's Angels surrounded them, snatched them up, and carried them over to Tophet, wherein they cast each one.[35] These enemies would forever be an abhorrence to all flesh, for when people went up to Jerusalem in the days to come, they would go out and look upon the corpses of the men who had transgressed against their maker, these whose worm would never die and whose fire would not be quenched.[36]

Yeshua then nodded to one of his principal Angels, who came and took the key from his hand and touched the ground. Immediately there appeared a wide door lying flat upon the earth. The Angel inserted the key and lifted open the massive door of the Abyss, letting thick smoke billow out from the awful pit.[37]

Ben and Kristiana held their breath in anticipation of what would happen next. They looked up to see a mighty Angel leading Lucifer by the chain over to the opening of the Abyss. Behind him came millions of other Angels leading other prisoners, Lucifer's millions of Watchers, who also were bound with weighty, unbreakable chains. These who had been exalted ones in the heavenly realms[38] were now brought low. These wicked spirits who had ruled the earth invisibly behind the covering of the veil, these mighty cosmic rulers of darkness who were the rulers and principalities of the past age had finally been arrested. The Angels herded their captives through the suffocating smoke to the dark and foreboding mouth of the pit.[39] The ones who long ago had begged Yeshua not to send them into the Abyss[40] now faced their inevitable, dreaded, and impending doom.

It was only fitting that they taste the torment, agony, and humiliation of that place.[41] The Adamites anxiously waited to see justice meted out to Lucifer and his legions who had unleashed horrendous plagues upon the earth. It was by mingling his own seed[42] that Lucifer had violated one of Adonai's fundamental directives, which was that everything was to reproduce according to its own kind.[43] Before the deluge certain rebel Watchers had left their first abode, going beyond the sphere of authority Adonai had given them, and consequently Adonai had chained them in prisons of darkness.[44] Now that same fate awaited them all.

"I shall return to free you from the darkness and evil which Adonai created!"[45] Lucifer had the audacity to boast even on the edge of the Abyss. Yeshua again nodded to his Angels and they thrust him into the darkness.

"Above the stars of Adonai, I will still set up my throne ... " Lucifer's slander was silenced as he plummeted into the Abyss. The other Angels likewise dragged their captives—fighting against their chains and chafing their necks in futile attempts to break free—and hurled them into the depths of the darkness.[46]

"You too have become as weak as we!" came the cry of derision from those condemned to that place, whom the Abyss stirred up to meet Lucifer. "You have become like us! You have become just like us![47] Despite all of your boasting you are still brought down to the Abyss!" They mocked him as he fell, bound in chains, further and further until at last he hit bottom. Surrounded by impenetrable darkness and sinking into the floor, Lucifer could feel a blanket of creeping maggots beneath him, which eventually enveloped him and also became a cover over him. His chain, fastened tightly to the floor, prevented him from moving.

"The one who caused the earth to tremble, who shook its kingdoms," they chided, "the one who declared that he himself would sit on the mountain of the congregation with the King is finally cut down to the ground and thrown into the Abyss."[48]

"Look how the oppressor has met his end!" people on the surface whispered, overwhelmed by the magnitude of the moment. "Hostility has ceased!"[49]

The whispers then erupted into shouts of joy. "Finally, the world is free!"

Cheers rang out and the immortals began to sing to King Yeshua a new song of praise for the amazing deeds he had performed. What seemed like billions were singing this song, their voices all in perfect harmony, in perfect balance; each singer hearing the intonation of the others and the clear articulation of every word.

"Sing to Adonai, all the earth! Sing to Adonai! Praise his name! Announce every day how he delivers, how his right hand and his mighty arm accomplish deliverance! Tell the nations about his splendor! Tell all the nations about his amazing deeds!"[50]

Then another melody from the Hebrews arose, complementing the first: "Adonai has demonstrated his power to deliver; in the sight of the nations he has revealed his justice. He remains loyal and faithful to the family of the Hebrews. All the ends of the earth see our King deliver us."[51]

Some among the nations joined in praising the King of all the earth and broke into a shout of joyful adoration: "Great is our King! He is more awesome than all of the worthless so-called gods of the nations! After all, it was he who made the sky and from him that its majestic splendor continually radiates."[52]

The Hebrews especially were overjoyed by the events of that day. With gladness of heart they praised Yeshua and called to the families of the nations: "Ascribe to the King the splendor he deserves! Worship him! Tremble before him, all the earth. Yeshua reigns![53] The world is established; it cannot be moved. He has judged the nations fairly."[54]

Caleb questioned an Angel standing next to him: "The authority of the Watchers was removed but they were not immediately overcome by Yeshua's fire.[55] Why was that?"

The Angel explained, "In order that true peace and harmony can be experienced on the earth during the next thousand years, Lucifer and his Watchers have been locked away in the Abyss. During this time their lives will be prolonged but they will not be able to deceive the nations. Then after many days in their dungeon of darkness they will be granted the space of one year before their predicted end will come."[56]

The Angel speaking with Caleb noticed Nebuchadnezzar, former king of Babel, celebrating the goodness of Adonai as the door of the Abyss closed over Lucifer and his Watchers. "Blessings, praise, and honor," he was shouting, "to the one who lives forever, for his sovereignty is eternal. His kingdom continues from generation to generation. All who live on the earth are nothing compared to him. He does what he wishes with the heavenly armies and with those who live on the planet. Everything he does is true, his ways are just, and he is able to humble those who walk in pride."[57] Nebuchadnezzar marveled at the tremendous mercy of Adonai that had been extended to him.[58]

Nebuchadnezzar smiled at the Angel—the same one who had given the decree for him to roam with the beasts of the earth for seven seasons[59]—and the Angel smiled back. Both understood that Nebuchadnezzar's fate could have been sealed with Lucifer had not Adonai allowed him to be humbled.

"Judgment has been executed on Lucifer, his Watchers, and Therion and Oracle!" Adam along with many others shouted in affirmation, endorsing the just actions of the King. David added: "The judgments of the King are true and altogether righteous."[60] Then an Angel echoed, "Even so, Yeshua, true and righteous are your judgments."[61]

◎ ◎ ◎ ◎ ◎

Ben and Kristiana smiled as they saw people everywhere dancing and rejoicing in great jubilation over the judgment of those who had destroyed the earth.[62] For the first time since the Fall, the earth was at rest. Except for the hearts of the mortals, who were now more rare than the gold of Ophir,[63] there no longer was anything defiled or corrupt; no longer were any creatures in rebellion against the King. What joy, what elation! No longer would the wicked prevail[64] for the kingdom of Yeshua finally had come.

26
Restoration

YESHUA PROCLAIMED IN a mighty voice: "Look, my beloved! I am making all things new, for I have created new heavens and a new earth.[1] I will open up rivers on the barren heights and fountains in the midst of the valleys."[2]

Adam finally had a moment to relish the fact that the earth had been restored as quickly as it had become corrupted. The curse on the ground had been removed! It was no longer in a state of disintegration and degeneration; rather it was in a state of generation. Thus the earth did not have any vegetation on it, just like on day three of creation, but was fertile with potential, ready to be restored to the pristine beauty it had when Adonai first created it.

Adam walked up to Caleb, who was astounded by all of the glorious things that were happening but unable to comprehend what it all meant. Adam explained: "As those who had remained were caught up to meet Yeshua in the air and were then transformed in the blink of an eye,[3] likewise the earth was restored just as swiftly."

"So it was because of this fiery purifying process that heaven had to receive him until the times of restoration of all things,"[4] Caleb surmised. "When the veil between the domains was removed, the earth immediately began to melt[5] and the elements in the rocks, the grass, the trees, and even the dirt itself were purified from the decay that had permeated the earth for those six thousand years."

"Yes," Adam replied. "Anything that was profaned and defiled was incompatible with Yeshua's fire and power and great glory. This is the reason that when he returned Yeshua still needed to be veiled in clouds[6] and thick darkness;[7] otherwise, his enemies would have been instantly eviscerated.[8]

"The *adamáh*, from which I was drawn and with which I had been intrinsically and inseparably joined," continued Adam, "was destabilized through my action, which left an indelible mark. When the sons of Adonai were manifested, the whole creation was gloriously liberated and the *adamáh* as well as the rocks, trees, and vegetation were essentially restabilized."[9]

Adam broke into song, delighting in the amazing rescue Adonai had accomplished to save him and his progeny.

He looked over at Eve, remembering that fateful day some six thousand years ago and the deep despair they both had felt as they desperately longed to be free—and now they were!

The wicked one had been judged and imprisoned, and their bodies were not only as good as they had been before but better—all because of Yeshua. Eve smiled knowingly at Adam and he smiled back—each of them understanding perfectly the other's thoughts: their children were free and their hearts were full. Never had there been such a joyous celebration! The thrill they felt was overwhelming—and rightly so, for the world had nearly been lost forever in Lucifer's jaws of death.

Adam thought back to the day of his creation, how he opened his eyes and beheld the very one who had formed him with his own hands. As an immortal, Eve followed his thoughts as if they were her own. Adam and Eve uniquely appreciated the present victory in a way that no one else could, for had Lucifer won, the earth would have been in a perpetual state of death and decay and eventually would have become nothing more than a cold, lifeless ball floating in the blackness of space until even the sun and all the stars in the universe burned out. It was through just one person, Adam, that wickedness entered the world, and death through wickedness, and so death spread to all people. Everyone committed wickedness[10] because through Adam all suffered death.[11]

"Father," Adam had said,[12] admiring the indescribable beauty of Adonai's face. His glorious light radiated upon his new creation. Adam could see the love in Adonai's eyes, expressing the depth of his tender care for him, his son. Adam stood up from the ground full of life, full of joy. Surveying his surroundings he saw the beautiful Garden with its magnificent trees already there to give him delectable food. His Father had provided everything for him.

"My son," Adonai had instructed, "you may eat of any and every tree of the Garden except that one," he said, pointing to the Tree of the Knowledge of Good and Evil, "because on the day that you eat of it you will die."[13]

Then Adonai put Adam into a deep sleep and, when he awoke, surprised him with a suitable new companion fashioned from his own DNA. "This is bone from my bones," Adam observed, comparing her hand with his, "and flesh from my flesh,"[14] he added, caressing her delicate face, a lovely complement to his own. Looking deeply into her eyes he said, "I will call you Eve!"[15]

Eve somberly reflected on that dark day when a bad choice had resulted in death and on the many tears that had been shed not only in the aftermath but also throughout their more than nine hundred years of life on the earth. She and Adam had seen the glories of the City, yet forfeited their opportunity to partake of it. The sting of death had been more acute for them than for their children who had never known bliss.

Even her relationship with Adam was fractured on that day. Oh, how he had betrayed her, the one he was supposed to protect! Instead of guarding and cherishing the companion Adonai had given him, he had cast all the blame on her; yet he was the one who had the power to intercede and plead on her behalf to Adonai.[16]

Adam remembered Eve's reaction and her bitter tears.[17] *How could I have blamed her for what I did?* he asked himself, looking back at the wife he had betrayed. "Adonai made her from my own body. She was formed to be my special counterpart but I turned against her. I have denied my own flesh!"[18] He hung his head in despair, lamenting the grief his action had caused her and the pain that untold generations yet to come would suffer.

Adam and Eve both remembered that day as if it were yesterday. *I am lost! I am ruined!*[19] had been Adam's initial thought as he felt the first hot tear ever to run down his cheek and began to understand—though too late—the repercussions of his action: the entire creation, the *adamáh*, had become subject to the bondage of corruption, and death would be his fate. Overwhelmed with sorrow, Adam had wondered, *Who will rescue me from this body that is infected by death? And who will liberate* [20] *the entire creation, which is linked to my fate? Already I perceive it is groaning and longing to be free from the bondage of corruption.*[21] How his heart had ached as he bore the weight of the consequences of his action.

But now all of that pain, sorrow, regret, and resentment was gone. Adam and Eve no longer needed to hope or wait to be rescued for their deliverer had come.

As a tear of joy rolled down Eve's cheek a tear fell from Adam's eyes as well. At that moment Yeshua went to Eve, stretched out his powerful hand, and gently wiped away the tear from her face. He then turned to Adam and did the same.[22]

There was a moment of silence as Eve and Adam looked

into Yeshua's eyes of fire, remembering when the two of them had been banished from Eden and the great despair they felt that day.

At last Eve spoke: "Through Adam all suffered death. So too in you, Yeshua, all have been made truly alive![23] You have opened for me, for Adam, and for our children the gates of virtue and mercy so that we may enter through them," she said with gratitude, "to give thanks to Adonai."[24] Looking first at Adam and then at all their kindred, she raised her voice in praise and said, "This is the day that Adonai has made; let us rejoice and be glad in it!"[25]

Suddenly people started coming back to life who had been beheaded on account of their testimony about Yeshua and their testimony of the word of Adonai, who had not worshiped Therion or his image and had not received his mark on their foreheads or hands; they would rule with Yeshua for a thousand years. Such was the first resurrection. How blessed and holy are those who participated in the first resurrection because the second death had no power over them. They were priests of Adonai and Yeshua and they would rule with him for a thousand years.[26] The wicked, who had died previously, would not come back to life until the thousand years were over.[27]

All were speaking in the same pure language for the first time in nearly four thousand years.[28] All were clapping their hands and extolling Yeshua for what he had done. All were singing different songs which, when heard all together, blended together beautifully in a magnificent musical canon or medley.

One group was crying out for the sky to rejoice, for the earth to be glad, and for the sea and everything in it to shout. While some immortals were playing harps, trumpets, and ram's horns,[29] others called for all creation to celebrate—fields, plants, flowers, even the trees of the forest to shout with joy before the King because he had come to judge the world in fairness, to judge the nations in keeping with his justice.[30] "Let the sea and everything in it shout, along with the world and those who live in it!"[31]

Suddenly, a massive structure began to descend from overhead. There it was in all its glory! The Mountain of Jerusalem, the City of the King, the Heavenly Jerusalem[32] with firm foundations, whose architect and builder was Adonai, the Mountain-City where Lucifer had been before the Fall, was returning to earth.[33] Millions stared in awe as the holy city, New Jerusalem, came down with Adonai out of heaven, prepared like a bride adorned for her husband.[34] Abraham watched with utmost satisfaction as the City for which he had waited came near.[35] Jacob stared in amazement at seeing the Mountain-City from which the Angels had ascended and descended come to the earth.[36]

As the city approached the earth, Adonai cried out in a caring yet commanding voice that had the sound of a great waterfall: "Awake, awake! Put on your strength, O Jerusalem; put on your beautiful garments, O Jerusalem, the holy city! For the uncircumcised and the unclean shall no longer come to you. Sing and rejoice, O daughter of Jerusalem! Behold, I have come and I will dwell in your midst.[37] This is the place of my throne and the place of the soles of my feet, here I will dwell in your midst forever."[38]

This was the culmination of history that Adonai had long awaited. Finally the time had come that he could openly dwell with his people in the place he had desired to be his home, as he had said: "This is my home where I will live forever. I will live here, for this is the place I desired.[39] I, Adonai, your King, am dwelling in Jerusalem, my holy mountain. Jerusalem is now devoted and no foreigner will ever pass through again."[40] Forever on that part of the earth the City of the King of armies will be, and he will reign on the Mountain of Jerusalem and before his elders gloriously.[41,]

Proceeding from the very throne of Adonai and of Yeshua at the apex of the mountain was a torrent of the pure Water of Life, clear as crystal.[42] The water collected in a pool before the throne and looked like a sea of glass.[43] From there it began to flow down the mountain to the ground below, branching off into multiple streams and making glad the City of Adonai, the holy habitation of the Most High.[44]

The rushing waters cascading to the earth resounded like thunder as they flowed down from Adonai, the source, to the *adamáh*, bringing life to the fertile but naked and uninhabited planet. As the earth drank in the water, all the seeds that lay latent in the soil, now free from decay and degeneration, began to sprout.[45] Grass, trees, flowers, and vines sprang up everywhere. Cactus plants covered with purple and yellow flowers arose out of the earth. The spiky needles characteristic of the previous age were now soft and pliable; degeneration was nonexistent and so too were the thorns and thistles.[46]

Adam examined the plants with great satisfaction; what a relief to witness the *adamáh* restored and the results of his rebellion finally done away with.[47] Instead of thorn bushes, pine trees appeared, and instead of briers, myrtles grew up.[48] The barren globe blossomed like a rose and the dry land rejoiced with gladness. The glory of Lebanon was given to it, the splendor of Carmel and Sharon; the splendor of Adonai was seen everywhere.[49]

Michael noted a correlation with day three of creation,[50] when seed-bearing plants and trees sprang up instantly from the earth.[51] As Adonai first had created everything with its seed within, ready to germinate, so he had caused it to be once more in the regeneration of all things.

Living waters flowed from Jerusalem, half toward the eastern sea and half toward the western sea;[52] all the brooks of Judah were flooded with water from the fountain that flowed from the house of Adonai.[53] The River ran toward the eastern territories all the way to the Salt Sea, where the salt water turned fresh. It happened that wherever the

River flowed, everything lived! Because of this revitalizing water the Salt Sea received, it was able to support all kinds of living creatures that thrived abundantly.

Yeshua's eyes swept compassionately over the Hebrews, his elect, his chosen, as he said, "Do not remember the former things; do not dwell on things past. Watch! I am about to do something new! And now it is springing up— do you not recognize it? I'm making a way in the wilderness and paths in the desert."[54]

The Hebrews were painfully aware that they formerly had forsaken Adonai, the fountain of living waters, and had hewn for themselves cisterns—broken cisterns that could hold no water.[55] Now they rejoiced and were abundantly satisfied with the fullness of his house as he gave them to drink from the River of his pleasures. Indeed, with him was the Fountain of Life, and it was in his light that they saw light.[56]

Adam was greatly relieved that the earth no longer would withhold its bounty but henceforth would yield in abundance—especially for the Hebrews.[57] Yeshua, son of Adonai had opened up rivers on the barren heights and fountains in the midst of the valleys. He had turned the desert into pools and the parched land into springs of water! Stately cedars shot up from the dry ground, along with acacia, myrtle, and olive trees. He planted cypresses in the desert, box trees, and pine trees together.[58]

Caleb was just trying to take it all in. On every lofty mountain and every high hill were brooks and canals running with water,[59] as far as his mortal eyes could see. He suddenly realized that the hand of Adonai had created[60] something new.[61] He took a few more steps through the countryside, barren only a few moments earlier but now adorned with roses, amaryllis, tuberose, and narcissus. He inhaled their sweet, fresh perfume as if taking his first breath. He noticed that, unlike in the previous age just past, all the vegetation now had a lovely glow about it.

The red roses had a ruby radiance and the cacti had an emerald iridescence.

Adam looked at Eve and smiled; the earth had been restored to the way it was so long ago, and the DNA of every living thing was absorbing and re-emitting Adonai's light just as in the beginning.[62]

Isaiah the prophet, elated to see the realization of things Adonai had shown him many years before, burst out in a loud voice, "Shout for joy, you heavens, for Yeshua, son of Adonai has done it! Shout aloud, you depths of the earth! Burst out with singing, you mountains, you forests, and all you trees! For Adonai has redeemed Jacob and is now displaying his glory in Israel. He carries out the words of his servants and fulfills the predictions of his messengers who say of Jerusalem, 'It will be inhabited,' and of the cities of Judah, 'They shall be rebuilt,' and of her ruins, 'I will raise them up.'"[63] The waste places of the earthly Jerusalem burst forth in joyful song. Adonai has comforted his people and he has redeemed Jerusalem.[64]

The depths of the earth and the mountains and the former waste places all resonated with a sound like singing; not like that of a son of Adam or the utterance of an animal, but rather, a low, steady hum.[65] A gentle and comforting timbre ever in harmony with the song of the King and the songs of the other creatures, it was something like the bagpipe, which produces a pleasing undertone that fills the other notes played over it—though the sound of the bagpipe can hardly compare to the subtle resonance of the earth.

Even the light of the moon and the sun were different than in the previous age: the light of the moon was like the light of the sun and the sun's light was seven times brighter, like the light of seven full days.[66] Adonai, the one sitting on the throne, said, "See, I am making all things new!"[67]

An unknown voice filled with gladness suddenly cried out from among the throngs of millions and millions of people and Angels surrounding Adonai's throne: "*Hallelu-*Yah! *Hallelu* Adonai from heaven; praise him in the highest places. Praise him all his Angels; praise him sun and moon, all you shining stars, you heaven of heavens. *Hallelu*-Yah! Praise the name of Adonai, for he himself gave the command that they be created. He set them in place to last forever and ever; he gave the command and will not rescind it. *Hallelu* Adonai, you from the earth, you creatures of the sea, and all you depths; fire, hail, snow, fog, and windstorm that carry out his command, mountains and every hill, fruit trees and cedars, living creatures and livestock, insects and flying birds, earthly kings and all peoples, nobles and officials of the earth, young men and young women alike, along with older people and children. *Hallelu* the name of Adonai, for his name alone is lifted up; his majesty transcends earth and heaven."[68]

The mortal Caleb, meanwhile, laughed at the sight of animals nudging each other, baby elephants and kid goats rousing tigers to play, lambs lying down next to wolves and being cuddled as if they were pups. Many different species of animals seemed to be enjoying one another. Even the mighty lions no longer were looking for something to eat but were enjoying the freedom to frolic.

"What formerly was a meal now can be a best friend!" Adam remarked to Caleb, who had been joined by Hosea. "What a change from the former days when lions chased calves and children only to eat them.

"Adonai has made a covenant on behalf of the Hebrews with the wild animals, the birds of the air, and the creatures that crawl on the ground; he has abolished the warrior's bow and sword from the land so that they may live in peace. Never again will there be wild beasts and now they can live securely in the wilderness and sleep in the forests.[69]

"Now the lions and calves will be led by little children and those born in this age will never know that the animals used to be ferocious killers. Your children," he explained to Caleb, "when they are just toddlers two or three years old, will go out to play with the bears and lions as if they were the stuffed teddy bears of the former age. They will even go up to the cobra's den and stick in their hands in search of a lost toy or a bug and the snake will not strike."[70] Adam watched nostalgically as a wolf and a lamb grazed together on a nearby hill, and beyond them a lion ate straw like an ox.[71]

"I remember after my Fall looking mournfully at the playful creatures, lamenting in my heart, knowing that as time progressed and nutrients became scarce they would become savage beasts, killing and eating one another. The wolves that so happily wagged their tails when I named them did not lie down and cuddle with the fluffy lambs; rather, driven by the pain of starvation they started savagely tearing the docile creatures to pieces. And the leopards that once had playfully crept up on the goats and chased them as they jumped from rock to rock, eventually crept up on them and slashed their throats in order to satisfy their hunger.

"Then my eyes caught sight of the lions, which until then had grazed on grass peacefully together with the ox. My heart was filled with foreboding as I considered their fate. Not long thereafter they lashed out at the ox with their sharp claws, then pounced on it, brought it to the ground, and sank their fangs into its sturdy neck, cutting through its skin until the blood, the life-force, was gone, and then they devoured it.[72] I felt deep regret as the greatest of the living creatures, the Behemoth and Leviathan, two of the largest dinosaurs, moved about, for I knew that they too eventually would devour and be devoured.

"From now on," Adam continued, "the wild animals, owls, and jackals will honor Adonai because he provides water in the desert and streams in the wilderness to give drink to his people, the chosen ones, the Hebrews, the people whom he formed for himself so that they may speak his praise.[73] Now the animals will neither harm nor destroy on his holy mountain, for the earth will be full of the knowledge of Adonai, as the waters cover the sea.[74]

"For you mortals," Adam said to Caleb, "he will also provide rain for your seed that you sow in the ground, and the food that comes from the ground will be rich and abundant. Your cattle will graze in broad meadows, and oxen and donkeys that work the ground will eat seasoned fodder that workers will winnow with shovels and forks."[75]

27
Yeshua's Song

"NOW I SHALL rest," Yeshua said, "because I have prepared and established Jerusalem and have made it a song of praise throughout the earth. I have sworn by my right hand and by my mighty arm: 'I will never again give your grain as food for your enemies; never again will foreigners drink your new wine for which you have toiled; but surely those who harvest it will eat it and praise the name of Adonai, and those who gather it will drink it in the courts of my sanctuary.'"[1]

Then Yeshua began to sing about the New Jerusalem, his bride,[2] for this was the moment that he had waited for. He had vowed to remain silent until Jerusalem's vindication should shine out like brightness and her salvation like a burning torch.[3] The earthly City, which had suffered tremendous humiliation, at last had been vindicated in the sight of the nations and in the sight of all kings.

Yeshua opened his mouth and declared, "You shall call Jerusalem by a new name, for it will be a crown of splendor and a royal diadem held by my hand. No longer shall it be called 'Deserted,' nor shall the land of the Hebrews any longer be called 'Desolate'; but people will call you *Hephzibah,* 'my delight is in her,' and your land *Beulah,* 'married' — for I am delighting in you, and your land is now married.

Just as a young man marries a young woman, so your sons will marry you; and just as a bridegroom rejoices over his bride, so I, your King, am rejoicing over you.[4] This city shall henceforth be called 'the City of Truth, the Mountain of Adonai of armies, the holy mountain.'[5] It shall even be called 'Adonai Our Righteousness.'"[6]

The moment the city touched the earth, a delightful fragrance of something like myrrh and aloes and cassia,[7] emanating from Yeshua himself,[8] wafted over the land and the people.

"Rejoice!" Yeshua said, "Rejoice, you childless woman, who could not give birth to any children! Break into song and shout, you who feel no pains of childbirth! For, the children of the deserted woman are now more numerous, than the children of the woman who had a husband.[9] You will spread out to the right hand and to the left, and your descendants will possess the nations and will populate the deserted towns. Do not be afraid," he comforted them, "because you will not be ashamed; do not fear shame, for you will not be humiliated. You will now forget the disgrace of your youth for I, your Maker, am your husband; I have called you back like a wife deserted and grieved in spirit. For a brief moment I abandoned you but now I have gathered you with great compassion." The look in his eyes conveyed his profound love and commitment. "I hid my face from you for a moment in a surge of anger, but I will have compassion on you with my everlasting and gracious love," Yeshua proclaimed to the lower Jerusalem.[10]

"O afflicted one, passed back and forth and not comforted," Yeshua called out: "Look! I have set your stones in antimony and laid your foundations with sapphires. I have made your battlements of rubies, your gates of jewels, and your walls of precious stones. Now all your children will be taught by Adonai, and great will be your children's prosperity.[11] I will make you my wife forever," he vowed to Jerusalem. "I will make you my wife in a way that is righteous, in a manner that is just, with a love that is gracious, and with a motive that is mercy.[12] I will make you my queen, my wife, forever because of my faithfulness, and you shall now know your King."[13]

Hosea the prophet sighed deeply with satisfaction and then noticed Caleb, son of Reu'el, watching in awe at the amazing sight. "For six thousand years," Hosea began to say, "the heavenly Jerusalem was behind the veil, right above the earthly Jerusalem, just as our people[14] described it: "*Yerushalayim l'ma'alah.*"[15]

"Yes," Caleb acknowledged, "I now clearly see the existence of the two cities and that the dual nature of their reality is apparently contained in the name *Yerushalayim.*"[16]

"And now I clearly see the fulfillment of the word that Adonai gave to me so many centuries ago," Hosea stated aloud for the sake of his counterpart who was a mere babe by comparison of years.

"I do not understand, though, how Jerusalem, the City, can be the bride of Yeshua,"[17] Caleb said.

"You see," replied the prophet, "in the previous age Adonai divorced himself from the lower Jerusalem in three ways: from the land, from the city structures and buildings, and from the inhabitants. He said 'she is not my wife, and I am not her husband.' Because the inhabitants of the City refused to turn from their adulterous attitudes and actions, Adonai said he would strip her naked and make her land a wilderness, cause her to die of thirst, and refuse to take pity on her offspring for they were children of prostitution. Sadly, Jerusalem did commit prostitution by giving her allegiance to Lucifer and his Watchers in worshiping all the false gods they pretended to be."[18]

"That is when," Caleb interjected, "she deceived herself into believing the false gods were the ones who had given the increase rather than Adonai."

"Indeed," Hosea agreed; she stubbornly refused to recognize that it was Adonai who provided her grain, wine, and oil, and it was he who gave her silver even as her inhabitants crafted idols for Baal. But after Adonai had punished the lower Jerusalem,[19] he promised to allure her and in the wilderness speak to her heart. He would restore her and she would call him *Ishi,* 'my husband,' and no longer *ba'ali,* 'my master'; then the names of the false gods would be forever forgotten."[20]

"So the time for fulfillment of the promise which Adonai has long awaited has finally arrived!" Caleb exclaimed. "Yeshua is to take his bride. At his first coming, we sons of Abraham, Isaac, and Jacob, whom he had selected to be the recipients of the oracles of Adonai and whom he had elected[21] and claimed as his own inheritance,[22] did not, for the most part, receive him.[23] Instead, many—especially among the leadership—made light of his coming, made various excuses[24] and went their own ways—one to his farm, another to his business. They were the ones who had been invited to the wedding but proved themselves unworthy.[25] Now we Hebrews, the few chosen along with the many who were called—those of the nations grafted in to the commonwealth of Israel—are the invited guests whereas all the immortals are now invited to become part of the New Jerusalem, the Bride of Yeshua."[26]

"Yes," said Hosea; "that's how I see it, too. Adonai declared that the Hebrews would marry[27] Jerusalem, which may explain why the gates bear the names of the twelve clans and the wall of the City has twelve foundations inscribed with the names of the twelve apostles."[28]

One of the daughters of Jacob burst forth in song and many others quickly joined in: "Yeshua has acquitted us and turned back our adversaries. Our King is among us; we will not fear disaster anymore. We will not be afraid and we will not lose courage!"[29]

◎ ◎ ◎ ◎ ◎

Kristiana let go of the AEFOD so that she and Ben could discuss all they had seen. "Ben, I think I understand now," she gasped. "Cities comprise a geographical location plus earth, soil, and rocks, upon which are buildings and roads; and cities are populated with people. Many people used to come to visit the Jerusalem below where Caleb lived. They had to travel to the City from distant countries. They saw the sights and they interacted with the Jerusalemites who gave the City life. So too it is with the New Jerusalem, this Mountain-City, the bride of Yeshua[30]—it is a geographic location in the land of the Hebrews. It has towers, walls, gates, and streets and, very important, it has inhabitants who make it their home."

"It also is like the waters of Noah," Ben contributed. "Just as Adonai swore that the waters would never again cover the earth, so has he sworn that he will not be angry with the City.[31] The mountains collapsed and the hills reeled at Yeshua's return, but his gracious love will not depart from the City; neither will his covenant of peace be broken."[32]

"Yeshua did it!" cheered Kristiana. "He brought together in himself all things behind the veil and all things on the earth.[33] Because the veil was removed, and all of the profane elements and people were removed, and the curse was also removed, it was possible for the City of Adonai to be on the earth and for the King to dwell with the Adamites once again. His self-imposed exile could end.[34] I get it!" she exclaimed. And then she wondered, *what could possibly be next?*

28
Yeshua's Inheritance

WHEN ADONAI SPOKE to Yeshua in a mighty voice like the sound of many rushing waters, everyone around the throne immediately grew still.

"I have given the nations as your inheritance and the ends of the earth as your possession, for you broke them with an iron rod; you shattered them like pottery.[1] See now, I have extended your mighty scepter from Jerusalem; rule in the midst of your enemies![2] To you I have bestowed dominion, along with glory and a kingdom, so that all peoples, nations, and languages should serve you. Your dominion is an everlasting dominion—it will never, ever pass away—and your kingdom is one that will never be destroyed."[3]

Isaiah the prophet smiled as he witnessed the fulfillment of the word he had received millennia before—the child that had been born was finally reigning as the King of kings; the government would be upon his shoulders. Here, before the world, was he whose name was Wonderful Counselor, Mighty One, Father of eternity,[4] Prince of Peace.[5]

Turning to the mortals of the nations, Adonai said, "Behold, O nations; I have set my King on Jerusalem, my holy mountain.[6] He has brought an end to wars throughout the earth; he shattered the bows, broke the spears, and burned the shields with fire.[7] He will arbitrate between many peoples and settle disputes between many distant nations.[8] He will not judge by what his eyes see, nor decide disputes by what his ears hear, but with righteousness he will judge the needy and decide with equity for the poor. He is the one who has struck the earth with the rod of his mouth and killed the wicked with the breath of his lips.[9]

"Your King will speak peace to the nations.[10] He rules from sea to sea, from the river Euphrates to the ends of the earth.[11] Of the growth of his government and peace there will be no end. He will rule over his kingdom, sitting on the throne of David, to establish it and to uphold it with justice and righteousness from this time forward and forevermore. He will rule over the house of Jacob forever with everything under his feet. I have left nothing outside of his control.[12] By my zeal, I, the King of the Heavenly Armies, have accomplished this.[13] Behold, Yeshua, your king!"

At the moment Adonai said the name of Yeshua, every Hebrew and all the inhabitants of the earth, mortals and immortals, fell to their knees before him.[14] Before them sat Yeshua, the mighty conqueror of the Abyss and death,[15] the one who cast Lucifer down into the dungeon, bound with unbreakable chains.[16]

Then they all in one accord, without hesitation, swore an oath of allegiance, crying out: "Yeshua, the Anointed, is Lord!"[17] Cheers and praise resounded, for all were filled with joy to have such a glorious and wonderful King who would faithfully judge, seek justice, be swift to do what was right from a throne established in gracious love.[18]

"Let the Twelve stand before me," Yeshua gently commanded.[19]

John, Thomas, Jacob, Andrew, and the others quickly approached his throne.

Simon Peter was in awe of the gloriously arrayed and powerful King enthroned before him. Peter thought of the question he had asked nearly two thousand years earlier: "We have left everything and followed you. So what will we get?" Yeshua had said, "I tell all of you with certainty that when the Son of Man sits on his glorious throne in the renewed creation, you who have followed me will also sit on twelve thrones, governing the twelve clans of the Hebrews. In fact, everyone who has left his homes, brothers, sisters, father, mother, children, or fields because of my name will receive a hundred times as much and will inherit eternal life."[20] Peter was overwhelmed at the realization of that promise. *He has given me the honor of sitting as judge over the Hebrews? I denied him but he has given me life abundantly!* Then Yeshua's eyes of fire locked onto his.

"Don't remember the former things," Yeshua said to Peter. "Don't dwell on things past; the former things will not be remembered, nor will they come to mind!"[21]

The Twelve beheld thrones prepared for each of them and took their royal seats.

"I authorize you to judge over the mortal Hebrews,"[22] Yeshua declared.

A great throng of people stood before them and cheered. Among the onlookers was the mother of the sons of Zebedee, smiling as only a proud mother could. She remembered how kind Yeshua had been to her when she bowed down before him to ask a favor and then audaciously demanded, "Promise that in your kingdom these two sons of mine will sit on your right and on your left."[23] At the time she had no idea what she was really asking, and things did not proceed as she had expected. Nevertheless, here now were her sons, ruling and reigning with the King of kings and the Lord of lords, part of the Twelve who would govern the affairs of the Adamite Hebrews for the thousand-year reign of Yeshua.[24]

Another throne was set in place awaiting its master when David,[25] the great shepherd king, entered through the portico of the gate from outside.[26] Approaching Yeshua, he fell at the feet of the one who came from his loins and yet was before him.[27] Yeshua thundered to the witnesses in front of him, "I swore that David would never be without a man sitting on the throne of the house of the Hebrews.[28] I now appoint one shepherd over the land of the Hebrews: my servant David. He will feed them, he will look after them and serve as their shepherd." Yeshua placed a crown of gold on his head[29] and then announced: "I, Yeshua, shall be their high King and my servant David will rule among them as Prince."[30]

"You have executed kings in the day of your wrath," David responded; "you have judged among the nations and filled valleys with corpses, and you have executed the heads of many countries.[31] Therefore, who am I and what is my family that you have brought me this far?[32] What can I say? You know what I am really like! For the sake of your promise and according to your will you have done all these great things that you showed me beforehand.[33] How great you are, O King! There is no other like you! You have given me eternal blessings and have made me glad with the joy of your presence.[34] May your name be honored forever! All the world will say, 'Adonai the Almighty is King!' because the dynasty of your servant has been established in your presence."[35]

The millions of onlookers rejoiced and began to sing an ancient song written by David in the King's honor thousands of years ago in anticipation of the time that Yeshua would return with the clouds of heaven.[36]

"I love you, Adonai; I love you Adonai, my strength. Adonai, my rock, my fortress, my deliverer, my mighty one, my stronghold in whom I take refuge, my shield, the glory of my salvation, and my high tower."

The song came straight from the heart as they remembered their own history and offered adoration to the one who was worthy, for he had delivered them from their enemies and from death itself.

"In my distress," they sang, "I cried to Adonai; to my Mighty One I cried for help. From his temple he heard my voice; my cry reached his ears."

Their song crescendoed as they recounted the return of the great King to the earth to rescue them.

"The world shook and trembled; the foundations of the mountains quaked; they shook because he was angry. In his anger smoke poured out of his nostrils, and consuming fire from his mouth; coals were lit from it. He bent the sky and descended, and darkness was under his feet. He rode upon a cherub and flew; he soared upon the wings of the wind."

"He made darkness his hiding place; dark waters and thick clouds were his canopy surrounding him. The brightness before him scattered the thick clouds. Then Adonai thundered in the heavens and sounded aloud, calling for hailstones and flashes of fire. He shot his arrows and scattered them; with many lightning bolts he frightened them. Then the channels of the sea could be seen and at your rebuke, LORD, the foundations of the earth were uncovered, by the blast from the breath of your nostrils."[37]

Eve looked toward the descending Mountain-City, "This is Adonai's gate—the righteous will enter through it,"[38] she said and then added: "I will praise you because you have answered me and you have become my *yeshuáh*."[39]

29

The Marriage Supper

THE HEART OF every person standing before Yeshua swelled in anticipation. How blessed were those who were called to the marriage supper of Yeshua![1] They were glad and rejoiced and gave Him glory! Before them was the beloved of Yeshua, the New Jerusalem, adorned as a beautiful bride.[2] All who had put on the garment of *yeshuáh*,[3] the wedding garment,[4] were eager to enter into the city, the bride of Yeshua. Many would come from east and west and sit down with Abraham, Isaac, and Jacob in the kingdom. To the ones who rejected the word of Adonai, however, the door was shut.[5]

"How blessed are those who wash their robes so that they may have the right to the Tree of Life and may go through the gates into the city!"[6] said Yeshua, having been given all authority over heaven and earth.[7]

Adam smiled and closed his eyes, bathing in the joy of that time. It was a wonderful moment and there was something special about the transition—just like the eager expectancy of a bridegroom on the eve of his wedding, so was the anticipation of the marriage supper of the King.

Those who had new bodies and wore robes of light began to enter through[8] the mammoth gates of solid pearl and walked on streets of purest gold to a magnificent hall.

Ezekiel the prophet stayed toward the back of the happy throng in order to take in the sight before him. Breathing in the pleasant scent, he gazed in amazement at the colossal size of the Mountain-City.[9] It dwarfed Mount Everest by many orders of magnitude! He observed how the heavenly Jerusalem, the City of Adonai,[10] was the great mountain with a city structure on it—the very one he had seen in the vision.[11] It was square[12] at its base with angled sides rising up to the apex. Each edge of the pyramid was about a hundred and seventy-two miles long.[13] As seen now, resting upon the earth, the City seemed to take on a new aspect. It was as if Ezekiel were seeing it for the first time, even though he had been with Adonai ever since Yeshua had liberated those who belonged to him from the good side of the Abyss.[14]

The prophet lifted his chin to look almost straight up into the sky at the apex of the city. The City's elevation was imposing; it reached up into the ionosphere![15] He noted the City's sheer perfection: it was unparalleled in beauty and from there Adonai's splendid fiery-lightning power emanated.[16] He and the other ancient prophets delighted in seeing it, as did all those on the face of the earth.[17]

Still spellbound by the enormity of the city, Ezekiel scanned its radiant walls studded with precious gem-stones,[18] refracting the vibrant colors of Adonai's glory. He then focused on the exits of the city, which he had seen before.[19] There were three gates on the four sides of the city, twelve in all; each guarded by an Angel and each named after one of the twelve clans of Jacob.[20] Each gate measured almost three[21] miles across, commensurate with the immensity of the City. These gates, made of solid pearl, would never be shut because it was never night there.[22]

John, like Ezekiel, had also stayed back so that he could more fully appreciate certain aspects of the City he had seen in the visions given to him. Adonai had posted watchmen on the walls who had not kept silent day or night, giving Adonai no rest until he had made Jerusalem a song of praise throughout the earth. These were now silent, for indeed Adonai had faithfully fulfilled his promise.[23] At last, the mountain of the house of Adonai[24] was established as the highest of the mountains; it was lifted up above the hills and eventually the peoples would flow to it.

Lucifer had attempted to establish himself on top of the Mountain-City and to establish his own law,[25] but Adonai's law and word triumphantly would go forth nonetheless from the Jerusalem mountain, the New Jerusalem.[26] It was finally back where it had been when Adam was created, never again to be separated from the planet.

At that moment someone cried out in a loud voice, "Behold, the tabernacle of Adonai is with men, and he will dwell with them, and they shall be his people. Adonai himself will be with them and will be their King."[27]

A lovely strain could be heard throughout the City—it was Adonai's song of rejoicing. As a bridegroom rejoices over his bride, so Adonai was rejoicing over Jerusalem.[28]

John and Ezekiel finally entered through the mammoth gates of solid pearl and walked on the translucent streets of gold, clear as crystal, into the banquet hall.[29] The walls were adorned with every kind of gem so that as Yeshua entered, his light created a kaleidoscope of colors. Before them were many, many ornately fashioned tables. No one hesitated about where to sit, for all seemed to know where they belonged. The two men decided to sit at the same table.

Eve, overwhelmed by the grandeur of the hall and the euphoria welling up within her, exclaimed, "He has brought me to the banquet hall, and his banner over me is love! I belong to my beloved, and his desire is for me. He has set me as a seal over his heart, as a seal on his arm. The flames of love are flames of fire, a blaze that comes from the King; neither mighty waters nor flooding rivers could ever extinguish the love that I feel for him."[30]

When Adam and Eve took their seats, Yeshua sat down next to them and smiled. Amazingly, Yeshua appeared to be sitting at every table, so that each individual was able to enjoy intimate companionship with the King. How he was able to do this was beyond understanding.

Yeshua looked deeply into Eve's eyes, taking her hand in his and, simultaneously reaching out his hand to every other guest, whispered to all, "I love you."[31]

The tables were all arrayed with an abundance of the choicest foods[32] and well-aged wine, which Adonai had made for everyone to enjoy.[33] As he reached out his hand to take hold of the cup, every eye was upon him.

John, who had been with him the night of his betrayal, instantly recalled the night Yeshua had celebrated Passover with the Twelve, and the words he issued at the drinking of the third cup of wine: "I tell all of you, I will never again drink the fruit of the vine until that day when I drink it with you once again in my Father's kingdom."[34] He had done the same with the cup after supper, saying, "This cup is the new covenant sealed by my blood, which is being poured out for you."[35] John's eyes met Yeshua's as he said, "Drink and eat freely,[36] my friends!"

The marriage banquet continued for seven days during the days of Sukkot. Never in all of human history had there been a more joyous time. For some, having lived in the previous age, eating for pleasure without concern about any undesirable effects was especially exciting. Adonai had always intended for food to be a joy.[37] It was because of decay and degeneration that food, especially the overconsumption of it, had done damage.

The delight of dwelling in the City of Adonai was even greater than the joy of seeing Lucifer and his forces destroyed. Everything was happening precisely according to what Adonai had declared: his servants would eat, but the wicked would go hungry; his servants would drink, but the wicked would go thirsty; his servants would rejoice, but the wicked would be put to shame. Yes, his servants would sing in gladness of heart, but the wicked would cry for help in anguish of heart and howl in brokenness of spirit.[38]

The immortals sang and danced and ate with their Lord in utmost joy and satisfaction.

@ @ @ @ @

As the scene disappeared, Kristiana's face froze. "Ben!" she whispered, lowering the AEFOD. The two of them were still in the grove where they had been going through the Chronicles. "I have a feeling that someone is looking for us!"

30
Adonai's Evil Secret

"WHAT MAKES YOU say that? Who do you think is looking for us?" Ben asked Kristiana, putting the AEFOD in his pocket.

In the stillness of the grove, they could hear someone coming and were paralyzed with fear. Prince Yaván, one of Lucifer's top commanders, looked around outside the grove before ducking down through the opening to check who might be inside. Ben and Kristiana stayed completely still as the Prince looked from side to side. Ben stared at him, fearful of what would happen. The Prince seemed to look right through them. Ben's heart was pounding. After a few moments, he perceived that the Prince—looking straight at them—was unable to see them, even though they were right in front of him.

The Prince pulled his head back and turned to go check out other areas.

After several minutes passed, Kristiana finally dared to let out a sigh of relief.

"I don't understand what happened!" she exclaimed. "He was staring right at us!"

"I know; I know!" Ben replied. "I looked into his eyes but he didn't see us. I wonder why not."

"Well … ," Kristiana paused to consider how she could

express what she was thinking, "maybe because we know the secrets of the past we were somehow invisible to him."[1]

"Or maybe," Ben added, "we have discovered enough that the Way is open to us. We can see the King's Highway when we couldn't before."

"That's right! And if we're invisible then we can just walk up to the King's Highway and get on it without being noticed!" Kristiana deduced.

"I don't know," Ben replied reluctantly. "It's hard to imagine that no one would see us."

"Well, then how else can we access it?" asked Kristiana. "Time is running out and we need to get into the City soon."

"What about the rest of the Chronicles ... ?" he asked.

Kristiana quickly slipped through the opening without responding. Ben held back for a moment, thinking about the wisdom of her plan, then ducked out and gave Kristiana a disapproving look, though he knew they probably had no other option. Ben did not notice when they left the grove that the AEFOD had slipped out of his pocket and fallen to the ground.

They both looked at each other and started walking for the highway as quickly and softly as they could go. They reached the crowd and stopped, wondering how they would get through the thick sea of villagers and then past Lucifer without bumping someone or making any noise.

In an instant, the sky darkened and thousands of shining Watchers flew directly overhead and then landed all around the villagers. Ben, giving Kristiana a grimace, could not help noticing the fear on her face.

All the villagers looked up, startled by the thousands of shining, blue-hued Watchers.

"Adonai has kept a secret from you," Lucifer announced. Ben surveyed the crowd of thousands of his fellow citizens, waiting in great anticipation to hear what Adonai had been holding back from them.

Lucifer lowered his voice to capture their attention: "O most noble citizens of Yaván, I was the one who showed Adam and Eve how to have their eyes opened to the secret knowledge.

"If I had not acted decisively those many years ago, you would not be standing here right now. You see, I revealed to your ancestors the secret that Adonai had withheld. They took my counsel and their eyes were opened; thus they were able to achieve self-actualizaton and become like Adonai. Had they not taken my good counsel, then your forebears would never have attained such a glorious civilization, glorious indeed—which, with my help, you can rebuild and make a name for yourselves.[2]

"Not surprisingly, though, Adonai retaliated by sending them away from the Garden of Eden and put a veil between the domain of Adam and himself, leaving Adam desolate and in need of the Covering in order to come near Adonai. My kingdom has never been so restrictive; you may come as you are and do whatever is best in your own eyes."

Lucifer gave an affected sigh of distress. "Oh, the many secrets that have been withheld from you! You see, not only did the Hebrews—whom Adonai elected to be his special treasure above all the peoples on the earth[3] — commit great evils ... " Lucifer paused to savor the even more insidious slander that he was about to utter: "You see, I have been mistakenly attributed as being the creator of evil and darkness. But that is simply not the case. I dare say it took one greater than I to start such a cruel and defamatory rumor. I, like you, am a victim of a tyrannical system created by Adonai himself!" With feigned passion Lucifer raised his hands, palms to the sky, in an air of desperation; then he lowered his head, seeming to hesitate but then finally forced to reveal the harsh reality. "Adonai declared and recorded in the Chronicles themselves:

"'*Yotzer or uvoreh khoshekh, oseh shalom uvoreh ra, ani Adonai oseh khol eleh*: Forming light, and creating darkness;

making peace, and creating evil—I, Adonai, do all these things.'[4]

"Adonai, you see, is the creator of darkness and the instigator of evil!"

Practically everyone gasped in disbelief.

"I implore you to acknowledge that I am the one who is telling you the truth. It is recorded in the Chronicles." Lucifer paused to give his spellbound audience time to digest what he had just said.

Ben was shocked and unsure of what it all meant. Kristiana looked at him quizzically.

Lucifer subtly and methodically continued his diatribe as if he were an innocent man defending himself against an accusation of guilt. "I have been on the other side and I have seen the plan that the King has for you, which is why I have now been fighting for seven thousand years to bring freedom to the Adamites. It was one thousand years ago that I was locked away unjustly and without a trial. The whole world desired my help and now has gathered with me to oppose the tyranny of Yeshua."[5]

Ben broke out in a cold sweat at this new revelation. *Could it be,* he wondered, *that Adonai is the creator of evil?*

Just then a butterfly—the same one he had seen at first —flitted past them.

Korah had been waiting for the right moment to voice his opinion. "My ancient sentiments were correct; we shall always be second class.... " He paused, reconsidering his words, "No. We shall merely be slaves to the Hebrews and pawns of the King. Now is our time to fight. We may never have another chance. See how other mighty warrior nations around the world are awakening! We too are discovering that we are mighty and powerful.[6] Yes, greater are we than he who sits on the throne![7]

"It is as Lucifer has rightfully spoken. The Hebrews have been elected to be Adonai's people and the selected inheritors of the King, though utterly unworthy to receive such an honor for they are no better than any other nation. It is merely because the King made a promise to Abraham, Isaac, and Jacob.

"Brothers, sisters, elders and youths, hear me!" Korah declared. "We cannot have Yeshua reign over us.[8] Is he not the creator of evil itself? Is that evil not evident by his unjustly requiring us to be servants of a nation that is worse than we?

"Lucifer has shared with us Adonai's one great weakness, so now you understand our simple but unbeatable strategy. Therefore, join the ranks of our heroic ancestors who risked their lives for freedom so that they might have true liberty from the oppression of the present King. By joining Lucifer we can bring true justice to the cosmos so that each of you can do what is right in your own eyes!"[9]

Prince Yaván walked to the front of the platform. "If you are serious about freedom and justice, then join your brothers, the other nations of the world. If you believe that it is not right to be the slaves of a nation that continually broke the commandments of the King, then join us. If you believe the King created you for a greater purpose, then come. Let us demonstrate that we can govern ourselves by doing what is right in our own eyes. Are you with us?" he shouted.

Immediately the villagers cried out, "We will not have Yeshua, son of Adonai, rule over us. We want our freedom!"[10] Immediately upon hearing this acknowledgement, each Watcher snatched up one of the mortals and shot into the sky, heading toward the City.

In the blink of an eye, everyone was gone—everyone except Ben and Kristiana.

31
Kristiana's Dilemma

BEN AND KRISTIANA looked at each other, utterly amazed. The King's Highway lay before them completely open and unobstructed. Kristiana was pleased that her daring to head for the Highway was paying off so well. Seeing the smirk on his face, Kristiana knew that Ben was conceding she had been right.

They sprinted to the Highway. It was made of pure crystal and was almost completely transparent, twenty feet wide and elevated roughly ten feet off the ground. They looked at each other, unsure how to climb on to it.

"We need a ladder," Kristiana said.

"Wait a second," Ben replied. "That can't be how people have reached it for the past thousand years. Let's think about what we know."

"Well, Yeshua created it and it is set apart for the redeemed," Kristiana recalled.

"For those *redeemed*," Ben remembered the words that Michael had said to him. "No one unclean is able to journey on the King's Highway. It is only for those authorized to travel on it, for those who have pledged allegiance to Yeshua." Kristiana, waiting patiently for Ben to say something more, was startled to hear him exclaim: "We mortals *may* travel on the Highway if we are loyal to the King!" With that insight he realized that a very important clue in their search for the Key, words spoken to him earlier by Michael, now had significance and meaning which he was able to understand.[1]

"Well, we must not be loyal because there appears to be no way to get up to it from this platform we are standing on." Kristiana sighed.

"We need to find the Key," Ben remembered, "but there is no time and we haven't seen anything that resembles a Key."

"You had better go on without me," she said candidly.

"What are you talking about?" Ben asked, shocked at what he had just heard.

"How can I pledge loyalty to Adonai after learning that he is really the creator of evil!" she said. "Why would I even want to do such a thing?" she asked, exasperated.

Ben, too, was very troubled by the most recent revelation. There was no getting around it; the Chronicles plainly stated that Adonai, not Lucifer, was the creator of evil. He sat down to ponder this further. "Wait!" he said. "We have the AEFOD! We can take another look and surely the answer will come." He reached into his pocket to retrieve it but found nothing. Quickly he checked his other pocket, and then his face fell.

"What's wrong?" asked Kristiana.

"I can't find it!" Ben looked around on the ground and then ran back to the grove as fast as he could. Kristiana could see him thoroughly combing the area. After several minutes he finally gave up and returned, dejected. He sat down on the platform, silent until finally he lifted his head, turned to her and said, "The AEFOD is gone. Lost."

"Why do we need it?" she asked, still put off by what Lucifer had quoted from the Chronicles.

Ben stood up abruptly. "Your question is well taken, but I think I know the answer from all we have discovered so far!"

Kristiana rolled her eyes.

"Before this present age of peace—and even before the previous age with its rulers and empires and the peoples with their great towers and monuments, before the former judgment through the deluge, even before Adam, before the Angels, and before Lucifer, before the differentiation, before anything was, before the blackness of the void— there was Adonai, the King, the self-existent and eternal One who was, and is, and is to come. He is the one now seated on the throne from whom fire and lightning come forth."[2]

"And?" Kristiana asked impatiently.

"When he made the void of the heavens, it didn't have his light and so for the first time ever, there was darkness. Do you understand? Adonai is light and there is no darkness in him at all, so that means that he actually created the darkness![3]

"You see," Ben continued, "the absence of his blazing light in the newly created void was something new and different, which is why the King said in the Chronicles, 'I form the light and create darkness.' Until that moment, darkness—or the absence of light—did not exist."

"So you are saying that until Adonai conceived of the absence of light, there was no such thing as darkness; it was his idea," Kristiana restated. "But we are concerned with evil, not darkness!"

"Well, just as there was no darkness until Adonai made it possible," Ben explained, "likewise there was no ability to choose something contrary to his desire until he basically created the potential for others to have a will. Before the creation, his was the only will in existence.

"Evil is what made choosing contrary to Adonai's will even possible," he continued. "Remember how Lucifer presented the fact that Adonai created both darkness and evil?"

She nodded affirmatively.

"What Lucifer failed to state was how Adonai defined evil, which was revealed in the Chronicles: 'they did what was evil in my eyes and chose what I took no pleasure in.'[4] Evil is by definition doing something Adonai doesn't like and until he created the potential to choose, it didn't exist."

Ben was pleased to think he had successfully communicated a complex and lofty concept.

His explanation seemed to satisfy Kristiana. "It makes sense that evil is really nothing more than making a choice to do something contrary to the wishes and desires of Adonai," she said. "Well, then, since he made the choice possible, is it right to say that Adonai was responsible for Lucifer's rebellion?"

"No, not at all," Ben corrected her gently, realizing there was more to explain. "Creating the parameter, the possibility, is far different than causing someone to act in such a way. Adonai had to give each of us the opportunity to choose *against* Him if any of us would clearly choose *for* Him. Without truly being given the option, none of us could experience the joy of freedom and real love."

"Wait a second!" Ben suddenly ran off to his house and returned almost immediately carrying golden plates. "To put it another way ... ," he said, arranging the plates on the platform. "Imagine if a king were to set before you ten dishes of the most excellent quality and then tell you that you may eat of any you choose because they all had his approval. No matter which plate you were to choose, you would be choosing in accordance with his desire. But if one of the plates contained poisonous food and he warned you that if you were to eat it you would die—and that option would not have his approval because he loved you and did not want you to die—then you would be forced to either believe him and heed his warning or not believe him and disregard his warning. By heeding his warning and not eating from the poisonous dish you would have exercised your own will and demonstrated that you believed him and wanted to align yourself with his will and wisdom. Choosing to eat the poisonous food, on the other hand, would be exercising your will in opposition to his."

Kristiana gave a half smile in response to Ben's overly detailed explanation. "But Adonai is the one who put the Tree of the Knowledge of Good and Evil in the Garden," she demurred. "So how is he not responsible for Adam and Eve's fall? And should Lucifer really be blamed for encouraging them to exercise their freedom to choose?"

"In order for Adonai's creatures to truly love him, the option to reject him had to be present," Ben countered. "Thus Lucifer, the Angels, Adam and Eve—all had to have the opportunity to choose *against* his will in order to be able to choose the opposite and thereby express their desire to love him.

"Lucifer was determined to put an end to the ones made of dust whom he was supposed to serve, yet a direct attack was impossible. However, if Adam were to eat from the Tree of the Knowledge of Good and Evil, which Adonai had forbidden, he would then commit himself and all of his future progeny to perpetual death.[5]

"The shrewdness of his scheme was actually in telling the *truth* about the purpose of the tree, but mixing it with a lie!" Ben exclaimed. "Adonai put the tree in the Garden to give them a choice. Adam and Eve could have rejected Lucifer's suggestion and chosen not to eat. Had they done so, they would have acquired what Adonai wanted to give them: volition—the freedom to choose.[6]

"Adonai was able to create them with the capacity of choice. Yet choice inherently must be exercised by each individual. So by making a choice, either in accordance with Adonai's desire or contrary to his desire, is the means by which they were activated and their eyes were opened. Being able to freely choose made them like Adonai, which Adonai desired very much."

"Therefore," Kristiana interjected, "Adonai could not make them choose; they had to choose freely, without any compulsion on Adonai's part. Adonai greatly desired Adam and Eve, as well as the Angels, to be like him because being like him, in his likeness, and a partaker of the divine nature was a good thing.[7] The Tree of the Knowledge of Good and Evil was *good*," Kristiana concluded.

"The lie was that they would not die," Ben said, still solving the riddle. "That's only the half of it! Lucifer realized that not only would Adam and the world be compromised materially, but once Adam violated the directive of Adonai, then Adonai would be bound by his own integrity to follow through with his admonition."

"Which is, of course, why Lucifer was so deliriously elated over the success of his plan," Kristiana added.

"He was not able to actually touch Adam," Ben continued, "or force him to do anything, if he were to remain unprosecutable; he merely gave a suggestion[8] and then Adam dug his own grave, leaving Lucifer legally free and clear!"

"Of course," said Kristiana, "Adonai would be upset, but because he was obligated by his integrity to keep his own law, Lucifer therefore had legal protection against the repercussions of the crisis he had just precipitated."

"Adam ought to have rejected the thing that the King did not delight in." Ben said. "Had he done so, Adonai still would have declared, 'Look, Adam has now become like one of us, knowing good and evil' yet without corruption; and then Adonai could have said, 'Now, let him stretch out his hand, take from the Tree of Life, and live forever.'"[9]

Kristiana had to let that sink in for awhile. "Lucifer knew that Adonai, by his great power and outstretched arm, made the earth, mankind, and the animals; and he gave full dominion over all of it in perpetuity to Adam.[10] So Lucifer must have secretly devised a plan to bring about the death of Adam as well as the whole earth by enticing them to violate Adonai's directive not to eat of the Tree of the Knowledge of Good and Evil. He had to be well aware that there would then be a legal debt, like a lien upon the earth, which would somehow have to be balanced or paid. Once Adam forfeited his right to dominion over the earth by violating Adonai's directive, Lucifer could occupy and rule over the earth instead of its legal and rightful possessor.

"Ultimately, it was Yeshua who demonstrated how fully Adonai was committed[11] to Adam and all of his sons by doing all that was necessary to remove the lien and pay the debt that Adam had incurred.[12] Yeshua, the express image of his father Adonai,[13] who existed in Adonai's own form and shared with him equality, demonstrated that he—unlike Lucifer—was willing to serve ones lesser than himself. He did so by emptying himself and taking the form of a servant, sharing the likeness of Adam, and then giving up his life."[14]

"All right then, I am ready to pledge," Kristiana said emphatically as she reached for Ben's hand.

"Yeshua," Ben began humbly, "we acknowledge that we are unworthy to set foot on your Highway for we have not been loyal to you. We ask you to forgive us of the treasonous acts we have done and wrong thoughts we have had." He stopped to think of what else he ought to say. "We now pledge our fidelity to you and only you."

"Agreed," said Kristiana wholeheartedly.

Immediately, stairs began to unfold downward to the platform. Made of purest crystal, they were virtually invisible. Ben looked at Kristiana, beaming, and kept holding her hand tightly as they started up the stairs together.

When they reached the top, they started walking in the direction of the City. Even though they were walking at a normal pace, somehow the highway transported them much faster than they could physically move. Saying nothing for what seemed like hours, the two of them were simply glad to finally be on their way to the City of Adonai.

32

The King's Highway

BEN AND KRISTIANA walked briskly past many villages that once had been loyal to Adonai. Some were very different from their village of Koinonia, now full of dry vegetation.

The two of them stopped occasionally along the road to eat from the gardens with plants and trees full of lush ripe fruit of all sorts.[1] In addition to the fruit trees, there were towering cedars and redwoods.

As they walked they heard the song of the trees,[2] a percussive drum-like tapping. This distinctively delightful sound had not been heard in Koinonia for centuries. It grew louder the closer Ben and Kristiana drew to the land of the Hebrews and to the City of Adonai. Even the song of the fields, a deep humming sound emitting from the ground[3]—inaudible to mortals in the previous age—was more lovely and pronounced the closer they came to their destination. The sound was reminiscent of the low undertone of the Scottish bagpipe of the former age, only more gentle and comforting, and it was always in harmony with the song of the King.[4]

Crossing over into the region of Asher in the land of the Hebrews, Ben and Kristiana were struck by the beauty and bounty of the terrain. In village after village, they saw the effect of the righteousness of the kingdom, which was peace, quietness, and confidence forever. The dwelling places were serene and secure, and the resting places were undisturbed. Seed had been planted in every field and cattle, flocks, and donkeys ranged freely.[5] Nearly every hill in the region of Asher was covered with luxuriant vines full of succulent grapes.

"All the cities that were destroyed and the places that were devastated during the time of the Hebrews' Trouble have been restored!"[6] Ben noted. "The proverb that Antipas told us about this region obviously is true: 'wine will drip from the mountains and flow from the hills.'"[7]

"Clearly, what the people have done has been blessed," said Kristiana. "They did not build houses only to have strangers live in them, or plant vineyards only to have others eat their fruit. Adonai has blessed them and their children. Before they called to him, Adonai promised to respond, and while they were still speaking, he heard."[8]

But where is everyone? Ben wondered. "These must be the homes of those who are loyal to Yeshua, but all the people are gone."

"They must be celebrating the feasts!" Kristiana realized. "Just like Antipas said that our village used to do."

Ben and Kristiana kept walking until they came to the place where the Highway merged from the east. "This place seems familiar," Ben thought aloud.

"But neither of us has ever left our village. How could you know this place?" Kristiana asked.

Ben walked a bit further, trying to remember. "I know! Antipas spoke about going up for the feasts and the time he met Caleb, son of Reu'el, with his family—the one we saw in the Chronicles.

"He said it was here that he met Caleb, son of Reu'el, and his family, who had gone on a journey in joy and were returning in peace. Antipas told me that the tree branches swayed, as if waving applause, when Caleb and his family crossed over the border.[9] He and his clan were accompanied by groups of people from at least ten nations, truth seekers from the north and from the west and from the land of Sinim. These people from the nations would say to Caleb, grasping his sleeve, 'Let us go with you, for we have heard that Adonai is with you.'[10] For the rest of the journey they surrounded Caleb and his wife, asking them questions about Adonai and what it was like to stand before Yeshua.[11] Those without little ones of their own were carrying Caleb's young sons in their arms and daughters on their shoulders."[12]

Ben and Kristiana passed under a fig tree with low-hanging limbs. "This must be the tree Antipas spoke of, where they rested and remembered how the joyous feasts of Adonai[13] have always been in his heart. He said they played their flutes and sang the rest of the way to the City.[14]

"Antipas also told me that my ancestor Matai could see in Caleb's eyes a humility and meekness which comes only from persevering through difficult trials."

"Well, we can certainly attest to that," Kristiana said. "You and I saw the awful things that the survivors of the time of the Hebrews' Trouble went through."[15]

"Yes; after that time it was said that the Hebrews were the kindest mortals on the earth," Ben continued, "because Adonai had taken away from their midst those who were puffed up with pride so that none who were haughty remained on his holy mountain. He had left in their midst a lowly remnant who trusted in the name of Adonai. This remnant of the Hebrews would do no unrighteousness, speak no lies, nor would a deceitful tongue be found in their mouths."[16]

Ben and Kristiana came through a thick canopy of trees and were utterly amazed. For the first time in their lives—and with their own eyes—they could see the beloved City. They lifted their heads, peering almost straight up into the sky, looking for the apex of the City.

The City of Adonai was so massive that its pinnacle, jutting up above the highest clouds,[17] extended beyond the ionosphere.[18] Glorious, brilliant rays of light in millions of shades of color, refracting the light of Adonai, radiated in all directions and illuminated the earth.

Kristiana had seen the City in the Chronicles but until now that she stood before it, she could never have imagined its splendor and majesty. This was the City that had been veiled for so many years, visible only to those who had eyes to see into the spiritual realm.

Ben thought of the prophets, of Stephen, John, Paul, and possibly others who had seen it in the Spirit but not in the flesh. Here he was seeing it in the flesh. He found it hard to believe that he too had finally come to Mount Jerusalem, the City of the Living Adonai, the heavenly Jerusalem,[19] the eternal home that Abraham awaited when he looked forward to the City with permanent foundations, whose architect and builder is the King.[20]

"Ben," Kristiana whispered, "what an awesome sight! We are seeing the King's holy mountain ... so beautiful in elevation! Truly it is the joy of the whole earth. And Jerusalem is the City of the great King,[21] unparalleled in beauty! From there his glorious fiery-lightning power emanates!"[22]

A gentle call could be heard in the wind—as it had been for the past one thousand years—beckoning, "Come! Let everyone who hears say, 'Come!' Let everyone who is thirsty, come! Let anyone who desires the Water of Life take of it freely, as a gift!"[23]

"Do you hear that?" Kristiana asked, looking at Ben.

"Yes!" he said. "That is the Spirit and the Bride extending the invitation even at this moment to those who are shaking their fists at Adonai!"

"Glorious things are spoken of you, City of Adonai,"[24] Ben declared, "yet what I had envisioned hardly compares to the magnificence of actually seeing his holy mountain."[25]

"So beautifully situated is Mount Jerusalem, the City of the great King, the joy of the whole earth!" Kristiana exclaimed. "And how wonderful it is to think that Adonai dwells there, in the midst of Jerusalem, the City of Truth. Surely within the citadels of the City we will find our refuge."

"I wouldn't be surprised," Ben mused, "if the followers of Lucifer, when they see the formidable city, flee in fear."[26]

He smiled at Kristiana and caught her smiling back. Their fond exchange ended when they saw that the hordes of Lucifer had completely surrounded the camp of saints and the beloved City on every side, and there was no way around them. Tears began to roll down Kristiana's cheek.

"What's wrong?" asked Ben, confused by her tears. "We're almost there!"

"It looks like there's no hope for us now. The City is too far away from where we are now, and Lucifer and his forces will soon be closing in on it. Besides, we don't even have the Key yet. We'll never be able to get in."

Ben's mind raced as he reviewed all he had seen and learned. "Michael told me the Key is the means by which access to the City is granted. He said Lucifer has attempted to destroy the Key and would try to steal it from us."

"Where could it possibly be?" Kristiana asked.

Ben thought for a moment before saying, somewhat tentatively, "I think I know."

"Where?" asked Kristiana, glad for a glimmer of hope.

"I don't think the Key is a *thing*; I think it's more of a *quality*."

"What do you mean?" she shot back.

"To be admitted into the City we must be conformed to Adonai's image."[27]

Kristiana gave Ben a quizzical look.

"Think about it," he said, reasoning aloud. "Adonai is so powerful that there is nothing he can't do; yet despite his limitless power, his glorious appearance, his knowledge of all things, and the many good gifts he gave his sons,[28] there was one thing he could not—he would not—do, and that was ... demand their love."[29]

"I'm not sure that I'm following you," Kristiana said.

"Well, even though Adonai could easily give anything and everything to his sons, for them to reciprocate his love, they had to be given the opportunity to reject not only his gifts but also his companionship; they had to be allowed to choose in the same way that Adam in the Garden was allowed to choose."[30]

"But what does this have to do with the Key?" Kristiana could not see the connection.

"Let's consider what we've learned," said Ben. The pieces were coming together in his mind. "Lucifer shared the external image of Adonai but refused to be like Adonai internally.[31] Adonai does not look at the outside; he looks at the inside of a person, at the heart. As the highest in rank, power, wisdom, and beauty, Lucifer needed to love by serving Adam, who was helpless and frail, in order to become like Adonai."[32]

"Whoever desires to be first," Kristiana recalled from the Chronicles, "must be the servant of all."

"Exactly! Yeshua lived that out in washing the feet of others,"[33] Ben added. "He ultimately emptied himself, made himself of no reputation, and gave his life-force in exchange for many."[34]

Kristiana remembered something else she and Ben had learned from the Chronicles: "Yeshua showed that there is no greater love than for one to lay down his life for another."[35]

Ben followed her train of thought: "The Angels were supposed to help those who were to inherit salvation;[36] that was their intended role. The creation of Adam gave them the opportunity to show love by serving someone lesser and weaker than themselves. But instead, they chose pride and self-exaltation. Adam and Eve needed to partake of the Tree of Life[37] in order to live forever. Once they had eaten from the Tree of Life, they would have been as strong as the Angels[38]—and even greater, because they had been created body and soul and infused with Adonai's Spirit.[39] For Adam and Eve, as well as for the Angels, making a choice allowed them to be like their creator—which is what he wanted for them—regardless of the outcome of their choices."[40]

"By aligning with his will and rejecting evil, which is essentially anything that displeases Adonai, they could have enjoyed pleasures at his right hand forever,"[41] said Kristiana.

"That's right!" Ben replied.

"If the Angels could have expressed love as Yeshua did," she continued, "which required serving and giving, then there could have been a meaningful and mutual relationship between Adonai and his creatures. Unlike human kings throughout history who have lorded their power and authority over others, demanding submission and obedience,[42] Adonai has not forced anyone, because love never demands its own way.[43] It was this aspect of love that Lucifer rejected," Kristiana realized.

"Ugh!" said Ben. "Now I understand that Lucifer's goal is not really to *liberate* us, as he likes to say, but to *use* us and then consume our life-force for his own benefit!" The realization hit home.

"And what about the Key?" Kristiana asked. "We have to have the Key!"

"The Key … is simply being willing to lay down your life, as Yeshua did, and become a servant."

◎ ◎ ◎ ◎ ◎

A wave of fear swept over Ben as he looked at the sea of Adamites—billions of them—who had answered the call of Lucifer.[44]

Kristiana reached out and took his hand. Ben wondered whether the two of them would make it; they couldn't possibly have much time left.

33
Mortal Danger

"I FEEL A great heaviness, like never before in my life," Kristiana whispered to Ben.

"I feel it too, though I can't really describe it," he said. "It's oppressive, like ... darkness and, and ... "

Ben finally was able to identify the weight that seemed to have settled on the world: "It feels like death! We must be very careful. Antipas warned not to turn to the right or to the left, and turn away from evil."[1]

On either side of the elevated highway were millions of Adamites as far as the eye could see. The blood of slaughtered pigs was oozing out from thousands of makeshift altars and the foul smell was inescapable.[2] Some of the Adamites lay prostrate around the altars, and next to each stood one of Lucifer's Watchers.

A cacophony of cries and shouts rang out: "Thank you for freeing us!" people were shrieking. "You are worthy of our praise because you ascended from the Abyss to save us!" they were shouting.

Some of the Adamites rose and began to dance in an ecstatic trance-like frenzy. The Watchers seemed to stand taller and stronger as long as this went on, and the blue hue of Lucifer's pretentious pride glowed brighter with every drop of blood spilled as an offering to him.

To escape danger and death, Ben and Kristiana were determined to follow the instructions Antipas had given: "Turn not to the right or to the left and turn away from evil."[3] So they continued going forward, focused on their goal of reaching the City—that is, until their attention was drawn toward the faces of some Adamites from their own village of Koinonia.

It seemed unbelievable that their own families and friends had been transformed into the brutal monsters Ben and Kristiana now saw feasting and delighting in their new master.[4] At every altar the same thing was happening: a Watcher pointed to a particular Adamite, who was immediately bound and placed on the altar. The Watcher incited the crowd, saying, "It is necessary that one should be sacrificed in order that *all* of you may thrive!"

Kristiana, revolted by what she was witnessing, whispered, "Vindicate us, Yeshua, for we have walked in our integrity. We have put our trust in you. We will not slip!" Then into Ben's ear she whispered again, "I know they can't see us, but still—let's hurry!"

The crowd roared in deranged delight as one of the Adamites started to plunge a knife into the human sacrifice bound on the altar.

"No!" Ben shouted with all of his might, causing the Adamites below to see him and Kristiana, though they had not been able to see them before.

Suddenly, Korah, the self-appointed leader from their village, shouted, "It's Ben and he has Kristiana!"

"Hey, Ben," someone else shouted, "where are you two going?"

"Join us," others in the group said.

"We cannot, for we have devoted ourselves to the service of the King and to be his subjects," Ben answered.

"No!" several of them yelled. "We are about to liberate ourselves from the oppression of Yeshua! We will no longer be his slaves! No longer shall Adonai withhold what is rightfully ours! The wealth of the city shall be ours."[5] They looked with envy toward the City.

"Lucifer has beguiled you," Ben cried over the clamor. "In the previous age, Adonai's eternal power and divine nature were understood and observed by what he made, so that people were without excuse. Yet now the honorable King dwells before us, so how much greater shall your condemnation be—for although you have known Adonai, you have neither glorified him as King nor have given thanks to him. Instead, you have turned away from him, your thoughts have turned to worthless things, and your senseless hearts have been darkened. You claim to be wise, yet you have become fools."[6]

"You're wrong, Ben!" they shouted back. "Lucifer has devised a plan that cannot fail[7]—come and we will show you how we will overthrow Yeshua and break his shackles!" The thought of breaking free from Yeshua brought loud cheering from the crowd.

"You have exchanged the truth for a lie," Ben yelled. "Now you are worshiping and serving a creature rather than the creator,[8] who is the eternal one. Look at you! You have become filled with every kind of evil and depravity. Although you know Adonai's just requirement, that those who practice wicked things deserve to die, you not only do such things but you even applaud others who practice them."[9]

Ben's piercing words provoked rage.

"Stop offering blood to the Watchers!" Ben pleaded. His voice could hardly be heard over the jeers of the angry mob. "Why should you yoke yourselves with rebellious Angels rather than the true creator of all?"[10]

"These sacrifices are in preparation for the battle," cried Korah, ignoring the warning. "For the past thousand years Adonai has required a sacrifice from us that he may be strong. So too does Lucifer require the same. Each of us has slaughtered swine in his honor!" he said, pointing to the thousands of makeshift altars with blood flowing from the victims in homage to Lucifer and his Angels.

"Adonai has never demanded the slaughter of animals for his own benefit; it has been for the mortals," countered Ben. "The animals' blood, their life-force, has covered us these past thousand years so that Adonai's blazing fire and lightning, his essence, should not destroy us. If it were not for these offerings and the Covering they provide, we all would have been lost. Adonai does not need the blood, nor does he delight in it.[11] The Covering is so that we can live in proximity to Adonai, but it shall soon be no more!

"Lucifer, though, has needed the life-force to sustain him. When he was banished from Adonai's presence he became grotesque and disfigured because his bond to the source of life was severed. Unlike Adam our father, he could not gain any power from the dirt, the *adamáh*. Even though his body is transdimensional and will never fail in the same way as Adam's, he still needs energy; so he takes nourishment from the life-force of the animals—or even from the Adamites!"[12] Ben was repulsed by his own words.

"Adonai's establishment of the Covering and offering is for mortals, not for Adonai! Lucifer and all of these Watchers, however, are demanding that the life-force of a creature be given as tribute to themselves. They are like roaring lions, seeking whom they might consume[13] to momentarily put themselves at ease. But the reality is that their desire for more will never be satiated![14] They despise you, yet they need you to willingly offer up the life-force of another being so they can receive nourishment from it. This is why Adonai specifically instructed the Hebrews to no longer offer the life-force to the rebellious Angels!"[15]

"Go preach somewhere else!" Korah said, pinning Ben with his gaze. "Do you really believe that we need to put our faces down and lick the dust of the Hebrews' feet[16] in light of all they have done? Is it right that the abundance of the sea be turned to them or the wealth of the nations?[17] Is it right that we should build up the Hebrews' walls or that the kings of the nations should serve them?[18] Do you think that the nation or kingdom which does not serve them should perish and be utterly ruined?"[19] he demanded.

"Adonai our creator is the rightful King," Ben answered, "and it is he alone whom you should serve.[20] Lucifer has twisted the words of the Chronicles ... "

Kristiana glanced into the crowd and was dismayed to see her father. This man she dearly loved had been dreadfully deceived. Suddenly she found herself heading in his direction.

"Father!" she shouted down from the King's Highway. "Come with us! We are going to the City. You too can enjoy the wonderful goodness of Adonai."

"Oh, my daughter," he responded tenderly, and then began weaving through the crowd toward the side of the Highway, which only moments before had been invisible. "How I have wanted to see you again. Come closer that I may touch your hand. This Highway you are on does not permit me to come to you. Reach down your hand that I may touch you again, my child."

Kristiana knelt down on the Highway, extended her hands and reached down as her father reached up, but it was impossible to bridge the distance between them. Without delay, Prince Parás came and effortlessly lifted him so that his head was raised just above the Highway. Now when Kristiana stretched out her hands, her father was able to grab hold of them.

"Oh, Kristiana, my dear child ... " her father's voice was filled with tenderness, "you have no future with Adonai! It is just as we have long suspected in our hearts. Adonai demands that the older serve the younger and the stronger serve the weaker[21]—what a backward and illogical way! Lucifer has valiantly fought in the past for freedom from Adonai's oppression, and he is now fighting again for the good of us all!

"In the previous age Lucifer was continually before the throne of Adonai, day and night, calling for the end of blatant favoritism toward the unworthy Hebrews![22] He brought true and accurate charges of their crimes before Adonai, reminding him of how they broke his laws again and again.

"Under Lucifer's leadership we can finally do as we please and no longer have to live according to Adonai's standards." He pleaded with his daughter as if his very life depended on her joining him. "Please, please do not travel with Oni, the son of affliction!" he begged, pointing disdainfully at Ben. "Come down here and join us. We will win our freedom and enjoy the spoils of victory. Then you too will be able to do what is right in your own eyes!"

"No, father," with sad resolution she responded—emboldened by her new discoveries and declarations—to this man who had influenced her thinking for so long. "Do not commit this great offense. Adonai is not our enemy! He is the rightful king for he is the creator of all. His ways are good. Should we not all serve one another? Come with us, father. It is not too late for you. If you turn away from the deceptions of Lucifer's and accept Yeshua as your King, you can join us on his Highway and Adonai will receive you as his own."

"No!" he argued with a vehemence that startled his daughter. "Adonai is unfair to the other peoples for he himself said that he will never rescind his promise; only if the ordinances of the sun, moon, and stars depart from before him would the seed of the Hebrews also cease from being a nation. He also said only if heaven above could be measured and the foundations of the earth searched out beneath would he ever cast off all the seed of the Hebrews for all that they have done![23]

"How could you want this one whose way is unjust to rule over us?[24] Lucifer is our only hope; he is our liberator! For a thousand years he was consumed only with thoughts of how he could finally set things right—how he could shatter our chains and set us free.[25] And now he has confirmed my suspicions that Adonai wants us to be slaves forever. But our deliverance has come! With Lucifer's help we will break loose and finally be free to do as we want," he ranted. "We will not grovel at the feet of the King!"

Kristiana pulled back. "Father, what you say makes no sense. You have been blinded by Lucifer's lies. I cannot, I will not, go with you."

Her father tightened his grip on her hands to her astonishment forcibly yanked her off the Highway.

Ben could not believe what he was seeing as he looked down in horror at Kristiana, who was lying on the ground, severely bruised from the fall.

From there she could see Korah approaching. "Kristiana, you know better than to talk back to your father!" The two men helped her to her feet.

"Give her back!" Ben cried, frantically trying to figure out what to do.

Korah then fixed his eyes on Ben: "*You* may *leave!*" he snarled. "Go to your precious Yeshua. We shall come knocking at the gates soon enough."

Ben was speechless. He remembered the admonition of Antipas to hurry to the City because time was short. So if he attempted to help Kristiana, then he might not make it to the gates before it was too late. He looked toward the City longingly.

Observing Ben's deliberation and perceiving his dilemma, Korah interposed: "I guarantee you safe passage to the gates. We shall not interfere with your reaching the City. We promised Kristiana's father that we would help him recover his daughter and that we have done. Now … go," he nodded as if dismissing a lowly servant.

Ben looked at Kristiana then turned and started toward the City. Her heart sank as she watched him walk away. Never had she felt so abandoned and afraid.

As soon as Ben was out of range, Korah began issuing orders to his attendants: "Bind her! She will be a prime offering to Lord Lucifer to strengthen him for ascending the Mountain of Adonai."

Kristiana's father shuddered at the pronouncement but was too cowardly to intervene. "Prepare the altar and the knife," Korah commanded.

Walking quickly, Ben thought about the Key and how Adonai had provided everything for Adam in order that he might choose to love him in return. Adonai had given the Angels the opportunity to love by serving one weaker and younger and so demonstrate that more happiness comes from giving than receiving.[26]

Then Ben abruptly turned around, his heart racing and his stomach burning, convinced he had to help Kristiana; determined not to turn his back on the one entrusted to him as Adam had done to Eve.

"No!" He screamed with all his might, leaping off the edge of the Highway and landing on top of Korah.

In seconds, the lawless crowd pulled him off of Korah and slammed him to the ground. An angry mob kicked and punched him repeatedly in the face, stomach, back— releasing their pent-up hatred toward their Maker. Some picked up rocks and hurled them at Ben, hitting him over and over again, battering his body almost beyond recognition. Lying on the ground in a pool of his own blood, Ben could hear Korah barking the order to bind him for sacrifice.

At that moment Lucifer appeared from somewhere in the crowd.

34

Lucifer's Secret Plan

"BRAVO, BEN-ONI!" Lucifer cackled, clapping his hands as he walked up to Ben, who was collapsed on the ground. "Bravo, my boy! You have learned the ways of your master well! Let me see," he mocked, "I think he said it something like this, 'There is no greater love than to lay down your life for another.'[1] Is that what made you think you would save your girlfriend?" he taunted. "Well, now you both will die and we will still take the City!"

The perverse pleasure Lucifer derived from Ben's plight evoked the ecstasy of his fondest memory: "Oh, the exhilaration of seeing Yeshua lay down his life for his friends. Some friends! A so-called friend who betrayed him with a kiss, another friend who denied him repeatedly, and others who scattered and deserted him. Even the leaders of his own people delivered him up to death. With every lash that ripped apart his pathetic flesh and with every strike of the hammer that slammed in the nails, I could finally unleash my true feelings! *Raca!*" he scoffed. "And *you*, you young fool, as I delighted in draining Yeshua's life from him, so I will delight in extracting yours."

"You are a liar and have been from the beginning," Ben countered. "Yeshua chose to relinquish his life-force at the right time to fulfill the lien that Adam had incurred.[2]

255

No one took his life from him, but he, incredibly, laid it down by his own choice, and he had the power to take it up again!"[3]

Ben grimaced in pain from the many blows and rocks that had been hurled against him. "That one heroic act by Yeshua allowed Adam and his sons to leave the Abyss, to be with Adonai again, and made the way for Adonai to end his self-imposed exile from the earth. That was also the beginning of the end of *your* kingdom. How foolish of you to think you can defeat Adonai. He will see you coming and simply laugh at you in derision.[4] This will be your final rebellion."[5]

Lucifer edged closer to Ben—squinting because of the blood oozing from his head wounds—looked him squarely in the face and glowered: "No, Ben-Oni. *You* were not paying attention when I explained the means of assured and undeniable victory."

The Adversary snarled like a hungry lion taunting his prey. "Adonai is confounding and his ways are incomprehensible, with the strong serving the weak, the older serving the younger, the greatest of all being a lowly slave.[6] He knows my thoughts, but it makes no difference. Look around and see, Ben-Oni! You have chosen the wrong side. Clearly the Adamites are displeased with the current administration; our numbers have become like the sands of the sea!"[7]

"And what will you fight with?" Ben ventured.

"Ben, Ben-Oni," the would-be usurper condescended. "Again, you clearly were not paying attention to my sagacious strategy; no, you were off studying the Chronicles with your witless girlfriend!" Lucifer jeered. Then to Ben's consternation, he produced the AEFOD, which a villager had retrieved, and proceeded to break it in two with his bare hands.

"They have nothing to fight with because—as part of the wedding preparations, which you witnessed in the

Chronicles—Adonai banished from the land the warrior's bow, sword, and every weapon of warfare[8] that I and my Watchers introduced to the Adamites long ago. These were converted into plowshares, and the spears into pruning hooks. You see, never again shall anyone train for war.[9]

"Understand, Ben, that during my unjust incarceration in the Abyss I calculated all conceivable scenarios and their potential outcomes. Not one single detail has eluded my shrewdness; there is nothing I have not thought of."

Ben looked over at Kristiana, lying limp on the ground, bruised and bloody, and then back at Lucifer, whose plan sounded flawless. There seemed to be no escape.

"I just can't believe that Adonai expected me to serve your kind ... so utterly weak and without understanding." Lucifer leaned over and muttered, "Ben-Oni, the weapons of our warfare are not those that mortals once used: physical swords and shields used to bludgeon, maim, and behead,"[10] He said with a malicious smile. "You see, the battle has never been about flesh and blood.[11] The only weapon we need to wield is the cunning to controvert his decrees. Yes, just one contradiction and Adonai will be unworthy of ruling.[12] When I make Adonai a liar—that will be my finest hour, the culmination of the plans I have carefully laid for the past seven thousand years to finally and forever throw off his yoke of oppression."[13]

At this, Ben breathed out a warning: "Your pride will be your downfall."[14]

"And your confidence in your capricious King will be *yours*!" Lucifer countered. "Look, ... he promised that all those who trust in him would not be put to shame.[15] But there you are, broken and left for dead outside the gates![16] You were willing to lay down your life, but what good has it done you?[17] You and your girlfriend are going to die!"

Prince Parás strode briskly to Lucifer and spoke telepathically for the sake of privacy: "My lord, I fear any further delay could derail our plan."

Lucifer glared at him. "Nonsense!" he retorted, before turning back to Ben on the ground.

"Ben-Oni, since you are as good as dead anyway, I will let you in on the key to my brilliant strategy. You know that it is stated in the Chronicles: 'There shall by no means enter the City anything that defiles or causes an abomination or a lie, but only those who are written in Yeshua's Book of Life.'[18] It also is stated that in order to go through the gates into the City, one must wash his robes and then take of the leaves of the Tree of Life.[19]

"So, you see, when just one—any one—of all these who are with us," he said with a grand sweeping gesture toward the surrounding throngs, "enters in through those *pearly* gates, then Adonai will be proven a liar. One foot across the city gates and we will have a legal victory, and that is all we need."

Lucifer then lifted Ben up by the nape of the neck and turned him toward the City. "Look, Ben-Oni. Do you see that gate straight ahead? There are eleven more, three on each side of the City. Even though it is surrounded by illustrious walls of jasper rising two hundred fifty feet high, its gates are never shut![20] Each gate measures about three miles and is wide open all the time! Like a mighty tsunami, I and all of these freedom fighters will storm past the thresholds and invade Adonai's beloved City. When even a single defiled foot touches the holy threshold, the very place where he said nothing unclean would ever enter,[21] then it's over!" he boasted as he dropped Ben back to the earth so hard that it knocked the wind out of him.

"Are you too blind to see, Ben-Oni, that Adonai has boxed himself in by his own integrity and his own laws? He is not an Adamite that he should lie or change his mind. Whatever he declares, he must also do.[22] My strategy to thwart him is simple ... so ingeniously simple."

Ben was vexed in spirit at the revelation of the plan.

Korah, standing next to Lucifer the whole time, eagerly

added: "Lucifer has pledged to us that he will secure our rights ... well, not yours—you'll be dead. But no longer shall we be referred to as dogs![23] When our feet step across the threshold, Lucifer will be our advocate; he will have legal grounds for demanding that the Maker grant us access to the Tree of Life. Then we will be like the Most High. We shall live forever and shall no longer be slaves to the Hebrews!"

Lucifer looked with lust toward the City from which he had been banished seven millennia earlier.[24] Throughout the entire mountain-like structure were towers studded with gems and pinnacles of rubies. Everything in view was overlaid with gold so pure that it looked translucent.[25] With gleeful anticipation he thought, *soon it will all be mine, and I will be King*!

But his reverie was interrupted by Korah: "This same plan worked in the past, and it will bring us victory again today," he said, with a dismissive glance at Ben. "Ages ago Lucifer successfully launched a legal war against Adonai and demonstrated the folly of his way, in which the weak are valued over the strong."

With false humility Lucifer recounted, "I merely asked the wife of Dusty, father of your sorry race, a simple question. I never touched him nor did I *cause* him to do anything. No; he committed his own treason and as a result he was no longer able to have dominion over the earth. Consequently the earth fell under my domain where I, more magnanimous than Adonai, let everyone do what was right in their own eyes."[26]

"What a priceless moment it was when the dirtbags realized that eating the fruit had cost them *everything*," Prince Yaván added callously.

Lucifer went on to boast, "Ben-Oni, it was so easy to convince them to violate Adonai's directive—which only proved my point that they were not worthy to be served by me. They and all of you are worthless pieces of dirt, bits of dust destined to disintegrate back into the ground from where you came."

Korah seemed disconcerted by hearing this admission of Lucifer's true feelings.

"There had never been a question in my mind that Adonai was worthy of my service," Lucifer elaborated. "He is powerful and mighty, full of energy and fire! But what could have come over him that he should create such frail creatures and expect the mighty Angels—especially *me*—to serve *them*! Just as I extricated myself then from having to serve them long ago, so I will liberate everyone now from having to obey the oppressive rules of Adonai. And finally, all will serve *me*!"[27]

Lucifer continued his argument *ad nauseam*: "My kingdom went unchallenged for four thousand years until the stupendous countermove by Adonai. Now lest you have any delusions, let me assure you that nothing of the sort can happen again. The Chronicles clearly state that Yeshua died once and only once for the treason of Adam.[28] Therefore, it is impossible that he could die again to offset the present rebellion.[29] Remember, Ben-Oni, we need only one foot across the threshold of the great City, and there are multitudes with us.[30] One foot, just one foot, and we will checkmate the King. We will create a stalemate that not even he himself, with all of his power, will be able to resolve. Once we accomplish our goal, he will not be able to smite us now, just as he could not smite me seven thousand years ago. He later played his Ace and now has nothing left; there is nothing further he can do."

"Never in the past," Prince Yaván pointed out, "would Adonai arbitrarily undo his own decrees, nor will he do so today. This works to our advantage, for once he is proven a liar, he no longer will have the right to be ruler!"

Ben began to hyperventilate. Lucifer seemed to be unbeatable. Ben's heart ached more from hearing the plan than from the physical suffering he was enduring. He had not imagined that Lucifer could outmaneuver Adonai, nor had he ever conceived that his own death would be as awful as this.

"Who will save you now, Oni?" Korah chided. "Where is your beloved Yeshua now?" he mocked. "Obviously he has forgotten you; he has hidden his face from you."[31]

Just then an attendant approached Lucifer. "Master, the altar is ready. Shall I slay them for you now?"

"Leave them for the time being; I do not need their strength," Lucifer replied. "Never have I been more ready to attack than at this moment. Let us delay no longer! Their destruction can be part of our victory celebration."

A loud blast came from one of the rebel Watchers, signaling to all that it was time to move out.

Lucifer the glorious Angel was suddenly transformed into a repulsive and hideous monstrosity[32]—a grotesque, fiery red and charcoal black figure, dragon-like,[33] with inky, almond-shaped eyes. He had morphed back into his true self, for he needed all of his strength at this moment and would spend no energy on maintaining the façade. Likewise, the appearance of every Watcher around him was no longer that of a holy Angel, for each had reverted to his real nature.

"My battle with the tyrant has cost me my beauty and left me disfigured.[34] Surely you now can see how completely committed I am to our success," he shouted to the fired-up forces that followed him.

Ben watched with trepidation as Lucifer and all the rebels moved into position around the City.

35
Transformation

BEN LOOKED OVER at Kristiana, who could barely manage to mouth the words "Thank you." Bound and severely wounded, both of them found it nearly impossible to move.

Ben lamented all that had happened. His spirit was overwhelmed, his mind filled with doubt and confusion, and his heart distressed.[1] All the words of Antipas ran through his head as he tried to make sense of his situation. What had he done wrong?

The minutes dragged on as he thought about their journey, both in the Chronicles and on the King's Highway. Ben remembered the words of Antipas: "Rejoice! Even though for a little while you have to suffer various kinds of trials, your genuine faith will result in praise, glory, and honor."[2]

It made no sense to him. Thinking of how Lucifer had afflicted them and trapped them in his diabolic scheme made him despondent.

"I did what you commanded, Yeshua!" Ben said. "I laid down my life for another. So why do you stand far away in our time of distress? Do you not see? Have you truly abandoned us?"[3] Choking on his own blood, he was unable to say any more.

Just then a strong wind blew over them and a deep-blue butterfly fluttered past Kristiana. "Ben, Ben, look— it's the butterfly!" she whispered with the little strength she had left. "When I called on Adonai, I saw the butterfly, and that was what led me to you!"

The butterfly floated over them and landed on Ben's leg. Staring at it intently, he wondering what it meant.

"Ben," Kristiana said faintly. "When I witnessed your sacrifice on my behalf, I finally understood what the Key *really* is. You were right; it is not a thing but a quality. But I see there is something more: It is rare for anyone to die for a righteous person—though somebody might be brave enough to die for a good person—yet you were willing to die for me. Thank you! But the Key isn't what *you* did for *me*," she said, still struggling to speak. "It was what *Yeshua* did for *us*, you and me!"[4]

Ben immediately realized that Kristiana was correct. His sacrifice, though commendable, suddenly felt insignificant compared to that of Yeshua. Looking toward the City, Ben said, "You were beaten, mocked, and cruelly killed on account of *my* treachery!"[5] For the first time he understood: "You, O great King, suffered for my sedition once and for all. You, the innocent, died for me, the guilty!

"I have spoken foolish things; I am a man of unclean lips.[6] Rescue us not according to *our* righteousness but according to *your* great mercy!" he pleaded with all the strength he could muster, "O Yeshua, we seek refuge in you. Snatch us away from the gates of death.[7] Bring us to your City that where you are we may be too.[8] There let us drink of the Water of Life and partake of the leaves of the Tree of Life." A peace beyond any he had ever imagined[9] settled over Ben and he was filled with a joy that transcended all the pain he was enduring.

"Kristiana ... ," Ben had started to say, when an unseen hand instantly lifted their bodies off the ground and into the air. Fast as lightning they flew, over Lucifer and his rebel throngs, to a gate just outside the city. The soft and gentle call of the Spirit and the Bride yet permeated the air, just as it had for the last thousand years. It beckoned, "Come! Let everyone who hears this say, 'Come!' Let everyone who is thirsty, come! Let anyone who wants the Water of Life take it as a gift!"[10]

Ben and Kristiana found themselves in the River of the Water of Life, which sparkled like crystal and proceeded from the very throne of Adonai and of Yeshua from the apex of the mountain.[11] The water rose up to their heads and then completely submerged them. They began to panic because they could not breathe, but then they heard Yeshua's reassuring voice saying, "Do not fear. Drink in the water from the River of my pleasures."[12]

Ben opened his mouth and let the ambrosial flow go down from his throat into his innermost being. Any sensation of thirst was gone. He remembered all of his ancestors who—after living as mortals for at least one hundred years, having children, and building houses—had come to Jerusalem to get their new bodies, as he was doing now. He looked over at Yeshua, who had made this fountain freely available to anyone who thirsted for it.[13] The fountain was opened for the house of David and for the inhabitants of Jerusalem, for the cleansing of wrongdoing and uncleanness.[14]

At once Ben and Kristiana each could feel the potential of death, which had ever permeated their being, begin to dissipate as every cell in their body was being healed by the water.[15] The error in their genetic code, like some awful venom, was eradicated. They shared the same freshness that Adam felt on his first day—although Ben imagined his own experience exceeded that, for Adam had known nothing but perfection, whereas he was passing from death to life.[16]

He and Kristiana came up out of the water healed, the many wounds inflicted upon them during the attacks by the embittered followers of Lucifer completely gone. Filled with greater strength than they had ever thought possible, they were as Adam was before the Fall.[17]

Kristiana saw a woman by the River's edge stoop down and cup the living water in her hand. The woman had compassionate eyes and was shining brightly, even like the sun,[18] as did all the immortals. Noticing the gratitude in her eyes, Kristiana knew immediately that she was the woman at the well when Yeshua had passed through Samaria. Letting the water in her hand sift through her fingers back into the River, she began ever so softly to lift up her voice in praise to the one on the throne who, so many years before, had told her everything that she had ever done.[19]

Her song was one of thanksgiving for the mercy of the King—how he had put away her rebellion, which had been before him every day.[20] She adored the King with gladness of heart: *Hineh el yeshuatí evtakh velo efkhád, ki ozí vezimrat-yah Yahveh vayehí li lishuáh.* "Look! The King, yes the King is my *yeshuáh*; I will trust, and not be afraid. For Yeshua is my strength and my song, and he has become my *yeshuáh*." Stretching her hands out toward the throne of the King, from which the water originated and emanated,[21] she celebrated, "I will draw water joyfully from the wells of *yeshuáh*,[22] for here is the fountain of living water that springs up into immortality, just as he said."[23]

Soon others joined in: "Give thanks to the King; call on his name. Make known his actions among the nations. Proclaim that his name is exalted. Sing praises to Adonai because he has acted gloriously. He is made known in the whole world. Shout aloud, and sing for joy, you who live in Jerusalem, for great in your midst is the Holy One of Israel!"[24]

"To enter the city," Yeshua said, "you must be transformed from your bodies of flesh and blood to bodies like the Angels, glorious and not made of dust;[25] yours must be conformed to my own glorious body[26] as you become partakers of my divine nature,[27] free from corruption. You must be born again[28] by taking of the Tree of Life and be transformed as were Antipas and all of your clan who came before."

The Tree of Life was in the midst of the street of the City and on either side of the River. [29] "Now," said Yeshua, "both of you, stretch out your hands and take and eat leaves from the Tree of Life, which are for your healing; and live forever!"[30]

Kristiana's heart leapt for joy as she stretched out her hand and plucked off a leaf from the same Tree of Life that had been in Eden with Adam and Eve!

Ben examined a leaf and his thoughts went immediately to the original Tree. Amazingly, it was as if he and Kristiana were holding the AEFOD again, back in the Chronicles: "Adam, where are you?" He could sense the sadness of Adonai on that day long ago when he looked plaintively at his dear children, face to face for the last time before he was obligated to remove himself from them—and from the earth, lest his splendor and radiance destroy it.

Ben understood: the desire of Adonai was to walk with Adam and his sons as an expression of love. He wanted to make his home with them and share his heart; he wanted them to be where he was[31] for he had always desired to live and walk among them, to be their King and Father, and they his people.[32] He realized that Adonai was forced to abandon the earth, putting up a veil of separation, lest his own glory, like a stream of sulfur,[33] destroy that which he had created. Because of Adonai's great mercy and love for his creation he entered into a self-imposed exile rather than let everything be incinerated.[34]

Suddenly Ben and Kristiana both perceived Michael and Gabriel in the past, standing next to the Tree of Life, surrounded by the four cherubim,[35] who appeared like blazing torches.[36] These four passed from one to another the fiery whirling sword[37] with such speed that it looked like lightning and indeed became an impenetrable wall of fiery-lightning.

"Lucifer's strategy worked, despite his humiliation," Michael said in shock. "Death is now permanent and irreversible according to Lucifer's scheme. Will Adonai ever be able to undo it? I can only wonder what hope there is for Adam and Eve and their race now that the way to the Tree of Life has been blocked. So long as Adam and his sons are separated through degeneration, Adonai can never reassert his presence on the earth because his omnipotent power would destroy it."

Kristiana looked again at the leaf in her hand. How amazing that it could transform a person from the essence of dirt, *adamáh,* to that of spirit, like an Angel.[38] Such a transformation could not be undone, and whatever state a person was in when they partook of the fruit would be their permanent state forever and ever. It was for that reason Adonai had placed the cherubim around the tree to guard it at all costs.[39] Therefore, the mortals could not eat from the Tree of Life until they had washed their garments, had bathed in the Water of Life, and had drunk from it.[40] Once they had washed their robes, however, they had the right to the Tree of Life and could enter through the gates into the City of Adonai because they then had a body made of spirit, as the Angels.

For the first time Ben appreciated that Adonai so swiftly protected Adam and Eve from eating from the Tree of Life. Had Adam taken of its fruit, he would have forever been in a state of death, because combining these opposing forces, life with the knowledge of good and evil, would have rendered him intrinsically unsustainable, in a state of infinite incompatibility.

Had Adam eaten from the Tree in the beginning, he would have been transformed into the likeness of an Angel,[41] defiant and accursed as Lucifer and the rebellious

Watchers. He would have lingered in the gloom of shades and shadows, constantly in death, yearning to be free of its grip yet with no hope of remedy from his dire existence.[42]

Ben gazed at the River of Life, now clearly understanding the predicament that Lucifer had engendered, which Yeshua had overcome through his sacrifice and restoration of hope to the hopeless. Yeshua made a way for an Adamite to transition from a body of dirt to a body of spirit and thus be able to enter the presence of Adonai—first, by bathing and drinking of the Water of Life, which only Adonai could provide, for the cleansing and healing of their bodies; and then, by eating of the Tree of Life, completing the transformation and optimizing them for life in Adonai's kingdom.

Ben and Kristiana ate the leaves and in moments their entire composition changed from the inside out. Every cell in the old body, made of carbon, was transformed. The *adamáh*, soil or dirt, was transformed into spirit—immortal and resplendent.[43] They looked at each other and then at themselves, delighted by their glorious new bodies, which death would never destroy, which no weakness would ever diminish. They were radiating light, and it was the light coming from Adonai!

They had been made new. They were direct creations of Adonai,[44] their new bodies conformed to his glorious body. They would always live in the light of his presence, with no veil between them any longer.[45] At last they each had their wedding garment—the garment of *yeshuáh*.[46]

Kristiana's appearance took Ben's breath away. Her body was dazzling. Light radiated from her exquisite face, creating a glorious corona of life,[47] shining and sparkling with emerald-hued crystal and accents of topaz, yellow pearls, and other magnificent gems. Her feet and arms were shining like gleaming metal,[48] and her clothing was brighter[49] than the purest snow; as lovely as the stars of heaven, gleaming like the rays of the sun. Truly, she had been conformed to the image of Adonai[50] and had become a partaker of the divine nature.[51] She would never die, for she was an immortal daughter of Adonai.[52]

Ben then considered his own body. The newness of it stunned him so that he grabbed one hand with the other, just to see how his new limbs felt. The sensation of touch was more real than ever. His body was tangible and physical but no longer degradable. He was experiencing an altogether new and wonderful mode of existence.

Besides that, Ben sensed an extraordinary connection to all around him. Now not only could he see Kristiana's beautiful new body but he could actually look into her heart. He knew her deeply and personally, as she also knew him. They now had the ability to appreciate each other to the very depths of their souls. Each could fully enjoy the essence of the other.

Instantly, Ben understood that this is the way it would be with all in Yeshua's kingdom ... knowing fully and being fully known.

36
The Purging

THERE STOOD YESHUA in all of his blazing glory!
Ben and Kristiana, in their innermost being, compre-
hended the magnificence and magnitude of the one they
stood before. With utmost adoration they knelt with faces
to the ground as images and sensations filled their minds
in ways never before imagined.

They traveled back before the current age of splendor,
before the age of shadow with its rulers and empires, before Lucifer. Back before the blackness of the void, before
the differentiation, before anything at all—there he was!
Yeshua! The very image, the perfect expression of Adonai,
the King, the Self-Existent One who was and is and is to
come. With fire proceeding out from before him and fierce
lightning lashing out,[1] clothed in light, he exuded absolute
power and goodness all at once—this One who spoke the
worlds and the Angels into existence![2]

Ben and Kristiana braced themselves, unsure what to
expect.[3] Both cringed as Yeshua's fire began to rage around
them, burning away like wood, hay, and stubble the worthless deeds done in their Adamite bodies as every action
was tested and revealed by the fire of Yeshua.[4] Like stepping into a hot bath, there was a moment of discomfort but
then pure delight as only their worthwhile deeds remained.

"Ben, Kristiana!" Yeshua spoke. Lifting their heads from where they knelt before him, they saw for the first time the holes in his feet. Looking up further they saw the holes in his hands. In stark contrast to the glorious form of the King standing before them, they were overwhlemed in their innermost being by a keen awareness, a vision as it were, of Yeshua in the past.

So appalling was his appearance that had they not now themselves been granted to see it experientially, they could never have envisioned the horror of it. Beaten and bloodied, they saw him staggering on a rocky hill, his broken body crushed under the weight of a beam of wood. His flesh was ripped apart, his features disfigured beyond recognition, and his form marred beyond human likeness.[5] Oddly, a crown of thorns punctured the top of his head.

At that moment both Ben and Kristiana came to a full realization of all that had been necessary to open the way to the Tree of Life. "Yeshua, you were beaten for me!"[6] Ben exclaimed. "I see the price you paid for me, the great penalty for all my misdeeds. I have spoken foolish things;[7] I am a man of unclean lips.[8] I give all honor and praise to you, O great King, who suffered for my treason once and for all—you, the innocent, for me, the guilty!"

In the vision they could see into the dimly lit place of rest in the Abyss. The ground began to quake[9] and Yeshua stood in that place. Ben and Kristiana had seen this in the Chronicles but now it became a reality to them; it was not only Adam's story but also their own. They saw, as if they were present, Yeshua approach the great chasm separating those who were waiting for him from those who were not.[10] He looked deep into the darkness, to the lowest rung of the Abyss, where the rebellious Angels were locked up awaiting the judgment of the great day.[11]

"It … is … done!" he thundered triumphantly.[12] The Watchers attempted to lift their necks to see their conqueror but the unbreakable, eternal chains bound them so tightly that they could not move. They remained speechless, not daring to open their mouths.[13]

"Your stronghold is finally broken!" the thundering voice of Yeshua announced in that place of gloom. "Lucifer, the ruler of the earth, is judged and shall be cast out.[14] The power of death—which he wielded to keep the Adamites in bondage and in fear of death all their lives[15]—I have removed from him! And you yourselves also are judged along with your leader!"

Yeshua then proclaimed to the rebels, "All authority in both the upper and lower domains[16] belongs to me. Understand this: no one took my life from me; I laid it down of my own free will," he stated unequivocally. "I had the authority to lay it down, and I had the authority to take it back again!"[17]

Ben and Kristiana felt a rush of elation as they heard Yeshua declare his victory over the rebels of the past.

"I did it for the joy that now is mine,"[18] Yeshua spoke in the present to Ben and Kristiana with the same joy he had when he created Adam in the beginning.

Standing before him, now able to withstand the medium of fire that forever would envelop them, Ben and Kristiana looked down and discovered that their garments were layered with gold, silver, and precious stones similar to the stones that were Lucifer's covering before he rebelled.[19]

To each of them, Yeshua handed a white stone with writing on it.

Ben was overwhelmed by what he read. No longer was he "Ben-Oni, son of my affliction." On his stone was written the first part of his name, "Ben," followed by a new last part, "Yamin."[20] He was "son of my right hand" to the King of kings, creator of heaven and earth! He looked gratefully at Yeshua, his heart nearly bursting with joy. The pain of rejection—by his fellow villagers, by his brothers and sister, by his own father—which long had lodged like an arrow in his heart, was gone forever!

Yeshua smiled at Ben-Yamin in delight.

Kristiana too was profoundly touched by what was written on her stone. Her new name, which only she and Yeshua would know, was Eliana-Abigail, "my God answered, my father's joy." Seeing the tears that began to flow down her face, Yeshua wiped them away and drew her close.

"Well done, Ben." Yeshua said. "Well done, Kristiana. You have been faithful in a little; I will entrust to you much. Enter now into the joy of Adonai!"[21]

Ben and Kristiana, strong and resolute, for the first time in their new bodies walked toward the open and welcoming mammoth gate of solid pearl.[22] Many other immortal Adamites also were entering along with them, traveling on translucent golden streets. They saw that the walls of the City were decorated with all kinds of gorgeous gems that refracted the light of Adonai and Yeshua in a kaleidoscope of colors. Once inside they could see millions and millions of Immortals—among them Antipas, Adam, and Caleb—along with innumerable Angels looking down from the magnificent walls and towers.

Antipas, seeing them immediately as they entered, was delighted that Ben and Kristiana had found the Key. For their part, they were amazed that they now had the ability to know and appreciate Antipas in a way that far exceeded the introduction they had to him in the Chronicles. This cognizance was a gift of their new existence, which surpassed all that they could have ever thought or imagined.[23]

Enchanted by the grandeur of the City and captivated by the King, Kristiana burst forth in euphoria: "His banner over me is love! I belong to my beloved, and his desire is for me. He has set me like a seal over his heart, like a seal on his arm. The flames of love are flames of fire, a blaze that comes from the King and not even mighty bodies of water or flooding rivers extinguish this love that I feel for him!"[24]

Ben was surprised to hear Adam speak to him—audibly or inaudibly, he did not know. As if they had always known each other, Adam shared with Ben his thoughts and desires. Ben expressed his feelings of amazing oneness with Adam.[25] "You are right!" Adam responded joyously.

"What do you mean?" asked Ben, not really surprised that Adam knew his mind; since the beginning of this perfect new life somehow he realized that all in Yeshua's kingdom would have this ability.[26] Still, it took some getting used to.

"Eve and I especially reveled in the moment of our new bodies—perhaps more than any other. She and I were the only two humans whose existence began in perfection. None of our sons and daughters ever knew what it was like to enter the world in perfect health, to have never felt pain or ever hungered. I radiated the light of Adonai from my creation, until I chose what he had forbidden.[27] For the rest of my days on the earth my soul was perturbed; oh, how I longed to be restored to perfection!"

Upon hearing this, Abraham, who was nearby, shared his insights: "It is like two men, one poor from birth and one rich from birth, who both fall on hard times. Neither is happy with his situation but since the poor man knows nothing but his poverty, for him, there is little change."

"Exactly!" Adam responded. "I knew what it was like to absorb the light and goodness of Adonai, so bearing the consequence of being deprived of his light was particularly painful for me."

"And later, when Moses was on the Mountain of Sinai," Abraham made the connection, "he was given only as much as he could handle because he was born corrupted."[28]

"Indeed." Adam completely understood the analogy. "Before I was corrupted I radiated the light of Adonai in its entirety. From the day that it began to fade, I longed for his light and goodness to be restored in me. But I was painfully aware that I would never be able to experience the fullness of his presence as long as I remained in a state of corruption."[29]

"Now I understand why you so wildly shouted for joy when Yeshua rescued you from the Abyss," Ben said.

"Now that everything has been accomplished," Adam said with satisfaction, "all those millennia I waited to receive my renewed body seem like only a moment."

Antipas appeared next to them. "Come," he said, "the end approaches." Instantly, all of them ascended a tower to see Lucifer and his hordes advancing.

37

The Beloved City Surrounded

LUCIFER THE SLANDERER, the dragon of old, and his hordes flowed like an ocean of ants over the broad plain of the earth, surrounding the dwellings of the Hebrews and the beloved City.[1] The rumble of their feet created dissonance with Adonai's joyful melodies permeating the air over the beloved City and being received with great jubilation, like a lover successfully wooing the heart of his beloved.[2]

Lucifer paid no attention to the sun setting behind him but focused squarely on the City ahead. He and his forces halted about a thousand feet from the open gates. Just as he had calculated during his confinement in the Abyss, no army was there to meet them because all weapons and warfare had long been banished.[3]

Bent on conquest, Lucifer broke into a malicious grin at the thought of finally beating his ancient foe. "Mark well this day," he boasted to the billions of Adamites and the Watchers behind him. "On this the tenth day of the one-thousand-and-first year since Yeshua established *his* kingdom, I shall at last establish *my* everlasting kingdom and Adonai's shall fall!"

Adam and the inhabitants of the New Jerusalem[4] stood on terraces of the City's lower towers, gazing many miles down upon the broad plain of the earth below.[5] He was dismayed to see that after more than one thousand years of Yeshua's reign, where justice had been like a sash around his waist and integrity like a belt around his hips,[6] so many of his mortal sons would listen to Lucifer, the slanderer, and attempt to oust Adonai from his own City.[7]

"The utter ingratitude they display toward their maker and rightful King is outrageous!" he exclaimed to Ben and all who were with him on the terrace. "Just as a furnace is for refining gold, Adonai is testing hearts[8] to expose those who remain defiant toward him, even after all these years of bliss. All who have paid attention to Lucifer's counsel have done so because they themselves are liars, eager to listen to Lucifer's slander!"[9] Adam shook his head sadly. "How foolish are those that follow the Adversary, for he can give them nothing but enslavement in darkness, despair, and death—as he did for six thousand years before Yeshua's kingdom was established."

Caleb looked down at Lucifer approaching the gates. He remembered many years ago, shortly after the commencement of Yeshua's kingdom, the day his son turned seven, that they had gone to the temple and offered an animal for him and his family to a priest, a son of Levi.

"Father," his oldest son had asked. "Why do we need to bring an offering every year? Didn't King Yeshua relinquish his own life-force long ago so that we could be with him?"

"After Adam's downfall," Caleb had explained, "the Covering made it possible for Adam and his progeny to be in close proximity to Adonai. The skin of the creature, which Adonai had killed, clothed their bodies with protection against the world that had become hostile toward them. But it was the life-force, the blood of the creature, which Adonai used to cover Adam and Eve, that permitted them a certain proximity to him.[10] It was like a force field, so called in the previous age in the study of physics, a shield of energy that protects a person or object from harmful effects. The covering from the life-force of the creature was used to temporarily shield the recipient from the fiery-lightning presence of Adonai. The creature which Adonai had caused to come up out of the dirt, the *adamáh*, was given in exchange for Adam and Eve so that they could draw near to Adonai.[11]

"Most of humanity refused to avail themselves of the Covering, though many who were wise did choose to use it. Some of those were Noah, Melchizedek, Abraham, Isaac, and Jacob. In the days of Moses, Adonai told him and the children of Jacob to make a copy, a shadow, of Adonai's throne room behind the veil.[12] He instructed that they make a veil of blue, purple, and scarlet and fine linen woven with a skillful design of cherubim.[13]

"Behind the veil Adonai manifested his fiery-lightning presence,[14] and once a year a special liaison, called a *kohen*, went in to bring the life-force as a Covering for many.[15] Before he could do that, however, he first had to prepare himself to go into the place where Adonai's fiery-lightning dwelt. Like a technician entering a cleanroom, the *kohen* had to be physically uncontaminated. He could not be ill or have any chronic disease,[16] nor could he have touched anything impure.[17] He had to bathe himself and put on specialized attire; he was not allowed to wear his regular clothing.[18] All of this preparation was necessary for his task, but yet insufficient. He still had to have a Covering for himself in order to create an energy shield[19] that would protect him from the fiery-lightning energy of Adonai."

"But why must we mortals now bring an offering year after year?" Caleb's son had persisted.

"You see, the Covering lasts only one year and thus must be continually repeated[20] because the life-force of the creature cannot in actuality reverse the effect of the treason that Adam committed."[21]

Caleb had continued to explain, "It was King Yeshua who cleared the debt incurred by Adam against our race when he died on the tree so that at the appointed time, all who thirst may partake of the Fountain of Life.

"After the new earth was created, Adonai decreed that all Adamites could live as mortals for one hundred years before choosing to become immortal.[22] A day is coming, however," Caleb had said, "when death will be done away with forever[23] and the Covering will end. No mortal will be able to remain in Adonai's presence, for the corruptible must put on incorruption, and this Adamite body *must* put on immortality or it shall be lost … forever."[24]

Ben apprehended Caleb's memory and understood the implications. It was then that he noticed Lucifer turn around to face the City.

Lucifer lifted his head up to Adonai's throne and spoke directly to him, knowing that Adonai could read his every thought. "You are about to have an insurmountable crisis on your hands when our feet cross over your precious gates and at that point, the earth will be mine forever, never to return into your hands. All of your options are exhausted. Nothing you do can stop me this time! Finally, after these seven millennia, my struggle with you, my irrational and unreasonable Maker, is at an end. I shall forever shake off the shackles of your[25] absurdly inverted kingdom, where the strong protect the weak and the older serve the younger![26]

"My patience has paid off for at last I shall have the freedom to rule as I see fit—'do as you will' shall be the whole of my law. Now prepare yourself, for I am about to rise in the sky far above your Angels. I will erect my throne and take my seat on your holy mountain—there in your great City, on the mountain of the assembly, on the farthest sides of the north.[27] I will ascend above the clouds, and there I will be second to none but equal with you in authority.[28]

"You have lost!" Lucifer shook his fist at Adonai. "We shall demonstrate you to be a liar and thus by virtue of your own word, which you have chosen to place above your name,[29] you will be forced into exile from your beloved City. You cannot simply undo the action I am about to take or you will be proven a liar—and if you can be proven a liar then you have no right to be ruler. Either way, you have lost! Now my authority can never be challenged and the entire cosmos will be mine forever."

At that moment, Adonai, shining like jasper, enthroned on the pinnacle of the city, simply laughed at Lucifer and the nations with him that would feebly attempt to dethrone him.[30]

"You were in Eden, my paradise,"[31] he said with a commanding voice that made Lucifer's sound like the squeaking of a mouse. "Everything I created was yours to enjoy.[32] Of all the Angels that I called into existence,[33] none was more wonderful than you. You served as the paradigm against which the others were measured. You were the sum of perfection, full of wisdom and perfect in beauty. I covered you with stones of dazzling colors and you had matchless splendor![34] I withheld no quality of beauty when I created you. I equipped you with tambourines and pipes so that you could make joyous and majestic music.[35]

"I entrusted you with everything. No Angel had more authority in my City than you.[36] I set you apart as the anointed Angel cherub; I placed you here, on my holy mountain, my City Jerusalem. You walked in the midst of the cherubim.[37] Despite all this you desired to rise higher still," Adonai declared.

"Of all my sons, you should have known that to be like me means assuming the role of a servant and giving of yourself to those with lesser abilities and riches—to those who can never repay you. In so doing, you would have been given greater honor, because all who humble themselves I have promised to exalt at the right time.[38] But pride has been your necklace and violence has covered you like a garment.[39] Harboring deceit within yourself, you have disguised the hate behind your words.[40] You have sought to exalt yourself, thinking only of your own life; yet you shall lose it in the end. And what profit is there in gaining the world and losing your life?[41]

"Through the abundance of your slandering you became filled with violence and committed treason those seven thousand years ago.[42] And by your endless defamation[43] of my good name and character, you persuaded many of my sons, my Angels, to turn against me.[44] You plotted and executed the death of Adam and Eve, whom I redeemed. Your role, and that of all of the Angels, was to watch over them[45] and guide and assist them as needed.[46] They afforded you an opportunity to choose to love by serving someone lesser and weaker than yourself. Had you chosen to do so, you would have discovered that there is no greater joy than to give,[47] for it truly is more blessed to give than to receive. But you refused to learn from me and thus forfeited the opportunity to be like me."

"The greater serving the lesser is foolish!"[48] retorted Lucifer. "Adam should be serving *me*!" Then with a roar like a fierce lion he defied Adonai: "We will not have this One to rule over us!"[49] and thrust his hand toward the sky.

These pompous words energized the rebel forces like a shockwave. Lucifer then led the charge toward the City gates; his disfigured reptilian Watchers were close behind, followed by Korah and his rebels from the village of Koinonia. They were running and shouting with all their might in wild anticipation of taking the City.

38
The Moment of Truth

ADONAI'S HOLY ANGELS, with implacable faces, followed orders not to engage the enemy, not to speak to them or try to resist them.

Adonai looked from the height of his sanctuary down upon the earth and saw all the Adamites who had joined Lucifer[1] rushing toward the open gates of the City. For long ages Adonai had stretched out his hands to an obstinate people, who walked in a way that was not good, following their own devices and provoking him to his face continually. He scoffed at them, knowing they had sealed their fate. "These are smoke in my nostrils," Adonai said, impervious to the sheer number of forces coming against him.[2]

The last rays of the setting sun disappeared when the rebel hordes were approximately thirty feet from the gates of the City. One year had passed since Lucifer had been released from the Abyss. It was finally time for him to attempt the coup he had so painstakingly planned.

Also, in keeping with the provision of Adonai, it was time for the efficacy of the Covering, instituted exactly one year earlier, to expire.[3] That Covering was what made it possible for those who had not taken of the River of Life and of the Tree of Life, and thereby received new bodies, to survive even in proximity to the fire of the King.

But now the clock ran out. When the last second ticked off—at that very instant—the Covering, which had been as it were a force field protecting each person from Adonai, suddenly evaporated.

Without warning, as Lucifer and his myriad followers were on the verge of crossing the threshold of the City, Adonai easily breathed out lightning bolts and tongues of electrified fire that swept over the unsuspecting hordes like a curtain of blistering liquid with the intensity of many suns.

The fire of Adonai also scorched the monstrous spirit-body of Lucifer. As the fire swept over his sunken cheeks and eye sockets, obscuring his pitch black almond-shaped eyes, and then spread over his shriveled arms and legs, he remembered that he had once been a burning one,[4] a flame of fire,[5] with Adonai's light radiating from him.[6] How he hated Adonai, who had removed the glorious fire from within him and was now tormenting him with that very same fire!

Lucifer crumpled to the ground in a ruinous heap, writhing in pain, cinders flaking off his body, as the whole world watched.[7] Michael, Gabriel, Adam, the Twenty-four Elders, all of the mighty Angels, and every immortal, including Ben and Kristiana, all were appalled and horrified to see how his shameless self-exaltation had caused him, who had appeared so appealing, to become visibly loathsome and disgusting.[8]

An Angel descended from the City and picked him up, writhing in agony from Adonai's fire, and took him to Tophet, a broad and deep burial pit prepared specifically for Lucifer millennia before. Therion and Oracle along with all those who had taken the mark of Therion[9] were already there, where they had been tortured by the breath of Adonai and the blast of his anger day and night for the previous thousand years. This would continue to be their fate forever and ever.[10]

Looking down into Tophet Lucifer frantically assessed the reality before him: his great name and memory would indeed be blotted out—he who was all-wise in his own eyes, the one who had been the sum of perfection,[11] the one who was convinced that everyone else should serve him!

The Angel opened his hand and released Lucifer as if he were rubbish, a useless piece of straw. "No!" he shrieked. The defeated usurper could not stand the thought that all the nations now saw him come to a dreadful end; he would be no more forever.[12] "I am like the Most High!" he absurdly maintained even while plunging into the pit.

There, in Tophet, where there was wailing and gnashing of teeth,[13] this prideful one would forever be debased. There, for all eternity, the inhabitants of the new heavens and the new earth—from one New Moon to another and from one Sabbath to another—would go out and look upon him, now the lowest of the low, and the corpses of all who were guilty of malfeasance against Adonai being tormented in the fire that is never quenched and consumed by worms that never die.[14]

Adonai's army of Angels hastily retrieved and then deposited into the Tophet the smoldering, ashen bodies of the rebels who had all been instantly incinerated by Adonai's fire on every side of the City.[15]

"And thus ends Lucifer's rebellion!" Adam shouted ecstactically. "All who had the audacity to march against the King with wicked intent are now like stubble. Lucifer, in his overweening arrogance and unbridled ambition, and those who followed him disregarded the very essence of Adonai—he examines the righteous but hates the wicked and those who love violence. He radiates lightning and fire[16] and rains burning coals and sulfur on the wicked; a scorching wind is their destiny!"[17]

With Lucifer deposited into the pit, Adonai gave the command and bodies began to rise up out of the ground and from under the waters. The sea gave up the dead who were in it, and Death and Hades delivered up the dead in them.[18] It was the appointed time for the dead Adamites to be raised to everlasting shame and contempt.[19]

Their bodies all floated rapidly toward the massive white throne of Yeshua,[20] whom Adonai had authorized to be the judge of all.[21] Yeshua sat gloriously before his millions of servants,[22] and the Twenty-four Elders were all around him.[23] Millions and millions of raised Adamites, some of them formerly weak and some once great and mighty while they had lived on the earth, stood trembling in terror before Yeshua,[24] the very One from whose face earth and heaven had rolled up like a scroll and fled away when he saved the Hebrews.[25]

Several Angels stood close to the throne, holding the voluminous books by which the dead were to be judged according to their works as written in the official record.[26]

The inhabitants of Chorazin, Bethsaida, and Capernaum, in agonizing fear before Yeshua, his eyes like flaming fire, thought of the many miracles he had performed in their midst and how they had refused to accept him and repent. Had Yeshua performed those same miracles in Sodom, it would have remained; yet the inhabitants of these cities had rejected Yeshua and now their penalty was due.[27]

There before the throne were also the rich man who had called out to Abraham from the netherworld[28] and the traitor Judas who had betrayed Yeshua with a kiss.[29] Many who in the previous life had been great kings and warriors enjoying honor and riches were now brought one by one before the noble and exalted King to be judged—each one according to his own actions.[30]

Everyone before the throne who had known what was required of him—what the Master wanted—yet failed to prepare himself would receive a greater condemnation; the one who erred in ignorance, a lesser condemnation.[31]

An Angel standing next to the throne verified for all the

dead present that their names were not found in the Book of Life; therefore, bare and exposed to the stream of fire that proceeded from Yeshua's throne,[32] they all collapsed in excruciating pain. Swiftly the holy Angels came to retrieve and transport these who were to join Lucifer in Tophet, the lake of fire.[33] Many Angels made many trips until all the dead had been judged and removed from the presence of Yeshua.

"The age of choosing in opposition to the wishes of Adonai has now ended!" Adam announced to Ben, Kristiana, Caleb, Antipas, and his other companions on top of the tower, all marveling at what Yeshua had done. "Never again will anyone choose contrary to his wishes, for the only remaining options are those that are wholly aligned with the desire of Adonai. His torrent of fire and his surging power envelop everything so that those who have put on the garment of *yeshuáh* rejoice, and those who have not—those without his Covering—writhe in agony.

"Lucifer and his Angels will be no more forever.[34] Everyone who has refused to welcome and embrace the love of Yeshua has forfeited his own life, despite the many solemn warnings Adonai gave because of his patience.[35] Even Death and the Abyss[36] have been cast into the fiery torrent."[37] Adam's mind retraced the past seven thousand years plus one, starting with his rebellion in the Garden —which had resulted in his death and Lucifer's dominion over the earth—and through the ages up to this, the most triumphant moment of all time, when the eternal purpose was fulfilled and the power of Death was vanquished.[38]

"Even though Adonai is self-existent, all-powerful, and all-knowing," Adam expounded, "his humble nature made him stoop to wash the feet of those closest to him, as an example, so that they would do the same for one another. But Lucifer, the great Slanderer, refused to 'wash the feet' of others[39] for he was more interested in saving his own life, honor, and rank," said Adam, looking toward Tophet.

"He was unwilling to lose those things he valued in order to serve lesser beings. If he had been willing to humble himself, however, he would have gained the full satisfaction that can be found only in obedience."

"Joy!" Kristiana exclaimed in appreciation of what she herself had gained. "What profit could there be in having all of the material things Adonai created without drawing near to him and having a relationship with him?"[40]

"Adonai knew that to cherish oneself more than others would lead only to destruction," said Ben, contemplating Lucifer's end.

"Thus, you see," Adam continued, "being subservient to Adonai was not enough; beyond that is the need to follow his example of servanthood. That is the path of life and obedience, for which we receive honor from Adonai ... "[41]

"... and in his presence," said Eve, finishing Adam's sentence, "we have fullness of joy and pleasures at his right hand forevermore!"[42]

39

Jubilee

A GREAT TRUMPET blast filled the air announcing the beginning of Jubilee. "Come on!" Adam said to Ben, Kristiana, Caleb, Antipas, and all who had stood with him on the tower. They were being called to ascend to the apex of the City.

Ben looked incredulously at Kristiana who shrugged and smiled gamely as if to say, "Let's go!" Together, they rose effortlessly into the air. Basking in the gentle wind they could feel on their faces and reveling in their freedom from the bonds of earth, they went up and up, higher and higher, to the loftiest platform of the City.

There Ben and Kristiana beheld a most glorious sight— the throne of Adonai surrounded by the Twenty-four Elders. Already, a thousand million Adamites and Angels were standing or hovering around the throne. All eyes were fixed on the one seated upon it as everyone awaited what was about to take place.

Yeshua then stood up before his father's throne. Turning toward it, he stretched out his arms, palms open, and declared triumphantly: "Father, I have put an end to all rival thrones, dominions, principalities, and powers. I have put every rebel under my feet, and finally I have destroyed death, the last enemy!"[1]

Ben was overcome with awe as he thought about the incredible work Yeshua had accomplished and the amazing obstacles he had overcome along the way.

"Father, I now deliver to you the kingdom, all power and authority,[2] and all things, which you placed under my feet,[3] that you may be all in all!"

Upon hearing these words, which greatly pleased the Father, every single voice resounded in praise to the King. Ben was intrigued that he could sing powerfully, in perfect harmony, and also distinguish the unique sound of every other individual voice among the billions of worshipers before the throne.

Hallelu-Yah! *Hallelu* Adonai from heaven; praise him in the highest places. *Halleluhu*, all his Angels; praise him, all his armies! *Hallelu* Adonai, you heaven of heavens, and you waters above the heavens. *Hallelu-Yah*, sun and moon; praise him, all you shining stars.[4]

Then another strain could be heard, complementing the first:

Sing to Adonai, all the earth! Sing to Adonai! Praise his name! Announce every day how he rescues, how his right hand and his mighty arm accomplish deliverance! Tell the nations about his splendor! Tell all the nations about his amazing deeds![5]

Still another was added, amplifying the first two:

Ascribe to Adonai the splendor and majesty he deserves! Adonai reigns! Worship him in holy attire! Tremble before him, all the earth. Let the rivers clap their hands! Let the mountains sing in unison before Adonai![6] The world is established, it cannot be moved. He has judged the nations with fairness.[7]

The glad song was sustained for five days, from Yom Kippur to Sukkot, but it seemed to be not nearly enough. When Adam, Ben, Kristiana, and the others returned to the earth, still rejoicing over the final victory, they were delighted to find that nothing remained which could defile outside the gates of the City!

Adam looked out at the multitude of his descendants. "Adonai did it, just as he promised! He has made us all to be like him, not only in his glorious appearance but also in his qualities of joy, peace, patience, and kindness ... "

"Yes, and goodness, faithfulness, gentleness, and self-control ..."[8] Eve chimed in.

"And, of course, his greatest quality," Kristiana added, "which is love!"

"We are all like him," she continued, pursuing Adam's train of thought; "we are all conformed to his glorious body and are partakers of the divine nature. And we are all conformed to his character![9] How amazing it is to think that now not even one person in the kingdom is looking out for his own interests above the interests of others."

Ben heartily agreed. "We are individuals, yet we are like-minded, having the same love, being of one heart and one mind. Nothing is ever done through selfish ambition or conceit; rather, in lowliness of mind, each one esteems others as better than himself. We all have put on tender mercies, kindness, humility, meekness, and patience."[10]

Eve added her insights: "None of us think more highly of ourselves than we ought to.[11] None of us are prideful because of what we have received, as Lucifer was! How could we not recognize that tangible gifts are simply expressions of love from Adonai?"

At that point everyone intuitively knew that Adam was wanting to speak; so they gladly gave him, their formerly carbon-based father, the opportunity.

"We now possess all the qualities that Adonai desired to pass on to us in the first place. Forever will he be infinitely greater than we, his creatures, yet we all now possess qualities similar to his own so that he can relate to us as friends and companions. It is his good pleasure, moreover, to give us the kingdom!"[12]

Adam lifted his eyes to the pinnacle of the City where Adonai's throne was. "I now understand that even though Adonai has always been highly exalted, he has nonetheless paid attention to the low and humble among us who were originally made of dust."[13]

It now began to make sense to Adam why Adonai had not simply destroyed him when he rebelled—or Lucifer either, for that matter. "Adonai is love!" he shouted, overcome by the fullness of Adonai's goodness. "Now everyone's heart is loving like Adonai's; so we are constantly patient and kind. We are never envious or boastful or proud or rude and, like Adonai, we do not demand our own way. As our example, when he walked on the earth he was not arrogant or irritable; he kept no record of wrongs committed against him; he was never glad about injustice but rejoiced whenever truth won out—qualities we now fully share!"

Eve fully shared in Adam's satisfaction. "The love of Adonai remained steadfast through seven thousand years of adverse circumstances,[14] and now he has made us like himself," she said, looking over the vast multitude of their descendants. "Forevermore we will each reflect on only what is true, honorable, and fair; on what is pure, acceptable, and commendable; on what is excellent and worthy of praise."[15]

The others were silent as Adam considered the nature of their relationship with Adonai: "As our creator, he has not demanded submission and obedience nor has he lorded his power, authority, and prerogative over us. Never has he forced anyone to adore him. He has not demanded his own way,[16] and no one in the kingdom is here under compulsion."

Adam paused as the implication of what he had just said sank in. "What it means is that everyone here has freely chosen to be with him and to be his friend."

This realization had such a profound impact on Adam that he then mouthed, as if speaking to himself: "Adonai has a kingdom full of servants by our own choosing! The very thing that Lucifer rebelled against—serving someone weaker than himself as an expression of love—is something that we have freely chosen. Everyone in the kingdom is fully and willingly in harmony with Adonai. All of us are sympathetic, humble, and compassionate.[17] We cherish one another as brothers and we love one another intensely, with pure hearts,[18] so that Adonai himself can now make his home with us and dwell with all of us. He will walk among us as our King and as our friend!"[19]

40
A Walk in the Garden

ADAM SUDDENLY SAW Adonai walking toward him and Eve, an engaging smile beaming from his brilliant face. "There you are! I recall that awhile ago we were about to go for a walk. Would you care to join me?"

Adam and Eve grinned at his wit. "Yes, of course; we would be delighted!"[1]

Adonai then looked at Ben, Kristiana, Caleb, Abraham, and countless more of his friends. "Walk with me!" he invited. In a way that only he could do, Adonai was with each of them individually and personally, and yet all were together at the same time. Somehow it did not seem as if one became lost in the crowd.

They walked leisurely through the lush green garden just outside the City. It was full of giant redwoods, expansive ferns, and an abundance of flowers of every hue, exuding all kinds of fragrant aromas. The flora glowed more brightly as Adonai approached. Mockingbirds, nightingales, robins and other songbirds sang overhead, and their arboreal companions—squirrels, sloths, monkeys, and raccoons—intently watched the giver of life pass by.[2] Everything that had breath sang its own harmonious song in honor of the great King.[3] David the prince, great musician that he was, also heard and was enraptured.

Eve stopped to admire a hillside of roses she had never seen before. Bowing down to breathe in their fragrance, she smiled at Adonai in appreciation of the sweet aroma he had given them. "I knew you would like it," he smiled lovingly back at her. Then Eve saw a tree with thousands of beautiful blue morpho butterflies like the ones she had enjoyed in the Garden of Eden. Ben saw them too and remembered how Adonai had incorporated them into his own story as well.

He will never leave us nor forsake us, Ben thought.

When they came to the dwelling place of the great elephants, Adam started scratching the top of the tongues of the great creatures, which he happened to discover that they loved[4] while still in the Garden.

Adonai and his friends laughed heartily.

"Why did you make them like that?" Ben could not help asking.

Adonai simply shrugged and said with a playful smile, "For my good pleasure—and yours as well!"

As they continued along, the conversation turned to the memory of their former trials, how difficult they had been at the time and how Adonai had worked all things together for good. Now they were merely distant memories seen as insignificant in comparison with the refining effect they had on every single person's character.

Ben could only smile at the delight he was experiencing. The sufferings of the past were not worthy to be compared with the glory that has been revealed to us."[5] Ben suddenly sensed Paul, the one whom Yeshua had so greatly used in the previous age; speak directly to his mind: "The light, temporary nature of our suffering has produced for us an everlasting weight of glory, far beyond any comparison!" he said.[6] "Being here with Adonai, with you, and with everyone, was worth every trial that I endured."

The friends of Adonai were so filled with joy over the vast and endless pleasures before them that they often would burst into a chorus of gratitude for Adonai's mighty works to the children of men.[7] As a human father found enjoyment in his children's musical expression, so likewise Adonai took pleasure in his sons' and daughters' songs of praise.

They continued walking until they came to a place no one had seen before. They all stopped and studied the ark of Noah, making all sorts of new discoveries while Adonai watched them with great satisfaction.[8]

Further along the way, Caleb stopped to admire a pride of lions. He walked up to one of them and stroked it between the ears. As the giant feline purred, he turned to Adonai and said, "I have always loved the playfulness of cats, no matter their size!" He remembered the many cats of Jerusalem in the previous age.

As Caleb started to pet the cat's stomach, it suddenly reared up, thrust back its ears, and pounced on Caleb as if playing a game of cat and mouse in which he was the mouse! Knocking him to the ground, it then began to lick his face with its rough tongue. Adonai laughed as Caleb tussled with the big kitty. Another lion joined in by jumping on Ben.

"Did you make him do that?" bantered Ben, pushing the other lion off of him.

"No!" Adonai shook his head, still laughing.

Ben and Caleb together charged Adonai. Growling and pretending to be lions, they jumped on him like children[9] attempting to get on their dad's back. Adonai enjoyed humoring them and then they all collapsed into laughter.[10]

Those who witnessed all this rejoiced at the thought of forever being with their gracious father, who had loved them so much he was willing to send Yeshua so that everyone who believed in him could be here.[11]

After the laughter subsided, Adonai looked each of his precious children in the eye and whispered, "I love you! I am glad that you are mine."[12]

A few moments later, Ben, still lying on the ground, looked up into the sky and saw trillions of stars. "Do you really know each of them by name?" he asked.

Adonai nodded his head affirmatively.

"Will you explain to me how that is?"

"Come, Ben-Yamin; I have much to show you! And to all who desire to know, I say, 'Come!'"

Epilogue

The Path of Destiny

"ANTIPAS," SAID BEN, as they walked on one of the golden streets in the midst of the City many decades after Lucifer's final rebellion. "I had to walk on the King's Highway and be transformed by taking of the Water of Life and the leaves of the Tree of Life to enter into the City. How was it that you were able to enter when those things were not accessible to you in your mortal lifetime?"

"I heard the message that Yeshua had died and rose again for my misdeeds, for my sins. I realized that I had disobeyed his directives many, many times and that by myself I would never be able to overcome my evil. So I accepted the fact that Yeshua shed his blood as a payment sufficient to cover my wrongdoing. My acceptance was all that was necessary to get a new body so that I could stand in his fiery-lightning presence."

"But you were not able to actually go to see Yeshua in your mortal lifetime," Ben contemplated.

"True; I lived and died in expectation of the future resurrection. In fact, everyone who lived in that era had the opportunity to live and die with the expectation of resurrection. Ben, every person who has ever lived is a part of the Chronicles, which have no end. Adonai has invited each one to join him, to be a part of his kingdom, to have a place at his table, to receive a new body, and to walk with him forever."

"What was necessary in the previous age for people to secure their place in Adonai's kingdom?"

"It was very simple. They had to choose between one of two paths: the path of life or the path of death," Antipas answered Ben.

"To gain access to the path of life, a person had to admit how he or she had broken the directives—the commandments of Adonai, repent from such evil, and ask Yeshua the great son of Adonai, our King and Savior, for a pardon.[1] Those who were wise would seek out this path."

"Choosing the path of life was to follow in the footsteps of Peter, Paul, Moses, David, and countless others. On that path a person would be in Adonai's presence, where there is fullness of joy and at his right hand pleasures forevermore,"[2] he said, motioning toward the glories of the City.

"Of course," Antipas continued, "a person could also choose to reject Adonai, the rightful King. By refusing to turn from his evil but, rather, doing what was right in his own eyes, he was deceiving himself and ultimately choosing the path of death."

"And choosing that path," Ben surmised, "would be to follow in the footsteps of Lucifer, Therion, Oracle, Korah, and all who rebelled."

"Correct!" Antipas answered. "And none returned who ventured to go that way, nor did they reach the path of life."[3]

"The path they chose led to everlasting shame and contempt,"[4] Ben said as he reflected on Lucifer's ultimate demise.

Antipas looked out from the City to the earth below and thought of all the people in the previous age who had come to the same crossroads. "Everyone, including myself, had to choose. As it is written in the Chronicles, 'Heaven and earth are witnesses today against you, that Adonai has set before you life and death, blessing and cursing. Choose life!'"[5]

ENDNOTES

Prologue

1 Ps 19:1-3; 148:3, 6; Isa 30:26; 24:23
2 Jer 31:35-37; Rev 21:2
3 Ps 48:2; Isa 14:13
4 Isa 54:11-13
5 Isa 30:25
6 Isa 41:18-20; 65:17
7 Zeph 3:17

Chapter 1

1 Mat 13:43
2 Dan 10:6-7
3 Rev 19:8
4 Dan 12:3; Luke 20:35-36; Phil 3:21; 2Tim 4:8; 2Pet 1:4
5 Ezek 40:6-16; 42:16-20
6 Rev 22:1-2, 14; Ezek 47:1
7 Rev 4:6
8 Ps 46:4
9 Zech 14:8, 10; Joel 3:18; Ezek 47:1
10 2Kgs 6:17
11 Isa 14:15
12 Jude 1:6; 2Pet 2:4
13 Rev 16:10
14 Rev 9:1-2
15 Rev 20:1-2
16 Heb 2:14, 15
17 Rev 1:18
18 Rev 5:3, 5
19 Isa 14:11
20 Rev 20:1-3
21 Isa 11:3-5
22 Jer 17:9
23 Ps 2:3
24 Rev 20:7-8
25 Num 23:19
26 Ps 138:2
27 Isa 14:13
28 1Pet 5:8
29 2Cor 11:14
30 Rev 9:1-2
31 Rom 1:29
32 Isa 11:6-9
33 Ezek 28:12-18
34 Ps 82:1
35 Ezek 28:14, 16
36 Gen 3:6
37 Jas 1:14-15
38 Prov 10:18; Rom 1:30; 2Tim 3:3; 1Pet 2:1; Col 3:8
39 Ps 36:8-9
40 Jer 2:13; Zech 14:8, 10

Chapter 2

1 John 8:44
2 Rev 2:13
3 Phil 2:4
4 Isa 65:22
5 Rev 20:6
6 Isa 2:3; Zech 8:21
7 Mic 4:3
8 Isa 65:21; Gen 3:19
9 Isa 43:18; Isa 65:20; Zech 13:1
10 John 3:19
11 Rom 1:30
12 Mark 9:35; 10:44; 1Cor 1:18
13 Isa 14:12-14; 66:4
14 Gen 2:7
15 Ps 8
16 Ps 104:4
17 Heb 1:14
18 Ezek 28:12-19
19 Mark 9:35; 10:44; Heb 1:14
20 In 1923 Ukrainian biologist Alexander Gurwitsh discovered that living things such as onions and yeast produce an ultra-weak photon emission. This discovery was confirmed circa 1950 by Russian scientists who identified an "ultraweak photon emission" from living organisms, and was further confirmed independently of the previous finding by Italian nuclear physicists L. Colli et al., who in 1955 "by chance discovered a 'bioluminescence' of seedlings." See also Douglas Hamp, *Corrupting the Image,* Defender Publishing, 2011, p. 58
21 Prov 13:9; 20:20; 24:20; Job 18:5; 21:17; Dan 12:3; Mat 13:43; Rev 19:8; Gen 3:8
22 Exod 34:29-33
23 Rom 6:10; Heb 9:28; 1Pet 3:18
24 Heb 6:6
25 2Tim 4:10

Chapter 3

1 Judg 17:6
2 1Kgs 6:15
3 Isa 66:23
4 Zech 14:16
5 Acts 5:3-11
6 John 12:32
7 Prov 6:17

[8] Lev 10:2; Isa 65:20; 66:24; Ps 97:3; 2Thes 1:8
[9] Zech 14:17-19
[10] Mat 11:30
[11] Isa 11:4
[12] Ps 2:3

Chapter 4

[1] Dan 10:6
[2] Ezek 28:12-18
[3] Prov 18:17
[4] Prov 22:1
[5] Ps 2:9; Rev 2:27; 12:5; 19:15
[6] 1Cor 2:15
[7] 1Cor 11:31
[8] Heb 5:14
[9] Jud 17:6
[10] Gen 25:23
[11] Heb 1:14
[12] Ps 146:9; Mat 5:44-46; Jas 1:27
[13] Mat 20:16
[14] Mark 9:35
[15] Ezek 28:12-16
[16] Prov 26:28
[17] Luke 4:5
[18] Job 40, 41
[19] Ps 148:2-6
[20] Ezek 28:12
[21] The first part of chapter 28 penned by the prophet Ezekiel is about a prince of Tyre, and the latter part of the chapter speaks of him who ruled Tyre in the spiritual realm—that is the true king of Tyre, who is Lucifer. The tenth chapter of the prophet Daniel describes how an angel of the Lord was withstood by the prince of Persia and also the kings of Persia. Michael went to help him, for he had been struggling alone for twenty-one days with the kings of Persia, who are angels. Angels are greater in power and might (2Pet 2:11) than humans. One angel was able to destroy 185,000 Assyrian warriors in one night (2Kings 19:35). Since one angel would easily be able to escape from ten human kings, the ten Persian kings thus must have been supernatural. The king of Tyre is the principality behind the earthly city of Tyre.
[22] Ezek 28:12-13
[23] Here Daniel is visited by an angel (clearly not Jesus, God himself, for this angel was withstood for some time by the prince of Persia and by the kings of Persia).

[24] Dan 10:5-15
[25] Ezek 28:12-13; Isa 14:11
[26] Ezek 28:12. Dr. Bill Gallagher has positively demonstrated that the Hebrew *Heilel* is synonymous with the Akkadian *Ellil/Lucifer* and Sumerian *Enlil*. In his article *On the Identity of Helel Ben Sahar of Isaiah 14:12-15* he shows that the Hebrew *Heilel* is equivalent phonetically to the Akkadian *Lucifer* (or *Ellil*). He states: "One could reasonably expect *hll* to be the West Semitic form of *Lucifer*. As the Ebla tablets suggest, *Heilel* came into West Semitic directly from Sumerian." W. R. Gallagher, UF 26 (1994), pp. 131–46. (Isa 14:12)
[27] The original Hebrew *khashmal* has been variously translated as color of amber (KJV), bronze (ISV), or gleaming metal (ESV 2011). The Theological Wordbook of the Old Testament translates the word as "a shining substance, amber or electrum." *Electricity* is a fair translation. Also, according to the Treasury of Scripture Knowledge, "Amber is a hard, inflammable, bituminous substance of a beautiful yellow color, very transparent, and susceptible of an exquisite polish. When rubbed, it is highly endowed with electricity; a name which the moderns have formed from its Greek name [*elektron*]" (TSK, Ezek 8:2).
[28] Ezek 1:4-14
[29] Ezek 28:18
[30] John 14
[31] Deut 4:19
[32] Isa 42:8
[33] Deut 4:16-1
[34] Heb 1:14
[35] Mat 6:24
[36] Rom 3:14

Chapter 5

[1] Ps 48:1-3
[2] Isa 54:11-12
[3] Ps 48:12-13
[4] Rev 21:16
[5] Isa 65:20
[6] Gen 18:23
[7] Gen 19
[8] Ps 82:1
[9] Rev 21:10
[10] Exod 24:9-10; Ezek 1:26
[11] Rev 4:5
[12] Isa 24:23

[13] Ezek 1:13-14
[14] Dan 7:9-10
[15] Ezek 1:26
[16] Gen 1:26
[17] Exod 24:9-10; Ps 94:9; Isa 66:2
[18] Ezek 1:26-28
[19] Dan 7:9-10
[20] Isa 24:23; Rev 21:23
[21] Rev 4:3
[22] Rev 22:1
[23] Rev 4:6
[24] Ps 46:4
[25] Rev 14:4
[26] Isa 6:3-4
[27] Rev 4:5-11
[28] Ezek 2:1; Dan 10:11; Exod 12:8; John 15:15
[29] Rev 20:3, 8
[30] Ps 2:3
[31] Rom 1:20-25; John 8:44
[32] Ezek 18:23-24
[33] 1Tim 2:4
[34] John 8:32
[35] Rev 20:2; Dan 7:10
[36] John 8:44
[37] Isa 35:8
[38] 2Pet 1:4
[39] Zech 13:1
[40] Ezek 47:12; Rev 22:2
[41] Rev 22:14
[42] Isa 6:1-8; Ezek 1:26-28

Chapter 6

[1] Deut 9:1
[2] Ezek 27:25
[3] Exod 32:1-8; 19:8
[4] Ezek 37:25
[5] Deut 9:6
[6] Exod 32:9
[7] Num 14:11-12
[8] Deut 12:31; 18:10; 2Kgs 16:3; 17:17; 21:6; Ezek 16:21
[9] Prov 26:28
[10] Isa 49:23
[11] Isa 60:6
[12] Isa 61:6
[13] Isa 60:10-12; Rev 21:25-26

Chapter 7

[1] Rev 20:7-9
[2] Dan 10
[3] Zech 14:17
[4] Zech 14:16-19
[5] Heb 13:2
[6] Isa 65:24
[7] John 3:19-21

[8] Isa 35:8-10
[9] Ps 2:9

Chapter 8

[1] They are referred to as Angels and *angeloi* (messengers) as well as cherubim and seraphim (fiery ones— seemingly a variation of cherubim). Their creation took place sometime after the initial creation of the heavens and the earth, though the exact moment is not abundantly clear in the manuscripts.
[2] Ps 148:1, 2; Gen 6:1-4; Job 1:6; 38:7
[3] Ezek 1:26-28; Dan 7:9-10
[4] Ps 104:2
[5] 1Tim 6:16; Heb 10:27; Exod 24:17; Num 11:1; 16:35; Deut 4:24; 9:3; Ps 50:3; 97:3; Isa 66:15; Dan 7:9; 2Thes 1:8; Ex 33:20
[6] Gen 1:26
[7] Ps 104:1-4
[8] Ps 148:2-6
[9] Dan 10:1-6; Rev 22:8
[10] Rev 10:1; 22:8-9
[11] Jude 1:9; Rev 22:9
[12] Isa 46:9
[13] Dan 12:1
[14] There were things that he and the other Angels could learn through experiencing life; likewise, there were things that they desired to look into (1Pet 1:12) and there were things yet to be revealed (Eph 3:9-10). Therefore, God created the Angels while he was still forming the earth. They sang and rejoiced as they beheld the creator transform the topsy-turvy watery mass into a solid ball of dirt, forming the foundations of the planet, and then stretch a line upon it (Job 38:4-7, Gen 1:9-10); that is, the point at which night and day meet, casting a line upon its face. Michael, Lucifer, and the other Angels had great reason to be continually in awe of God, and of the things which he decreed and established that would never pass away— the sun, moon, and stars (Ps 148:3-6), the planet (Ps 78:69) and everything in it, along with the seas and everything in them—as well as the life he would keep on giving (Neh 9:6). Truly, heaven and the highest heavens could not contain God (1Kgs 8:27).

[15] Seraphim literally means "burning ones" (Ps 104:4; Heb 1:7; Isa 6:2; Rev 4:8; Ezek 28:12).

[16] Ezek 1:13

[17] Ezek 28:12-13; Isa 14:11

[18] The stones of fire were described by one of the prophets of the Archives while he sat by the river Chebar, in the land of Babel and saw a great storm coming toward him from the north, driving before it a huge cloud that flashed with lightning and shone with brilliant light. The fire inside the cloud glowed with electricity.

[19] Ezek 1:4-14

[20] Ezek 28:18

[21] Gen 39:8-9; Ezek 28:14, 16; 1Tim 3:1, 6; Titus 1:7-8

[22] Ezek 28:14; Ps 48:1; Heb 12:22

[23] Ps 148:6

[24] Ps 104:14, 17-18; Gen 1:11-25

[25] The Theological Wordbook of the Old Testament defines and describes the connection between Adam and the soil: 'ădāmâ, ground, land, planet. Originally this word signified the red arable soil…. The Bible makes much of the interrelationship between man ('ādām) and the ground ('ădāmâ). That this might be vivid in the mind of the reader we will transliterate the words in the following discussion. Initially, God made 'ādām out of the 'ădāmâ to till the 'ădāmâ (Gen 3:23, to bring forth life). The 'ădāmâ was God's possession and under his care (Gen 2:6). Thus, the first 'ādām (the man, Adam) and his family were to act as God's servants by obeying him in maintaining the divinely created and intended relationships vertically and horizontally. As long as this condition was sustained, God caused the 'ădāmâ to give its fruitfulness (blessing) to 'ādām. Then came sin. The unit 'ādām (Adam and Eve; see also (Rom 5:12) violated the created structure. The 'ădāmâ, henceforth, rather than freely giving fruit brought forth thorns and thistles (Gen 3:17). Since 'ādām had disrupted the perfect paradisiacal life-producing state, he was driven off the paradisiacal 'ădāmâ and sentenced to return to the 'ădāmâ (Gen 3:19). He was driven to it rather than it being given to him" (TWOT, 'ădāmâ).

[26] The manuscripts don't specifically state this, but in light of the fact that the Angels rejoiced at the foundation of the planet (Job 38:6-7), they must certainly have witnessed the creation of Adam as well.

[27] Gen 2:7

[28] Read *Corrupting the Image* for a detailed explanation of biophotons and Adám's body of light. A free chapter is available at www.douglashamp.com.

[29] John 20:22

[30] Gen 1:26; Ps 24

[31] Ps 48:1; 132:13; Isa 2:2; 25:7; 62:5, Ezek 28:14, 16; 40:2; Zech 8:3; Joel 3:17; Mic 4:1; Heb 12:22; Rev 3:12; 14:1; 21:10

[32] Jas 1:15

[33] Isa 14:12-14

[34] Ps 82:1

[35] Ezek 28:12-14

[36] Mark 9:35; 10:44; 1Cor 1:18

[37] Isa 66:4. Though the ancient manuscripts of the Bible do not indicate precise reasoning, it can be construed from the totality of the texts, as I have attempted to do. The actual event must have been even more subtle and compelling than I am able to portray.

[38] Job 31:16-17, 21; Ps 146:9; Mat 25:36; Mark 9:35; James 1:27

[39] Dan 4:17

[40] Ps 91:11; 103:20; Dan 6:22; Mat 4:11

[41] Ezek 28:14, 16; 1Tim 3:1, 6; Titus 1:7-8

[42] Jas 1:17

[43] Rom 12:4

[44] Rom 12:1, 3

[45] Jas 3:14-17; Ezek 28:16-17

[46] Prov 18:12

[47] Prov 16:18

[48] 2Sam 15:4

[49] Jas 1:15

[50] The word *rakhal* means "to go back and forth" and is the root of the word Lucifer ("slanderer").

[51] Ps 148:6

[52] 2Pet 2:11

[53] Deut 4:19

[54] Deut 4:16-18

[55] Isa 42:8

[56] Heb 1:14

[57] Rom 3:13

[58] Prov 6:19; 10:18; 26:24

[59] Prov 10:12; Rev 12:4

[60] Ezek 28:16

[61] Rev 12:4

Chapter 9

1 Rev 19:8
2 Dan 10:6-7
3 Mat 13:43
4 Phil 3:21
5 2Pet 1:4; Luke 20:35-36; Dan 12:3
6 Isa 35:8
7 Isa 19:23-25
8 Rev 21:1
9 See *Corrupting the Image:* Adam's Bio-photons and Future Bodies of Light.
10 Isa 30:26
11 http://www.nytimes.com/2012/05 /17/science/bodies-inert-they-moved-a-robot-with-their-minds.html?_r=0
12 Ezek 1:27; Ps 97:4; Rev 4:5. Electricity is a fair translation. According to the Treasury of Scripture Knowledge (TSK), "Amber is a hard, inflammable, bituminous substance, of a beautiful yellow color, very transparent, and susceptible of an exquisite polish. When rubbed it is highly endowed with electricity; a name which the moderns have formed from its Greek name [*elektron*]. But, as amber becomes dim as soon as it feels the fire, and is speedily consumed, it is probable that the original [*chashmal*], which Bochart derives from the Chaldee [*nechash*] copper, and [*melala*] gold, was a mixed metal, similar to that which the Greeks called [*elektron*] electrum, as the LXX and Vulgate render, from its resemblance to amber in color" (TSK, on Ezekiel 8:2).
13 See "Thought Activated Computers Planned," Indo Asian News Service, IndiaBroad, Mon 23 Aug 2010; http://in .news.yahoo.com/thought-activated-computers-planned.html.
14 Rev 5:8
15 Rev 8:3-5
16 Mic 4:3
17 Gen 3:19
18 Zech 8:21
19 Isa 2:3
20 Ezek 43:1
21 Ezek 43:2; Zech 6:13
22 Ezek 44:2
23 2Kgs 6:17
24 Ezek 40:6-11
25 Zech 14:20
26 Isa 65:23
27 Ps 90:10
28 Isa 65:20

29 Num 32:11, 13; 14:29; Exod 30:14
30 Isa 65:20, 22
31 Num 14:29, 33
32 Isa 65:20; Zech 13:1; Ezek 47:1-12; Rev 22:1-2
33 Ps 72:10; Isa 60:5, 11
34 Rev 21:24, 26
35 Isa 61:7
36 Mat 24:21; Dan 12:1

Chapter 10

1 Mat 4:9
2 2Cor 11:14
3 Taken from "Instructions to the 23 Supreme Councils of the World," by Albert Pike, July 14, 1889; http://www.bible believers.org.au/mason1.htm
4 Isa 45:7
5 Prov 6:17
6 Job 1:11
7 Job 2:5
8 1John 2:18
9 Gen 1:24
10 Gen 6:1-4; Dan 2:43; 2Pet 2:4; Jude 1:6-7
11 In 2Cor 5:2 the apostle Paul writes of the putting off of the earthly habitation (physical body) and the putting on of a heavenly habitation (spiritual body). The Greek word *oiketerion* (οἰκητήριον, habitation) is the same word used in 2Pet 2:4: "For we know that if our earthly house, [this] tent, is destroyed, we have a building from God, a house not made with hands, eternal in the heavens. For in this we groan, earnestly desiring to be clothed with our habitation which is from heaven, if indeed, having been clothed, we shall not be found naked. For we who are in [this] tent groan, being burdened, not because we want to be unclothed, but further clothed, that mortality may be swallowed up by life."
12 Dan 2:43
13 Rev 20:1-2
14 Rev 12:12
15 Ezek 43:7
16 Dan 7:25; Rev 13
17 2Tim 3:2-5; Jas 3:14-15
18 Manly P. Hall, *The Lost Keys of Freemasonry*, Macoy Publishing and Masonic Supply Co. Richmond, Va., 1976, p. 65.
19 Ibid.
20 Rom 1:29-31; Phil 2:3-4

21 Gen 3:15
22 Dan 8:10-12; Rev 17:12
23 2Kgs 6:17
24 Mat 4:9
25 Dan 8:10-11; Rev 17:12
26 2Thes 2:3-4, 9; Rev 13:2, 4
27 Manly P. Hall, *The Lost Keys of Freemasonry*, Macoy Publishing and Masonic Supply Co. Richmond, Va., 1976, p. 65.
28 Rev 13:2, 4
29 Dan 8:10-11; Rev 17:12
30 Dan 7:8; 8:9-10
31 Rev 13:1, Dan 7:11; 2Thes 2:3; Gen 3:15
32 Mat 4:8
33 Heb 2:14-15
34 Deut 32:10; Zech 8:10

Chapter 11

1 The original *Yerushalayim* has a dual ending which signifies 'two of something'—thus it follows that there must be a pair of cities; one above and one below. We see evidence of this in Galatians 4:26 "but the Jerusalem above is free, which is the mother of us all."
2 Heb 1:14; Ps 146:9; Mat 5:44-46; Jas 1:27; Mark 9:35
3 Ezek 28:12-18
4 Gen 6:12
5 Gen 9:15
6 Gen 6:4
7 Amos 2:9
8 Num 13:33
9 Gen 12:2-3
10 Mat 24:24
11 Rev 13:6
12 2Thes 2:3-4
13 Jerry Rabow, *50 Jewish Messiahs*, Gefen Publishing, Jerusalem, 2002, p. 95.
14 Ibid., p. 110.
15 Barry Chamish points out in his seminal work *Shabtai Tzvi, Labor Zionism, and the Holocaust*: "This is Rabbi Antelman's central assertion—that Shabbataism was the polar opposite of Judaism, that Shabatai Zvi's program was to destroy all the tenets of the Torah and replace them with their opposites. Incredibly, more than half the Jews of the world at the time believed he would be revealed as their promised messiah." Barry Chamish: *Shabtai Tzvi, Labor Zionism, and the Holocaust*, Lulu Press, 2005, p. 287.

16 Mat 24:12
17 Albert Pike, *Morals and Dogma of the Ancient and Accepted Scottish Rite of Freemasonry*, p. 321, 19th Degree of Grand Pontiff. See also http://www.cutting edge.org/free11.html
18 *Encyclopaedia of Freemasonry*, by Albert Mackey, MD, 33rd and Charles T. McClenachan, 33rd revised edition, by Edward L. Hawkins, 30th and William J. Hughan, 32nd, Volume II, M-Z, published by The Masonic History Company, Chicago, New York, London, 1873; A.G. Mackey, 1927, by the Masonic History Company. See also *The Holy Bible: The Great Light in Masonry, King James Version, Temple Illustrated Edition*, A. J. Holman Company, 1968, Foreword entitled, "The Bible and King Solomon's Temple in Masonry," by John Wesley Kelchner.
19 http://townhall.com/columnists/dennisprager/2006/01/24/explaining_jews,_part_ii_why_are_most_jews_secular/page/full/
20 http://www.moshiach.com/index.php?option=com_content&task=view&id=269&Itemid=30. See also http://www.mechon-mamre.org/jewfaq/mashiach.htm
21 Ps 97:2-3
22 Exod 19:18, 22
23 Rev 15:8; 16:1; 21:22
24 Heb 9:11-12, 26
25 Heb 9:12, 26
26 Gen 11:4
27 Ps 97:2
28 Dan 9:27; Mat 24:15; 2Thes 2:4; Rev 13:14-15; 14:9, 11
29 Dan 12:11; Mat 24:15-21
30 Isa 6:2
31 Rev 15:8

Chapter 12

1 Rev 5:1-5
2 Isa 26:21
3 Rev 11:3-6
4 Isa 28:15
5 Joel 1:15
6 Joel 2:1-5
7 Joel 2:6, 10
8 Dan 9:26-27
9 Isa 28:16-18
10 Exodus Rabba 35, a Talmudic passage
11 Hos 5:15
12 Mat 23:39
13 Hos 5:15

Chapter 13

1 Gen 28:12
2 Luke 21:29. See also Douglas Hamp, *Corrupting the Image*, Defender Publishing, 2011: The Budding of the Fig Tree.
3 Ezek 38–39
4 Rev 9:1
5 Gen 1:28; Ps 8:6
6 Rom 5:12, 17
7 Rev 5:1-3
8 Num 23:19; Heb 6:18; Tit 1:2
9 Isa 14:13-14
10 2Cor 12:9
11 Mark 9:35
12 Dan 11:38
13 Dan 9:27-28
14 1Thes 5:3
15 Juan Enriquez, Chairman and CEO of Biotechonomy. Retrieved on July 6, 2010 from http://arstechnica.com/science/news/2009/02/we-are-becoming-a-new-species-we-are-becoming-homo-evolutis.
16 Ibid.
17 "Life, Liberty and the Defense of Dignity: The Challenges of Bioethics former chairman of the President's Council on Bioethics," by Leon Kass. Retrieved Oct. 25, 2010 from http://www.aei.org/book/295; compare http://www.newswithviews.com/Horn/thomas121.htm.
18 Ibid.
19 Juan Enriquez, chairman and CEO of Biotechonomy. Retrieved July 6, 2010 from http://arstechnica.com/science/news/2009/02/we-are-becoming-a-new-species-we-are-becoming-homo-evolutis.
20 New Ager Thelma Terrell Tuella, Project World Evacuation, Inner Light Publications, 1993 edition.
21 Barbara Marciniak, *Bringers of the Dawn: Teachings from the Pleiadians*, Bear and Co., 1992.
22 New Ager Thelma Terrell Tuella, Project World Evacuation, Inner Light Publications, 1993 ed.
23 David Lewis, UFO: *End Time Delusion*, New Leaf Press, 1991, p. 46.
24 Dan 2:43
25 2Thes 2:10-12
26 http://profiles.nlm.nih.gov/ps/access/SCBCCP.pdf
27 John 3:19
28 Rev 20:4
29 Mat 24:21-22
30 "We are going to become Gods, period. [...] But if you are going to interfere with me [sic] becoming a God, you're going to have trouble. There'll be warfare." Richard Seed, TechnoCalyps, Part II—Preparing for the Singularity, Nov 14, 2008.
31 For further understanding refer to Douglas Hamp, *Corrupting the Image*, Defender Publishing, 2011; also, visit http://www.douglashamp.com/category/media/video/end-times-video/page/2/ and http://www.douglashamp.com/synthetic-biology-video-another-step-toward-the-mark-of-the-beast.
32 Jas 1:45

Chapter 14

1 Rev 11:19
2 John 5:43
3 "Tel Aviv was named the Best Gay City of 2011 in an American Airlines competition selecting the most popular destinations among LGTB tourists." http://www.ynetnews.com/articles/0,7340,L-4174274,00.html
4 Dan 9:26-27; Isa 28:15
5 Jer 50:7; Hos 1:9
6 Num 23:19; Heb 6:18; Tit 1:2
7 Gen 15
8 Ps 148:6
9 Isa 28:15, 18
10 Mat 23:39; Hos 5:15
11 Jer 31:31-34
12 Rom 11:2
13 Rev 12:7
14 Eph 6:12
15 2Cor 10:4-5
16 Jude 1:9
17 James 1:6-7
18 Mat 4:4, 7, 10
19 James 5:16
20 Ps 141:2
21 Rev 5:8; 8:3
22 Rev 8:3-5
23 See Douglas Hamp, *Corrupting the Image*, Defender Publishing, 2011, p. 152.
24 1Sam 17:45, 47
25 Eph 6:11-17
26 Hos 1:7
27 The name of the star is Wormwood.
28 Rev 8:10; Rev 12:9
29 Rev 6:13; Isa 34:4
30 Rev 12:10
31 Rev 13:1
32 Rev 8:10-11
33 Rom 8:22

[34] Mat 24:21; Dan 12:1
[35] Rev 12:13
[36] Rev 8:12; 16:10. Note: The book of Revelation is a series of visions that are not necessarily in chronological order.
[37] Rev 9:1-2
[38] Rev 13:1; 17:8

Chapter 15

[1] Dan 11:37-39
[2] 2Thes 2:4
[3] Gen 3:15
[4] Ps 2:3
[5] Rev 13:3-4
[6] Rev 13:17
[7] Rev 13:16
[8] Mat 24:15; Dan 11:31
[9] Isa 28:18-19
[10] Mat 24:16-18

Chapter 16

[1] Eph 4:8
[2] Mat 12:43
[3] John 12:31; 14:30; 16:11
[4] Dan 10:13, 20; Job 1:6-7
[5] Heb 9:16-17
[6] Col 2:14-15
[7] Mat 2:16
[8] Mat 4:1-11
[9] Mat 4:8-9
[10] John 12:31; 14:30; 16:11
[11] Exod 33:11; Lev 26:12; Rom 8:18; Mat 5:8; 18:10; 1Cor 13:12; 1John 3:2; Rev 7:14; 21:3; 22:4
[12] Rom 8:19-22; 2Pet 3:10; Rev 6:14; Isa 34:4
[13] Dan 7:18; Isa 60:14
[14] Isa 65:9
[15] Isa 65:22
[16] Job 1:12; 2:6
[17] Job 1:10
[18] Dan 12:1
[19] Jude 1:9
[20] Rom 11:19
[21] Eph 2:19
[22] 1Chr 16:13; Ps 33:12; 105:6, 43; 135:4; Isa 45:4; 65:9, 22; Deut 14:2
[23] Exod 15:15; 19:5; 34:9; Deut 4:20; 7:6; 9:26
[24] Eph 1:4; see Douglas Hamp, *Why God Did Not Elect Calvinists*, Part Two.
[25] Eph 3:6-10; 2:12-13, 19; 3:11
[26] Gen 12:1-2
[27] Rom 11:29; Gen 15
[28] Num 22:12, 18, 35; 24:10-13; Deut 23:5

[29] Num 24:14; 31:16; Mic 6:5; Rev 2:14
[30] Rom 2; Eph 2:12
[31] Rom 11:1-2; 16-24
[32] Dan 7:18; Deut 28:13; Isa 62:7
[33] He was proven accurate through the doctrine of Chrysostom Augustine and others who taught that the Hebrews had forfeited God's election and the nations, which had been brought into the commonwealth of Israel, had replaced the Hebrews! In time the nations persecuted God's people in the name of the very one who had come to restore them. The Bible is replete with passages where God said that he would never abandon his people, Israel (1Sam 12:22; Ps 94:14; Jer 31:35-37), whom he had foreknown and elected (Rom 11:1-2; 1Pet 1:2). Also, a plethora of evidence outside the Bible demonstrates how Lucifer was able to deceptively convince the nations which professed a relationship to Yeshua that they had replaced the Hebrews; e.g., *The Church Is Israel Now: The Transfer of Conditional Privilege*, by Calvin Charles D. Provan. ISBN 978-1-879998-39-1
[34] Dan 10:13
[35] John 1:11
[36] Heb 9:16-17
[37] Rom 11:18
[38] 1Sam 12:22; Ps 94:14; Jer 31:35-37; Rom 11:1-2
[39] Rom 11:13-18
[40] Mat 22:1-14
[41] See *Why God Did Not Elect Calvinists*, by Douglas Hamp, at www.douglashamp.com.

Chapter 17

[1] Joel 2:10; Isa 13:10; Mat 24:29
[2] Rev 16:10
[3] Rev 11:7-13
[4] Isa 24
[5] Rev 9:7-10
[6] Luke 21:26
[7] Isa 28:19-20
[8] Joel 2:28
[9] Rev 16:12
[10] Rev 9:15
[11] 2Pet 2:4; Jude 1:6
[12] Rev 9:14-19
[13] Rev 16:13-14
[14] Rev 9:14-19
[15] *50 Jewish Messiahs* by Jerry Rabow, Gefen Publishing, Jerusalem, 2002.

16 2Thes 2:11
17 Gen 3:15
18 See *Corrupting the Image*, Defender Publishing, 2011: Warnings from Ashtar.
19 John 5:43
20 1Thes 5:3
21 Dan 9:26-27; 12:11
22 Mat 24:24
23 Isa 28:18
24 Isa 28:21; Rom 8:28
25 Rev 13:13-17
26 Rev 14:9-11; Mat 25:41
27 See *Why God Did Not Elect Calvinists*, by Douglas Hamp, at www.douglas hamp.com.
28 Mat 24:24
29 Rev 13:4
30 Dan 7:18; Deut 28:13, 44
31 Ps 83:4
32 Deut 28:20, 25-29, 42, 49, 65-67

Chapter 18

1 Rom 11:1-2; 1Pet 1:2
2 Rev 12:17
3 Mat 24:16-18
4 Rev 12:12, 14
5 Dan 12:1
6 Mat 24:24
7 Rev 12:6
8 Dan 12:1; Rev 12:7
9 Rev 13:4
10 Numbers Rabba 11, from the Talmud.
11 "The fourteenth verse in the second chapter of Ruth is thus explained." Midrash Ruth 5, a Rabbinic source.
12 Isa 53:3
13 Isa 53:2-3
14 Isa 53:4-6
15 Isa 53:7-9
16 Isa 53:8-9
17 Heb 12:2
18 Joel 2:13
19 Zech 12:10, 12
20 Isa 66:2
21 Isa 53:10-12
22 Isa 40:1-2
23 Joel 2:14-17
24 Isa 40:27
25 Isa 49:13
26 Jer 31:35-37
27 Joel 2:32
28 Isa 49:23
29 Mat 23:39
30 Isa 25:9 Yeshuah = salvation

Chapter 19

1 Hos 6:1-3
2 Zech 12:8
3 Amos 2:9
4 Joel 2:30-31; Jer 4:28; Zech 14:6; Rev 16:10
5 Exod 14:2-4
6 Zech 13:8
7 Zech 14:2-4
8 Joel 3:11
9 Arema (a heap, pile [of sheaves], gai (valley) don (judgment) http://biblefocus.net/consider/v01Armageddon/Word-Armageddon-is-Hebrew-for-a-Place.html; compare (with *tzere*, impure) Jer. 50:26, a heap, e.g. of ruins, Neh. 3:34; of corn, Cant. 7:3; of sheaves, Ruth 3:7; from the root No. II. See also http://www.deafbible.org/Armageddon.htm. I discovered this information at http://biblefocus.net/consider/v01 Armageddon/Armageddon_To_Occur_In_The_ Valley_of.html (Mic 4:12). A metathesis appears to have occurred hence: *amir* versus *arema*—both meaning sheave or heap.
10 Ps 83:4
11 Joel 3:9
12 Rev 9:16-17; Dan 8:12
13 Rev 16:8-9
14 Joel 3:9-11
15 Mic 4:11
16 Ps 83:3
17 Rev 13:6
18 Gen 3:15; 6:4
19 Zech 14:2; Dan 7:21, 25; Rev 20:4
20 Deut 7:6; 9:26; 1Kgs 8:51
21 Joel 2:17
22 Mic 4:11
23 John 3:16
24 Rev 13:3-4
25 Mat 4:8-9
26 Rev 13:2, 7-8
27 Dan 7:25; 12:7; Rev 13:7
28 Dan 11:36
29 Dan 8:24
30 Dan 7:8; Rev 13:5-6
31 Prov 18:10
32 Ps 138:2; 22:5
33 Isa 62:11
34 Isa 12:2
35 Mat 23:39
36 Isa 49:23
37 Isa 25:9
38 Isa 49:15-17
39 Isa 40:28

Chapter 20

1. Isa 49:15-17
2. Isa 40:28
3. Rev 1:13-16
4. Isa 59:17; Mat 13:39; 24:42; Rev 14:16
5. Joel 3:16
6. Rev 5:8
7. Mat 23:39
8. Hos 5:15
9. John 1:10-11
10. Isa 61:3-4
11. Joel 2:18-19
12. Isa 59:15-16; Mat 13:39; 24:42; Rev 14:16
13. Joel 3
14. Hab 3:13
15. Mic 4:12
16. Dan 7:22
17. Zech 12:2-4
18. Rev 14:15
19. Joel 3:12-14
20. Mat 24:29-31; Isa 11:12
21. Mark 13:30
22. Mat 13:41
23. Isa 24:21
24. Isa 40:15, 17
25. 2Kgs 2:11; 6:17
26. Rev 1:16
27. Jude 1:14-15
28. Joel 3
29. Ruth 3:18
30. Dan 7:22
31. Isa 62:7
32. Deut 28:13, 44
33. Isa 34:8
34. Isa 40:50
35. Isa 64:1
36. Isa 59:18
37. Isa 63:5
38. Rev 16:17
39. Rev 11:15-19
40. Rev 22:20
41. Joel 3:16
42. Rev 19:14

Chapter 21

1. Gen 6:6
2. Gen 2:17
3. Gen 3:17-19
4. Rom 8:22
5. Rom 8:19-21
6. Gen 2:19
7. Nuclear physicist Dr. Robert Gentry discovered in granite rocks from around the world that a process of decay happened close to the formation of the planet. The decay (radioactive) process could not have been in effect before the Fall because God had declared everything to be very good. Dr. Gentry's discovery of the escaped alpha particles must be testimony to ruin at the Fall, when the planet became corrupted which would be liberated at the revealing of the sons of God. See Rom 8:19-22; see also Douglas Hamp, *The First Six Days*, Yoel Press, 2007.
8. Gen 3:19
9. Gen 3:24
10. Isa 34:4; Rev 6:14
11. Luke 3:38; John 1:18; 6:46; 1John 3:2
12. 2Kgs 6:17
13. Gen 3:15
14. John 8:44
15. Ps 49:7-9
16. Isa 30:33; Ezek 1:26-27; Dan 7:9-10
17. 2Pet 3:9
18. Exod 19:18; Deut 4:11; Ps 97:3-5, 104:32; 144:5; Dan 7:9-11
19. Exod 19:5; Deut 10:14; Ps 24:1; 50:12; 89:11
20. Mat 4:8-9; John 12:31; 14:30; 16:11; Acts 26:18; 2Cor 4:4; Col 1:13; 1John 4:4; 5:19
21. Exod 19:18; Ps 97:5; 104:32; Dan 7:9-10; Ezek 1:27
22. John 12:31; 14:30, 16:11; Heb 2:15
23. Ezek 28:18
24. Ezek 28:18
25. 1Pet 5:8
26. Prov 27:20; 30:15-16; Hab 2:4-5; Luke 11:24
27. Lev 17:11
28. Heb 10:4
29. Heb 9:6-10
30. Lev 17:7, 10-14; Ps 106:36-38
31. Lev 17:10-14
32. Lev 17:7; 1Cor 10:20
33. Mat 12:12
34. John 8:44; 10:10
35. See Douglas Hamp, *Corrupting the Image*, Defender Publishing, 2011, p. 137, for a detailed explanation of this verse (Gen 4:26).
36. Gen 6:5-6
37. Deut 18:10
38. Jer 32:35
39. Jer 7:31; 19:5
40. Deut 12:31; 18:10; 2Kgs 16:3; 17:17; 21:6
41. See Isa 57:5. The deception and cunning of Lucifer were so great that he was able even to cause many of

the Hebrews (whom God had chosen to be special guests at the restored kingdom) to offer their children to him and his Angels (Ezek 23:37). God took this offense so personally that he called the murdered children "my sons" (Ezek 16:21).

[42] Prov 27:20; 30:15-16; Hab 2:4-5; Luke 11:24

[43] See *Corrupting the Image*: Genetics of the Incarnation.

[44] Lev 25:47-55

Chapter 22

[1] The term "redeemed," from *ga'al*, refers to someone who has been delivered from danger. TWOT 300, *gā'al*: "The primary meaning of this root is to do the part of a kinsman and thus to redeem his kin from difficulty or danger. It is used with its derivatives 118 times. One difference between this root and the very similar root *pādâ*, 'redeem,' is that there is usually an emphasis in *gā'al* on the redemption being the privilege or duty of a near relative."

[2] Isa 35:8-10

[3] Gen 28:12

[4] Ps 78:23-25

[5] 2Kgs 6:16-17

[6] Ezek 1:1

[7] Mat 3:16

[8] John 1:51; Acts 7:55-56; 10:11; Rev 19:11

[9] Luke 12:49; 2Thes 1:7-9; Isa 40:5; 66:15, 18; Ezek 39:21; Mat 24:30

[10] Isa 66:15-16; Hab 3:3-9; Rev 19:14

[11] 2Thes 1:7-9; Rev 14:10

[12] Isa 66:15; 2Thes 1:7-8

[13] 2Pet 3:10

[14] Rev 1:16; 19:15, 21

[15] Isa 34:4; Rev 6:14; 2Pet 3:10; Hag 2:6; Isa 24:18

[16] 1Cor 13:12

[17] Isa 40:5; 66:18; Ezek 39:21; Mat 24:30; Luke 9:26

[18] Hab 3:6

[19] Rev 16:3; Isa 24

[20] Zech 12:2-3; Rev 19:19-20

[21] Ps 18:8; Rev 19:15; Mat 24:30, Ps 18:11; 97:25; 2Thes 1:7-8; Isa 66:15-16

[22] Rev 19:14; Mat 24:30

[23] Hab 3:4-13

[24] Mat 24:30

[25] Isa 19:1

[26] Ps 21:9

[27] Hab 3:1

[28] Deut 32:22

[29] 2Pet 3:10; Ps 144:5

[30] Ps 97:6

[31] Mat 24:27

[32] Hab 3:4-9

[33] Rev 1:7

[34] Ps 14:1

[35] Isa 51:6

[36] Mat 13:41

[37] Isa 33:14

[38] Rev 6:15-17; Isa 2:19

[39] See http://www.crystalinks.com/underground-bases.html with reference to places such as NORAD and Mount Weather.

[40] Isa 2:11; 13:11

[41] Isa 2:19; Rev 6:14-17

[42] Hab 3:3

[43] Dan 9:27; 11:31; 12:11; Mat 24:15; 2Thes 2:4

Chapter 23

[1] Zech 12:5-6

[2] Mic 4:13

[3] Zech 12:7-8

[4] Isa 63:5

[5] Ps 144:5

[6] Isa 2:13-19; Rev 6:14; 16:18, 20

[7] Hab 3:10

[8] Isa 24:19-20

[9] Isa 40:31

[10] Isa 40:31; Zech 14:5

[11] Mat 24:29-31; Isa 11:12

[12] Hab 3:13

[13] Isa 63:1-6

[14] Ps 97:3

[15] Hab 3:4-13

[16] Zech 14:13

[17] Hab 3:14

[18] Zech 14:12

[19] Hab 3:4-13

[20] Isa 63:1-6

[21] Hab 3:13

[22] Hab 3:11

[23] Amos 2:9

[24] See *Corrupting the Image*: Amorim were Nephilim.

[25] Josh 10:13

[26] Josh 10:14

[27] Rev 14:19-20

[28] Since liquid is measured in volume, the 83 miles in Revelation 14 must be the cube of 5.7 miles. A horse's bridle is approximately 5 feet high; the distance from Jerusalem to Azal is unclear.

[29] Isa 24:21-22; 34:5; Ps 7:13; 18:14; 77:17; 144:6

30 Mat 24:29
31 Deut 32:41
32 Jer 10:10-11; Ps 7:13; Dan 7:12
33 Rev 20:1-2; Jude 1:6
34 Isa 13:9-11
35 Isa 2:12
36 Isa 2:17

Chapter 24

1 Jer 4:23; Isa 24
2 Ps 144:5
3 Rev 16:3-5
4 Isa 26:21
5 Jer 4:23-27
6 Isa 24:6; 13:12
7 Ps 97
8 Rom 8:20
9 1Pet 2:24
10 Exod 15:3; Zech 14:3
11 Isa 63:1-6; Rev 12:18; Jer 31:35-37
12 Rev 19:17-18

Chapter 25

1 Dan 7:10
2 Dan 7:9-10, 13
3 John 5:22-23
4 Zech 13:8
5 Mat 25:32-36
6 Joel 3:2
7 Mat 25:37-40
8 Rev 19:12
9 2Thes 2:4
10 Rev 13:16
11 Ps 83:4; Micah 4:11
12 Ps 18:8
13 Rom 11:36
14 Col 1:16-17
15 Dan 11:36-37; Rev 13:6
16 Mic 4:1
17 Mark 8:36
18 Phil 2:10-11
19 Isa 30:33; Dan 7:11; Isa 11:4
20 Gehenna was also where formerly some of the Hebrews murdered their children by delivering them to be sacrificed by burning to the god Molech.
21 Rev 19:20
22 Rev 19:20; 20:10; 14:11; Mat 13:42
23 Joel 3:2
24 Matt 25:41-45
25 Joel 3:2-3
26 Rev 14:9-10
27 Rev 16:15
28 Ps 17:15; 1Cor 15:49; Phil 3:21
29 Ps 16:17
30 Isa 30:33

31 Mat 25:41
32 Mat 13:50
33 Isa 33:14
34 Mal 4:1; Job 4:9; Ps 97:3
35 Mat 13:41-42; 22:13
36 Isa 66:23-24
37 Rev 9:2
38 Eph 6:12
39 Isa 24:21-22
40 Luke 8:31
41 It appears that through his cunningness and legalism Lucifer had not technically violated any specific command of God for the previous six thousand years. Certainly he had lied and had pride in his heart, yet there was no one action that he had done to another for which he could be incriminated. The downfall of Adam came by a mere question, which was slander to be sure, yet nevertheless, Adam broke the command and not Lucifer. When he afflicted Job he first obtained permission from God. His great cunning was posing questions to the sons of Adam rather than making a direct attack.
42 Gen 3:15
43 Gen 1:11, 24
44 Jude 1:6
45 Isa 45:7
46 Isa 14:13; 24:22; Dan 7:12
47 Isa 14:10
48 Isa 14:9-16
49 Isa 14:4
50 Ps 96:3; 145:5
51 Isa 52:10
52 Jer 10:11
53 Ps 98:8
54 Ps 96:1-10
55 Dan 7:12
56 Isa 24:21-22; Dan 7:12; Rev 20:3
57 Dan 4:34-37
58 Luke 7:47
59 Dan 4:16
60 Ps 19:8
61 Rev 16:7
62 Rev 11:18
63 Isa 13:12
64 Isa 11

Chapter 26

1 Rev 21:5; Isa 65:17
2 Isa 41:18-20
3 1Cor 15:52; 1Thes 4:17
4 Acts 3:20-21
5 2Pet 3:10

6 Mat 24:30

7 Ps 97:2

8 Ps 97:3; 21:9; 18:8; 50:3; Dan 7:10; Hab 3:5; Mal 4:1; Heb 12:29; Isa 66:16

9 Rom 8:19-22

10 Rom 5:12

11 1Cor 15:22

12 Luke 3:38

13 Gen 2:16-17

14 Gen 2:18, 23

15 Gen 3:20

16 Num 30:12

17 Rom 5:12; 8:21

18 Rom 7:24

19 Rom 8:19-22

20 Isa 6:5

21 Eph 5:28-29

22 Rev 7:17

23 1Cor 15:22

24 Ps 118:19

25 Ps 118:24

26 Rev 20:4-6

27 Rev 20:5

28 Zeph 3:9

29 Ps 98:5-6

30 Ps 96:11-13

31 Ps 98:5-7

32 Heb 12:22

33 Ezek 28:14, 16

34 Rev 21:2; Isa 62:5

35 Heb 11:10

36 Gen 28:12

37 Zech 2:10; Zech 8:3; Isa 52:1

38 Ezek 43:7

39 Ps 132:13-14

40 Joel 3:17

41 Isa 24:23

42 Rev 22:1

43 Rev 4:6

44 Ps 46:4

45 Ezek 47:9

46 Gen 3:18

47 Gen 3:17-19

48 Isa 55:13

49 Isa 35:1-2

50 The new earth was like the original earth. "In the Paradise of God (*en to☐i paradeiso☐i tou theou*) ... The abode of God and the home of the redeemed with Christ, not a mere intermediate state. It was originally a garden of delight and finally heaven itself (Trench), as here." Robertson's Word Pictures accessed on theWord Bible Software, note on Rev 2:7.

51 Gen 1:12

52 Zech 14:8, 10

53 Joel 3:18

54 Isa 43:18-19

55 Jer 2:13

56 Ps 36:8-9

57 Isa 65:19

58 Isa 41:18-20

59 Isa 30:25

60 For understanding of the linguistic features of creation, see Douglas Hamp, *The First Six Days*, Yoel Press, 2007.

61 Isa 41:18-20, 44:1-4

62 See Douglas Hamp, *Corrupting the Image*, Defender Publishing, 2011: Biophotons and Future Bodies of Light.

63 Isa 44:23, 26

64 Isa 52:9

65 Planet Speaks in an Inaudible Voice, by Gregory Mone 08.02.2007 http://discover magazine.com/2007/aug/planet-speaks-in-an-inaudible -voice/article_view?b_start:int=1&-C=

66 Isa 30:26

67 Rev 21:5

68 Ps 148:1-13

69 Ezek 34:25; Hos 2:18

70 Isa 11:6-8

71 Isa 65:25

72 Isa 11:6-7

73 Isa 43:20-22

74 Isa 11:6-9; 65:25

75 Isa 30:23-24

Chapter 27

1 Isa 62:7-9

2 Rev 21:9-10

3 Isa 62:1

4 Isa 62:2-5

5 Zech 8:3

6 Jer 33:16

7 Ps 45:8

8 2Cor 2:14-16

9 Gal 4:27

10 Isa 54:1-8

11 Isa 54:11-13

12 Hos 2:19

13 Hos 2:20

14 The original "Jerusalem" has a dual ending which signifies 'two of something—thus it follows that there must be a pair of cities; one above and one below. Evidence of this is given in Galatians 4:26: "but the Jerusalem above is free, which is the mother of us all." See also John Gill Commentary on Galatians 4:26, citing the Zohar in Gen. fol. 13. 2. & 16. 2. & 75. 4. & 77. 1. & 78. 2. & 114. 3. & 121. 1. & in

Exod. fol. 6. 1. & 92. 2. T. Bab. Taanith, fol. 5. 1. Gloss. in T. Bab. Sanhedrin, fol. 97. 2. Caphtor, fol. 14. 2. & 25. 2. & 65. 1. & 68. 2. & 71. 2. & 118. 2. Raziel, fol. 13. 1. & 27. 1. Tzeror Hammor, fol. 61. 3. & 150. 3. Nishmat Chayim, fol. 26. 2. Kimchi in Hos. xi. 19.

15 Gal 4:26: *amar ribi yehudah, asah hakkadosh baruch hu yerushalayim lema'lah, keneged yerushalayim shel matah* (Zohar: Noach, translation mine). Rabbi Yehuda: "The Holy One, blessed be he, made the Jerusalem above as a counterpart to the Jerusalem which is below." http://unityzohar.com/uzreadnu1.php?parid=18292

16 Isa 52:1

17 Rev 21:9-10

18 Hos 2:2-5

19 Hos 2:8, 13

20 Hos 2:14-17

21 1Chr 16:13; Ps 33:12; 105:6, 43; 135:4; Isa 45:4; 65:9, 22

22 Exod 34:9; Deut 4:40; 7:6; 9:26, 29; 32:9; 1Kings 8:51-53; Ps 28:9; 33:12; 68:9; 74:2; 78:62; 79:1; 94:14; Isa 63: 17; Jer 10:16; 51:19; Zech 2:12

23 John 1:11

24 Luke 14:18-20

25 Mat 22:5, 8

26 Mat 22:1-14; Rev 19:9; 21:9-10

27 From the Hebrew word *ba'al,* meaning to marry, lord over, rule, possess, own (refer to TWOT).

28 Ezek 48:31; Rev 21:12-14

29 Zeph 3:14-16

30 Rev 21:9-10

31 Isa 54:9

32 Isa 54:10

33 Eph 1:10

34 Rev 7:17

Chapter 28

1 Ps 2:9

2 Ps 110:1-2

3 Dan 2:44; 7:14; Mat 28:18

4 See BDB — Aviad [דָ֒בִיעַ] means literally 'the father of forever.' Hence Yeshua is the father of eternity versus the everlasting father.

5 Isa 9:6

6 Ps 2:6

7 Ps 46:9

8 Mic 4:3

9 Isa 11:2-4

10 Zech 9:10

11 Ps 72:8

12 Heb 2:8; Eph 1:20-22

13 Isa 9:7

14 Phil 2:10; Isa 45:23

15 Rom 8:2

16 Rev 20:1-2

17 Phil 2:10; Isa 45:23

18 Isa 16:5

19 Luke 22:30

20 Mat 19:27-29

21 Isa 43:18; 65:17

22 Luke 22:30; Rev 20:4

23 Mat 20:20-21

24 Luke 22:30; Rev 20:4

25 Jer 33:15

26 Ezek 46:2

27 Ps 110:1; Mat 22:45

28 Jer 33:17

29 Ps 21:3

30 Ezek 34:23-24

31 Ps 110:2-6

32 2Sam 7:18

33 2Sam 7:18-22

34 Ps 21:6

35 2Sam 7:26

36 Mat 24:30

37 Ps 18:1-15

38 Ps 118:20

39 "my salvation," Ps 118:21

Chapter 29

1 Rev 19:9

2 Rev 19:8; 21:2, 9-10

3 Isa 61:10; Rom 13:14

4 Mat 22:13

5 Mat 8:11-12; 25:10

6 Rev 22:14

7 Mat 28:18

8 Rev 22:14; Mat 13:43; Dan 12:2-3

9 It is very odd that many translations of Ezek 40:2 have rendered the word as "on" or "upon." Ezekiel was not set *on* a mountain but set *toward* a mountain. Brown Driver Brigg's Hebrew-English Lexicon (BDB) states that the preposition *el* means (1) to, toward, unto (of motion) and never means "upon."

10 Heb 12:22; Ps 48:1-2; Rev 21:10

11 Ezek 40:1-3

12 Rev 21:16

13 In the vision there was an Angel whose appearance resembled glowing bronze and who had a measuring rod and line in his hand standing in the city gate (Ezek 40:3). Adonai wisely directed the Angel in Ezekiel's vision to measure the city's gates (Ezek 48: 30-31), and in John's day an Angel to

measure the city and the walls. Now that it was actually before him on the earth, he was astounded by its magnitude. He observed how its base was laid out as a square, with its length equal to its breadth and its height being equal to one of the sides. The Angel had measured the City to be 1,380 miles, which may be understood as the sum total of all the edges. For details, see companion book *The New Heavens and Earth*.

[14] 2Cor 5:8
[15] Ps 48:2
[16] Ps 50:2
[17] Ps 48:2
[18] Isa 54:12
[19] Ezek 48:30-31
[20] Ezek 48:31; Rev 21:11-12
[21] The text of Ezek 48:30 says the exits (*totzaot*) of the city measured 4500 rods (1 rod = 10 feet). There were three gates on each side of the city, therefore each gate measured 1500 rods (4500/3). Converted into miles each gate was 2.84 miles. Each of the gates is named after one of the twelve tribes of Jacob as indicated in the text of Rev 21:12-13.
[22] Rev 21:25
[23] Isa 62:6-7
[24] *Har beit Yahveh*
[25] Mic 4:1; Isa 14:13; Ezek 28:13-16
[26] Mic 4:2; also Isa 2:2-3
[27] Rev 21:3
[28] Zeph 3:17; Isa 62:5
[29] Rev 21:21
[30] Song 2:4; 7:10; 8:6-7
[31] Deut 7:8; 10:15; Malachi 1:2; John 3:16; Rom 5:8; Titus 3:4; 1John 4:19
[32] Ps 63:5
[33] Isa 25:6
[34] Mat 26:29
[35] Luke 22:20
[36] Isa 55:1
[37] Gen 2:9, 16
[38] Isa 65:11-15

Chapter 30

[1] Ps 69:23
[2] Gen 11:4
[3] Deut 7:6; 14:2
[4] Isa 45:7
[5] Rev 16:14; 19:19
[6] Zech 4:6
[7] 1John 4:4
[8] Luke 19:17

[9] Judg 17:6
[10] Luke 19:14

Chapter 31

[1] Isa 35:8-10
[2] Ezek 1:26-28; Dan 7:9-10
[3] Isa 45:7; 1John 1:5
[4] Isa 66:4
[5] Rom 5:12; 1Cor 15:21-22
[6] Gen 3:22
[7] Ps 17:15; 2Pet 1:4; 1John 3:2
[8] Gen 3:1-5
[9] Gen 3:22
[10] Jer 27:5
[11] The word *agape* means fully committed to something, wholly devoted and dedicated.
[12] John 3:16; 15:13
[13] Heb 1:3; Col 1:15
[14] Phil 2:6-8; Isa 53:10

Chapter 32

[1] Joel 3:18
[2] http://boingboing.net/2010/03/18/bioacoustician-berni.html
[3] Planet Speaks in an Inaudible Voice, by Gregory Mone 08.02.2007 http://discover magazine.com /2007/aug/planet-speaks-in-an-inaudible -voice/article_view?b_start:int=1&-C=;Scientists Hear the Song of the Planet, http://www. catholic.org/technology/story.php?id=447865
[4] 1Chr 16:33; Zeph 3:17
[5] Isa 32:17-20
[6] Isa 61:4; Amos 9:14
[7] Amos 9:13; Isa 61:5
[8] Isa 65:21-24
[9] Isa 55:12
[10] Isa 49:12, 22
[11] Zech 8:23
[12] Isa 49:22
[13] Zech 3:10; Mic 4:4
[14] Isa 30:29
[15] Isa 4:3-4; Zech 13:8
[16] Zeph 3:11-13
[17] Isa 14:13
[18] Ps 48:2
[19] Heb 12:22
[20] Heb 11:9-10
[21] Ps 48:1-2
[22] Ps 50:2
[23] Rev 22:17
[24] Ps 87:3
[25] Ps 48:1
[26] Ps 48:1-3, 5, 12-13
[27] Rom 8:29; Ps 17:15
[28] Gen 1:31

29 1John 4:8; Exod 34:6-7; Ps 86:5, 15; 2Cor 13:11; Eph 2:4
30 Isa 45:7
31 2Sam 16:7
32 Gen 3:22
33 John 13:14-15
34 Mat 20:25-28; John 3:16; Rom 5:8; Phil 2:7
35 John 15:13
36 Heb 1:14
37 Gen 3:22
38 Luke 20:35-36
39 Mat 10:28; Gen 2:7; John 20:22
40 Gen 3:22
41 Ps 16:11
42 Mat 20:25-28
43 1Cor 13:5
44 Rev 20:8

Chapter 33

1 Prov 4:27
2 Rev 22:15
3 Prov 4:27
4 Ps 26:1; Exod 32:6
5 Prov 1:11-13
6 Rom 1:19-22
7 Ps 64:5-6
8 Ps 90:2
9 Rom 1:25, 28-32
10 Lev 17:7; Deut 32:17; 1Cor 10:20
11 Ps 51:16
12 Lev 17:7, 10-14; Ps 106:36-38
13 1Pet 5:8
14 Prov 27:20; 30:15-16; Hab 2:4-6; Luk 11:24
15 Lev 17:7; 1Cor 10:20
16 Isa 49:23
17 Isa 60:6
18 Isa 60:10-11; Rev 21:25-26
19 Isa 60:12
20 Exod 20:3-5
21 Luke 22:26-27
22 Rev 12:10
23 Jer 31:37
24 Ps 2:3
25 Luke 19:14
26 Acts 20:35

Chapter 34

1 John 15:13
2 Luke 22:26-27
3 John 17:24
4 John 10:18
5 Ps 2:4
6 John 12:31; 16:11
7 Rev 20:8
8 Hos 2:18; Zech 9:10

9 Mic 4:3; Isa 2:4
10 2Cor 10:4
11 Eph 6:12
12 Ps 138:2
13 Ps 2:3
14 Prov 16:18
15 Rom 9:33; 10:11; 1Pet 2:6
16 Rev 22:15
17 John 15:13
18 Rev 21:27
19 Rev 22:14
20 Isa 60:11; Rev 21:25
21 Rev 21:27
22 Num 23:19; Heb 6:18; Tit 1:2
23 Rev 22:15
24 Isa 14:12; Ezek 28:12-18; 40:2
25 Ps 48:1; Isa 2:3; 54:12; Heb 12:22; Rev 14:1; 21:10, 16, 18-20
26 Judges 17:6
27 Exod 34:29-33
28 Rom 6:10; Heb 9:28; 1Pet 3:18
29 Heb 6:6
30 Rev 20:8
31 Ps 10:11
32 Lucifer's disfigurement was noted in other commentators of the ancient manuscripts. "This is he who was hidden in the serpent, and who deceived you, and *stripped you of the garment of light and glory in which you were.* This is he who promised you majesty and divinity. Where, then, is the beauty that was on him? Where is his divinity? Where is his light? Where is the glory that rested on him? ... his figure is hideous; he is become abominable among angels; and he has come to be called Lucifer." *Pseudepigrapha—Lost Books of Eden: The First Book of the Life of Adam and Eve,* chapter LI, pp. 2, 5, 6-7 (emphasis mine).
33 Ezek 28:17; Rev 12:3; 20:2
34 Ezek 28:17

Chapter 35

1 Ps 143:3-4
2 1Pet 1:6-7
3 Ps 10:1-2
4 Rom 5:7-8
5 Isa 53
6 1Pet 3:18; Mat 12:36; 2Cor 5:10
7 Ps 9:13; 7:1-2
8 John 14:3
9 Phil 4:7
10 Rev 22:17
11 Ezek 47:2-12; Rev 22:1
12 Ps 36:8; Rev 22:17; Zech 13:1

13 Rev 21:6
14 Zech 13:1
15 John 4:14; Rev 22:1, Ezek 47:9
16 John 5:24
17 Gen 3:22
18 Mat 13:39
19 John 4:29
20 Ps 7:11
21 Rev 22:1; John 4:10, 14
22 Isa 12
23 John 4:14
24 Isa 12:1-6
25 Luke 20:35-36
26 Phil 3:21
27 2Pet 1:4
28 John 3:5-7
29 Ezek 47:12; Rev 22:2, 14
30 Gen 3:22; Rev 22:2; Ezek 47:12
31 John 14:3, 23
32 2Cor 6:16
33 Isa 30:33; Ezek 1:26-27; Dan 7:9
34 Ex 19:18; Deut 4:11; Ps 97:3-5; 104:32; 144:5; Dan 7:9-11
35 The original Hebrew in Genesis 3:24 has the definite article "*the* cherubim." These are the very cherubim Ezekiel saw in his vision by the river Chebar.
36 Gen 3:23-24
37 Genesis 3:24 "the sword" (singular)
38 Luke 20:35-36; Rev 2:7; 22:2
39 Gen 3:24
40 Zech 13:1; Rev 22:14, 17; John 4:14
41 Luke 20:35-36
42 Rev 9:6
43 1Cor 15:52
44 Exod 34:29; 2Cor 5:17; Gal 6:15
45 Phil 3:21; Rev 21:3
46 Mat 22:11-12; Isa 61:10
47 Mat 13:43; Jas 1:12; 1Cor 9:25; 1Pet 5:4
48 Dan 10:6-7
49 Rev 19:8
50 Phil 3:21
51 2Pet 1:4; Luke 20:35-36; Dan 12:3
52 Luke 20:35-36

Chapter 36

1 Ezek 1:26-28; Dan 7:9-10
2 Ps 148:2-6
3 Heb 10:31; 2Cor 5:10
4 1Cor 3:12-15
5 Isa 53
6 1Pet 3:18; 2Cor 5:10
7 Mat 12:36
8 Isa 6:5
9 Mat 27:54
10 Luke 16:23
11 Gen 6:1-4; Dan 2:43; 1Pet 3:20; 2Pet 2:4; Jude 1:6-7

12 John 19:30
13 Jude 1:6-7; Isa 52:15
14 John 12:31; John 14:30; 16:11
15 Heb 2:14-15
16 Mat 28:18
17 John 10:18
18 Heb 12:2
19 Ezek 28:13
20 Rev 2:17
21 Mat 25:23
22 Rev 21:21
23 1 Cor 2:9
24 Song 2:4; 7:10; 8:6-7
25 John 17:21
26 1Cor 13:12
27 Dan 12:3; Rev 19:8, Mat 13:33
28 Exod 33:20
29 Rev 14:10; Isa 30:33; Mat 25:41

Chapter 37

1 Rev 20:9
2 Zeph 3:17
3 Hos 2:18
4 Ps 48:1; Isa 2:3; Ezek 40:2; Heb 12: 22; Rev 14:1; 21:10, 16
5 Rev 20: 9
6 Isa 11:5
7 Isa 14:13-14; Rev 20:7-9; Ps 2:1-3
8 Jer 20:12
9 Prov 17:3-4; Isa 65:20; Jer 17:9
10 Lev 17:11, 14
11 Lev 17:11
12 Heb 8:5
13 Exod 26:31; 26:35
14 Ex 25:22; Num 7:8-9; 2 Kings 19:15; Ezek 10:1-19
15 Heb 9:7
16 Lev 13:11; 2 Chron 23:19
17 Lev 11:24
18 Lev 16:4
19 Lev 16:6; Heb 7:27; 9:7
20 Heb 9:6-10
21 Heb 10:4
22 Isa 65:20; Zech 13:1
23 1Cor 15:25; Rev 20:13
24 1Cor 15:53
25 Ps 2:1, 3
26 Ps 37:11; Isa 11:4; Zeph 3:12; Mat 5:5
27 Isa 14:13; Ps 48:1-3
28 Isa 14:14
29 Ps 138:2
30 Ps 2:4; Rev 21:23; Isa 24:23
31 Ezek 28:13
32 Luke 15:31
33 Ps 148:2-6
34 The breastplate worn by the high priest in the temple was a picture of what Adonai clothed Lucifer in.

35 Ezek 28:12-13; Isa 14:11
36 Gen 39:8-9; Ezek 28:14, 16; 1Tim 3:1, 6; Titus 1:7-8
37 Ezek 28:14; Ps 48:1; Heb 12:22
38 Luke 14:10-14; 18:14; 1Pet 5:6
39 Ps 73:6
40 Prov 26:24
41 Mat 16:25
42 Ezek 28:16
43 Lev 19:16; Ezek 28:16
44 Rev 12:4
45 Dan 4:17
46 Ps 91:11; 103:20; Dan 6:22; Mat 4:11
47 Acts 20:35
48 Mark 9:35; 10:44; 1Cor 1:18
49 Luke 19:14

Chapter 38

1 Ps 33:13-14; 102:19
2 Isa 65:2-5; Ps 2:4
3 Dan 7:12; Heb 9:7, 25
4 Isa 6:2; Rev 4:8. *Seraphim* literally means "burning ones."
5 Ps 104:4; Heb 1:7
6 Ezek 1:13
7 Ezek 28:18; Rev 20:8-9
8 Ezek 28:17, 19
9 Rev 14:10; 20:10; Isa 30:33; Mat 3:12; 25:41
10 Rev 20:10; Job 4:9
11 Ps 9:6; 103:13; Prov 10:7; Isa 26:14; Ezek 28:12-13
12 Ezek 28:18-19
13 Matt 13:42, 50
14 Isaiah 66:22-24; Mark 9:43-47; 2Thes 1:9
15 Num 16:21, 45; Josh 24:20; 2Kings 1: 10, 12; Neh 9:31; Lam 3:22; 4:6; Ps 97:3; Job 4:9
16 Ezek 1:26-28; 2 Sam 22:9; Ps 18:8; 97:3-4; Job 41:20; Dan 7:9-10
17 Ps 11:5-6
18 Rev 20:12
19 Dan 12:2; Mat 25:41
20 Rev 20:11; 2Pet 3:10
21 John 5:27
22 Dan 7:10; Isa 24:23
23 Isa 24:23; Rev 4:4; 20:4
24 Rev 20:12
25 Rev 20:11
26 Rev 20:12; 13:8; Dan 7:10
27 Mat 11:21-24
28 Luke 22:47-48
29 Luke 16:19-31
30 Mat 16:27
31 Luke 12:48
32 Dan 7:11; Rev 19:20; 20:15

33 Isa 30:33; Mat 25:41
34 Ezek 28:19
35 John 12:47-48; Ezek 28:19
36 Rev 20:14-15
37 The Bible suggests that these were in fact angels and not just concepts or states of being.
38 1Cor 15:26
39 John 13:14-15
40 Mat 16:25-26
41 John 12:25-26
42 Ps 16:11

Chapter 39

1 1Cor 15:24-26; Col 1:16; Eph 6:12
2 Mat 28:18
3 1Cor 15:24, 28; Eph 1:20-22
4 Ps 148:1-4
5 Ps 96:3; 145:5
6 Ps 98:8
7 Ps 96:1-10
8 Gal 5:22-23
9 Phil 3:21; 2Pet 1:4; 2Cor 13:14
10 Phil 2:2-4; Col 3:12
11 Rom 12:3
12 John 15:15; Luke 12:32
13 Ps 138:6; 1Cor 15:47-48
14 1Cor 13:4-7
15 Phil 4:8
16 Mat 20:25-28; 1Cor 13:5
17 1Pet 3:8
18 1Pet 1:22
19 Lev 26:12; Rev 7:14; 21:3

Chapter 40

1 Gen 3:8
2 Neh 9:6
3 Ps 150:6; Rev 5:13
4 http://www.animalcircuses.com/news.aspx?headlineid=21
5 Rom 8:18, 28
6 2Cor 4:17
7 Ps 107:8
8 Prov 25:2; Deut 29:29; Rom 11:33
9 Mark 10:14-16
10 Isa 65:19; 35:10; 51:11
11 John 3:16
12 Deut 7:8; Isa 43:1; Mat 7:11; Ps 103:13

Epilogue

1 Rom 3:23; 6:23; 5:8; 10:9-13
2 Ps 16:11
3 Prov 2:19
4 Dan 12:2
5 Deut 30:19

About the Author

Douglas Hamp, author of *Discovering the Language of Jesus, The First Six Days,* and *Corrupting the Image,* earned his MA in the Hebrew Bible and the Ancient Near East from the Hebrew University of Jerusalem, Israel. During his three years in Israel, he studied both modern and biblical Hebrew, biblical Aramaic, Koine Greek, and other ancient languages as well as ancient texts and the archeology of the Bible. He served as an assistant pastor at Calvary Chapel Costa Mesa for more than six years, where he taught at the School of Ministry, the Spanish School of Ministry, and Calvary Chapel Bible College Graduate School.

Douglas has given numerous lectures on biblical languages, creationism, and prophecy in the United States and internationally and has been a featured speaker at many conferences and churches.

Douglas has been a guest on both radio and television programs including Coast to Coast with George Noory (10 million listeners), Prophecy in the News with Gary Stearman (2 million viewers), and Southwest Radio Church with Noah Hutchings. Several times he has been a guest pastor on Pastors Perspective (KWVE radio broadcast on about four hundred stations nationwide) and has been a contributor to The Update on KWVE as well as dozens of other radio programs (FM, AM, and blogtalk) nationwide.

Douglas has been endorsed by Dr. John Morris, president of the Institute for Creation Research; Ken Ham, founder and president, Answers in Genesis and the Creation Museum; Joseph Farah, chief executive officer of WorldNetDaily.com; Carl Westerlund, ThM, director of Calvary Chapel Costa Mesa School of Ministry and Graduate

School; Dr. Stan Sholar, retired aerospace engineer; Dr. Bill Spear, director of Mountain Ministries, Dillon, Colorado; Pastor Chuck Smith, Calvary Chapel Costa Mesa; Albert Cerussi, congregational co-leader of Ben David Messianic Congregation; and Dr. David Lehman, Bible researcher and lecturer.

Douglas Hamp is a committed follower of Yeshua (Jesus). You can invite Douglas to share *The Millennium Chronicles* presentations with your church or group by contacting him at douglas@douglashamp.com or by calling 949-273-0120. You can view other materials he has made available at his website: www.douglashamp.com.

Resources by Douglas Hamp

The Final Rebellion: Satan's Assault Against the New Jerusalem

Douglas examines the Scriptural clues of Satan's final rebellion when the 1,000 years have expired and he along with the nations come up against the beloved city.

The Millennium: Heaven on Earth? (DVD)

If the earth is destroyed and the heavens pass away at the second coming of Jesus, then what will there be during the Millennium?

The Second Coming and the Battle of Armageddon: A Graphic New Look (DVD)

The Battle of Armageddon is often portrayed as taking place in the north of Israel, between nations. Could there be another way to see it?

Corrupting the Image
paperback, by Douglas Hamp

According to the prophecy of Genesis 3:15, the serpent will one day mix his seed as a counterfeit of the incarnation. Jesus told us that the last days will be like the days of Noah when, according to Genesis, fallen angels mixed their seed with humanity.

Corrupting the Image Class Lectures (MP3 CD)

In this 13-week 2-credit class recorded at Calvary Chapel Bible College in Costa Mesa, CA, author Douglas Hamp teaches directly from the book *Corrupting the Image*.

Discovering the Language of Jesus
paperback, by Douglas Hamp

For the last 150 years, both popular and academic views have asserted that Jesus spoke Aramaic as his primary language of communication since Hebrew supposedly died out after the children of Israel were taken into Babylonian captivity.

Rise of the Nephilim (DVD)

In the days of Noah and afterward, fallen angels fathered hybrid creatures called Nephilim. The genetic mingling of human and demonic could not be tolerated in the days of Noah or when the Israelites came into Canaan.

The Angelic Domain and the Fall of Satan (DVD)

In this PowerPoint–enhanced study Bible teacher Douglas Hamp examines perennial and profound questions from the evidence of Scripture: What is time? Were the angels created before or after Genesis 1:1?

The Antichrist, Freemasons, and the Third Temple (DVD)

What is the meaning behind 2 Thessalonians 2:4, where the Antichrist sits in the temple, declaring himself to be god?

The Fall Feasts and the Budding of the Fig Tree (DVD)

There are seven feasts of the Lord. On Passover Jesus died; during the Feast of Unleavened Bread He was in the tomb; on Firstfruits He rose, and on Shavuot (Pentecost) the Holy Spirit came. Therefore, should we anticipate something significant to happen on each of the three remaining feasts?

The First Six Days
paperback, by Douglas Hamp

If God really created through evolution then why does God say that He created everything in only six days? Are those days literal days or are they really indefinite periods of time as Progressive Creationism claims?

The Genetics of the Incarnation and of the Resurrection (DVD)

God made Adam in his image and likeness, but what *is* that image? Did God breathe into Adam the same spirit Jesus breathed into the disciples? If we will be covered in light in the age to come, and did Adam also have a covering of light?

The Language of Creation (DVD)

What can we learn from the language of creation? Evolution has made many believers reinterpret the literal reading of the text. Through a detailed analysis of the Hebrew words we can confidently reassert that God created in six literal days only thousands of years ago.

The Messianic Age: The Millennium and Beyond (CD)

Much of our eschatology rightly deals with the events that lead up to the Second Coming of Jesus, but little attention is given to looking at the events that happen thereafter. This discussion explores the wonders of the Messianic Age / Millennium from a bibliocentric perspective.

Made in the USA
Charleston, SC
17 September 2014